GENOCIDE OF ONE

GENOCIDE OF ONE

KAZUAKI TAKANO

Translated by Philip Gabriel

MULHOLLAND
BOOKS

HODDER

First published in Great Britain in 2014 by Mulholland Books
An imprint of Hodder & Stoughton
An Hachette UK company

1

First published as *Jenosaido* in Japan in 2011 by Kadokawa Shoten

A CIP catalogue record for this title is available from the British Library

Trade Paperback ISBN 978 1 444 75951 8
Ebook ISBN ISBN 978 1 444 75952 5

Printed and bound by Clays Ltd, St Ives plc

Hodder & Stoughton policy is to use papers that are natural,
renewable and recyclable products and made from wood grown
in sustainable forests. The logging and manufacturing processes
are expected to conform to the environmental regulations
of the country of origin.

Hodder & Stoughton Ltd
338 Euston Road
London NW1 3BH

www.hodder.co.uk

GENOCIDE OF ONE

PROLOGUE

THIS MANSION NEVER felt like home, no matter how many years he lived in it. He never slept well here; his sleep was shallow at best, and it wasn't just because he was getting older. Today, after another restless night, Gregory S. Burns awoke to the ringing of his usual morning wake-up call.

He exchanged a few words with the operator but stayed in bed, enjoying a precious few minutes of reprieve. Eventually—reluctantly—he got up, stretched his arms high above his head, and yawned deeply. He stepped into the shower, keeping the water cool to help clear his head, then changed into the suit his wife had laid out for him.

In the dining room his wife and two daughters had started breakfast. His daughters, just up and in a bad mood, were running through a litany of complaints about their school. He half listened and made the appropriate noises so they knew he wasn't totally ignoring them. Fortunately, his wife no longer had sharp words for him when he neglected his family, a small concession he'd won after a long-running battle.

His home and workplace were connected: all he had to do was step into the hall, and he was in a public space. He picked up the forty-pound briefcase at his feet and stepped out of the room. As the ominous nickname of the case—the nuclear football—implied, it contained within it the trigger that could destroy mankind, the device that Burns would need if he were to order a nuclear attack.

"Good morning, Mr. President."

Naval Commander Samuel Gibson approached him. Gibson was rated Yankee White, the highest security clearance.

"Good morning, Sam."

Gibson took the briefcase from Burns and snapped the metal cuff around his own wrist, chaining the case to himself. Burns and Gibson proceeded downstairs, where they were joined by Secret Service agents, and together they headed for the West Wing. On the way a National Security Agency official met them and handed Burns a small plastic card, code-named Biscuit. The card was coded with a series of random numbers that made up that day's nuclear launch code. Inputting these numbers into the keyboard inside the nuclear football would authenticate any launch order. Burns put the card in his wallet, then put the wallet in the inside pocket of his jacket.

The Oval Office looked out onto the sunny Rose Garden. Burns waited as his daily briefing staff assembled. As they were cleared to enter they came in—the vice president, the White House chief of staff, the national security adviser, the director of national intelligence, and the director of the CIA.

They settled down onto the sofas, exchanging greetings, and Burns noticed one more person in the room than usual, a middle-aged man seated farthest from him—Dr. Melvin Gardner, his science and technology adviser. Gardner was hunched over, clearly ill at ease. With his genial, intelligent eyes below his silver hair and his low-key, subdued appearance, he looked ill suited to be joining a group that included the most powerful man on the planet.

"Good morning, Dr. Gardner," Burns said quietly.

"Good morning, Mr. President."

With Gardner's smile the atmosphere relaxed ever so slightly. Of all the men in the room, only Gardner had this quality, this air, of being harmless. Innocent, even.

"Mr. Watkins asked me to sit in," Gardner explained.

Burns glanced at Charles Watkins, his director of national intelligence.

"We need Dr. Gardner's advice," Watkins said.

Burns nodded, careful not to let his disapproval show. If Watkins wanted Gardner to sit in on the briefing, he should have gotten his permission beforehand. The post of director of national intelligence was new, and Watkins was newly appointed, but Burns was already irritated by the way the man was constantly taking authority into his own hands.

Well, we'll eventually find out why Gardner was called here, Burns thought, collecting himself. In recent years he'd worked hard at controlling his sudden outbursts of temper.

"Sir, the daily intelligence briefing," Watkins said, pulling some papers out of a leather binder. This was a summary, prepared by the intelligence community, detailing activities over the last twenty-four hours.

The first two items dealt with the wars Burns had begun in the Middle East. The wars in Iraq and Afghanistan weren't going well. Security in Iraq was deteriorating, while in Afghanistan hidden terrorist cells were still at large, and US casualties were mounting. The number of US war dead and Burns's rising unpopularity were both trending upward. Burns now regretted having swallowed whole his defense secretary's advice, which put only a fifth of the number of troops on the ground that the army chief of staff had requested. One hundred thousand US troops had been enough to overthrow the dictator and take over this small country, but they were unequal to the task of restoring order now that they were an occupation force.

The third item was an even more disturbing report. The CIA suspected that there were double agents at work among their paramilitary personnel in the Middle East.

The director of the CIA, Robert Holland, asked for permission to speak. "We're seeing a type of intelligence leak we've never seen before. If our suspicions are correct, there is one individual who is leaking intelligence, not to an enemy country but to a human rights organization."

"An NGO?"

"Correct. He's leaking intelligence about our extraordinary renditions program."

Burns looked sullen as he listened to the details. "Let's get the counsel to the president involved before we discuss this again."

"Of course," Holland said.

The fourth item concerned a leader of one of the coalition countries who was suffering from depression and unable to carry out his duties. The report stated that it was only a matter of time before there was a change in leadership, but that this shouldn't affect the country's friendly relations with the United States.

They turned the page to the next two items on the report, and as

Burns listened to the explanations they arrived at the final page and the following heading:

The Possibility of the Extinction of the Human Race: A New Life Form Appears in Africa

Burns looked up from his binder. "What is this? A Hollywood screenplay?"

Only the chief of staff smiled at the president's little joke. The others were silent, unable to hide their bewilderment. Burns fixed his gaze on the director of national intelligence. Watkins held his gaze without flinching. "It's a report from the NSA," he said.

Burns suddenly recalled an earlier incident in which a deadly virus outbreak had occurred in Reston, a DC suburb. The US Army Medical Research Institute of Infectious Diseases and the Centers for Disease Control had worked together to contain the deadly virus, a form of Ebola. This incident must be something similar.

He read on.

A new type of life-form has appeared in the tropical rain forests of the Democratic Republic of the Congo. If it spreads, this life-form will pose a threat to the United States and may lead to the extinction of all mankind. This type of situation has already been mentioned in the Heisman Report from the Schneider Institute, which was submitted in 1975. . . .

Burns carefully read through the information and then leaned back on the sofa. It was clear now why the science and technology adviser had been summoned to the meeting.

He couldn't help making a sarcastic joke.

"Are you sure they didn't mistake Islamic extremists for this new life-form?"

Watkins remained matter-of-fact. "This is reliable intel. We've had specialists analyze it, and they believe—"

"Enough," Burns said, interrupting. He found the report offensive. Not just the contents but its very existence, which he couldn't stomach. "I'd like to hear what Dr. Gardner has to say."

All eyes turned to the hesitant-looking older scientist. With the president in such a foul mood, Gardner found himself stammering. "It's been predicted since—since the second half of the twentieth century that—something like this might happen. The Heisman Report mentioned in your intelligence summary was written in response to discussion about this possibility."

Burns was surprised at the seriousness of his reply. The scientist's thoughts on this seemed to exceed anything a layman could fathom. Still, Burns couldn't get rid of a deep sense of unease. A new life-form that leads mankind to extinction? Who in his right mind could believe that?

"And you find this intelligence reliable?" Burns asked him.

"I can't refute it."

"I have a copy of the Heisman Report right here," Watkins said, taking out a new document from his folder. "I've marked the relevant section. Section five."

Burns read over this report from a quarter of a century earlier. Gardner waited for him to finish, then spoke. "The intelligence we have now is indirect. Other than the person sending the report, no one else has confirmed this new life-form. I think it would be worth sending personnel from the United States to check out what's actually going on."

"At this point it should be easy to take care of," Watkins added. "And it wouldn't cost much. A few million dollars should be sufficient. But we'd have to make sure it's kept entirely confidential."

"Do you have a plan in mind?" Burns asked.

"I've ordered the Schneider Institute to put together an action plan. I should have options on my desk by the weekend."

Burns thought it over. He couldn't see a downside. For the president of a nation at war, it was best to handle any extraneous problems immediately. And this whole issue was something he found particularly loathsome. "All right. Let me see the options as soon as you get them."

"Yes, sir."

The morning meeting was concluded, but these same issues were raised again at the nine o'clock cabinet meeting. There the secretary of defense, Geoffrey Lattimer, summarized the final issue—*a biological problem*—after a quick, two-minute discussion. "This is the kind of stupid thing that should be left up to the Schneider Institute," he said dismissively.

At the president's urging they bowed their heads in prayer to close the meeting.

A CIA staffer came into the Cabinet Room after the meeting broke up and collected all the copies of the president's daily briefing. All briefing materials were top secret and were archived at Langley. Only ten people in the entire world knew what had been discussed at this meeting in the late summer of 2004.

PART 1

THE HEISMAN REPORT

1.

THE CONVOY OF three armored Suburbans barreled through the swirling dust. The last SUV had its rear hatch open, a legless sofa set up on the bed, facing the rear. On this jury-rigged gunnery platform sat Jonathan "Hawk" Yeager, eyes scanning the road behind the vehicle.

They were five minutes out from their barracks in the Green Zone. Yeager was on his last mission before his three-month tour in Baghdad came to an end.

Western Shield, his employer, assigned him and his colleagues to protection detail the whole time they'd been in Iraq. Yeager and his team provided security for VIPs from around the world: reporters from the United States, an executive of a British oil company inspecting postwar reconstruction efforts, diplomats from a small Asian country.

The Iraqi sun had been piercingly hot when Yeager had begun his tour, but now, three months later, the heat had abated. It was so cool, in fact, that by late afternoon he was starting to feel the chill, despite the body armor and tactical gear. If the temperature dropped any lower, he knew this gritty, low-slung city would look even bleaker and more desolate. Not that he was looking forward to the one-month leave he was about to begin tomorrow. If anything, the thought depressed him, and he wished he could stay put. For Yeager, this city, far removed from the peace that civilized people took for granted, was a kind of nihilistic playground, an escape from the reality that faced him at home.

An armored chopper grazing past the rooftops. Mortar rounds whizzing by, shattering the quiet of the night. The hollowed-out shell of a tank in a barren, sandy field. And the Tigris River, its surface littered with dead bodies.

In its 5,200-year history this cradle of civilization had seen countless wars and now, at the beginning of the twenty-first century, invasion by yet another enemy army. This invading foreign country claimed to be driven by ideology, but its real objectives were obvious: the vast oil deposits that lay beneath Iraqi soil.

Yeager knew the war wasn't about justice. Not that he cared one way or the other. All that mattered was that there was a job here, work that paid well. But seeing his family meant confronting a reality far harsher than anything he came across in Iraq. As long as he was in Baghdad he could avoid having to face his son and could use the excuse that he was doing his duty.

Sporadic gunfire echoed in the distance. M16 assault rifles. Yeager heard no answering AK-47s and knew it wasn't a real firefight.

He turned his gaze and saw a small car separate itself from the other vehicles far behind them and accelerate in his direction. Through his sunglasses Yeager checked out the vehicle, a battered Japanese sedan. Baghdad was crawling with them—little nondescript cars that terrorists loved to use for their suicide attacks. No one ever seemed to notice them until they exploded.

An adrenaline rush narrowed his field of vision. This main road their convoy was on was designated a kill zone. In the briefing before their mission they'd heard a report on how dangerous it was and how in the last thirty days the insurgents had switched from attacking US troops to targeting private defense contractors. A dozen or so security personnel had been killed along this short stretch of road alone.

His radio crackled with a report from the lead SUV. *"A suspicious vehicle up ahead on the right. Stopped under the overpass. It wasn't there this morning."*

Very likely the car contained an IED. Insurgents were probably nearby, impatient to set off a remote-control device. These explosives might be improvised, but they packed enough force to blow an armored car to shreds.

"Should we turn back?"

"Hold on," Yeager said into his wireless mike. "A car's coming our way from the rear."

The Japanese car was only fifty yards back now.

Get away! Yeager waved his M4 carbine at the car and signaled with his left arm for them to back off. But the car only sped up.

"Check the jamming device," the convoy leader, McPherson, yelled. The insurgents often used cell phones to trigger IEDs, and the jamming device could jam the signal.

"Jamming device is activated," the lead SUV reported.

"Keep going," McPherson ordered. *"And get rid of that car."*

"Roger that," Yeager replied and yelled at the car to move away.

But the car didn't obey. Through the dusty windshield the hostile face of the Iraqi driver glared back at him. Following the rules of engagement for security contractors, Yeager squeezed off a few rounds. The four shots struck the pavement near the car's bumper, sending fragments of concrete flying.

The warning shots didn't slow down the small car. Yeager raised his carbine and aimed for the hood of the car.

"Watch out for an IED!"

Seconds after McPherson yelled this through the radio, a low, rumbling explosion rocked the SUV. The bomb hadn't exploded in front of them but on the road a couple hundred meters to the rear, past where Yeager's carbine was pointed. A single date palm alongside the road was wreathed in black smoke. Another hate-filled religious fanatic bites the dust, Yeager thought. Just another day in Baghdad. But if the car following them exploded like that, they'd be scraping up pieces of him off the road.

Yeager didn't squeeze off a standard second warning shot, but drew a bead on the driver with his M4, the red laser beam inscribing a circle right between the Iraqi's eyes.

Don't close your eyes! Yeager yelled silently. Don't show me that pathetic expression bombers show just before they blow. Or else you're dead meat.

For the first time, the Iraqi driver looked afraid. Was he planning to die? Just as Yeager increased pressure on the trigger, the man's face in his scope shrank away. The sedan was slowing down.

For a moment darkness fell over them as the convoy slipped beneath the overpass. The suspicious vehicle under the bridge didn't explode.

Yeager waited for the car following them to change direction. "All clear," he reported.

"Roger that," McPherson replied from the lead SUV. *"Returning to base."*

Maybe the driver of the sedan wasn't a terrorist but just an ordinary citizen trying to challenge the Americans. And maybe the car stopped below the underpass wasn't booby-trapped but had simply broken down.

All Yeager knew was the terrible hatred directed at him, the rush of fear, and that he'd been a second away from gunning down a person he'd never even talked to.

The three armored SUVs passed the American checkpoint, wound their way through the detour set up to stop VBIEDs, and entered the Green Zone. The zone was in central Baghdad, surrounding the palace of the former dictator.

The Western Shield barracks was along the road, not far from the palace. It was a long, two-story, concrete-block building covered in peeling paint. There were so many rooms in the building he wondered what it had been used for before it was rented out to the private contractor. Housing for government employees? Or a school dorm? No one had a clue.

The convoy pulled up in the front yard, and the six security guards clambered out. All six, including Yeager, were former Special Forces— Green Berets. They exchanged a few fist bumps in honor of a completed mission as a maintenance crew ran out. The crew discovered a bullet hole from a high-powered rifle in the body of the lead car, but that didn't faze any of them. Par for the course.

"Hey, Hawk!" McPherson called out to Yeager as he was going inside. "No need to file a shooting incident report. Tonight we're partying on the roof."

"Roger that," Yeager said, smiling his thanks. McPherson must be planning a farewell party for him. Tomorrow a replacement would show up, and Yeager would be out of here. Standard rotation for this company was three months on, one month off. The next time he came back there would be no guarantee he'd be with the same crew or on the same assignment. And depending on where the bullets chanced to fly, he might never see any of his crewmates again.

"Where're you going on leave? Back home?"

"No; Lisbon."

McPherson knew the reason he was going to Portugal and nodded. "Hope it works out."

"Yeah. Me, too."

Yeager went up to his second-floor room, laid his M4 on the bed, stripped off his tactical gear, and stowed it in his locker. He'd relinquish his ammo and all the rest of the gear when he left and would just take along a backpack containing his few private effects.

Yeager paused and looked at the family photo taped to his locker door. It was taken six years ago at their home in North Carolina. Back in happier times. Yeager, his wife, Lydia, and their son, Justin, were seated on a sofa, smiling at the camera. Justin, seated on his father's lap, was so small he could almost have disappeared in Yeager's arms. Justin had his father's dark brown hair and his mother's blue eyes. When he smiled impishly he looked like Lydia, but when he was in a bad mood he looked just like a miniature version of his tough-guy dad, the former Green Beret. Yeager and his wife often wondered which of them he'd take after when he grew up.

Yeager stuck the photo in a half-read paperback, took out his cell phone, and called his wife in Lisbon. There was a three-hour time difference. Lunchtime would just be over there, and he knew he wouldn't get her the first time. So he left a voice message, asking her to call him back. He finished cleaning the M4 then went downstairs, cell phone and laptop in hand.

The small rec room was always crowded. It was outfitted with an old TV, a sofa and love seat, a coffeemaker, and some computers, which anyone could use. A couple of guys were at the screens, scrolling through porn sites and joking around. Yeager went to a different station and plugged in his laptop to a high-speed line. He knew he'd be disappointed, but he checked an academic search engine anyway.

As expected, nothing. No reports on any dramatic new treatment for PAECS—pulmonary alveolar epithelial cell sclerosis. "Yeager."

Yeager looked back to the doorway and saw Al Stephano, manager of the barracks, motioning to him. "Hawk, could you step into my office? You got a visitor."

"Me?" Wondering who could be visiting him, Yeager walked to Stephano's office at the foot of the stairs.

When he went in, a middle-aged man stood up from the sofa. He was about six feet tall, the same height as Yeager, and was dressed the same as the security guards—in a T-shirt and cargo pants. The man was a couple of decades older than Yeager, in his fifties. He had the stern look of a soldier, coupled with a faint smile. He held out his hand.

"This is William Liban, the director of Western Shield," Stephano explained.

Yeager knew the name. The private defense contractor that employed Yeager was founded by former Delta Force members, and Liban was the company's number two man. The secret to Western Shield's rapid success lay in the tight relationship between its executives and the military. Liban clearly had combat experience, yet he lacked the hard, aggressive demeanor of most Special Forces veterans.

Keep things formal and noncommittal, Yeager told himself as he shook his hand. "Very nice to meet you, Mr. Liban. Jonathan Yeager."

"Do you have a call sign?" Liban asked.

"They call me Hawk."

"Hawk, take a seat and let's talk." Liban motioned to the sofa and turned to Stephano. "Could we have the room?"

"Of course," Stephano said, and left his office.

When they were alone Liban gazed around the small room as though he were noticing it for the first time.

"Is this room secure?"

"As long as Stephano doesn't have his ear glued to the door."

Liban didn't crack a smile. "Good. Let me get right to it. Can you postpone your leave?"

"What's this about?"

"I'm hoping you could work one more month."

Yeager imagined what Lydia would say if he told her his trip to Lisbon had to be delayed.

"It's a good job. The pay's fifteen hundred dollars a day."

This was more than twice what he was getting now. This put him on his guard. Why would the company's number two executive fly all the way here to offer him a job? "Is it in Hillah?"

"Excuse me?"

Hillah was the most dangerous front in Iraq. "Is the job in Hillah?"

"No; the assignment isn't here. It's in another country. There'll be twenty days' prep time, then the mission should take, at most, ten days. You might even be done in five. But you're guaranteed thirty days' pay, no matter how short it turns out to be."

Forty-five thousand dollars for a month's work—not bad at all. Right now the Yeager family needed as much money as they could get. "What kind of assignment are we talking about?"

"I can't go into the details, but I can say this: the assignment originates with one of the coalition forces, not from someplace like Russia or China. Or North Korea. Also, it's not that dangerous a job. At least it's safer than being in Baghdad. And this assignment won't benefit any one particular country. If anything, you'll be doing a service to mankind."

Yeager couldn't fathom what the job could be, but at least it didn't seem overly risky. "Then why's the pay so high?" he asked.

A trace of disgust showed in the deep lines around Liban's eyes. "I was hoping you'd read between the lines. It's kind of a—dirty job."

A dirty job. An assassination. One that wouldn't benefit one particular country. But weren't all assassinations political?

"If you take the job, we'll need you to sign an agreement. Then once you start training we'll read you in. But understand that after you've signed the agreement and are briefed on the details, there's no backing out."

"You're worried about a leak? You shouldn't be. I have top secret clearance."

US military intelligence is divided into three clearance levels: confidential, secret, and top secret. A strict background check is required for clearance at each level, including a polygraph test. Even after he left the army Yeager had kept up his TS clearance, for without it he wouldn't be able to work at some of the assignments portioned out to security companies by the Defense Department.

"Look, I know your background. Ex–Special Forces, totally reliable. It's just that in this case we have to be extra cautious about security."

Liban's vague words gave Yeager another hint. This former Delta Force executive was talking about a job that required a higher level of security than what a TS clearance could provide. It required TS/SI, top secret/special intelligence, or TS/SCI, top secret/sensitive compartmented information. From what Liban was hinting at, this might even be an SAP, a special access program, the kind of operation with the most tightly controlled intelligence access of all—an assassination authorized by the White House, for example. But then why not assign Delta Force or Navy SEAL Team 6 to do it? This wasn't the kind of job you give to a private defense contractor.

"What do you think?" Liban said, urging him to make a decision. "Would you like to sign on?"

Yeager had a strange feeling. The same feeling he had when he was a teenager and his parents divorced and he had to choose which one to live with. The same sense of indecision he'd felt when, in the face of an urgent need to make up his mind, he'd decided, just before graduating from high school, to enter the army in order to be eligible for a scholarship later to go to college. He knew he was standing at a decisive crossroads. Whichever choice he made, he knew it would change his life forever.

"If you have any questions, now's the time. I'll answer as much as I can."

"You sure it isn't dangerous?"

"As long as you don't screw up."

"Is this a one-man job?"

"No. You'll be in a four-man team."

A four-man team was the smallest operational unit the Special Forces used.

"The rest of the terms of employment are the same as usual. We'll provide the weapons, and if you were to die during the operation the Defense Base Act will provide sixty-four thousand dollars to your family."

"Can I see the agreement?"

Liban smiled approvingly and took a document out of his briefcase. "You shouldn't hesitate. Trust your luck. You're a lucky guy."

"Me? Lucky?" Yeager gave a lopsided, half-sarcastic grin. "I always saw myself as the unlucky type."

"No, not at all. You're a survivor," Liban said, his mouth drawn. "We had six other candidates for this job, but all of them died. They died in firefights, one after another. The insurgents have been targeting security personnel a lot these days."

Yeager nodded.

"Today was the first time I was finally able to meet one of our candidates face-to-face."

Yeager considered the figures, hoping they'd wipe out the ominous feeling he had. Forty-five thousand dollars a month. Could he really turn an offer like that down? So what if it was a dirty job? He was just a replaceable tool anyway, no different from the gun in his hands. Even if he were to kill somebody, you couldn't blame the gun. The one who's to blame is the one who really pulls the trigger, the person who actually orders the murder.

Yeager scanned the agreement. It didn't provide any new clues. He just had to make up his mind and sign.

Liban held out a pen. As Yeager reached for it he felt a vibration in his shirt pocket and stopped.

"Excuse me," he said. He took out the cell phone and checked the screen. Lydia was calling back from Lisbon. "I'd like to check with my wife first. I told her I'd be seeing her tomorrow."

Liban looked like a hunter about to lose his prey. "Sure; go ahead."

Yeager pushed the call button. Before he said a word he heard Lydia's small voice. It held the despair and hopelessness he'd heard so many times before.

"Jon? It's me. I don't know what to do."

"What's wrong?"

She swallowed back her tears. "They put Justin in intensive care."

There goes more money, Yeager thought. I guess I have no choice but to sign. "Calm down, Lydia. We've been through this before, and he always gets better."

"This time's different. There's blood in his phlegm."

This was a sign that his son's disease was reaching its terminal stage. A chill ran up Yeager's spine. He motioned to Liban that he was stepping out, then he left the office. The stairs next to the hallway were noisy as security personnel rushed up and down.

"You sure about this?"

"I saw it myself. A red line like a piece of lint."

"A red line," Yeager muttered. "What does Dr. Garrado say?" Garrado, Justin's Portuguese attending physician, was one of the world's leading experts on PAECS.

Yeager couldn't make out Lydia's words through her sobs. He could picture her, wiping away the tears. "What is Dr. Garrado's opinion?" he asked again.

"He says that Justin's heart and liver are failing... that he doesn't have much time left."

Yeager forced his frozen mind to think, to review what he knew about the disease. Once a patient started hemorrhaging from the lungs, he had about a month left.

"You'll be here tomorrow, won't you?" Lydia sobbed, as if imploring him.

I have to see my son before it's too late, Yeager thought. But how the hell are we going to pay for his treatment? Yeager stared at the closed door of the office. He tried his best to hold up, but had reached the limits of his strength. His mind was hovering on the verge of chaos.

Why am I standing here in the hallway of a dirty barracks in Baghdad clutching this phone? he asked himself. Why the hell am I here?

"Jon?" his wife's sobbing voice reached him. "Jon? Are you there?"

2.

MISFORTUNE LOOKS VERY different when seen from the inside.

The hearse carrying his father's body wound its way through the narrow streets of the shopping district in the city of Atsugi, in Kanagawa Prefecture. Kento Koga was in a black limousine provided by the funeral home, slowly following behind the hearse.

It was early afternoon on a weekday. In the gentle winter sunshine, not one of the shoppers paused to look at the line of black cars as they passed by. And not a single one was sympathetic to the shock the young man was feeling.

Ever since he heard about the sudden death of his father, Seiji, Kento was unsure of his own feelings, as if all that kept him going emotionally had collapsed. Five days ago, when he'd rushed to the hospital and was told that the cause of death was an aneurysm of the thoracic aorta, he and his mother hadn't dissolved in tears. Ever since, they'd felt passive, inert, as if watching events sweep over them. His father's older brother and other relatives who'd hurried in from Yamanashi Prefecture took over all the arrangements for the funeral without ever being asked. It was obvious to them that they couldn't count much on the widow, a full-time housewife, or her thin, slight, graduate-student son.

Kento had never really respected his father. Seiji had always been so negative about everything, a man with a warped, jaundiced view of life. He had a respectable position, for sure—he was a full professor at a university—but Kento always viewed him as a poor example of an adult. So he was taken by complete surprise when, a half hour ago, as they were placing flowers inside his father's coffin, he'd burst into tears. It wasn't grief that brought this on, he thought as he wiped away the tears behind his glasses, but more a visceral reaction brought on by the blood ties they shared.

The coffin lid was closed; the body, surrounded by colorful flowers, lost to sight forever. This was the last time Kento would ever see him, this professor with long, haggard features. They'd known each other for but a brief twenty-four years.

The line of cars carrying the bereaved relatives and funeral home staff pulled up to the crematorium building, and the coffin was placed inside the incinerator. There were two types of incinerators, one more expensive than the other, and Seiji's coffin was in the cheaper one. Even in death they rank people according to how much they can afford, Kento thought, bristling at the Japanese view of life and death.

The thirty or so relatives and friends in the funeral party headed to the waiting room on the second floor. Only Kento stayed behind, staring at the tightly shut door of the incinerator. Inside, his father's body was consumed by flames. A passage from a book came to Kento, a science text he'd read in junior high.

The iron flowing in your blood was made in a supernova explosion some 4.6 billion years ago. Floating through the vastness of space, it became part of the earth as the solar system came into being, and now, through food, it has become part of your body. To carry this idea further, the hydrogen and other elements found throughout your body were created at the birth of the universe. They've existed for 13.7 billion years, along with the universe, and are now a part of you.

Now the time had arrived for all the elements in his father's body to return to the place from which they'd come. These scientific facts helped, a little, as he struggled to cope.

Kento left the incinerator and climbed the staircase in the spacious entry hall to the waiting room.

The group of mourners was seated in a circle in the middle of the large room, which was covered with tatami. The mourners sat on floor cushions placed next to low tables. Kento's mother, Kaori, couldn't hide her exhaustion but was still holding up. She was seated formally, politely thanking all her husband's friends and relatives who came to express their condolences.

Kento's grandparents were there, too, from Kofu, as well as his uncle and his family. The Kogas were a fairly well-to-do merchant family from Kofu, in Yamanashi, and though they'd recently been losing customers to a large supermarket that had moved into the neighborhood, Kento's uncle, who had taken over the family business, managed to keep their store going. It was the second son in the family, Seiji, who was the odd man out, for after attending a local university he'd gone on to graduate school in Tokyo, finished his doctorate, and stayed on as a researcher at the university instead of seeking a job in industry.

Kento never felt comfortable with his father's side of the family. He stood there for a moment, wondering where he should sit, finally settling down on a cushion in the farthest corner of the room.

"Hello, Kento."

From across the table a thin man, hair streaked with gray, was speaking to him—his father's friend, a newspaper reporter named Sugai. Sugai had visited their house in Atsugi a number of times, so Kento knew who he was.

"Haven't seen you in a while. You've really grown," Sugai said, coming around the table and sitting beside him. "You're in grad school now?"

"That's right."

"What are you studying?"

"I'm in a pharmaceuticals chemistry lab, working on organic synthesis," Kento said curtly.

He tried to make it clear he wasn't in the mood to talk, but Sugai went on anyway. "What exactly do you do?"

Kento reluctantly explained. "We use computers to design new drugs, which are then created based on these plans. We combine all sorts of compounds."

"Shaking a test tube in a lab?"

"You could say that."

"Sounds like research that helps people."

"I suppose so..." The words of praise made Kento uncomfortable. "Anyway, it's all I know how to do."

Sugai inclined his head, puzzled. He might be a reporter, but he seemed unable to bring to light the doubts Kento held, deep down, about his own abilities and aptitude for the work he was doing. At this point Kento wasn't anyone special, and Sugai didn't figure that would ever change.

"Scientific research in Japan has some serious fundamental problems, so we're counting on you" was all Sugai said.

Fundamental problems. The guy's a science reporter at a major newspaper, yet he has no idea what he's talking about, Kento thought angrily. Something about Sugai rubbed him the wrong way. He couldn't pinpoint it, but his kindness came off sounding more like hostility, and Kento ended up feeling slighted.

Ten years ago his father's research had been written up in the science columns of all the big newspapers. It was the first and only time Seiji, in his role as scientist, had been in the spotlight. Sugai had written the column. The term *environmental hormones* was sweeping the nation, and in his research at the university lab his father had determined that the ingredients in a particular controversial synthetic detergent didn't harm the human endocrine system. REPORT BY PROFESSOR SEIJI KOGA OF TAMA POLYTECHNIC, the bold headlines had said, and when he saw this it was the first and only time in his life that Kento was proud of his father. But his newfound respect soon faded when he found out that his father had accepted a large research grant from the detergent's manufacturer.

Seiji's field had been virology, so why had he, this one time, done research into materials that disrupted the endocrine system? And was his research really objective? Had he skewed the data to pander to the company that was shelling out all this research money?

Since then researchers throughout the world had looked into the effects of environmental hormones on the body but had never found conclusive proof that they were harmful. But their conclusions were less than satisfying, because they still couldn't state categorically that the hormones were harmless. The whole thing illustrated the limits of science, Kento had decided. But still, the incident had engendered a dislike toward his father and a distrust that he couldn't shake. And he'd lumped Sugai, who'd written the article, in the same category—people who lived in a corrupt adult world.

"It's a real shame. He still had so many good years ahead of him," Sugai said, clearly shocked at the sudden death of a friend the same age as he.

"Thank you for coming all the way to be with us."

"It's the least I could do," Sugai said, his head bowed.

To fill in the lull in the conversation Kento picked up the teapot on the table and poured them each a cup of tea.

Sugai sipped and reminisced about Seiji. They were all the stereotypical anecdotes you'd expect from a cheap TV drama—about how his father had been well respected at work, how deep down he must have been so proud of his son. It made Kento feel all the more how dull and prosaic his father's life had been.

Finally out of topics, Sugai changed the subject. "Someone said you're going to do the memorial service for your father as soon as we finish our tea."

"That's right."

"I have to be going just after that. So I'd better ask you now, before I forget."

"Forget what?"

"Have you ever heard of the Heisman Report?"

"Heisman Report?" Must be some sort of academic paper, though he'd never heard of any researcher named Heisman. "No, I've never heard of it."

"Your father asked me to look into it, and I was wondering what I should do now."

"What's the Heisman Report?"

"It was a report to the president of the United States from an American think tank thirty years ago. Your father wanted to know the details."

Must have something to do with a viral epidemic, his father's field. "I can't help you there," Kento said.

His tone was unexpectedly detached, and Sugai, seemingly surprised, stared at him. "I understand. Don't worry about it, then."

Kento didn't care what Sugai thought of him. The relationship between a father and son was nobody else's business. Parents and children with a perfect relationship were a myth, anyway.

The funeral director soon came to assemble them. The mourners, who had been talking in hushed, subdued tones, shuffled to their feet and followed him downstairs.

Kento stood in front of the incinerator and received the bones of his father. The whitish bones laid out so simply, so bleakly, before him told a graphic tale of how a single human being had now vanished from the earth.

His grandparents and his uncle were sobbing quietly. And Kento, for only the second time since his father had died, found himself crying, too.

The memorial service soon followed, and then the ceremonies for sending the departed on his way were over.

The alarm clock buzzed Kento awake early the next morning, and after a quick breakfast he left his parents' home, located in a subdivision in Atsugi. He had to get back to his grad-student life, back to his one-room apartment and a life of following the instructions of an assistant professor, slogging through one boring experiment after another.

As he walked out of the typical three-bedroom house into the cold morning air, Kento started to worry about his mother, who was alone now. His mother's parents would be staying with her for a while, but after they went home she'd be all by herself. It was impossible for him to imagine what must be going through her mind now that she was widowed at the age of fifty-four.

As he'd left she said, "Stop by and see me some time."

"Okay. Will do," he replied, and set off for Hon-Atsugi station.

The university Kento attended, the Tokyo University of Humanities and Science, was located on the other side of Tokyo from Atsugi, in Kinshi-cho, the town closest to Chiba Prefecture. Fifteen thousand students attended the school, which was a fifteen-minute walk from Kinshi-cho station. As you walked northeast from the station you came to a canal called the Yokojikken River, which divided the campus in two: the science campus was on the left bank and the humanities campus was on the right. Only the medical faculty, with the university hospital, was separate; it was located closer to the station. The university boasted a ninety-year history, but with the steady reconstruction over the years even the extensive farmlands that used to exist there—part of the school of agriculture—were covered over by new school buildings. Like universities within Tokyo itself, the campus was dreary, a sprawl of uninspired concrete structures.

From his parents' home the journey took two hours, with one change of trains, so Kento had plenty of time to think about his future. His family's financial situation worried him most. When he was in his second year of studying for his MA, Kento had decided not to look for a job but go right into the doctoral program, which meant he would have to rely on his family for three more years' worth of tuition and living expenses.

One of his friends, a student in the humanities, teased him for still sponging off his parents, lecturing him on the need to go out and get a part-time job, but this was a typical way of thinking for humanities students—they just played around and never studied. Almost all the classes in the pharmacy school were required, and dropping even one unit meant you'd flunk out. After you passed the national pharmacy licensing exam and the graduation exams, what faced you in grad school was a life spent running experiments and nothing else. Days so unbelievably hectic that *harsh* didn't come close to describing them. *Unimaginable* was more like it. In the pharmaceuticals research lab that Kento belonged to, you were stuck in the lab every weekday running tests, from 10:00 a.m. until far into the night. The only days off were Sundays and holidays, but tests often ran late, and half those days off were still spent in the lab. Lengthy vacations were out of the question, and if you could get five days off in a row for the summer Obon festival or New Year's, you considered yourself lucky. You spent nine years like this to get to, finally, become a "doctor." A part-time job? Give me a break.

Until a month ago he could have still gotten a full-time job instead of staying in research. Kento cursed his bad timing. Either way would have been fine with him. He'd gone on to the doctoral program because he didn't feel ready to go out into the world, not because he was all fired up to work in research. Quite the opposite: ever since he entered university he'd felt out of place, as if he'd made a wrong choice. He never really enjoyed pharmacology or organic synthesis, but he had continued with it simply because he had no other skills. He could picture it well—twenty years from now he'd wind up just like his father, a boring researcher in some backwater branch of science.

Kento arrived on campus, and as he passed through the back entrance to the science and engineering quad and headed toward the pharmacology building, his pace grew dull and heavy. The more he thought about the drab path he was headed down in life, the heavier his steps had become, but he finally managed to pull himself together and speed up.

He climbed the linoleum steps to the third floor, to the Sonoda Lab, named after his supervisor. He walked down a corridor and opened a door onto another short corridor. On either side were small rooms, some with lockers; one of them was a seminar room. At the end of the corridor was Professor Sonoda's office, and to the left was the research lab.

Kento, dressed in jeans and a sweatshirt, took off his down jacket, hung it up in one of the lockers, and looked into the professor's office. The door was open, and Professor Sonoda was there, dressed in his usual shirt and tie.

"Good morning," Kento said, and went inside.

Professor Sonoda glanced up from a stack of papers on his desk, and when he saw it was Kento he looked concerned. Professor Sonoda was normally a lively person, much more energetic than you would expect from a man in his late fifties, ever ready to urge on his young grad students. But now he wore a grave, solicitous look.

"I'm so sorry to hear what happened," he said. "How are you holding up?"

"Okay, I think," Kento replied, and thanked him for sending flowers to the funeral.

"I never had the pleasure of meeting your father," Professor Sonoda said. "But because we were in the same line of work it really hit home. It's a terrible loss."

Kento was genuinely grateful for his supervisor's kind words. Professor Sonoda was an elite researcher who had developed numerous new drugs for major pharmaceuticals companies, yet he somehow managed to find time in his busy research schedule to write academic papers, which had led to his being appointed professor at the university. He was also exceptionally adept at winning major grants to conduct joint research projects with drug manufacturers. Kento had often compared his father unfavorably with the professor, wondering why his father couldn't be more like him.

Not wanting to bring back sad memories, Professor Sonoda changed the subject. "So are you ready to come back?"

"Yes, I—" Kento said, and stopped. Other than the formal interment of his father's bones, was there anything else he still had to do? "I still might have to ask for a few days off."

"Of course; that would be fine. Don't hesitate to ask."

"Thank you. I appreciate it."

"Well, work awaits," the professor said, smiling encouragingly, and saw him out.

The lab the grad students worked in was, perhaps, too enormous to be labeled a room. It was a gigantic space as big as four junior high or high school classrooms put together. There were four lab benches in the middle, covered with various testing equipment and jars of chemical compounds, and along three of the walls there were grad-student workstations and draft chambers with industrial exhaust fans. The scene verged on the chaotic, but somehow the functional beauty of it all had its own special power and appeal.

The Sonoda Lab was focused on developing new drugs to combat autoimmune diseases. The professor, his assistant professor, and some twenty grad students were all dedicated to the task, but at this time of year, in January, the lab was relatively quiet. Undergrads who worked in the lab were preparing for the national pharmacy license exam, while the recently graduated MA students were mostly out on job interviews.

"Kento, I'm really sorry to hear about your father," Kento's immediate supervisor, Nishioka, said. He was a second-year PhD student. His eyes were red, as if he'd been crying, but it wasn't from tears of sympathy: it was because he had spent another long, sleepless night in the lab.

"Thank you for your text message," Kento said, remembering the condolences Nishioka had sent.

"I'm sorry I couldn't make the wake."

"Everybody's busy, so I can't expect them to attend. I should be the one to apologize, for taking five days off."

"No; don't worry about that," Nishioka said, blinking his bloodshot eyes.

Other colleagues came up one by one to express warm words of sympathy. Even the female grad students, normally so brisk and businesslike, were unusually kind as they spoke with him. Kento realized that he'd made it this far as a researcher through the help of all these colleagues.

Kento stood at his workstation and got back to work. Organic synthesis focuses on creating carbon-based compounds. Carbon has, as it were, four hands with which to connect up with other elements. Oxygen has two. When these elements combine, two oxygen atoms link up with a carbon atom, creating CO_2, namely, carbon dioxide. But organic synthesis is not, unfortunately, this easy. It is much more challenging to build new organic compounds from simpler building blocks. Many reaction conditions can influence the results: the chemical concentration, the order of addition, the temperature, the type of catalyst, and the reaction solvent, to name a few. In Professor Sonoda's lab researchers were constantly looking for molecular structures with druglike activity, which they could further modify to create new pharmacologic agents.

Kento's present research involved working with a basic core structure consisting of carbon, oxygen, and nitrogen molecules and adding other functional groups to it. The assistant professor had taped the recipe onto his workstation—instructions on the steps he should take to get the reaction they were looking for. Pharmacology experiments had something in common with cooking. The connection wasn't clear, but the fact remained that there were far more women in the pharmacy schools than men. In some universities it was up to 90 percent. At the graduate-school level, too—unusual for the sciences—nearly half the students were female.

It took Kento the rest of the morning to get his reagents and lab equipment set up and to prepare for the first reaction. While he waited for the results, he went to his desk by the window and flipped open his laptop. As expected, he'd received several sympathy e-mails. He was grateful to his friends for their thoughts. He read through them, answering each one. When he got to the last message, he froze. The sender's name startled him: Seiji Koga, Tama Polytechnic University.

He checked the name again, and a chill ran up his spine.

The e-mail was from his dead father.

He almost shouted out in surprise, then glanced around him. The other students were deep into their own experiments, none of them paying him any attention.

Kento pushed his narrow glasses up higher on his nose and gazed at the screen. The message had been sent today, at exactly twelve midnight. More than five days after his father had passed away. The subject heading read:

To Kento, from Dad

It didn't seem to be a virus e-mail or spam masquerading as a message from his father. Was this somebody's idea of a prank?

Kento checked that his security software was running and opened the message. Small, nine-point script came up on the display.

Dear Kento,

If you get this message it means I've been away from you and your mother for more than five days. But no need to worry. I should be back in a couple of days.

Back? Back from *what?* From the dead? Kento read on.

Figuring I wouldn't be able to get home for a while, I have something I need you to do.

Open the book you dropped a Popsicle on.

And don't tell your mother or anyone else about this message.

That's all.

The message ended there.

Short, but cryptic. It looked like a farewell note, but his father didn't seem to be thinking he might die when he wrote it. Had he really sent this? Had he used software that lets you send a message at a predetermined time? If he really set this up himself, it obviously meant he'd anticipated he'd be away from them. But why? Kento was clueless.

Kento reread the final lines.

Open the book you dropped a Popsicle on.

Popsicle? He pondered this for a moment, and then it hit him, and he knew the message had to be from his father. Back when he was in elementary school, his father had decided to give him some extra lessons during summer vacation and had reviewed the periodic table of the elements with him in a science reference book. As Kento was looking at it, the Popsicle he'd been licking slipped off its stick and plopped onto the page, staining the box representing zinc — Zn — a strawberry color. Only his father knew about this.

The book must still be back home, on a shelf in his father's study. He considered calling his mother to have her check it out, but his father's instructions brought him up short.

Don't tell your mother or anyone else.

If he was going to obey his late father's wishes, it meant he'd have to go all the way home again, another two-hour train ride.

Kento leaned back in his chair. What could possibly be hidden away in that sticky, stained old book?

3.

YEAGER FLEW INTO the Republic of South Africa, changing planes in Johannesburg and arriving in Cape Town. In the Southern Hemisphere it was the middle of summer. He was met at the airport by a car from a local private defense contractor, Zeta Security, and driven to a training facility in the suburbs.

South Africa was where the first private defense contractors had begun. In its initial stages this new business—providing paid military services—had success in putting an end to some of the civil wars that raged on the African continent. But the practice had also led to some bloodthirsty mercenaries grabbing the wealth of certain countries by force so that the winning side could gain control of valuable mineral resources. The South African government passed an antimercenary law prohibiting South African defense contractors from operating in foreign countries, but under the pretext of aiding in the reconstruction efforts in Iraq a number of new private defense contractors had sprung up, Zeta Security among them. Zeta was a subcontractor for Yeager's employer, Western Shield.

The view outside changed as they drove, first through a beautiful, seaside city, then through wide-open plains filled with vineyards, and finally up into hills. Yeager, seated in the back of the van, still struggled with whether he'd made the right decision.

In Baghdad he'd made up his mind to turn down the job offer and fly to Lisbon to be with his wife and son. But after he spoke with Lydia and Dr. Garrado, he found out how enormously expensive it was going to be to keep Justin alive for the final days of his life. Over the past four years, as they paid for the advanced medical treatment for Justin abroad, Yeager and his wife had reached the limit of what they could borrow.

Even if it meant he couldn't be with Justin as much as he should, Yeager was at the point where he needed to earn some serious money.

Dr. Garrado was their last hope. Most children with PAECS die before they reach the age of six. No one has ever survived until the age of nine. But using every possible treatment in his repertoire, Dr. Garrado, one of a handful of experts on the disease, had kept Justin, now age eight, alive. When terminal symptoms appear the patient usually has only a month to live, but Yeager was counting on Dr. Garrado to keep Justin alive a few more months. As soon as he finished this assignment he could race off to see him and make it in time. And spend his son's final days with him.

But what would happen to him after Justin passed? What choice would Lydia make?

They'd been on the verge of divorce several times. When Justin was two and had started having breathing problems, the doctor at the army hospital had first told them their son's disease was a single gene disorder. "People get two sets of genes from their parents," he'd explained. "So even if one set is abnormal, the other will cover for it and allow things to function normally. Sometimes, though, a person gets abnormal genes from both parents, and a disease results. In your son's case there's a mutation in one part of the genes that create the lungs, which results in difficulties in absorbing oxygen."

Yeager felt like he was being blamed for the condition. And Lydia probably felt the same way. As if he could read their thoughts, the doctor added, "This isn't anybody's fault. It's more like plain bad luck. Everyone has some abnormal genes, some more than others. In this case, unfortunately, two abnormal genes happened to be in the same location."

But Yeager found this bad luck hard to accept. If only he hadn't married Lydia, then his child wouldn't be suffering like this. And Lydia must have had similar thoughts about her husband. The blame went back and forth, one of them attacking the other, barbed words flying fast and furious, cutting them to the quick. They knew these fights only made them more miserable, but they couldn't stop.

It was only a matter of time before their marriage fell apart. Right around this period was when they first heard of Dr. Antonio Garrado at the Lisbon University Medical Center, who specialized in the disease. But their military health insurance didn't cover treatment abroad, and Yeager's E-9 sergeant major salary wasn't enough to pay for the expensive treatment.

One day, after Yeager had finished a long tour and had returned home, he and Lydia were having their usual fight when he suggested they get divorced. Lydia, though, wouldn't agree to it. She insisted that they stick it out for three more years. Wiping away her tears with her fingertips, a characteristic gesture, she said, "Ever since he was little, Justin's been suffering because of this disease. He doesn't have even one happy memory. And you want us to get divorced and make his life even more miserable?"

Lydia's words struck a chord. Yeager's own parents had broken up when he was a child.

Then, after spending a short time home on leave, he left on another deployment. There, in Afghanistan, as part of a forward observation team, he met a man on contract from a private defense contractor. A former SEAL member, the man told him he'd be happy to introduce Yeager to his employers if he were interested.

It was the perfect chance. Private contractors didn't get benefits or retirement, but their salary was more than three times that of his army pay, and he'd be able to earn at least one hundred and fifty thousand dollars a year. He waited until the so-called stop loss period was lifted, during which his term of service could be extended beyond the contracted-for end date, then resigned from the army and moved his wife and son to Portugal.

Three more years, Lydia had said, but thankfully Dr. Garrado had been able to extend that to five. Now, though, with Justin coughing up blood, the end was, at most, a few weeks away.

Yeager was determined to keep their family going until their son had passed, but after Justin was gone Yeager was sure he would end up alone—a mercenary who fought for money, not for country.

"Here we are. Company headquarters."

The driver's voice brought Yeager back to the present. He glanced at his watch and saw that the trip from the airport had taken more than an hour. The Zeta Security four-wheel-drive vehicle passed through the sentry gate and entered the company grounds. It was a large base, in dry, hilly country, cordoned off by security fencing. The compound contained a main building, training grounds, and a runway long enough to accommodate cargo planes during takeoff and landing.

The headquarters was a spacious, three-story, cream-colored Mediterranean-style building that nicely belied the shady image associated with private defense contractors. From the outside, Yeager thought, it looked more like some chic hotel.

As he got out of the van, Yeager put on his game face. It was show-time—time to put the harsh realities of his life behind.

He lugged his backpack and sports bag into the lobby, where a tall man with a mustache came out to greet him. He was dressed in khaki from head to toe—military without a doubt, a hard look in his eyes, as though he'd forgotten how to smile. "Mike Singleton, director of operations," the man said in a South African accent. "The rest of your team is already here. I'll show you to your room."

Yeager followed him to the back of the building. They walked down a mazelike corridor, past numbered rooms. Singleton halted in front of room 109, knocked, and opened the door.

The room was a typical four-man layout, with bunk beds along the walls on each side and individual lockers on the far wall, straight ahead. The only new item in the room was a small writing desk. The three men who had been standing in the room, talking among themselves, looked toward the door as soon as it opened.

"Gentlemen," Singleton said. "Let me introduce one of your team members. Jonathan Yeager, call sign Hawk." The men's expressions were a little tense at this first meeting. For Yeager these were critical new colleagues, his new comrades in arms.

"We assemble at seventeen hundred hours in the second-floor briefing room," Singleton added, and left.

"Hi, Hawk," one of the men said. He was slim, calm-looking, and appeared to be in his twenties—on the young side for a private defense contractor. In situations like these invariably the friendliest man introduced himself first, the most somber man last. "Scott Meyers, call sign Blanket."

"Nice to meet you." Yeager smiled at the call sign and shook his hand.

The next man to shake his hand was about the same age. "Warren Garrett. No call sign."

He figured Garrett for a thoughtful staff officer. An unpretentious type, but someone you could count on when things got rough.

Meyers and Garrett were both white, probably American, but the third man was Asian. He was short but hugely muscular, especially around the neck and shoulders, obviously on performance-enhancing drugs.

"Mikihiko Kashiwabara," he said.

"Miki—*heko*?" Yeager asked, and Meyers and Garrett laughed.

"Nobody can pronounce it," Garrett said. "Japanese names are impossible."

"What were you called on your last job?" Meyers asked. "Mickey?"

"Mick," the Japanese man said, disgust evident in his voice. Clearly not his favorite nickname.

"Mick it is, then," said Garrett.

Japanese weren't common among private defense contractors, and Yeager was impressed. "What did you do before you started this line of work?" he asked.

"I was in the French Foreign Legion," Mick replied in heavily accented English. "Before that I was with the Japan Self-Defense Force."

Yeager already saw a potential problem. Normally when a team of private contractors was put together the men were all from the same military background. Even within the United States, the army and the marines employed different tactics and weapons. Once they were in combat these differences could lead to confusion and even get a team killed, which is why private contractors were usually teamed up with people who had the same background and training.

"I was in the US Special Forces," Yeager said, trying to draw out the others.

"US Air Force for me," Meyers said. "Pararescue."

Pararescue jumpers were trained in advanced medical treatment and combat. Their motto was "That others may live." An unusual background for a private defense contractor.

"The marines, Force Recon," Garrett said.

The team was certainly a mixed bag. Yeager knew they'd have to coordinate code words and hand signals to use in a combat situation. And he'd have to make sure that Mick felt like part of the team.

The briefing room was a small, windowless room. Narrow desks lined up facing a whiteboard next to the wall.

Singleton strode in at exactly 1700. He glanced at Meyers, who was ready to take notes. "No notes in this briefing. You need to memorize all the info I give you."

Meyers quietly put away his pad and pen.

"I know you still don't know each other, so I'll introduce each of you and tell you what your individual assignments are. First of all, all of you are airborne certified. Yeager will be the team leader. He'll be in charge of weapons and sharpshooting. Your languages are English, Arabic, and Pashtun, too, I believe?"

"Correct," Yeager replied.

"In the present operation, though, we won't have need for those special skills." Singleton turned to the next man. "Meyers will be your medic. What other languages do you speak?"

"None, really," the young man answered. "A little medical terminology. That's about it."

Singleton stared hard at him for a moment. Yeager figured Singleton for a former member of the South African army.

"Garrett, you're in charge of communications. In addition to English you speak French and Arabic?"

Garrett wordlessly nodded.

"Finally, Kashiwabara," Singleton said, carefully sounding out the name. "You're in charge of explosives. You speak Japanese and French, but can you handle English?"

"I—think so," Mick replied.

Singleton looked a little concerned at the uncertain reply. "Let's take a look at your schedule," he went on.

Their training regimen would include forty-kilometer endurance marches every other day, training in Swahili, and inoculations against a variety of diseases, yellow fever included.

"Let's move on to your area of operations." Singleton walked over to a projector and punched up a PowerPoint presentation onto a large screen. The first slide was a map of Africa. He hovered his laser pointer over at the middle of the map. "You'll be inserted into the Democratic Republic of the Congo, known until recently as Zaire."

Yeager checked the location of the Congo. It was a large country right in the center of the continent, just below the equator. The country's border was long on the west, as it followed the Congo River, which ran past the capital, Kinshasa, all the way to the Atlantic Ocean, where it ended in a narrow strip. The different colors of the map showed the concentration of tropical rain forest within the Congo's borders. The country was covered in heavy forests.

"Gentlemen, you'll be inserted at the opposite end of the country from Kinshasa, in the eastern jungle region. It's a search and destroy mission. Your cover will be that you're working for an animal rights organization, so let your hair grow out. Your primary weapons will be limited to AK-47s and shotguns. We won't be distributing squad automatic weapons. I'll give details on the rest of your gear at a later briefing." Singleton looked at Meyers, the former pararescue jumper. "Meyers, are you familiar with Ebola hemorrhagic fever?"

"I am."

"Since this has to do with the mission, could you brief the team on this disease?"

Meyers looked a bit taken aback, but turned to the other members. "Ebola hemorrhagic fever is the most deadly infectious disease known to man. The virus destroys the cells of the body, including the brain. The internal organs and muscles dissolve while you're still alive. In a person infected with the disease all the bodily fluids infected by the virus gush out through the openings of the body—the ears, nose, mouth, and anus, and through the pores—and you die. The mortality rate for *Zaire ebolavirus* is ninety percent."

The soldiers listened without expression. Meyers stood and pointed to the map of the Congo on the screen. "The eastern region of the Congo, where we're going, is surrounded by Ebola hot zones, including those along the western part of the Ebola River and the border with southern Sudan, to the northeast. Kenya and Uganda, to the east, have also seen substrains of Ebola."

Yeager raised his hand. "What's the treatment?"

"There isn't any. Once infected, all you can do is pray."

"You said the mortality rate is ninety percent," Garrett said. "What about the remaining ten percent?"

"Their immune system somehow stands up to it, and they're able to survive."

"Hmm," Garrett responded softly.

"You'll be operating outside of the endemic area," Singleton said. "But you'll still need to take precautions. There's a high possibility that bats can carry the disease, so make sure you don't get bitten or come in contact with their droppings. Also, other primates can be infected, so stay clear of chimpanzees, gorillas, and small monkeys."

"If you get infected, what are the symptoms?" Yeager asked.

"Fever, vomiting, and other symptoms resembling malaria. But Ebola particularly affects the eyes and testicles."

The men grimaced for the first time.

"So if your eyes turn red, that could be a sign you're infected."

"I'd rather not have to check out anybody's balls," Meyers said, and everyone laughed.

Mick, who'd been silent until now, spoke up in his halting English. "Why doesn't that disease . . . spread all over the world? Like HIV?"

"That's a good question, Mick," Meyers said. "The virus's incubation period is too short. Once infected, you start showing symptoms in about seven days. Which means most patients die before they're able to infect others."

"I see."

"So you understand how frightening Ebola is now?"

The four men nodded. Though they didn't verbalize it, all of them had one question that they answered for themselves. If one of the team got infected during the operation, what was the protocol? There wouldn't be a rescue helicopter. They'd have to give him a needle and some morphine and leave him behind in the jungle. This was the fate of a mercenary in battle. In exchange for the good pay, they were expendable.

"I'd like to turn to the main topic today: the situation in the place you'll infiltrate, the Democratic Republic of the Congo." Singleton called up the next slide. The men were unprepared for the gruesome scene on the screen, a muddy road littered with bodies. Young people, old people, men, women. Some of them had their hands tied behind their backs, others were headless torsos.

"Genocide," Singleton intoned. "Right now the Congo is experiencing a large-scale conflict, one that's been dubbed the Great War in Africa. It's responsible for the highest number of dead since the Second World War—four million. Cease-fires have been broken over and over, and there's no end in sight."

As if reading the doubt in the men's expressions, Singleton went on. "This is really happening, believe me. It's just that the newspapers and TV aren't reporting it. Discrimination on the part of the media, you could say. The mass media in industrialized countries doesn't care how many Africans die. The genocide that occurs all the time there gets less coverage than when seven gorillas are killed. Of course Africans aren't an endangered species." Singleton smiled coldly.

"The root cause of the problems in the Congo can be traced back to colonial times. When Belgium controlled the country they pitted the two main tribes—the Tutsi and the Hutu, which up until then had gotten along peacefully—against each other. They arbitrarily gave preferential treatment to the Tutsi, which provoked resentment on the part of the Hutu. This tribal hatred festered until it broke out in genocide in Rwanda."

Yeager knew all about this conflict. The Hutu president's plane was shot down, and this caused the Hutu to start slaughtering the Tutsi. The state radio fanned the flames of the massacre, and thousands of ordinary citizens took up hatchets and cudgels and began murdering their neighbors. They aimed their attack at women and children in order to annihilate the Tutsi for all time. Murderous bands quickly sprang up, fueled not just by tribal hatred but also by the fear that if you didn't participate in the killing you'd be killed yourself, even if you were Hutu, and by the false rumor that anyone murdering a Tutsi would get his farmland. The slaughter became fierce, with victims paying their attackers to shoot them in the head instead of cutting them up with dull knives and leaving them to bleed to death. In the chaos many Hutu were mistaken for Tutsi and butchered.

A hundred days after the genocide began, a Tutsi-led military force was organized outside the country. They counterattacked, and finally the situation calmed down. But not before 10 percent of the population had been killed—some eight hundred thousand people.

"Rwanda became a Tutsi-controlled government, and peace returned, but so did historical revisionism, the claim that the genocide had never happened." Singleton smiled coldly again as he continued the briefing. "And that's it, as far as the rest of the world is concerned. But the tragedy has continued. That genocide touched off the Great War in Africa."

The PowerPoint slide changed to an enlarged view of the Congo region. Singleton's laser pointer flitted back and forth between Rwanda to the east and the Democratic Republic of the Congo to the west.

"One faction of the Hutu ringleaders of the Rwandan massacre escaped into the DRC and are still mounting cross-border attacks from there. The Congo government has turned a blind eye to this, which has enraged Rwanda. The conflict evolved into one between Rwanda and the Congo. Rwanda, in partnership with Uganda, also a Tutsi-led government, moved to overthrow the Congo dictatorship. They gave support to antigovernment guerrillas in eastern Congo, which began a rebel insurgency. Their plan was a great success. The rebel forces quickly moved west, overran the capital, drove out the dictator, and established a new regime. The new president was the leader of the rebel army supported by Rwanda. You'd think that would settle things, but that's when the situation turned into even more of a quagmire."

The slide changed to one that showed three maps, each tracing the power shifts among insurgent groups in the various regions of the Congo.

"The new president wanted to make it look like he wasn't a puppet of Rwanda, so he betrayed his Tutsi supporters and joined forces with the remaining Hutu armed groups in the east. Needless to say, this upset Rwanda, which, in concert with Uganda and Burundi, attacked in an attempt to overthrow him. The new government had its back to the wall, so it sought aid from outside and allied itself with Chad and other neighboring countries. That's how this massive war started, in 1998, with more than ten countries involved."

As Singleton finished, Yeager raised his hand. "Do the countries involved in the conflict have the financial resources to sustain such a huge war?" he asked.

A cold smile again came to Singleton's lips. "They all have their sponsors. Once the war began the real goal became clear—control of the resources that lie beneath the soil of the Congo. Diamonds, gold, oil, and rare earth metals used in computer components. The forces fighting in the Congo are keeping up this bloody conflict because of mineral resources, and more than a hundred European and Asian corporations have a financial stake in the outcome. Mining companies give military aid to the forces that plunder the resources and take their share from what's left over. Rwanda exports more minerals than they mine within their borders, and developed countries buy this up, even though they know it's been stolen. Hundreds of thousands of Congolese have died to supply the coltan used in cell phones. And superpowers like the United States and Russia support the Congolese government, while behind the scenes they also help fund Rwanda and Uganda—playing both sides so they can ensure that, no matter who wins, they protect their interest in Congo's mineral resources. If you consider all the funding that's coming into the conflict, most of the major powers are involved, and it's become a world war."

"What about human resources?" Garrett asked. "How do they maintain that many soldiers?"

"At first they drafted the unemployed, then the poor. If you're in the army, at least you get fed. But they still needed more troops, so they started kidnapping children. I want to emphasize that this is no longer a war between states. The majority of Congolese do not support this idiotic conflict. A handful of evil men—some two hundred in an armed group—have, for instance, created a ten-thousand-person army. And the Congolese government forces are no better. They attack their own country's villages, plunder everything in sight, and massacre the people." Singleton returned to the map. "Right now Congolese government forces control the west and south, but the northern and eastern regions are in chaos. Rwanda and Uganda, which are supposed to be allies, have split over who gets to control the mineral resources, and things have spun out of control. The eastern region, where you'll be going, has seen continuous war for more than twenty years, and it's reached the point where you can't tell friend from foe anymore. On top of this, racial hatred has festered, and you have genocide everywhere you turn. The UN has dispatched a peacekeeping force, but they can't keep an eye on this whole jungle region. It's just too huge."

"So whose side are we fighting on?" Yeager asked. "The UN?"

"You're not on any side. You'll infiltrate the jungle without any of the insurgent groups noticing your presence and carry out a mission that's not part of what's going on in this war."

"What, specifically?"

"I'm not at liberty to provide more details yet. For the time being, just focus on your training."

Yeager was reminded of his time in the army. *Don't question anything* was the rule drummed into the heads of all new recruits.

"In the Congo you won't find any cool new weapons; no pinpoint bombing tactics. No cause or ideology or patriotism behind all this. It's naked war, a power grab stripped of any pretense. It's a bloody struggle over minerals and racial hatred, in which people slaughter each other with machetes and small arms." Singleton's expression was stiff and un-readable again. He ended the briefing with these words:

"After you infiltrate the region, if you want to avoid seeing hell, don't go near any people."

4.

KENTO WAITED UNTIL Sunday before venturing to his parents' home in Atsugi. He was surprised at how still and quiet the house had become in
the days since he'd last been there.

His mother, Kaori, looked gaunt, but having her own parents there
was keeping her occupied.

Kento briefly chatted with them in the living room, then made his
way upstairs. There were three rooms on the second floor; the smallest
of them had been his father's study. Bookcases lined three of the walls,
and a desk stood in the middle of the room.

The room had his father's smell. Before he could get too sentimental,
though, his curiosity won out—the desire to know what was in the book
he'd *dropped a Popsicle on*. Kento scanned the bookcases and found it, on the
lowest shelf of the middle bookcase. *Chemistry Commentaries*, volume 1.

He opened the book and found that the pages had been neatly
scooped out. Hidden inside was an envelope, folded in two.

Kento picked up the envelope and stared at it intently. On the outside
were the words *To Kento* in his father's handwriting. Inside was an ATM
card and a one-page memo:

1. Get rid of this book and memo right away.
*2. There is a black laptop in the desk drawer. Take it and never let any-
one else have it.*

Kento opened the drawer and found a black tablet-size laptop. He
took it out and tried to power it up, but the blue screen came on and
the operating system did not boot up. Something must be wrong with
it, he thought. He did a force quit and went back to the memo.

*3. You can use the ATM card as needed. You probably haven't heard of
the account holder, but don't worry about it. The account has a balance of
¥5,000,000. The PIN number is Poppy's birthday.*

Kento stared in surprise at the ATM card, which was issued by a major bank.

The name on the card was Yoshinobu Suzuki. As his father had said,
it was a name he'd never heard of.

The PIN number is Poppy's birthday.

Poppy was a papillon puppy that they had when Kento was a child.
From the depths of a far-off memory, Kento was able to recall the
puppy's birthday—the one day a year when they gave him some special
treats. December 6. The number 1206 had to be the PIN.

If the account really had five million yen in it, that would be his
father's estate. Wouldn't he have to pay inheritance tax on it? Did his
father leave him this large amount of money to cover his tuition and
board?

Kento read on.

4. Go immediately to the following address:
1-8-3 Morikawa, Apt. 202, Machida City, Tokyo.
A key is taped underneath the first step of the stairs of the building.
*Keep everything you do from now on a secret. Do it alone, without
telling anyone.*
Don't tell your mother.
*Consider all means of communication you use—landlines, cell phones,
e-mail, and faxes—to be tapped.*

The memo ended there.

Kento frowned at this final instruction, which struck him as paranoid. Putting the memo in a book that only Kento would know about
also reflected his father's fear that his mail was being read. Apart from
the physical condition that brought on his death, had his father been
suffering from mental problems, too?

His father with a woman? News to him. "What kind of woman?"

"They said she was about forty, slim, with hair down to her shoulders."

It finally struck Kento what his mother had been imagining. "So what you're saying is . . ."

Kaori nodded, a trace of anxiety in her eyes.

"Wait a second," Kento stammered. "Y-you're saying Dad was . . ."

That was impossible. This university professor in his worn suit, chronically short of research funds? This small man so full of grievances and complaints? Maybe it was one final fling before he turned sixty. That seemed unlikely, yet it was much more probable than that he'd been deliberately murdered. Kento was disappointed at this sordid ending. Is that what his father was now asking him to do in this role-playing game? Clean up the traces of his affair?

"Let's not start imagining things," Kento said. "That woman was probably just somebody who happened to be there."

"I hope you're right," his mother said, and sighed.

On the train to Machida, Kento's mind wavered. His life had been turned upside down so quickly. For the first time ever he was seeing his parents as more than just his parents. He was seeing them as a married couple.

Until yesterday he'd thought he was already an adult, but these recent experiences probably marked the true end of adolescence. For better or for worse, it was through their deaths that parents taught their children their most important lessons.

Kento got off at the Machida station and headed for a bank. He was familiar with the area, which was about twenty minutes from his home. In high school he'd often gone there to buy books or see a movie. It was exactly halfway along his father's normal route to work. Where he'd rented an apartment, no doubt to rendezvous secretly with his lover.

The bank that had issued the ATM card had a branch next to a trendy shopping plaza. Kento went to the ATM, inserted the card into the machine, and punched in 1206. And sure enough, the balance was five million yen.

Kento was shocked. So his father did have hidden assets, secret savings he'd tucked away. The amount was so huge Kento was afraid to do anything other than confirm the balance. One more piece of evidence that his father had been having an affair.

Kento walked back to the station and checked the address his father had given him on a map of the area. Morikawa was on the other side of the railroad tracks, across from a bustling shopping and entertainment district.

As he made his way past office buildings and condos, he came upon a narrow alley. The building should be at the end of that. On the right side of the alley, which looked like a private road, was a concrete wall; on the left was a fence surrounding a gravel-topped parking area. Away from the activity of the shopping district, the place was quiet.

Kento made his way down the alley and found the building he was looking for. He came to a halt and gazed at the two-story wood-and-mortar apartment building.

The outside walls were cracked, the wooden window frames out of kilter, the outside staircase rusty.

The building was an antique, something left over from the previous century. The narrow ground around it was overgrown with weeds, as if the structure were ringed by a moat. Surrounded on both sides by taller, more modern buildings, it looked forlorn, forgotten, and alone, left behind by the wave of development in the neighborhood. It was a perfect place for keeping out of sight, but it was a little too eerie to bring a lover to. To put it crudely, the place was like a haunted house. In fact, Kento didn't sense the presence of another soul around him.

Gathering his courage, he walked across the weed-covered ground and up to the building. Judging from the number of windows, he figured there must be three apartments on each of the two floors. His father's memo had said it was apartment 202. Kento checked the mailboxes, but not a single one had a resident's name.

He went over to the outside staircase and, feeling like a thief, stuck his hand under the bottom step.

There was some tape there, and not just in one place. He ripped off the strips of tape and found a total of three keys. The almost morbid cautiousness his father had displayed only deepened the bad feeling Kento was getting.

He quietly went up the stairs. On the second-floor hallway were three doors in a row. Kento went to the middle one, apartment 202. There was no nameplate on the door, but there was a shiny new lock that looked recently installed. He tried each key in turn, looking for the right one, and finally was able to unlock the door.

The entranceway was tiny, barely large enough for one person to stand in. On the immediate right was a sink with a separate small water heater; on the left was a wooden door to what had to be the lavatory. Kento slipped off his shoes and stepped inside. At the end of a short hallway was a sliding door, behind which Kento, in his fevered imagination, pictured a double bed with gaudy sheets.

The room was pitch dark and unexpectedly warm. Kento could hear the faint hum of air from a heater. He fumbled for the switch and turned on the light. As the cheerless fluorescent light blinked into life, Kento stared in amazement at the sight before him.

This was no trysting place for lovers. It was a typical apartment-size room, and blackout curtains on the window blocked any outside light.

The middle of the room was taken up by a large dining table covered with lab equipment. On top was a white laptop and a bookshelf on which were stored chemical reagents, pipettes, Erlenmeyer flasks, a rotary evaporator, and an ultraviolet light. The refrigerator alongside one wall, too, wasn't a typical home fridge but the kind used in chemical experiments. The equipment was familiar, the type Kento used in his lab work. The lab was outfitted for experiments in Kento's own field, organic synthesis.

All this equipment must have cost a lot. On the floor lay a sleeping bag and a toothbrush-and-toothpaste set. Kento knew that whatever task awaited him here, he'd be staying over.

Just then he heard something rustle behind him, and he stiffened. On the wall opposite the window was a closet he hadn't noticed before, on the top shelf of which were a series of large, clear plastic cases. Cages for animals used in experiments, fitted out with a ventilation system and automatic feeders. Altogether he found forty mice, in four groups of ten each. The mice had apparently been living all this time in the closet of this run-down apartment. The twenty mice on the right-hand side looked weak. Kento wanted to help them, but never having done animal experiments himself, he wasn't sure how to proceed. The water feeders were empty, and he was going to fill them with water from the tap, but then he wondered whether he should used distilled water instead. He weighed what to do and in the end decided he'd buy some mineral water at a convenience store before he went back home.

Kento gazed around this odd little laboratory. Why had his father prepared this lab? Ah, he thought. There had to be a logbook. Sure enough, there was a large notebook, the kind researchers use, on the table.

He opened it and found an envelope inside. Inside was a message, a computer printout.

Kento:
I'm glad you made it this far. I imagine you were pretty surprised to see this weird little lab. Now comes the real work. For reasons of my own, there's some personal research I've been doing, and I'd like you to take over while I'm away.

While I'm away. It wasn't clear what he was referring to, though he clearly hadn't anticipated dying.

I'd like you to do the research alone. Don't tell anybody. But if you find yourself in danger, give it all up right away.

More paranoia. Kento frowned and read on.

First of all, the software you'll need for the research is in the white laptop, so use that. Do not ever hand over the small black laptop you took from my study at home to anyone. Keep it safe.

Kento sat down on the swivel stool at the table and placed the two laptops in front of him. One white, the other black. He switched on the larger of the two, the white one. He'd already tried the black one at his apartment and knew it wouldn't work, but he tried the power button again anyway. Maybe this smaller laptop contained private messages and e-mails. He still knew nothing about the woman who'd been with him at Mitaka station when his father had collapsed. He still wasn't convinced his father hadn't been carrying on an affair.

As he waited for the laptop to boot up, he read further in his father's message.

The research project:

1. I want you to design an agonist for an orphan receptor and synthesize it.
2. Details about the target GPCR are in the white laptop.
3. You have to complete the project by February 28.

Kento let out a groan. This was ridiculous. He read the instructions again, carefully, to make sure he was getting it. This was all a little out of his field.

The outer surfaces of cells have several types of receptors, all of which are proteins. As the name implies, receptors have pocketlike depressions that accept and bind to certain types of ligands and through this binding control cell function. This is how hormones are bound by the cells and how hormones influence cells to take a particular form and / or perform certain functions. For example, ligands in the form of male and female steroid hormones play a role in muscle development and skin conditioning.

The orphan receptors mentioned in his father's message are bodies whose function—and the ligands they bind with—are unknown. His father wanted him to find a material, an agonist, that would activate orphan receptors.

The GPCRs his father mentioned—G-protein-coupled receptors—are long, ropelike proteins that loop seven times inside the cell wall and out again, making a pocket in the middle. It is very hard to determine the pocket's shape, and designing a ligand to bond with it is extremely difficult.

To carry out his father's instructions would require a huge research organization—like a pharmaceuticals company—as well as top-flight researchers, more than a decade of work, and tens of billions of yen. Even then the hurdle would be so great the project might fail. Yet here his father was asking a second-year MA student, alone, with only five million yen to complete the task in a month. Was he crazy?

Did his father actually have any chance of succeeding? The clues to that would lie in the lab logbook, but the contents were way out of Kento's field of expertise.

There were only four pages of notes in the logbook. The first research goal, according to the notes, was to "design an agonist for the mutant type GPR769 and synthesize it."

Ah, Kento thought. So this mutant protein, GPR769, was the name of the target orphan receptor. The agonist was the drug that would bind with this receptor and activate the cell—in other words, an artificially created ligand. But that was as far as Kento could follow. The rest of the procedures read:

- Structural analysis of mutant type GPR769
- CADD (design in silico)
- Synthesize
- Binding assay in vitro
- In vivo activity assessment

Other than the part about synthesizing, this all required expertise in other disciplines, and Kento couldn't judge whether these were appropriate directions or not. But he did get the impression that his father had greatly underestimated the difficulties of drug development. Structural optimization of the synthesized compound, clinical trials on humans—these critical and time-consuming phases of development were entirely missing.

Kento suddenly wondered whether this mutant type GPR769 was not a human receptor at all. Maybe it was that of another living being. The term *mutant* made it clear that there had been a genetic mutation. What changes had this mutation brought about to the creature that had this receptor? If the creature involved wasn't a human, then he could understand omitting the clinical trials.

The two laptops his father had left him looked to be key. The white laptop, the one he was supposed to use in the research, ran on the Linux operating system—not a system familiar to researchers in organic synthesis. The other laptop remained, as before, frozen.

To carry out his father's last wishes he would need to enlist the aid of a third party, though this would go against his instructions to do the research alone.

Kento returned to the instructions his father had left and read the final item.

> I think I'll be back soon, but on the odd chance that I'm gone for a long time, let me say this:
> An American will show up at some point. Give this person the compound you've synthesized. You were in the English club at school, so you should be able to handle speaking in English. Unlike me. LOL.
> That's all.

Kento liked the light way the message ended, and he chuckled along with his father. *On the odd chance that I'm gone for a long time.* It turned out to be not a long time but forever. And who was this American he was supposed to meet? It was hard for him to believe that his father, so poor when it came to English conversation, had any American acquaintances.

One unanswered question led to another. The only thing he did know for sure was that his father had been trying to create a substance that could fit in the pocket of mutant GPR769. All Kento felt he could do at this point was see whether this was a realistic goal and go from there.

He stood up and put on his down jacket. As he was closing the logbook he noticed a phrase in English in the margins. The research notes were all written neatly in pen, but this was scribbled, lightly, in pencil.

Heisman Report #5

He'd heard these words before somewhere.
Heisman Report...
The face of the newspaper reporter came to mind.

5.

THE MEMBERS OF the war cabinet had assembled in the Situation Room, in the basement of the White House. Fluorescent lights overhead lit the long, narrow, windowless room, but this did nothing to dispel the oppressive atmosphere.

Everything in the room was neutral—the mahogany conference table, the black leather chairs, the dark suits of the officials seated there. The people and objects in the room sank back in a dull monotone, their outlines indistinct, an unpleasant, unearthly aura enveloping the place, as if the entire room were a single living creature.

This was partly because the leader of the world's greatest superpower, the embodiment of the nation's will, was distinctly short-tempered.

"So what's behind it?" President Burns asked. Seated at the head of the long conference table, he glared indignantly down the rows of officials. "For us to sustain this much damage there had to be an internal leak."

None of the cabinet members seemed willing to respond, so Burns indicated one of them. "I'm asking you, Charlie."

Watkins, the director of national intelligence, looked up from the summary report, which wasn't much help to him at this point. "It's exactly as you said: the number of fatalities among private defense contractors in Iraq has risen sharply, though in the past week it's returned to previous levels. I think our counterintelligence strategy is starting to pay off."

"You haven't answered my question. How is the enemy getting wind of our movements?"

How the insurgents in Baghdad were able to target private defense contractors so efficiently was a mystery to Watkins. But that shouldn't have been his responsibility. "When it comes to the movements of private defense contractors," he said, "I think the Pentagon knows more details than the intelligence community. The Defense Department should know about their action plans. Or else the State Department."

"Our investigations haven't revealed any problem," the secretary of defense, Lattimer, said with his usual frown.

Vice President Daniel Chamberlain shot back. "So I guess the CIA has underestimated the ability of Islamic militants to gather intelligence."

The participants were well aware of the dynamics involved here, for they'd experienced any number of glum meetings like this one. Before the meeting had even begun Chamberlain had, typically, made the intelligence community the scapegoat. In his world, everything was their fault.

"That's not the case," replied Robert Holland, the CIA director, who had been silent up to this point. With his silver hair and mustache, Holland had a mysterious air about him—perfect for the head of a spy organization. "Our analysis has been quite rigorous."

"What do you base that on?" Chamberlain demanded.

Lattimer broke in. "We should take that up in a separate meeting. The point is, private defense contractors are like canaries in mines. If some of them die, the American people don't care. But if US troops suffer the same level of casualties, public opinion will turn against us. The main thing is to avoid an increase in the number of KIAs in our official announcements."

Holland nodded reluctantly, wanting to get this pointless debate over as soon as possible. He shot a reproachful glance at the president's national security adviser, as if to remind him that dealing with any intradepartmental discord was his job.

"So I guess we're done here," Burns said, straightening up his files.

"There is one more item," Chief of Staff Michael Acres said. "The issue of the ICC, the International Criminal Court."

Burns let out a faint groan and turned to Thomas Wallace, his chief counsel. "How is it going with retracting our ratification?"

"The UN isn't accepting a US withdrawal from the treaty."

Burns let out a huge sigh. At the end of the last administration his predecessor had ratified an international treaty establishing the ICC. If the ratification went through, American citizens who committed war crimes could be tried in an international court. Burns had unilaterally withdrawn US ratification, a move that the UN had opposed. Who the hell do they think they are? Burns swore to himself.

"The only thing to do is draw up a bilateral immunity agreement," James Ballard, the secretary of state, added. A former military officer, now a pacifist, he had quickly found himself out of favor in the present administration but still made sure to faithfully carry out his duties. "If we do that, other countries won't be able to haul US citizens before the ICC."

"That's not enough," Burns said. "If a country won't sign a bilateral immunity agreement with us, I say we cut off all aid to them."

"Then that's the direction we'll take," Ballard said, keeping his own opinion to himself.

"Good. Gentlemen, you can get back to work," Burns said, closing the meeting.

On both sides of the long, narrow conference table cabinet members and advisers prepared to leave. Burns waited until the nearest seats were vacated and called his chief of staff over. "Get me Dr. Gardner."

"Yes sir," Acres replied, and picked up a secure phone line. "Have Dr. Gardner join us," he said into the receiver.

The aging scientist passed the exiting officials as he made his way into the Situation Room.

"Ah, Dr. Gardner. Sorry to have kept you on hold like that." Burns stood up and welcomed his science adviser. For the president, it was a relief to talk to someone he could let his guard down with. Sensing this affinity, perhaps, Gardner smiled gently as the president motioned him to take a seat.

CIA director Holland, who remained behind, mentally put aside the unpleasant barbs that had been directed at him in the meeting and turned with genuine personal interest to what Gardner had to say. As a simple avocation, Holland liked to read science journals written for nonspecialists, and he was particularly anxious about the special access program they had under way. In his mind, the administration underestimated the threat. If the new life-form mentioned in the president's daily briefing really did emerge, then not just the United States but all mankind would face a crisis that threatened its very survival. Even now, at this moment, this life-form was secretly growing deep in the jungles of the Democratic Republic of the Congo.

Before turning to the main topic, Burns brought up a different, more tractable subject. "What I asked you about the other day—what are they called again?"

"Embryonic stem cells."

"Right. Embryonic stem cells. You were advocating that we restart research?"

"Correct. If we don't, the United States will lose its competitive edge."

Burns couldn't get angry with Gardner, even when he voiced an opposing opinion right to his face. Burns's opposition to stem cell research wasn't based on scientific or moral grounds but on political considerations: a desire not to lose the support of conservative Christians. "This is a difficult issue," he said. "I appreciate your viewpoint, but after considerable thought, I can't change present policy."

"Naturally I'll respect your decision," Gardner said calmly. "But let's focus, then, on a related field. The twenty-first century is the age of biology. And we can't allow America to fall behind."

If only other officials would learn to respond like this, Burns mused. He directed his chief of staff to bring some coffee for Dr. Gardner. "So," he said deliberately. "How is our plan progressing?"

Gardner, the science adviser for the special access program, took a sip of his coffee. "We got off to a slow start, but we're back on track. Through the kindness of Secretary Lattimer we have a very nice facility set up at the Pentagon."

Kindness permeated Gardner's personality, but in the White House kindness wasn't what made things run. Burns couldn't help but smile at the thought, but when he saw that only Holland maintained a stern, serious expression, he wondered what was bothering the CIA director. "You're talking about the Office of Special Plans?"

"That's right. It's about this size," Gardner said, looking around the Situation Room. "We have videoconferencing equipment, monitors live-streaming information. The person in charge is an outstanding young man from the Schneider Institute. He's the one who came up with the options I submitted earlier. He's doing a very good job of presiding over all aspects of the operation."

"Yes, he's one of our best players," Lattimer added. "A top-level analyst in his thirties. He doesn't have much of a track record yet, but he's very promising."

Burns understood what lay behind these comments. In case the operation was botched, this man was the one they could force to take the fall. In truth, the present operation, based on the Heisman Report, was a fairly low priority among the black-ops programs under way.

"We've selected the people who will carry out the ground operation, and they're already training in South Africa."

"If that life-form exists, isn't it already a threat to the United States?" This was what concerned Burns.

"There's no need to worry. It hasn't grown to those proportions yet. It's in its infancy, you might say."

"I see. So we'd best get rid of it, as we planned."

"And we'll do just that," Gardner said, nodding.

For the very first time, Burns had an uncomfortable feeling about this science adviser he relied on so closely. Far from objecting to these dirty tactics, the normally placid, gentlemanly Gardner was doing his very best to see that the operation went forward as planned. Even for a scientist like Gardner, for whom religious dogma meant nothing, this life-form was disgusting and needed to be eradicated.

"Has Congress been informed of the operation?" Gardner asked.

"Just the budget for it," Vice President Chamberlain said. "The law requires us, thirty days before we commence an operation, to inform the top leaders of both houses of Congress of the amount of the budget. But we don't have to tell them any operational details. So they don't know what we're planning. We also aren't disclosing who's involved in the operation."

Gardner seemed relieved. For an academic, being part of a top-secret operation was the kind of thrilling experience that kept one awake at night, too excited to sleep. Burns couldn't suppress a smile. "With your help, Dr. Gardner, I think our plan will work out just fine."

Gardner nodded. "The head of the operation I mentioned has come up with a very elaborate, detailed strategy. We should be done with the operation within a month. You have my guarantee."

Holland, who'd been silently watching this exchange, nervously stroked his mustache, trying to shake the dismal feeling he had. Both the president and his science adviser underestimated their opponent. If that life-form were, by some chance, to come into contact with developed societies, the precarious balance that held the world together would easily fall to pieces.

Holland thought about the four men assembled in South Africa. And how they might well end up sacrificial victims so that mankind could avoid catastrophe.

6.

UP UNTIL NOW, the tougher the assignment the better. Life-threatening situations and physical pain only helped Yeager forget the painful realities of his life. But now, with his son only a month away from dying, even the harshest training failed to dull the agony.

Back when he was in the army, it was nothing for him to go on endurance marches of forty kilometers while lugging a forty-kilogram pack. But too much time on urban protection detail as a private defense contractor had left him soft, lacking in stamina. The group left the Zeta Security compound, hiked through hills over unpaved roads, and by the time they'd gone ten kilometers, Yeager was out of breath. With each step the heavy load on his back drained away his strength. The Southern Hemisphere sun, dazzling in the northern sky, evaporated in an instant the sweat he needed to maintain his body temperature. Just focus on the pain, he told himself as they marched in single file, Yeager in the leader's number two position. But from deep within him fragments of memories—recollections of the hardships he'd endured in life—rose up and then faded away.

Once, when he'd been seven—an age when he got upset at his sister for not playing war with him—his father had driven the four of them to visit relatives in Arkansas. They'd stayed at a motel along the way, and Yeager watched from the backseat as his father checked in at the desk. Two adults, a counter between them, just chatting. The billfold his father took out of his back pocket. The pen he was given to sign with. Yeager wondered when he would grow up to be a father, too, and do what his dad did.

But this adult he'd looked up to had abandoned his family. His mother had had to go to work as manager of a supermarket warehouse, a single mom struggling to raise her two children. When Yeager, just before graduating from high school, announced he was enlisting in the army, his normally strong mother looked defeated. At eighteen, Yeager couldn't understand the feelings she'd stored up in her heart for her son. It was only years later, when his own son was in a life-or-death struggle, that he began to understand what she'd gone through.

Ever since he could remember, Justin knew there was an enemy out there ready to snatch away his life. He knew, too, that he would have to fight this enemy alone. And that one day his strength would be exhausted, and he would die.

Whenever Yeager went to visit his son in the hospital he'd load up with toys—model cars, a laser pistol, the latest Transformer. He hoped to see his son happy, even for a moment. But Justin, permanently connected to an IV drip, never seemed to enjoy his presents. He'd hold a robot in his tiny hand and stare at it with sunken eyes, as if holding it was a painful duty he had to perform.

The scene left Yeager sensing the fragility of life. Five years from now only that plastic robot would remain behind. Justin would be just a memory.

More than anything in life, Yeager wanted to see his son smile. See him healthy and playful. Justin could spill his cup of milk on the table, scribble all over the walls of their house. He'd play catch with Justin whenever he wanted. If only he could be like other children, healthy again . . .

"Yeager."

Hearing the accented English, Yeager looked up. Mick, on point, had come to a halt.

"How about a break?" Mick suggested, though he didn't look like he needed one. Garrett and Meyers, though, bringing up the rear, looked worn out.

"Sounds good," Yeager said. "Let's take ten."

They got under the shade of a tree and lowered their backpacks. They cursed their aching bodies and the training, though with few of the swear words typical of soldiers. The members of this makeshift team, Yeager realized, were surprisingly well mannered. Normally he'd expect at least a couple of them to spew out a slew of four-letter words.

"I'm a little worried about this mission," Meyers said as he tugged off his trekking boots and slapped Band-Aids on his blistered feet. "Even when I was in the air force I never got real jungle training. I can't figure out why they picked me."

"Must mean it's an easy mission," Garrett said.

Without any details yet about their assignment, Yeager had no comment. "Mick, have you had any jungle training?" he asked.

"Yeah." The Japanese former Foreign Legionnaire nodded.

Garrett, the onetime marine and Force Recon member, should be used to operations in jungles as well. Yeager turned to Meyers. "What you need to fear in the jungle isn't wild animals but insects and smaller creatures. Mosquitoes can give you malaria, and fleas can lay eggs under your toenails. Snakes and scorpions, bees and spiders. You get bit, you could die. So the first thing is to make sure you use enough insect repellent. Not just on your skin but on your clothes, too. And you have to use a mosquito net."

"What about when you sleep? Do you use a tent, like when you bivouac?"

Yeager turned to Garrett. "How'd you handle it in the marines?"

"We, ah . . ." Garrett hesitated a moment. "We used a combat tent."

"A combat tent? In the jungle?"

"Only when we could get enough supplies," Garrett explained, unruffled.

"What we did was tie together tree branches to make a hammock," Mick interjected. "If you're up off the ground you don't worry about snakes and centipedes."

"That's what the British Special Air Service does, too," Garrett said.

Was Garrett really Force Recon? Yeager was starting to wonder. Some private defense contractors misrepresented their backgrounds, exaggerating their level of experience. The problem was, lies like that might get them killed. In a four-man team, if one member couldn't carry his weight, their fighting effectiveness was down by 25 percent.

Garrett looked so calm, though, that Yeager wasn't sure. Garrett wasn't the conceited type, but was too quiet and low-key to be a typical marine. From now on Yeager would keep an eye on the man's skill level.

The endurance march went an hour over the scheduled time, but they managed to finish. "It's your first one, so I guess that's to be expected,"

Singleton said as he welcomed them back to the training facility. He was clearly none too thrilled by their performance.

With great relief the four of them threw down their backpacks in their quarters and, without changing clothes, proceeded to the next item on the schedule.

Behind the Zeta Security headquarters building was a massive stretch of open ground crossed by a runway and bordered by airplane hangars and other training facilities. When Yeager and the others exited the rear of the headquarters they saw a forklift used to load cargo onto military transport planes. This was the first time they'd seen any personnel here other than Singleton. Yeager knew they were deliberately being kept isolated. The operation they were training for had to be a top-secret mission.

"I'd like to distribute your weapons now," Singleton said, and led them into a concrete warehouse.

The weapons storage facility was amazingly well stocked, not just with heavy artillery and small arms but also with rocket launchers, trench mortars, and parachutes used in airborne operations. In the hot zones they were used to, most people used weapons made in Eastern Europe or China, but here was a truly impressive array of weapons from around the world, including Western countries.

Singleton stood in front of a locker filled with assault rifles. "As I said before, your primary weapons will be AK-47s or hunting shotguns. Pick either one. Your backup weapon is a Glock 17."

Mick, their point man, picked a shotgun, but then turned to Singleton. "What is the possibility of . . . contact in the jungle?"

"Extremely low."

Mick returned the shotgun to the rack and exchanged it for a Kalashnikov.

The men were all outfitted with tactical vests, eight spare magazines each, and leg holsters for the 9mm semiautomatic Glocks. Yeager was filled with his usual sense of childish pride. It was a kind of inborn disease among men, he mused, that being outfitted with deadly weapons was all it took to feel omnipotent.

Singleton also distributed a military pouch to each of them. "Night-vision equipment and a silencer for your Glocks," he explained. "You'll be practicing a nighttime assault later this evening."

This was the first hint of detail about the operation he'd given them. Was the target an anti–US insurgent camp?

"Okay, time to hit the practice range."

There was an outdoor firing range on the opposite side of the runway. Yeager and the team shot at human-shaped targets as they did zero-point adjustment of their AK-47s—fine-tuning the rear sight so they were able to hit their target a hundred meters away, precisely where they aimed.

They moved on to training for a firefight. In both standing and prone positions they practiced shooting at human-shaped targets that popped up automatically around them. Yeager kept an eye on Garrett's skills and saw that he was perfectly adept. He was smooth, too, at reloading, and seemed to have had all the requisite training. So what was his background, anyway? Why did he have to lie about being an ex-marine?

Once they had used up their ammo, they were told to reassemble after sunset for night training. Then they went off to the dining hall, in the headquarters building, for a dinner break. While the four of them ate, they didn't see another soul. No one was in the kitchen, either. The meals were already laid out for them when they arrived.

Exactly an hour later they reassembled for nighttime assault training. For this they were loaded in a van and driven to a different training area. There was still some residual light left in the west when they set out, but by the time the van came to a halt it had been swallowed up in darkness. In the headlights of the van Yeager saw a building, the kind of shoot house used in hostage rescue training.

"Night vision gear on."

At Singleton's direction, they tugged on their goggles. The small amount of light around them was electrically amplified so that everything glowed in a green phosphorescence.

"Silencers on your Glocks, gentlemen."

The four men swiftly obeyed.

"Follow me."

Flashlight in hand, Singleton moved around behind the shoot house. It was in a square lot, a hundred meters on each side, and also in the lot were twelve domelike structures, lower than a person's height. The structures were reminiscent of igloos, and each had a hole in front that looked like an entrance.

"Here's what you're doing," Singleton said, his voice hushed, perhaps because of the surrounding darkness. "Consider those structures as tents. There are three or four targets in each. Assume they're asleep. Use your Glocks, with silencers, and take the targets out as quickly as you can."

Meyers shuddered slightly, but that was all the emotion anyone showed. The director of operations looked appraisingly at Yeager and the other three in turn. In the greenish glow of the night vision goggles, Singleton's face resembled that of some cruel, bloodthirsty killer.

"You have three minutes to decide on your plan and execute it."

Singleton, stopwatch in hand, stepped aside.

"We'll come at them from all four sides," Yeager immediately decided. The spherical tents formed two lines facing each other, six on each side. It was most efficient to attack each row from both the left and right.

"Can I ask a question?" Garrett said. "How should we handle it if anyone escapes?"

Yeager was upset with himself at this oversight. Even with the silencers the Glocks would make a sound—enough of a noise that nearby animals in the jungle at night would flee. "Good point. Two of us will attack from the north. The other two will stand in the open space and to the south and take out anyone who escapes."

"Who will lead the attack?" Meyers asked.

"I'll do it," Mick quickly replied.

Yeager, the team leader, instructed the others. "Garrett, you'll be in the open space. Meyers will stay on the south side. Mick and I will take care of the targets."

"Roger that," Meyers said quietly.

"Take your positions."

The team members dispersed to their assigned positions, trying to make as little noise as possible.

I'll have to kill about twenty people, Yeager calculated. It really is a dirty job, as they said. But who were the targets? Terrorists who've infiltrated the Congo? He figured he'd just have to believe what the executive from Western Shield had told him—that he'd be doing a service to mankind.

Yeager reached the tent on the end. Garrett and Meyers were already in place, waiting for the go sign. Yeager looked over at the other row of tents and through his night vision goggles saw Mick racing forward, crouched low, Glock in hand, ready to strike.

Yeager lowered his arm to signal the others to begin. He made sure that Mick had started and then slipped into the nearest tent. The entrance was at chest height, so he had to lean over, as if peering into a cellar. As soon as he saw human figures inside he pointed his weapon at them. But his trigger finger froze. They were mannequins of children. Small figures, from infants to those that looked about ten years old, were sprawled out on the ground.

From behind he heard the low, muffled report of four shots. Mick must have shot the people in the first tent. Despite the high stress, Yeager's finger moved reflexively. Fifteen years of army training had transformed his brain and his body so that in combat he was a merciless killing machine. Yeager's shots couldn't have been more perfect. Shot right through the middle of the forehead, the child mannequins jerked like living beings, then were still.

Mick had finished with two tents already and was starting on the third. Like an athlete, with no wasted motion, Yeager sprang to his next target. What started as training became a competition to see who could kill the quickest. Yeager played catch-up as both he and Mick sprayed the mute children with bullets. By the time he finished with the fourth tent he'd used fourteen bullets, and as he sped to the next one he quickly slammed in a fresh magazine. Eight shots later he'd dispatched the eight figures in the two remaining dwellings.

As Yeager and Mick met up at the open space Singleton barked out a command: "Garrett. Meyers. Confirm the kills."

The two ran off, Garrett checking the left-hand row of tents and Meyers checking those on the right, starting from the farthest end. This was the first time they realized what their target was. Garrett silently went from tent to tent, while Meyers listlessly shook his head.

They reported back to Singleton.

"No survivors."

"Mission complete."

Singleton looked at his stopwatch. "Nearly sixty seconds, start to finish. Next time around I'd like you to tighten that up. Tomorrow we'll use dummy ammunition and work on handling anybody who flees. That's it for today. You did a good job, for the first day."

They followed Singleton back to the van. The team members were silent. After they boarded and the rear door was closed Yeager finally spoke. "Hold on. I made a stupid rookie mistake. I dropped an empty magazine."

Singleton tsked and reset the parking brake.

"I'll be back in a second."

Yeager tugged on his night vision goggles again and raced back to the pitch-black training ground. He hovered around behind the tents, groping in the dirt with his trekking boots until he found a good spot. He knelt down, careful not to get his cargo pants dirty, and vomited out the entire contents of his stomach.

Can I really be this lucky? The young Ugandan man felt almost afraid. A huge amount of money had been deposited into the bank account he'd just opened—some two hundred million Ugandan shillings. In US dollars this came out to about $106,000. Three hundred times his yearly income.

It was all thanks to an Internet café in the capital, Kampala. The store was on a corner, at the end of a line of shops that stood at the foot of high-rise buildings. It was expensive, so he could only afford the café once a week, but the dozen computers there lured him into an exciting, unknown world.

At first he just surfed the Web from one site to another, but soon he got interested in studying computers and searched for information on programming. He was dying to study and learn. He'd had to quit junior high school to help with his parents' work, and he was frustrated at his present job—carpentry—and dreamed of someday working in the digital field.

As he played around in cyberspace he learned another use for the Internet. He registered with a social networking site, describing himself as a tour guide in Uganda. The guys he knew who worked with him at construction sites were from all over the country, and if he needed to he could pump them for knowledge of their hometowns. It was a sham, of course, but he didn't plan on getting caught.

For half a year he got no response. But suddenly, a month ago, he received an e-mail from an Englishman named Roger asking if he would be willing to take on a job "transporting a vehicle and food to your neighboring country, the Congo."

The Democratic Republic of the Congo was a bloody battlefield, and his first instinct was to turn down the offer. But the fee made his head spin.

We'll pay 100 million Ugandan shillings up front. We'll also pay 100 million for the purchase of a car and the materials we need transported. Once we determine that the job has been completed successfully, we will pay an additional 200 million shillings.

He thought this had to be some kind of joke, but then he considered that the total, which came to about $212,000, might not be out of the realm of possibility for a rich Englishman.

He e-mailed back, telling the man he'd take the job, and was directed to open an account at the Stanbic Bank and e-mail back the account number. And a short time later he had confirmed that the advance and the expense money, this huge amount of money, was in his account.

He withdrew a small amount from the account, just to make sure it wasn't all an illusion, and sure enough, the money appeared. The job was for real.

As he exited the bank he looked around, suddenly fearful that the money might be stolen. It didn't occur to him at that moment that the bulk of it was safe within the bank. He felt like the richest man in town. Uganda was steadily developing economically, but it was still a desperately poor country. Even in the capital, Kampala, where most people drove old Japanese cars, electricity was only available in limited areas. He walked down the streets of the city, packed with many different races of people, and thought about buying something nice for his parents and three younger sisters. It wasn't Christmas, so he wondered if it would look suspicious if he bought some expensive beef to bring home.

Before the young man returned home he stopped by the Internet café where his good fortune had all begun. He checked his e-mail and saw a message from Roger. This message, too, took him by surprise. Below a notification that the money had been transferred to his account, it read:

As you have probably already noticed, the job we're asking you to undertake involves some risk. So we'd like to give you a final chance to choose from one of the following two options:

1. Quit the job at this point. If you do, the 200 million Ugandan shillings in your account are yours to keep. There is no need to repay the money.

2. Continue with the job. On a date indicated by us, you will transport provisions and a four-wheel-drive vehicle in good condition to a disputed area in eastern Congo. Once you do this, we will honor our agreement and transfer an additional 200 million Ugandan shillings to your account.

Since your life may be in danger, consider this very carefully before you decide. However, we will not tolerate any attempt at deception. We await your prompt reply.

The young man couldn't believe his eyes. If he chose option 1, he could keep two hundred million shillings without doing a thing. He had no idea why they'd given him these options. It sounded like they were seriously worried about his safety.

The young Ugandan carpenter stood up, went over to the counter, and got a paper cup of cola. As he drank the carbonated drink he thought about his name, Sanyu—*good fortune*.

Mind made up, he went back to the computer and typed in a reply to Roger.

Option 2.

His adventure had begun.

7.

BACK AT THE Sonoda Lab on Monday morning, Kento used column chromatography to refine the compound he'd synthesized the previous week. He put a sample mixture in a long glass tube, dissolved it with chloroform, separated it, and made a clear stratum. Adding a solution containing 0.2 percent methanol was the key. After almost two years in the MA program, he was getting pretty adept at experiments.

Ready for a lunch break, Kento headed to the locker room. He put the laptops his father had left him inside his backpack and exited the lab.

The day before, on his way home from his father's private lab, he'd stopped at a real estate agency to ask about the apartment building. According to the agent, the worn-out old building was scheduled for demolition, and people were already being evicted. "If you move in now the rent would be a steal, but you'd have to move out in two months," the agent added. That explained why there seemed to be no one else around. His father clearly had chosen the apartment in order to remain anonymous. There must be a reason the research had to be done in secret.

After he got back to his own apartment, Kento had done an online search for the Heisman Report but came up empty-handed. He typed it in English, too, but again struck out. It was unusual for a search term to yield no relevant results at all. He wasn't thrilled about the idea, but if he wanted more information he'd have to ask Sugai, the reporter.

After he left the pharmacology building, Kento crossed the concrete bridge over the canal, heading toward the cafeteria on the humanities campus, a long-established routine for him. From far off he scanned the cafeteria through the window as he walked, wondering if the girl who was in the English club with him when he was an undergraduate was inside. Just then someone called out his name.

He turned and there she was, the girl he'd been looking for—Marina Kawai. He hadn't seen her for some time, and her hair was now down to her shoulders. Her large, bright eyes, though, were unchanged.

"Hi, Kento," Marina said. Kento wasn't tall, but she still had to look up at him. She had a heavy-looking bag slung over her shoulder, filled with books. "How have you been?"

"Ah—fine," Kento replied without thinking. He realized Marina hadn't heard about his father's death. Not wanting to break the mood, he went on. "How about you?"

"Same as always. Dueling with Carroll."

"Carroll?"

"Lewis Carroll."

"Ah," Kento said, pretending to understand. He figured she meant the author of *Alice in Wonderland*. Did English lit majors really study fairy tales? "What aspect of Carroll are you working on?"

"Right now," she said, with a mischievous smile, "'perhaps Looking-glass milk isn't good to drink...'" She said this in English, her pronunciation excellent.

"Hmm?" Kento asked. "What kind of milk?"

"Looking-glass milk. It's a line from *Through the Looking-Glass*."

"So you can't drink Looking-glass milk, huh?" Kento was surprised. He saw a direct connection between the world of English literature and science. "Was Lewis Carroll a scientist?"

"A mathematician. Why?"

Kento saw his chance to actually be of help in her research. "The sentence you quoted refers to a mirror-image isomer. It's a chemical compound with asymmetric carbon atoms. It's like your right hand and left hand—it's the same shape as other compounds but has two structures that don't overlap with them. Unless it's reflected in a mirror you won't get the same shape. In some cases the right-hand-shaped compound will be a medicine, the left-hand shape a poison. Thalidomide is one example. I think 'Looking-glass milk isn't good to drink' is referring to that."

Marina listened blankly to this. "Hmm" was all she said. "What kind of research are you doing now?"

"How should I put it?" he began, pushing his glasses up higher on his nose. He wanted to explain it as simply as he could. "I take the parent nucleus that one of the more advanced students provides and add various side chains to it. Amino groups, nitro groups, and so on."

"Sounds pretty hard."

"Yeah, it is."

"Well, I'd better be off to the library." She gave him another winning smile and walked off.

Kento watched her leave and felt a twinge of regret. *I'm making a drug that treats rheumatism.* That's what he should have said. That would have been easier to understand.

Still brooding, he went into the cafeteria and bought a ticket for a meal. The room was noisy, filled with humanities and science students. The humanities cafeteria had the reputation of serving better food, so students from both areas tended to congregate there.

He got his tray of food at the counter, and as he turned to look for a table a student by the window waved to him. It was Akihiro Doi, a friend from his undergraduate days. He was doing clinical research now, working on reconfiguring the DNA of E. coli to come up with a set type of protein.

"Hey there, stranger." Doi grinned as Kento sat down across from him. "I saw you over there."

"Saw what?" Kento asked, knowing full well the answer.

"She's in humanities, right? You guys going out?"

That's right, Kento wanted to brag, but he answered truthfully. "We maintain a Van der Waals contact distance."

"Ah," Doi lamented. "That's too bad."

"How about you? Any prospects?"

"There're some cute girls in our lab, but we have more of a metallic bond. We're just atoms moving in a group."

"It'd be nice if you could get a little covalent bonding going."

"You got that right."

The two of them were silent for a time, working through their minced-beef cutlets.

"But you know," Doi said, draining his miso soup, "girls like guys who are good talkers, but guys like us have actually been trained to be poor conversationalists."

"You think so?"

"You hold seminars in your lab, right?"

"Sure."

In Kento's lab they held weekly meetings dubbed thesis seminars. A student was asked to analyze a recent published research paper and explain it in front of the others. Any explanation that was overly subjective or had logical gaps would be mercilessly critiqued by the others, so you learned to choose your words very carefully. Without this kind of training, they would have a tough time as full-fledged scientists later on. As his late father used to put it, "In the humanities it's the ones who are good at lying and deceiving who move up in the world, but a scientist isn't allowed a single lie."

Unfortunately, one by-product of this training was that, even in social situations, Kento and his fellows tended to overthink things and explain everything from a scientific standpoint. Put them in a group of people eating cake and all they could think of would be the mechanism of taste receptors.

"I know what you mean," Kento said.

"Those who only try to say what's right seldom talk," Doi pronounced. "Plus girls in the humanities don't want to go out with guys involved in the three Ds anyway, right?"

Now he'd hit a nerve. The three Ds meant work that was difficult, dirty, and dangerous—a virtual synonym for research labs. And no wonder, for the researchers who worked there put in fourteen-hour days, had to deal with foul-smelling chemicals, and were required to wear sneakers so they could race out of the lab in case of an accident.

"Girls prefer the three Hs over the three Ds."

"Three Hs?"

"A guy with a high level of education, enough height, and a high salary."

The only one that applied to him, Kento, thought, was education.

Doi sighed. "It's pretty sad."

"You think so?"

Doi seemed surprised. "What, you agree with these awful criteria?"

"Well, think about it. It's a sort of biological imperative for females to choose strong males. And the human animal is no different. If women were to choose men who are the opposite of the three *H*s and produce offspring with them, civilization would go into a nosedive."

"Granted, but where does love fit in?" Doi seemed to be more of a romantic. "That twisted way of thinking won't make you very popular."

"Twisted? Me?"

"Yeah," Doi said with a nod. "You need to be more positive."

For a long time Kento had been thinking the same thing about himself—that he was unfortunate enough to have inherited his father's warped disposition.

"You gotta be a more upbeat, cheerful guy if you want to hook up with these humanities girls."

As he looked reproachfully at Doi, Kento suddenly realized that his friend was exactly the kind of person he was looking for.

"You know, there's something I wanted to ask you," he said, taking out his father's research notebook. "If you want to make an agonist for GPCR, are these the right steps?"

Doi stared steadily at the pages. "You want to make an agonist like this? Not a lead compound?"

"That's right. I'm not looking for candidates, but for a complete model."

"The only steps I understand are the last two." Doi pointed to "Binding assay in vitro" and "In vivo activity assessment."

Kento asked, "So are these two the verification processes for determining whether the synthesized compound will bind to the receptor?"

"Right. First you make a cell that has the target receptors and check the binding in vitro. The next step is to verify in vivo, using lab animals. For example, you recombine the genes of mice, create the entity that has the receptors you're looking for, then inject them with the synthesized compound."

Kento thought of the forty mice in that shabby apartment. "So these directions are correct?"

"No way," Doi said, shaking his head. "It's way too oversimplified. Plus there aren't any clinical trials listed. It looks pretty amateurish to me."

"I suppose so," Kento admitted. His father was a virologist, after all, so maybe that was only to be expected. "What about this?"

Kento took the white laptop out of his backpack and turned it on. "Can you handle Linux?"

"I'm okay with it," Doi said as he scanned through the computer. "There's a program here I've never seen before. GIFT. Heard of it?"

"No."

Doi booted up GIFT. A few seconds later, when the program came up on the screen, the two grad students let out a shout of surprise.

The screen was divided into three panels. One large pane on the right side displayed odd computer graphics. On top of gentle wave patterns were a number of projections, like thick flower petals, with a pocketlike cavity in the center. It was a mysterious-looking 3-D image, so detailed it looked like a photo.

Kento soon recognized what it was—an enlargement of a cell surface. This microscopic world, less than a micron in size, filled the screen.

"This is weird," Doi said, moving the cursor to point to the two frames on the left. "There's information here. This computer graphic is showing mutant GPR769."

Exactly the receptor I need, Kento thought. What my father wanted was the material that will bind with the pocket in the middle.

"The frame on the bottom is the sequence of the gene that will produce this receptor," Doi said, crossing his arms. "But do you have any idea how many types of G-protein-coupled receptors there are?"

"Seven or eight hundred?"

"Exactly. And out of all those, there's only one whose distinct form has ever been determined—a receptor in a cow's retinal cell. We can only deduce the structure of the other GPCRs by analogy. We look at how similar the gene base sequences are to guess what the complete product looks like. This model here is probably created in the same way, so I'm not sure how accurate it is."

"Does the software have any other functions?"

"That I'm not so sure about," Doi said, picking up the research notes again. "Maybe it's used for the first two items here."

Kento looked at the notes.

Structural analysis of mutant type GPR769

CADD (design in silico)

GIFT appeared to be software that used genetic information to predict what kind of protein would be created, depict the actual shape, and actually design the chemical structure of the material that would bind with it. "So you're saying if we follow this software's instructions we could create a drug?"

"There's something not right about it," Doi said. "I can't follow the calculations. If you want to know more about that, you have to have somebody else help you out."

"Who? Do you know anybody?"

"Let me see..." Doi stared off into space. "There *is* someone. An amazing guy doing physical chemistry drug development. An exchange student from Korea."

"Really," Kento said, interested.

"I heard him speak once on molecular dynamics simulation, and he made it really easy to understand."

"What about his Japanese?"

"He's fluent. Speaks English, too."

"Would you introduce me?"

"Sure. I'll find out when he's free." Doi glanced at his watch. It seemed like he needed to be getting back to his lab. He stood up, picked up his tray, and said, "Well, I'll call you."

"I appreciate it."

"Let's hope we've both got some covalent bonding in our futures." Doi laughed and headed off to return his tray.

Kento smiled and put the laptop back in his pack. One task down. Now he'd just have to wait for Doi to contact him about this Korean student.

There was one other thing he needed to take care of. He picked up his cell phone and dialed Sugai, the newspaper reporter, whose number his mother had given him the night before. But as he punched in the number of the science section of the *Toa* newspaper, he remembered his father's warning.

Consider all means of communication you use—landlines, cell phones, e-mail, and faxes—to be tapped.

No way, he told himself, but he still had the vague, uneasy feeling that he was being watched. He glanced around the cafeteria, but didn't see anyone suspicious. He shook off the feeling and punched in the number.

A young man's voice came on the line. "*Toa* newspaper, science section."

"Hello; my name is Koga. I was wondering if Mr. Sugai is there."

"Just a minute."

Kento regretted how curt he'd been with Sugai at his father's funeral and felt sheepish about contacting him. But Sugai was his only source of information.

"Hello?" he heard the reporter say.

"Hi, Mr. Sugai, this is Kento Koga. Thank you again for all you did at my father's funeral."

"Ah, Kento," Sugai said, his tone friendly.

Relieved, Kento went on. "I have something I'd like to ask you. It's about the Heisman Report you mentioned at the funeral."

"The Heisman Report? Well..." he said, and paused. "What are you doing tonight?"

"Tonight? I'll be in the lab until twelve."

"Can you get out for a while? If you meet me at the Kinshi-cho station, I'll buy you dinner."

"Yeah, okay," Kento said. It sounded like a lot of trouble, but he knew Sugai was just being kind. Kento quickly figured how he could make up the time he would lose with his experiments. "I should be able to get away at nine."

"Great. I'll see you at nine at the south entrance to the station. Bring your appetite."

Kinshi-cho was just outside Tokyo, the last shopping district before Chiba Prefecture. Unlike the Shinjuku or Shibuya districts, though, Kinshi-cho was located near residential areas, and the shopping district was a jumble—half entertainment district, half nice stores. Shady little bars dotted the street alongside a modern shopping mall complete with a supermarket and a Cineplex. There was even an outstanding concert hall, the kind that could host a world-class orchestra. The district was a mix, then, of high and low culture, the upscale rubbing elbows with the tawdry.

Kento stood outside the station, a cold wind blowing fiercely as he waited for Sugai. Whenever he pictured the reporter's face, he couldn't help recalling his father, especially his father's litany of complaints.

His father would often bemoan his lot in life when he was having a drink with dinner. People in the humanities earn five hundred thousand dollars more in their lifetimes than those in the sciences, he said. In other words, in a typical forty-year career a scientist had to advance the cause of science while earning more than ten thousand dollars per year less than people in the humanities.

"They never pay us a decent salary, and still they claim Japan is a science-centered nation. Bunch of assholes." His father, usually tipsy by this point, didn't hide his low opinion of Japan's politicians. "Guys in the humanities swipe all our work. The telephone, TV, the automobile, computers. These were all created by scientists. What have those sly bastards in humanities ever contributed to civilization?"

When he was in his teens, Kento found his father's discontent depressing. Later on, though, something happened—an event concerning the development of the blue light-emitting diode—that made him see that his father's opinions weren't so far off the mark.

Blue LED was supposed to be impossible, but when a technician successfully developed it, he and the company that employed him got into a legal dispute over it, which ended in a trial. In the first trial the plaintiff—the technician—was awarded two hundred million dollars, but in the second trial this judgment was overturned, and the company was ordered to pay the technician only six million dollars out of the $1.2 billion profit they got from his invention. The judgment was so out of line that one could only conclude that the judge had thrown judicial independence to the wind and was basically at the beck and call of the company executives.

Scientists and technicians were shell-shocked at the decision. An invention that brought in tens of billions of dollars to the industry was only worth, to its inventor, what a major league baseball player earned in a year. Many scientists saw the case as a turning point and predicted that Japan's international competitiveness would decline. In an age when a nation's power depended on its science and technology, treating its scientists and engineers so poorly was not the path to development. The day was not far off, they believed, when Japan would be outpaced by China, Korea, and India.

"Civilization can go to hell as far as I care," Kento's father once spat out, a malicious smirk on his face. "The only ones who can rebuild science and civilization are scientists. Humanities guys wouldn't be able to figure out electricity no matter how much time you gave them."

When Kento became an adult he started to feel there was some truth to what his father said. During his four years as a science undergraduate he'd been run ragged. His only outside activity, the English club, was something he could barely find time to attend. Students in the humanities, by contrast, skipped class and had a good time. At least it looked that way to Kento. If they really did earn five hundred thousand dollars more on average over the course of a lifetime, that was pretty hard to accept. Society seemed set up so people who skimmed off the top profited more than those who broke their backs actually creating things. Thinking this way, though, made Kento uncomfortable. Like the very skin he was born into, he knew how hard it would be to rid himself of this warped genetic inheritance from his father.

In front of the station, Kento stuck his numb hands deep into the pockets of his down jacket and remembered something that had been puzzling him for a while.

After yet another one of his father's drunken rants, Kento had once asked him, "If you hate your work so much, why don't you just quit?"

"I can't give up research," his father had replied.

"Why not?"

"Once you become a researcher, you'll understand." His father smiled, a contented expression lingering on his face, the kind of look he never showed his family.

What did that smile mean? What part of his inner life did it express? Kento was himself a researcher now, but he still didn't know the answer. All he'd learned by devoting himself to research was that people in the sciences are lousy at getting along in life.

A crowd of people spilled out of the station. Kento brushed aside his built-up discontent and scanned the passengers. Sugai appeared, giving a little wave as he approached.

Kento wove through the crowd as he went forward to greet him. "Sorry you had to come all the way out here," he said.

The middle-aged reporter was dressed casually in a sweater and jacket but no tie. He peered through his glasses at Kento. "You live alone," he said with a laugh. "So I figured you aren't eating all that well. What would you like? Meat? Fish? Chinese? Ethnic?"

Kento wasn't up on the latest food trends, so he chose something simple. "Meat sounds good."

"Great." Sugai scanned the buildings around the traffic circle in front of the station. "Let's do Mongolian barbecue."

Sugai took him to a nearby bar and grill. They sat down across from each other in a small, partitioned-off room and ordered their meals.

They drank mugs of beer and ate for a while, reminiscing about Kento's father until Sugai broached the reason for their meeting.

"So you were interested in the Heisman Report?"

Kento leaned forward. "In my father's lab notebook he'd written the name of the report, in English, and I was wondering what it was all about."

"In his lab book? Is that all it said?"

"It also said 'number five.' Heisman Report number five."

"I have a vague memory that that report was divided into five sections," Sugai said, looking up, as if searching his memory. "I think I mentioned that an American think tank had produced the report."

"You did. I figured it had to be related to my father's field, virology."

"It may have had a section about viruses," Sugai said, and looked back at Kento. "But in a word, the Heisman Report is about extinction—research into the extinction of the human race."

Kento reflexively stared at the reporter. "Extinction? Of the human race?"

"You're too young to remember this, but when the report was written some thirty years ago, the international situation was very tense. The United States and the Soviet Union were staring each other down, armed to the teeth with huge numbers of nuclear weapons. Everyone was terrified there would be a nuclear war that would destroy mankind."

"They were seriously afraid of that?"

"They were. This was the Cold War era. During the Cuban Missile Crisis the world came to the brink of a nuclear attack."

Kento was shocked. The whole thing sounded like science fiction.

"Physicists who had helped develop nuclear weapons predicted an all-out nuclear war and came up with something called the Dooms-day Clock, a kind of countdown to the destruction of mankind. By the time the first hydrogen bombs were successfully tested, the clock's hands were two minutes away from destruction. Fortunately, though, with the collapse of the Soviet Union, the hands of the clock were reset."

As the waiter took away their empty plates Sugai ordered another round of beers and went on. "The White House began research into possible causes for the extinction of mankind, including nuclear holocaust. They wanted to prepare for any potential crisis. A researcher named Joseph Heisman, who worked at a think tank, prepared a list of possible events that could cause the human race to be annihilated. And that became the Heisman Report."

"But why would my father be interested in that?"

"My guess is there had to be something in it related to your father's field. Something about viral infections."

"Like a lethal virus that wipes out everyone on the planet?"

"Exactly."

Could his father, of all people, have been fighting some unknown virus that pushed mankind to the edge of destruction? A professor always short of research funds, toiling away at a no-name university? He remembered his father's long, exhausted face and smiled. This was hardly the face of mankind's savior.

Sugai looked at him dubiously, and Kento quickly stopped smiling. "Do you know the details of what's in the report?"

"After your father asked me to look into it, I went through some old files but couldn't find anything. When it first came out, though, there were special reports on it in magazines."

Finding these magazines from thirty years ago wouldn't be easy, Kento thought.

"Our company should be able to track the report down," Sugai said. "When your father insisted on finding out more about it, I asked people at our Washington bureau. They said there should be an original copy in the National Archives."

"Could I ask you to continue looking into it?"

"I'll be hearing from them soon, and I'll let you know as soon as I get a copy."

"I really appreciate it."

After eating his fill of Mongolian barbecue, Kento thanked Sugai, said good-bye to him at the station, and walked back to his own apartment.

He hadn't drunk very much—he'd been too fascinated by the topic they'd been discussing—and his mind was still clear. He turned on the light in the room, switched on the heater, and sat down at the small desk next to the wall. He took out the two laptops from his backpack.

He tried to power up the black laptop, but again it wouldn't start up. He did a force quit and turned to the larger laptop.

This one started up fine. The screen showed the same 3-D image of an orphan receptor embedded on the surface of a cell.

Kento, struggling with the unfamiliar software and operating system, copied the base sequence of the mutant GPR769 onto an external hard drive. Next he connected his usual computer to the Internet.

He accessed a site that allowed searches of base sequences. Once you inputted a base sequence, the site would show genes that had a similar sequence.

He pasted the mutant GPR769 into the search window, clicked HU-MAN for the target organism, and did a BLAST (Basic Local Alignment Search Tool) protein data bank search. This wasn't his area of expertise, but he'd learned how to use it as an undergraduate. If the receptor in question were a protein involved in viral infection, this would link his father's research to the Heisman Report.

The search results came up, and Kento stared at the screen. The closest homology to mutant GPR769 was, naturally, GPR769. Of the nine hundred base sequences, only one had mutated. Because of this, only one of the amino acids that make up the receptor had been transposed.

Kento clicked on a link to find out more about the GPR769 receptor. The English, full of medical terminology, gave him some trouble, but he could make out the main points.

Type: Orphan

Function: Unknown

Ligand: Unknown

Cellular location: Surface of pulmonary alveolar epithelial cells

Mutation: If 117 leucine is replaced by serine, then pulmonary alveolar epithelial cell sclerosis occurs.

He'd never heard of the disease, so he searched to find out more.

Pulmonary Alveolar Epithelial Cell Sclerosis

Cause: Single gene disorder caused by autosomal recessive inheritance.

The gene mutation leading to pathogenesis is already identified. Substitution of 117 leucine with serine in the orphan receptor GPR769 leads to the diseased state.

Signs and symptoms: The pulmonary alveolar epithelial cells harden, resulting in labored breathing. Further complications are cor pulmonale, liver hypertrophy, and alveolar hemorrhage. The prognosis is poor. Age predilection is three, and the majority of patients die by six.

Treatment: Treatment of symptoms only. Administering of steroids, or bronchial lavage after general anesthesia.

Epidemiology: No geographical difference in outbreak. The disease affects 1.5 persons per 100,000.

This wasn't the information that Kento had expected. The disease was unrelated to viral infection and occurred when a person inherited a spontaneously mutated gene from his parents.

He felt like he'd swung at and missed a big fat pitch down the middle. A total miscalculation. It happened a lot in the lab, though. Whenever it did, his mentor, Dr. Sonoda, would invariably say the same thing: put away your preconceptions and see what actually occurred.

In other words, understand unexpected phenomena. Kento stood up from the desk and thought for a minute. What in the world could his father have been up to? Not that he had to think about it much, for the answer was clear.

I want you to design an agonist for an orphan receptor and synthesize it.

Kento realized he'd overlooked the most important part of the research his father had left behind. This involved knowledge that was out of his field, so he went over it many times to determine whether his conclusion was correct.

The function of GPR769 was not clear, but it was a receptor on the membrane of pulmonary alveolar epithelial cells. When GPR769 was dysfunctional it could lead to death, so the receptor served some function necessary to normal respiration. But for this receptor to function as intended, a ligand was needed.

Receptor ligands are molecules with physical and chemical properties that match perfectly those of the receptor's ligand binding site, and so they bind to the receptor and thereby activate it. Ligands are typically produced elsewhere in the body and are transported to the receptor by the blood. Once bound to the receptor on the outer surface of the cell membrane, the receptor-ligand complex is pulled into the cell interior through a coordinated sequence of events. In the cell interior the active tip of the receptor acts on many other proteins within the cell, thereby activating these proteins. These activated proteins in turn activate other proteins. In this way chemical signals are amplified and sent throughout the cell interior to act on diverse targets that modify the cell's overall function. In other words, binding of the ligand by the receptor works as a switch to get the cell operating in a certain way.

In the case of mutant GPR769, the substitution of serine for leucine at position 117 of the receptor results in a binding site that cannot bind the native ligand, and so the switch isn't turned on. Thus the lungs fail to function correctly, and you have the onset of disease. One way to regain normal lung function is to create a drug that can bind the mutant site and thus can serve as a ligand specific for mutant GPR769. Such a ligand would be an agonist, since it behaves in much the same way as the native ligand when bound to the nonmutant GPR769—that is, it activates certain cell functions as opposed to inhibiting them, as an antagonist would. This was precisely the agonist that Kento's father had been trying to create.

An agonist that would activate mutant GPR769.

Kento stood stock-still in front of the desk, mouth open.

It was a simple theory with no room for doubt. This agonist was none other than a remedy that would treat pulmonary alveolar epithelial cell sclerosis, an incurable disease that took the lives of children.

Kento was breathing hard. He followed the image on the computer screen and did some mental calculations. There were approximately one hundred thousand children on earth suffering from pulmonary alveolar epithelial cell sclerosis. Successfully creating this drug meant saving that many children around the world.

"A hundred thousand?" Kento yelled out, and looked around the cramped apartment. A grad student living in a tiny apartment in Kinshi-cho was going to save a hundred thousand children?

Was this what his father was doing? Using all his money to save dying children?

An American will show up at some point. Give this person the compound you've synthesized.

Kento imagined this American must be someone whose child suffered from the disease. This person would come, full of hope that his precious child could be saved from this terrible disease.

Hold on, Kento thought. The hurdles to pulling this off are too great. Even if a huge pharmaceuticals company put all its resources into it, producing a new drug like this would be extremely difficult. And all he had was this plan that his friend Doi had dubbed amateurish. Once the drug was synthesized, without clinical trials you wouldn't even know whether it was safe or not.

Why was a virologist like his father working so far out of his area? And what odds did he think he had of succeeding?

Kento knew he had as much of a chance of succeeding as a spider did in catching a huge fish in its web. But he decided that, for the time being, he'd give it a shot. He mentally ran down the list of his friends from his undergraduate days, trying to remember if he knew anyone who'd gone to med school.

8.

FOR YEAGER AND the team communication with the outside was strictly controlled. They couldn't use e-mail, and when they wanted to call their families they had to use the one phone in their room. Further, a clause in the contract they signed strictly forbade them from revealing where they were.

"This phone is routed through several lines," Garrett said. "If somebody monitored it they'd have a tough time tracing the call."

The phone in their room also served to strengthen team cohesion. Even if you didn't try to eavesdrop, you couldn't help picking up on private details of your roommates' lives. They all soon knew that Yeager's son was suffering from an incurable disease, that Meyers had become a private defense contractor to help out his parents, who'd lost money investing in real estate, that Garrett was saving his money to become an entrepreneur, and that Mick wasn't close enough to anyone to want to make any calls.

Yeager got more depressed with each call from Lydia. Justin's condition was worsening by the day. They'd been counting on Dr. Garrado to help extend his life at the end, but it wasn't working out that way. At this rate Justin might die before Yeager could finish this assignment.

"Why do you always have to be away on work when we need you here?" The two of them had made the decision together for him to take on this extra duty, but still Lydia berated her husband. "Can't you just quit and come here?"

That was impossible—he'd signed the agreement. Resigning now meant being hit with a massive penalty for breach of contract. Yeager was probably not the only one who was feeling the weight of having signed. It seemed to be weighing heavily on Meyers as well. Starting the day after their nighttime drill, the cutout targets on the firing range were changed to small figures the size of children. It was clear what this signified. Yeager and his team were to kill a group of children. At night they continued to visit that practice field and those tentlike structures and spray the mannequins of children with bullets.

On the fifth day, after morning physical workouts and shooting practice, the whole afternoon was set aside for classroom training. The team members expected they'd finally learn more details about the mission.

After blasting the small human targets to shreds on the firing range, the four of them were heading back to headquarters when Meyers spoke up.

"I never heard anything about something like this. Same with you guys, right?" Meyers, always cheerful, looked uncharacteristically disgusted. "What are you going to do if our mission really is to kill a bunch of children? Are you going to go through with it?"

Yeager, who felt like vomiting every night they ran through the drill, wanted to side with him. Justin's death was inevitable now. Was he taking the lives of so many children just to extend his own child's life by a few days?

Garrett and Mick were silent. "But all of us signed the agreement," Yeager said. "What else can we do?"

"This is our last chance. We can quit before we hear what the mission is. If we don't know the target, maybe they'll let us quit."

"I doubt it. If they were going to be that easy on us they wouldn't have made us sign the agreements."

"I doubt that agreement's even legal. If it came to a trial, I don't think the employer could say anything. You think they could testify that they ordered us to kill children but we refused?"

"I don't think defying them's the best strategy," Garrett said.

"Why not?" Meyers asked.

"Private defense contractors are all connected up through the Pentagon. If we break our contract, they'd drum us out of the industry. We'd be lucky to get a job in the parking lot at Walmart."

As professionals whose only skill was killing, the men felt utterly powerless and fell silent. Yeager was able to take down a person at five hundred meters with a single shot. Stab a man in the kidney from behind and kill him so quickly he didn't make a sound. This was the father Justin was so proud of. His son saw him as a hero fighting for peace, this father who had no place in a peaceful society. Every time he felt Justin's innocent respect for him, Yeager felt wretched, like a cheap impostor in a uniform.

"Besides," Garrett went on, "we've gotten ourselves into something heavy here. For all we know this is a White House–authorized assassination. A special access program, maybe. If it is, who knows what'll happen to anybody who tries to bail?"

"You're saying we might be murdered?"

"Or else labeled as terrorists and shipped off to someplace like Syria or Uzbekistan, where they have no qualms about torturing people." Garrett lowered his voice. "I can see the Burns administration doing that."

A cold wave of apprehension swept over the team. Meyers had brought up this topic before they went inside the building because he knew they were under close surveillance in their dorm room.

Yeager stood at the rear entrance to the headquarters building and thought of someone back in his hometown, a Vietnam vet named Jack Riley. Riley had sat on the porch of his broken-down old house on the edge of town, drinking beer all day. He didn't appear to have a job. To his neighbors he wasn't a hero back from battle but an eyesore.

On the day when the army recruiter had talked to him at high school, Yeager stopped by Riley's place on the way home. "I'm thinking of joining the army," he told him.

Riley stared at him with his rheumy yellow eyes. "It's up to you," he said.

Yeager didn't think so. It felt like the only choice he had.

"Let me tell you one thing about being a soldier," Riley said. "You go off to fight for your country. You kill the enemy. And only the good people carry around the guilt. Only the good people."

Seventeen-year-old Yeager didn't follow. "What do you mean?"

"There are people who have no problem hurting others and people who do."

The pile of beer cans at Riley's feet told him which type he was. So was this broken-down soldier, shunned by those around him, a good person?

If he slaughtered twenty children, Yeager thought, would he end up like Riley?

Once they were back in their room, Meyers said to the Japanese team member, "Mick, what do you think about this mission?"

"I'll do my duty," Mick replied. From day one he'd shown no compunction about blasting the mannequins to pieces. "They tell me to do it, I do it. That's my job. That's *our* job."

"You don't mind killing children?" Meyers asked, his voice carrying a trace of contempt.

Normally Mick was expressionless, but now a cold smile rose to his lips, as if he were on the verge of calling Meyers a coward. A change swept over Meyers's expression and Yeager, sensing danger, stepped in. "Hold on. We don't know yet that we're supposed to kill children. Let's not jump to any conclusions until we hear what this mission's all about."

Meyers looked disgusted. Just then the door opened and Singleton came in. The tall director of operations stared down at them and asked suspiciously, "What are you men up to?"

"We're going over tactics," Garrett replied. "Our backgrounds are all different, so we have some differences of opinion."

"Go have lunch. The afternoon briefing will give you all the details you'll need."

The four team members exchanged glances.

"Did you all understand the tactics I was talking about?" Yeager asked. "There's an optimum time to check out the enemy's moves."

"I get it," Meyers said. "It's too early to decide to withdraw."

"Exactly."

At 1:00 p.m., after lunch, the four men filed into the briefing room. Singleton was there ahead of them, alone as usual. Until they began their mission he was likely the only other person they would meet.

They sat down and Singleton began using his laptop to project a PowerPoint presentation on the screen at the front of the room.

"All right, take a look at this," he said. "Do you notice anything odd about this man?"

The screen showed a photo of an African man. He looked about thirty. Or maybe older, since he had some gray hair. He was wearing a worn-out shirt too big for him, and he faced the camera, a gentle look on his face. His neck was muscular, but his shoulders were narrow, so he didn't come across as especially brawny. His skin color was fairly light, and Yeager figured he must be from either the northernmost or southernmost region of Africa.

"Look at this one now," Singleton said, moving to a second photo. A giant was standing next to the African man from the first slide. He was a white man, so much larger than the African that they looked like an adult and a child standing together. The black man's head didn't even come up to the white man's chest.

"Remember this white man's face. His name is Nigel Pierce, and he's a professor of anthropology at a university on the East Coast of the United States."

Nigel Pierce was extremely slim. He was quite tan and had a beard. He looked to be in his forties and appeared more like an exhausted explorer than a scholar.

"By the way, Pierce is only one hundred and eighty-seven centimeters tall, about six feet one, the same as I am. The African man beside him is only one hundred and forty centimeters tall."

"Why so small?" Garrett asked.

"He's a Pygmy."

Seeing that they understood, Singleton continued. "The word *Pygmy* has negative connotations, but as you can see, Pygmies are just like normal people except smaller. Their skin color is light, similar to that of Asians, and anthropologists classify them differently from other Africans."

Singleton put on reading glasses and picked up a notebook. "What I'm going to tell you now is based on anthropology. I'm just telling you things I heard from others, so no pointed questions, if you don't mind."

Singleton smiled, as if this were some amusing joke, but the team members, none of whom had much affection for him, couldn't even manage an insincere smile.

Unperturbed, Singleton continued. "I doubt any of you in this room is typically conscious of this, but we belong to an agricultural people. We depend mainly for our staples on agricultural products. The Pygmies, on the other hand, are hunters. They live in the jungle and hunt animals to get the food they need."

Singleton advanced the PowerPoint presentation to the third slide: a map of Africa that had a special colored section running from east to west along the equator.

"This is the region the Pygmies inhabit. It overlaps the African tropical rain forest. No one knows why they evolved to be so small, but according to one theory it's an adaptation to their environment. Being so small allows them to move about unfettered, among thick, low-hanging branches. Until the age of about ten they grow just as we do, but then their growth stops. They live the rest of their lives with bodies the size of children."

Yeager suddenly realized something hidden behind this lecture on anthropology. The child-size targets they'd been using must be modeled on Pygmies. The thought lifted some of the depression he'd been feeling, but at the same time raised a new question. These people living deep in the jungle, far from civilization, are light-years away from the kind of work he did. Why did they have to kill them?

Garrett raised a hand. "What nationality are the Pygmies?"

"Nominally they belong to the country where they live, though actually they haven't been granted citizenship. Instead of citizenship they're divided into several tribes. The man in the first photo is from the Mbuti tribe. They live in the eastern Congo, in the jungles of the Ituri Forest."

The eastern Congo was where Yeager and the team were to be inserted. The briefing was finally getting down to essentials. "Is the Ituri Forest part of the Great War in Africa battle zone?"

Singleton smiled knowingly. "It is," he said. "It's not regular warfare but a guerrilla war. Nearby villages are ransacked, and there's genocide—one people murdering another. But that's not all. The troops fighting here, including the regular Congolese army, go into the jungle, hunt down Pygmies, and eat them."

"*What?!*" Meyers shouted.

"Cannibalism. The people in the region view Pygmies as subhuman. They also believe that if you eat their flesh the mysterious power of the jungle will come to reside within you. So they hunt them, slice them up, and cook them in pots. Add a little salt, apparently, and eat them. UN observation teams have confirmed this." The only one in the briefing room who didn't seem to find this disgusting was the person telling the story. "White colonists in Australia, too, used to love to hunt down the Aborigines. In Tasmania there's not a single Aborigine left. The whites wiped them out."

Singleton looked like one of the devil's own, apparently enjoying thoughts of how depraved humans could be. Yeager was growing worried about what would be revealed now about their mission.

"Okay, back to the Mbuti Pygmies."

Singleton clicked forward, and the screen showed an enlarged map of the eastern Democratic Republic of the Congo. A road about a hundred kilometers long stretched from north to south, with villages dotting the area alongside it. Beyond that was nothing else to indicate the presence of people. Most of the map was covered in green.

"Here's the Ituri Forest, where they live. The Mbuti live in so-called bands of several dozen people each. In the rainy season they live near farming villages, but now, in the dry season, they go into the jungle to hunt. They set up hunting camps, stay there for a set time, then move a few kilometers to the next camp. Moving around like that ensures they don't run out of food."

Eight spots were highlighted on the map, running east to west.

"These eight dots are the camps used by the so-called Kanga band of Pygmies, which is made up of around forty people. The area is approximately thirty-five kilometers from one end to the other. This will be your field of operations." Singleton looked at each one of them. "All right. Let's get into the details of the operation."

Yeager and the others shifted in their seats and listened carefully.

"The operation is code-named Guardian. You'll use fake names and pose as members of a wildlife conservation organization. You'll fly from Entebbe International Airport in Uganda to the Congo. We'll guide you to the infiltration point in the Ituri Forest, then you'll be on your own, with no more supplies. Make sure you have absolutely no contact with the locals. Move through the jungle without attracting the attention of the insurgents, locate the hunting camp where the band is, and wipe them out."

"Why?" Meyers asked, without raising his hand. "Why kill the Pygmies?"

"Let me finish," Singleton snapped. "We're planning ten days for the operation, but if things go as planned the whole thing should only take five days. We'll need you to take a video of the forty corpses to confirm the kills and transmit this digitally. Then you head to the rendezvous point we specify and we get you out of there by chopper. If you run into one of the insurgent groups along the way, there are no special rules of engagement. We'll leave that up to you."

Yeager raised his hand, and Singleton nodded. "Is the Kanga band the only group of Pygmies in the area of operations?"

"No. There are several other similar bands living about ten kilometers away."

"Then how do we tell one from the other? How do we know which is our target?"

"Nigel Pierce, the anthropologist, is the key. He's living with the Kanga band doing fieldwork. He believed the cease-fire would hold, and he went to the Congo, but once hostilities restarted he couldn't get out. The camp where Pierce is, that's your target."

"So we're supposed to take out Pierce, too?"

"Correct."

"We're going to kill an American?" Meyers said in low voice.

Singleton stared at the medic. "Why do we have to kill an American professor and the Pygmies? Here's why. Half a year ago a new type of virus was discovered in the jungle. Like the Ebola virus, the host isn't clear, but we do know it infects primates, including humans. The problem is the incubation period and the mortality rate. It takes two years from the time you're infected to the time you show symptoms, and the mortality rate is a hundred percent. In other words, there is plenty of time for an infected person to spread the virus, and once the symptoms appear, no one survives. If this virus were to spread outside this region there will be a pandemic, and the human race might be wiped out."

The team members were taken aback by this unexpected situation. Yeager finally could see the big picture. What he'd been told when he was recruited wasn't a lie after all. It was, indeed, a dirty job. Yet one that would do a service to mankind.

"Operation Guardian is how we're dealing with this danger. I'm sure you've figured this out already, but Nigel Pierce and the forty or so people of the Kanga band are the only known group infected by the virus."

"But why kill them?" Meyers argued. "Why not just isolate them?"

"A large-scale medical team can't be sent in—not in such a chaotic region, where more than twenty armed insurgent groups are battling it out. If they're going to send in a force it'd have to be an army, but other countries hesitate to do that because they'll be accused of participating in the war. And there's another reason we have to deal with this immediately. You'll recall the hunting down of Pygmies I spoke of. If the insurgents' cannibalism were to reach the Kanga band, what then? All the troops would be infected by the virus, and when they attack villages and rape the women and girls, the infection would spread even further. UN peacekeeping forces themselves sexually abuse local women, and then it would be only a matter of time before the virus makes the leap to other continents."

"If you're infected with the virus, what are the symptoms?"

"That I can't say. It's classified, so that's all the information I have."

"Hold on," Meyers said calmly now, so as to not upset the director of operations. "There's one piece of intelligence we still need. Isn't there a risk that we'll be infected during the mission?"

"We've taken preventive measures. The virus has one weak point. In the first month after a person contracts it, it can easily be stamped out with a drug." Singleton pulled out a small capsule from his shirt pocket. Inside the clear capsule they could see a white powder. "I can't reveal the origin of this, but an unnamed country's military research lab developed the medicine. Once you finish your mission you'll all take this medicine. But even with this drug you can't let your guard down. During the mission avoid any physical contact with your targets. Be careful not to get sprayed with any blood when you shoot them. Do that and you run no risk of infection."

"Is the medicine safe to take if we haven't been infected?"

"Of course. It won't harm you."

"I see," Garrett said, nodding.

The Q&A came to an end, and an oppressive silence hung over the room. Yeager could sense that the others had made their final decision to participate in the operation. Who came up with the idea for such a crappy mission? he wondered.

"I know you're not enthusiastic, but you have to understand that this situation is the result of a perfect storm of adverse conditions. If the Congo were a peaceful country it wouldn't have come to this. But right now there's not a moment to lose. We have to ensure that Operation Guardian is a success no matter what. Everything depends on the four of you." He went on, sounding more apprehensive. "Three final points. After you wipe out the Kanga band, you need to collect samples for research. You'll bring back several types of organs and blood samples. I'll give you the complete list later."

"And that would be my job?" Meyers gloomily asked.

"You other three will help him," Singleton said, indirectly answering Meyers's question. "And again, take all necessary precautions to avoid infection."

Yeager had a small question, one he thought was critical. "If we damage the bodies like that, don't we run the risk of blowing the secrecy of the mission? If a PKO happens onto the site they'll know this wasn't just some ordinary firefight."

"No need to worry. The local fighters don't just eat the flesh of the Pygmies; they also cut off pieces of them to use as charms. Any PKO'll think that's what happened."

"I see," Yeager said. They'd thought of everything.

"Now the second point. You need to confiscate Nigel Pierce's laptop and bring it back undamaged."

None of them knew what the point of that was, but they had no objection.

"And finally, the most important instruction of all. If during the operation you run across a living creature you've never seen before, kill it immediately."

What was he talking about?

Mick, who'd been quiet the whole time, thought maybe he'd misunderstood the English. "What did he say?" he asked. "Living creature we never saw before?"

"That's right. If you see a living being you've never seen before, you need to kill it right away."

"Do you mean the virus?"

"No—you can't see a virus. And a virus isn't a life-form anyway. What he means is an animal that has a shape, a form."

"I don't get it."

Yeager stepped in. "There must be lots of living things in the African jungle we've never seen before."

Garrett and Meyers cracked a smile, but Singleton remained serious. "Most of those are things you can imagine—butterflies, lizards, whatever. What I'm talking about is a special type of creature, something that doesn't fit into those categories."

"It would help if you could give us some more details."

"The client has restricted the amount of information," Singleton said, his expression uncertain. By client he meant the country that ordered the operation. Most likely meaning the White House. "I'm merely the messenger here. The creature is in the jungles of the Congo. And the chances that it's in the Kanga band's hunting camp are very high. It will appear like nothing that's ever been seen before. But it's not violent, and it moves slowly, so with your skills you should be able to take it out with a single shot. After you kill it, collect the whole body."

"But that can't be all—"

"That *is* all the information I've been given," Singleton said, abruptly closing the subject. "The most striking characteristic of this creature is that you'll know as soon as you spot it that it's a totally unknown type of being. It might confuse you when you see it, but the point is not to think about it. Don't ask yourself what sort of creature it is. Once you see it, just shoot it. That's Operation Guardian's highest-priority target."

9.

THE EVENING AFTER his dinner with Sugai, Kento interrupted his experiments, wolfed down a cup of instant noodles he'd bought at the campus store, and headed over to the Tokyo University of Humanities and Science hospital. The hospital was a twelve-story building a ten-minute walk from the science campus. Kento was going to see Yoshihara, an older student he'd met at parties a number of times back when they were in college.

He entered through the staff entrance at the rear of the complex, told the security guard whom he was visiting, and proceeded into the main building. Kento couldn't help but feel a bit uncomfortable. He'd convinced himself that the medical school was superior to the pharmacy school, and he could never shake his sense of inferiority.

In the elevator to the upper floors he remembered the orientation session he'd attended when he first entered college. The dean had proudly told the assembled students, "Even if you were to become doctors, the number of patients you could save in your lifetime would be, at most, around ten thousand. But as a drug researcher, if you develop a new drug, you can save more than one hundred thousand people."

Which was exactly the point, Kento thought. If he were to actually develop a drug that treated PAECS, he would not only save the one hundred thousand patients suffering from the disease worldwide but also help the children who might be born with the disease in the future. Kento hoped the dean's words would encourage him, but they fell short. He still felt helpless—the hurdles he was facing were just too high.

It's simply impossible, he thought. He shouldn't get his hopes up. He had to tell himself this; otherwise, when he failed, his disappointment would be all the greater.

He got off the elevator at the fifth floor and walked over to the pediatrics nurses' station. One of the busy nurses noticed him and asked if he was visiting someone.

"Yes, but not one of the patients," he replied. "I'm here to see Dr. Yoshihara."

The nurse nodded. "Dr. Yoshihara!" she called out to a white-coated cluster of people beyond the nurses' station.

"Yes?" a man with short hair replied, and turned around. It was Yoshihara. Up until high school, Kento had heard, Yoshihara had practiced kendo, a type of sword fighting. And now here he was, being addressed as Doctor.

"Hi, Kento! Haven't seen you in ages," he said in his characteristic low voice. He was dressed in a button-down shirt, tie, and white coat, and he appeared totally different from the way he looked back in college. Kento felt out of place in his jeans and worn-out down jacket.

"Sorry to bother you when you're so busy."

"No problem. Let's go over to the office," Yoshihara said. He left the nurses' station, taking Kento with him.

"So you're going to be a pediatrician?" Kento asked.

"I'm an intern now, so I do rotations in different departments. Pediatrics is okay, but it doesn't pay."

"Doesn't pay?"

"You don't earn enough for the effort you put into it is what I mean. If you plan to open up your own clinic, a different specialty would be better," Yoshihara said, turning to glance back at the pediatric wing. "When you meet a pediatrician you know for sure he's a dedicated doctor who isn't in it for the money. But I'm going into a different field."

As they waited for the elevator Yoshihara brought up the main reason for Kento's visit. "Lung sclerosis, isn't it?" he asked, using the shortened form of the name for the disease.

"That's right."

"Unfortunately there's nothing present-day medicine can do. All we can do is try symptomatic treatment and see how things go. It's just a question of how long you can extend the patient's life."

"So there's no cure?"

"None," Yoshihara said flatly.

"What about basic research?"

"There's one person, a Dr. Garrado in Portugal, who's trying to develop a remedy."

"A remedy?" Kento was surprised. This was unexpected news. "How far along is he?"

"That's really out of my field. Hold on a minute."

They got out at the sixth floor, and Yoshihara headed to a corner, following a sign that read MEDICAL OFFICE. There was a series of doors down the hallway, each labeled with a different medical specialty. Yoshihara went into the one marked PEDIATRICS. There were a number of desks, but since it was evening, only a handful of people were there. Yoshihara opened a locker and extracted a sheaf of papers from a shoulder bag.

"I downloaded some of the articles I found," he said.

"Thank you," Kento said, taking the printouts. He quickly glanced through them.

"They seem to be at a stage well before preclinical trials."

"So it appears."

Dr. Garrado, of the Lisbon University Medical Center, had already developed a model of the three-dimensional structure of mutant GPR769. Based on this he was trying to design a drug that would bond to the receptor and could be activated as a medicine. His work probably put him in the forefront, worldwide, of clinical application research in this field.

"He's gone as far as structural optimization of the lead compound."

"What's that?"

"He's found a compound that may act as a drug, and he's trying to configure its structure to maximize its pharmacological activity."

Garrado wasn't just outstripping him, he was already years ahead of Kento. Trying to catch a big fish with spider silk was, after all, probably an impossible task. The research Kento could do in the tiny room in the deteriorating apartment building was no match for Dr. Garrado's. Like Little Leaguers playing against a major league team.

"So he's on the verge of completing a drug to treat lung sclerosis?"

"No; that's still a few years away. Even if he's isolated the lead compound, the chances of coming up with a drug are one in a thousand. Assuming things go well it would take more than five years."

"So this won't help patients now?"

"No, it won't."

Yoshihara sighed. "Follow me," he said, and took off down the hallway. The sign above Kento's head read ICU.

"One of my patients is a child with lung sclerosis."

"Really?"

They went through the swinging doors into the ICU. One wall was a huge window, and behind it lay the most critically ill patients.

"The row on the left, third bed from the front," Yoshihara said quietly.

A little girl, six years old or so, lay among the adult patients. Her skin was pale and purplish, her eyes closed as she labored to breathe. The numerous IV drips around her showed how serious her condition was.

A nurse was near her bed, along with a woman in her thirties who was likely the girl's mother. The mother wore a mask to keep the room free of germs, but it was still clear that she was close to breaking down in tears.

The nurse lifted the tiny oxygen mask from the girl's face and wiped away the fresh blood that stained the skin around her mouth. Kento took a step back, shocked.

"She's terminal. She'll be dead in about a month."

It was so unfair. Faced with this hideous reality, Kento felt even more wretched. He wasn't able to save her. The miserable hovel of a lab became, in his mind, the reality of his father and of himself—and their inability to do anything about this girl's condition.

Perhaps out of a need to punish himself, Kento read the name of the patient on the nameplate. MAIKA KOBAYASHI, AGE 6. He knew he wouldn't forget that name as long as he lived. The name of the child he'd stood by and watched die.

"I'd like to earn money, sure, but I also want to save my patients," Yoshihara said. "You're in pharmacology, so you should develop a drug someday that will cure this disease."

"But doing it in a month is impossible." Kento thought of the limit of twenty-eight days his father had given him. One month from now.

The sun had long since set, and the temperature had dropped considerably. On the Yokojikken River, which paralleled the sidewalk, migrating winter birds floated on the surface, resting from their journey.

As he made his way back to his lab, hands stuck in the pockets of his down jacket, Kento hung his head like a wounded animal. He couldn't shake the image of the little girl on the verge of death.

She'd never done anything to deserve this, so why did she have to suffer? Why did she have to die at age six? Even a mediocre scientist such as he knew the answer to that one. Sometimes nature, indiscriminately, is unfair and cruel.

Researchers in pharmacology combat this threat, but what had he accomplished? In the six years since he'd entered college he'd wasted one day after another, with no sense of mission or purpose.

Still, knowing that, what was he able to accomplish from now on? Kento looked up at the night sky, hoping to shake off these gloomy feelings. Above him spread the universe—countless stars, light-years away, shining brightly.

A drug would someday be developed to cure PAECS. But that would be five years in the future, at least, not a month from now. He'd been given an impossible assignment. Crushed by a sense of impotence, Kento still couldn't shake his father's final message. His father wouldn't have spent such a huge sum of his own money to prepare that private lab without some confidence that he could successfully create the drug. All he could depend on now was the GIFT software installed in the laptop, though he wasn't sure of its function. And that Korean exchange student who'd done computerized drug development. Doi should be checking his schedule. Kento was about to phone Doi when he heard someone calling his name. He was so lost in thought that at first the voice didn't register. "Kento Koga?" he heard a second time, and came to a halt.

Kento had arrived at the rear of the pharmacology building on the science campus. At night it was usually deserted. The only light came from the fluorescent lights illuminating the distant bicycle parking area.

Kento looked out into the darkness, but he couldn't see anyone. It had been a woman's voice, but just as he was about to dismiss it and walk off he heard faint footsteps approaching from behind.

He turned to find a slim, middle-aged woman. She was dressed in a neutral-colored coat and wore no makeup. The kind of fresh, well-scrubbed look that women in the sciences often had.

"You're Kento Koga?" she asked in a faint voice.

Maybe she was someone on the science faculty. Still, she seemed a bit ghostly for that. "Yes, I'm Kento."

"I have something I need to talk with you about. Would you mind?"

Kento hesitated. "Uh . . ."

"Come with me," she said, and began leading him away from the campus.

"Wait a second. What's this about?"

"It's about your father."

"My father?"

The woman nodded, all the while staring straight at him.

"I need to talk with you about something."

"But how did you know I'm Seiji Koga's son?"

"Your father showed me a photo of you once. He was very proud of you."

That had to be a lie. Kento couldn't picture his father bragging about him.

"Please, follow me," the woman said, walking briskly. She seemed to be concerned about the voices of students filtering over from the bicycle parking lot.

"Where are we going?"

"It's cold out, so let's talk in the car."

"Car?" he repeated. By then they were outside the main gate. A minivan was parked on the narrow road alongside the wall that surrounded the campus. It was parked in the space between the streetlights, and all he could tell was that it was a dark color.

Kento stopped. He wasn't sure why, but he felt like if he got in the car he'd never see the campus again. "Can't you tell me here?"

"But I—"

"What about my father?" he asked, and as he did, a second question came to his confused mind. "Excuse me, but who *are* you?"

The woman looked away. "My name's Sakai. Your father helped me a lot."

"Miss Sakai? And your first name?"

"Yuri. Yuri Sakai."

Kento didn't recognize the name.

"Your father never mentioned me?"

"No, he didn't. What's this all about?"

Yuri Sakai glanced at the minivan. "I was shocked when I heard your father died."

What a strange way to express regret, Kento thought. Why hadn't she paid her respects at their home in Atsugi, as everyone else did? "What kind of relationship did you have with my father?" he asked.

"We did research on viruses together."

"At Tama Polytechnic?"

"I'm in a research facility outside the university."

"You mean joint research?"

"That's right. You really never heard anything about it?"

Kento could only nod. There was so much about his father's activities that was a riddle to him, so he couldn't determine whether she was telling the truth.

"I wanted to ask you about that research. I left some valuable experimental data with your father."

"Data?" For a moment Kento believed her. Nothing was more important to a researcher than their data.

"Did your father happen to leave behind a small laptop?"

Kento froze. She was talking about the laptop his father had left in his study, the one that wouldn't boot up.

Never let anyone else have it.

"N–no, I don't know anything about that," he answered, flustered. It was obvious how unsettled he was.

He pushed his glasses up higher on his nose, trying to regain his composure. Yuri looked at him, smiled, and chuckled quietly.

"You're just like your father."

Kento looked in surprise at her smile. He'd never expected this gloomy woman to smile. This straightforward, candid woman was, he noticed for the first time, rather pretty.

"Won't you come into the car to talk?" Yuri asked again. "It's warm inside."

But Kento couldn't believe this minivan with the tinted windows was really hers. He felt as if, at any moment, the doors would whip open and men would rush out at him. "I'm fine here. But what's all this about a black laptop?"

"I never said it was black."

Damn. He'd blown it again.

"But that is the one I'm talking about, the black laptop," she said, her look serious once more. "Your father left it to you, didn't he?"

Kento was at a loss. If he said any more he'd just be digging himself into a deeper hole.

"I'd like you to give me that laptop."

Kento thought it over for a moment, then decided to change his strategy. "Okay, you're right, I do have it. But my father told me not to give it to anyone."

"Of course he did. It contains data on research he was doing. In your own work you never take your experiment notes outside the lab, do you?"

It seemed like she knew what she was talking about. Maybe she really did work for a research institute.

"Your father was never expecting he'd die."

That much was true. The note his father had left behind was a strange sort of will, one that didn't take into account the possibility of death.

"Without that laptop I won't be able to continue my research. I need you to return it to me."

"Tell me about when my father collapsed at Mitaka station."

Yuri was about to say something but suddenly fell silent. She inclined her head slightly and cast him a sidelong glance.

"Did my father suffer?" he asked.

"I have no idea."

"But weren't you the one who called the ambulance?"

"No. That wasn't me," she said flatly. But Kento couldn't believe her. She was the last person ever to talk with his father. But then why would she have run away? There had to be a reason why she'd left his father behind.

"This is for your own good, too, Kento," Yuri said. "Give me back the laptop."

"My own good? What are you talking about?"

"I'm afraid I can't tell you."

"Then I'm not giving you the laptop."

Yuri was silent, her eyes unfocused, considering what to do. Kento stiffened, waiting for her next move. But she just looked up and said coolly, "All right. I understand."

Their conversation came to a sudden halt. Before he could stop her, Yuri strode off toward her van. He watched her, puzzled by the encounter. Should he have tried to keep her talking and find out more about her? Thinking he should at least get the license-plate number, Kento stepped forward toward the minivan. But as soon as he did, his heart started to pound, and he froze. Someone else was behind the tinted windows of the van.

Yuri wasn't alone.

Kento instinctively felt at risk. Yuri, hand on the door handle, turned around. Her stern look as she peered through the darkness shot right through him.

Kento backed off and stepped through the main gate. Behind the campus wall, the car out of sight, he felt, if anything, even more afraid. He turned around and hurried away. By the time he reached the pharmacology building, he was running. He raced up the stairs, heading for his lab and his colleagues. He stopped in the third-floor corridor and looked around, but no one seemed to be following him.

Maybe he was just imagining things. Or had he really been in danger?

Kento opened the door and went into Dr. Sonoda's lab. Some of the female researchers were relaxing in the seminar room, drinking tea. He could hear the assistant professor's voice calling out directions to someone and the clatter of lab equipment.

Relieved at being back in familiar surroundings, Kento suddenly thought of calling his father's office, and he took out his cell phone. It was just before 7:00 p.m., so someone should still be in the lab.

The phone rang twice, and someone answered. "Hello? Tama Polytechnic University." A man's voice.

"Is Professor Hamasaki in?"

"I'm Hamasaki."

"I'm Seiji Koga's son, Kento."

"Ah," the man said, no doubt recalling Kento greeting him at the funeral.

"There's something I'd like to ask you. While my father was alive, was he doing any joint research with an outside research institute?"

"Joint research? No, he wasn't."

"Are you familiar with a woman researcher named Yuri Sakai? She's about forty years old."

"No. I can't say I know her."

So Yuri had been lying. As he was wondering who she could possibly be, a sudden chill ran down his spine.

Consider all means of communication you use—landlines, cell phones, e-mail, and faxes—to be tapped.

What about this phone? Was it tapped? By Yuri Sakai?

"There is one thing," Hamasaki went on. "I don't know if it's relevant, but your father was planning to take a long-term leave of absence."

"A leave of absence?" Kento repeated, trying to calm down. "For how long?"

"One month, until February twenty-eighth. If he had lived, he would have begun the leave tomorrow. That's all I can think of that might be related to joint research."

So his father really had been seriously hoping to develop a drug to treat PAECS. He'd been planning to develop it by the end of February and then hand it over to the American. "Thank you," Kento said. "Sorry to bother you."

"No trouble at all. If I can be of any more help, please feel free to call," Hamasaki said, and hung up.

Even after he'd hung up the cell phone, Kento couldn't shake a queasy feeling. He left the seminar room and walked back to the lab, thinking of Yuri Sakai. All she seemed interested in was getting hold of the laptop. Not the computer he was using to develop the new drug but the other one, the one that wouldn't start up.

The answer to the riddle seemed to lie in the silent black laptop. What could possibly be recorded there?

10.

INSIDE HIS BULLETPROOF limousine, Defense Secretary Lattimer was in a foul mood—and had been since early morning. Why were all these stupid problems arising when he should be concentrating on force planning for Iraq?

"So what are you saying about this drug cartel underling?" He threw aside both the report in his hands and his patience. "Bullet points only, please."

Watkins, director of national intelligence, and Holland, the CIA director, were in the backseat, and both looked annoyed. It was too late to get back on the defense secretary's good side. They hated how he always blamed everything on a failure of the intelligence community.

"It wasn't some underling, it was a midlevel person," Holland replied. "A person who is, on paper, an executive in a phony company they set up. He was in a small plane on his way to the United States from Colombia when the pilot lost consciousness."

The pilot, perhaps because of some chronic condition, had lost consciousness for a short time, during which the plane made a rapid descent. The drug cartel member noticed what was happening, and by the time he grabbed the controls the plane was on the verge of crashing into the Atlantic. He managed to straighten out the plane, but that was the most he could do, since he didn't have a pilot's license. The plane deviated drastically from its original flight path until the pilot finally regained consciousness. Aghast at what he saw when he came to—they were barely skimming the surface of the ocean—he pulled back on the stick and climbed steeply, but this set off alarms all over the United States. The air defense radar system that covers a 450-kilometer area off Miami picked up the plane as an unidentified object. If the interceptors—US fighter jets—had scrambled ten minutes later, the president would have been rushed into Presidential Emergency Operations Center, the emergency bunker under the East Wing of the White House.

"It was a series of elementary mistakes," Holland said lightly. "NORAD has investigated the causes and reviewed the air defense system. It won't happen again."

"In that case take this report off our morning briefing," Lattimer said, handing back the document.

The limousine made its way through the steadily falling snow, and the massive St. Regis Hotel loomed into view. They were close to the White House. Lattimer hurriedly turned to the next briefing papers. The report concerned the shortcomings in Russia's counterintelligence measures and pointed out the vulnerabilities in Internet usage originating from its military communications network. Even if the Cold War was over, this wasn't the kind of news the president would be happy to hear, though it wouldn't necessarily displease him. Lattimer decided to keep it on the agenda.

An unnatural silence fell over the sealed interior of the car. Watkins and Holland didn't feel much like chatting with the secretary of defense, who had a tendency to meddle with the contents of the president's daily briefing.

Lattimer considered the final report, with its implications about US superiority in a cyberwar with the Russians. For all of human history, going back thousands of years, military force had decided the outcome of wars, but that was a thing of the past. Behind the brave and miserable fighting now lay another, more secret conflict: a struggle over information. Most conflicts today came down to a war of wits between cryptographers and analysts. Even in World War II, when the Allies defeated the Fascist powers, it was hard to say how the war would have wound up if the United States and Britain hadn't broken their enemies' codes. The whole world might very well have been conquered by Fascism. But in reality capturing the Enigma code had crushed the ambitions of the Third Reich, while breaking the Purple code led to the destruction of the Japanese Empire.

But since the activities behind these information wars were mainly kept under wraps, the story for public consumption was that the main actors in the victory were the scientists who developed radar technology and the atomic bomb. Thus World War II was dubbed the Physicists' War. Now, well over a half century later, with information technology having evolved so dramatically, a new category of conflict had arisen: cyberwarfare. The battlefield was no longer in the real world but in the realm of computer networks. Superior hacking technology was all it took to bring a superpower to its knees. Not just the infrastructure—power plants, water treatment facilities, traffic control—but also financial transactions and military command systems could all be fatally damaged through the computer networks that linked them. The United States had suffered numerous such attacks since the beginning of the century and had carried out similar attacks on potential enemy nations. And they weren't above deliberately violating a country's airspace to feel out its intercept capability. Any major conflict in the twenty-first century would be a "mathematicians' war."

"About the last point in the report," Lattimer said. "How far have we broken Russia's code?"

"You should ask the NSA," Holland replied, referring to his professional rival.

Finding this pretty rude, Watkins responded. "We have the upper hand, no doubt about it. Our ability to decipher public-key encryption, especially, is second to none."

"What is that?"

"The most common code used on the Internet. RSA code, for instance." Seeing that Lattimer wanted a more detailed explanation, he reluctantly continued. "RSA code uses prime numbers. Prime numbers are like five and seven—they can be divided only by one and themselves. Prime numbers are easy to multiply, but it's difficult to get back to the original number."

Lattimer frowned. "How so?"

"For instance," Watkins said, making a mental calculation, "for the number two hundred and three, it's hard to tell what its divisors are."

"For sure."

"The answer is seven and twenty-nine."

"I didn't know you were so good at math." As they often did, Lattimer's words of praise sounded more like sarcasm.

"Just something I picked up from the people at the NSA," Watkins said, parrying the remark. "In an RSA code, what's important is the two prime numbers used to calculate the product that becomes the public key. The two original prime numbers have to be kept secret and only used when decoding the encrypted message. With some mathematical creativity in selecting your prime numbers, you can make sure that a person who has the public key is unlikely to determine the original prime numbers and decrypt the message. But if the receiver has the original prime numbers used to generate the public key, they can easily decrypt the message. So it doesn't matter that the product of the prime numbers is made public, because it would be very hard for someone to factor the key into the correct original prime factors." The director of national intelligence shrugged. "If you want anything more than that, you'll have to ask a mathematician."

"Hold on. If you know the prime factors that are the key to the code, wouldn't you be able to break the code?"

"You would."

"Couldn't you just then multiply random prime numbers and eventually break the code?"

"In theory, yes. But there's no need to worry. They use tremendously long numbers. The RSA code used nowadays is so secure that you couldn't do the calculations unless you used the massive computers at the NSA."

"I see," Lattimer said. The NSA had more than three hundred supercomputers, so many that they no longer calculated them in terms of number of computers but in square footage. "They always want a huge budget."

"And first-class mathematicians as well." At this Watkins's expression grew gloomy. "This might be a groundless concern, but there is a problem with present-day codes. If a genius mathematician appeared who was able to devise a revolutionary computational process, Internet security would collapse in an instant. Even state secrets would leak out. One single genius could control the cyberwar and reign supreme."

"Could that actually happen?"

"Most experts say that computational procedure can't be found. But they have no mathematical proof of it. There's still a risk that a new method of prime factorization might be discovered."

The limousine had arrived at 1600 Pennsylvania Avenue. It entered through the Southwest Gate and pulled up next to the West Wing. In the moment before they got out of the car Lattimer broached another topic. "By the way, what's happening with getting rid of the monster?"

"Are you talking about Afghanistan?"

"No; the Congo."

"Ah." Watkins nodded.

Holland, extremely interested in the special access program, perked up his ears.

"As always, our child prodigy is in high spirits."

"You mean that young guy at the Schneider Institute?"

"He's pretty sharp. And he gets along well with Dr. Gardner."

"Have you heard any updates?"

Lattimer was secretary of defense, yet he apparently knew nothing about this special access program, which his own department was spearheading. Holland considered himself the only one who seemed to be taking the threat seriously.

"All the people in the Office of Special Plans have set their action time to Congo time," Watkins replied. "They've moved the mission up. The unit is quite an elite group, and they've finished their training ahead of schedule."

"An outstanding group?"

"From what I hear."

"It's a real shame," Lattimer said with a sigh. "But since the president made the decision there's nothing we can do about it."

"It's the right decision. The operation will be over in a couple of weeks. Just wait for the final report."

Watkins hadn't touched on anything of substance about the mission. Holland glanced at him. The director of national intelligence's composed expression made it clear that the subject was closed. In the present administration anyone who gave the president disappointing news brought disaster down on himself. And in the present special access program there were disturbing signs below the surface, but these needed to be suppressed. The counterintelligence operation in Japan would, no doubt, eventually reach the president's ear. Easygoing Dr. Gardner would no doubt let it slip.

★   ★   ★

Operation Guardian was moved up more than a week. Singleton decided this after seeing how well the training was going. The four-man team, because of their military training, quickly regained the stamina they'd need for a ten-day operation in the tropical rain forest.

Yeager was happy at the news. Now he could get back to Justin, in the hospital in Lisbon, even sooner.

None of the others was perturbed by the sudden change in orders. They simply got ready. They'd all been supplied with various equipment—hammock, maps, compass, canteen, GPS units, long-range recon rations. They were each given strict orders to carry enough antiviral antidote capsules, in a waterproof case, for all the other men, just in case someone lost his own. But since their cover story was that they were civilians, the only weapons they were allowed to carry openly were AK-47s. AK-47s could be picked up for less than a dollar in the Congo, and everyone had one. Their semiautomatic pistols and night vision equipment would be kept out of sight, packed away in their civilian backpacks. After consulting with Mick, Yeager also packed some grenades and a grenade launcher, so they would have the minimum firepower they would need if they made contact with one of the insurgent forces.

At the last briefing before they were to leave South Africa, they were given the necessary documents—fake passports, ID cards for the wildlife conservancy organization, yellow fever inoculation certificates, and several types of passes issued by the various military forces in the Democratic Republic of the Congo.

"Here's the situation on the ground," Singleton explained. "The Congolese government has sent a battalion-size force into the area, but the rebel forces still have the upper hand. There's a local military force in central Ituri, and a broad section of the north and south part of the region is under the control of Ugandan and Rwandan forces. If you come in contact with the rebel forces, make sure you show them the correct pass. If you can't tell who it is you're dealing with, then emphasize you're with the wildlife conservancy group. They don't want world opinion to run against them, so they are, on the surface, at least, adopting a pro-wildlife stance."

As Singleton had sarcastically told them once before, world opinion seemed more concerned with the fate of a couple thousand gorillas than it did with the lives of millions of human beings.

"The last thing I'll give you is cash, ten thousand US dollars each. Congolese officials and soldiers will do anything as long as you bribe them. Money will be a valuable weapon with the insurgents. You need to be prepared for both war and peace."

Each of the four mercenaries was given a stack of two hundred fifty-dollar bills. Added baggage.

"We've only spent a short time together, but I wish you all the best, and Godspeed."

Yeager and team shook hands, perfunctorily, with Singleton and set out from the Zeta Security building, leaving their personal possessions back in their room. The equipment and ammunition they'd just packed away would be sent on separately.

The four of them, on separate flights, flew to Kampala, the capital of Uganda.

This city on the banks of Lake Victoria was much more modern than Yeager had imagined. He'd never pictured high-rise buildings in the middle of the African continent. The city was almost right below the equator, but since it was at a high elevation the heat was not overpowering. He wanted to take a walk through the bustling city of one million people, but they'd been ordered to stay out of sight in their hotel rooms.

As the sun was setting Yeager's satellite phone rang once, then cut off. He left his decoy luggage in the hotel room and went out the front door of the hotel empty-handed. The main street was full of an endless stream of people making their way through clouds of diesel exhaust. Lights from the rows of shops along this central part of the capital lit up the people and cars that filled the streets.

Yeager noticed that traffic traveled on the left and remembered that Uganda was a former British colony. Everyone he passed called out *Mzungu, mzungu* to him—"white person" in Swahili. Everyone on the street was black, and he didn't come across a single Westerner or Asian. Not wanting to stand out so much, Yeager slipped into an alley behind the shopping street until he located the truck with the canvas canopy over the back and quickly climbed aboard.

A middle-aged African man was in the driver's seat. He wore an old shirt, and his arms were muscular. He looked like a civil servant, a man with a wife and family. In accented English he said, "Your key, please." Yeager took his hotel key out and handed it to him.

"I'll take care of checkout for you," the driver said as he slowly drove through the jammed street. He reached out his right hand. "I'm Thomas," he said.

Yeager shook his hand and told him the fake name on his passport, James Henderson. "Call me Jim," he said.

"All right, Jim. Here you are," he said, and passed Yeager a paper bag that was on the seat. "Dinner."

"Thanks." Inside the bag was a hamburger from a fast food chain Yeager had never heard of. A Ugandan franchise, apparently. He was hungry. He opened the bag and dug into the burger. "This is really good."

"Glad you like it," Thomas said, and smiled.

Yeager surmised that this friendly driver was a local CIA operative. No doubt Thomas wasn't his real name. But he didn't inquire any further. He knew no matter what he asked he wouldn't get the truth. The need-to-know principle on covert ops meant that no one was told more information than he absolutely had to know. Thomas, too, probably hadn't been told who this man calling himself Jim Henderson really was or why he was taking him to the war zone in the neighboring country. But as they talked, Yeager did find out that he was Ugandan.

"If only we had a decent government and education, this country could become an advanced nation," Thomas said with a sigh, his tone serious.

"But it's already developing, isn't it?"

This halfhearted compliment brought a hard-to-decipher smile. "For the last few years minerals from the Congo have been coming into our country," Thomas said.

Yeager remembered that Uganda was one of the countries involved in the Great War in Africa. "Looted material?"

"Exactly. If you count underground resources, the Congo is the wealthiest country in the world. The Ugandan army encouraged the racial killing in the eastern Congo and then took over in the name of restoring order. A lot of smuggling is still going on. Still..." Thomas made a wry face and continued. "I really hope this isn't what people judge Uganda on. It's the crazy leaders who decide we have to go to war, not the ordinary people."

"The same's true in America," Yeager replied. "And every other country."

It took an hour to get free of traffic. Yeager was surprised to find that none of the intersections in Uganda had traffic signals. A few kilometers more, and the face of the city changed completely. There was no electricity here, apparently, and the dim residential area looked overwhelmed by the broad, dark African night sky. As he saw the candlelight filtering out of the homes they passed, Yeager wondered what sort of lives these people led. Surviving tough times, struggling to make it from one day to the next. There might be a huge difference between them and Americans in terms of material wealth, but inside, as human beings, they were probably much the same.

The truck, moving along a red clay road, slowed down. The headlights illuminated a man standing beside the road. Garrett. Yeager slid over and greeted his team member as he got in the truck.

"How'd you get here?" Yeager asked.

Garrett smiled and pointed at something beyond the windshield. "Rode one of those."

A minivan tore down the opposite side of the road. The seven-passenger van was stuffed with twice that many people.

"It's a taxi. Quite the experience."

The canopy-back truck picked up speed and drove for close to an hour until it came to a deserted plain, where it came to a stop. The sound of the parking brake was swallowed up in the African darkness. For a moment Yeager was entranced by the star-filled sky. Each and every star that covered the heavens seemed to be murmuring to him, and he couldn't sense the quiet around him. The scene made him feel intuitively that the earth was merely a planet floating in the universe.

Thomas got out and, flashlight in hand, walked to the rear of the truck. The bed was loaded with stacks of wooden crates, but this was just on the outside. Beyond was an open space big enough for the men to lie down in. Thomas pulled aside a crate, and there were Meyers and

Mick, just getting to their feet. They'd been in the truck before Yeager had boarded.

"So we're finally taking a break?"

Thomas motioned to the four backpacks and AK-47s. "Your luggage is over there."

The mercenaries began preparations to cross the border. They put on tactical vests and leg holsters and strapped on pistols. They loaded their weapons, both pistols and rifles, getting them ready to fire. They stored the night vision goggles in pouches they would keep close at hand, but to save battery power they wouldn't use the goggles until it was absolutely necessary.

Next they sprayed insect repellent on their skin and clothes, even drenching their backpacks. Once these preparations were complete, Thomas took out portable transceivers from one of the crates and distributed them. They each checked the frequency, slipped the device in a shoulder pocket, and put on a headset.

"Are you all set?"

They nodded, and Thomas went back to the rear of the truck. He lifted up the heavy crates and made a double wall so the interior of the truck was out of sight. Using Meyers's penlight, the men sat down inside, leaning back against the crates on either side.

The engine started up again, and the truck lumbered into motion. Meyers turned off his light, and the back of the truck was pitch dark.

"What's in the crates?" Yeager asked.

"Scrap and all kinds of random stuff," Meyers's voice said. "At least they'll serve as sandbags if we need them."

Yeager shone his flashlight at the line of crates between him and the rear of the truck. There were narrow cracks deliberately left between the crates, perfect as gun ports. Thomas was a real professional.

They bounced around on the long journey, and every time they felt the road get smooth beneath the tires they knew they were passing through a village. Yeager tried to get some sleep, but only dozed fitfully.

About the time one day changed to the next the truck came to a halt, and Thomas whispered to them through their headsets. *"We're crossing out of Uganda."*

The four of them listened carefully for any sounds. Thomas was saying something, an exchange of words in Swahili. The other person must be a Ugandan border guard. Thomas got out of the truck and went off somewhere, but he soon was back and began driving again.

"We're out of the country," he reported. *"We're in the Congo neutral zone."*

Three kilometers ahead should be the Democratic Republic of the Congo. But a few minutes later the truck stopped again.

"One Congolese soldier, two boy soldiers, all with rifles."

Yeager and the others quietly picked up their AK-47s and got up on one knee in case they had to defend themselves.

High-pitched voices came from outside the driver's side. Boys' voices that had not yet changed. "Five hundred dollars," they were saying, over and over, obviously seeking a bribe. Thomas was saying something back to them in a determined tone, and finally the negotiations seemed to settle on *tumbako*—cigarettes—as payment to let them pass.

The truck moved on, but the four men in the back remained at the ready, waiting until they'd cleared the border. Finally the truck slowed down, and Thomas reported, *"Three soldiers with rifles. Immigration control station. There should be another dozen inside, but don't worry. I'll handle it."*

This area was under the control of insurgents who received aid from Uganda, so a Ugandan such as Thomas should be able to find a way to get through. Still, Yeager and his team switched on their night vision gear just in case. The world turned a phosphorescent green before their eyes. At Yeager's hand signal the other three took up positions at the wall of crates.

The truck halted. Thomas spoke briefly with someone through his window and then got out, probably to go to the immigration control office. But still they heard someone walking around the truck. Yeager peered through a crack between the crates.

A uniformed soldier was walking back and forth, obviously interested in the freight they were carrying. A second soldier appeared, and they started talking. Probably telling jokes, since they both started laughing. The two soldiers held on to the back of the truck and swung up inside.

Yeager motioned to Garrett and Mick that they would do the shooting. He and Meyers would drag the bodies into the back of the truck.

The soldiers lifted one of the near crates off the truck. They opened it, and when they found nothing of value inside they clucked their tongues in disappointment. Garrett and Mick planted themselves— their Glocks, fitted with silencers, held firmly in both hands. As soon as the soldiers removed the second row of crates and revealed the men's hiding place they'd put a bullet in each of their foreheads. Fortunately for all of them, though, the soldiers weren't so greedy. They put the crate back and leaped down from the truck.

Thomas was soon back. As before, he seemed to have deftly handled the soldiers seeking bribes, this time apparently handing over a bit of cash, and was now safely back in the driver's seat.

The engine gave a low growl as it started up, and Yeager and the others settled back as it began to move. Thomas came on the radio. *"We're in the Congo now. This isn't the time of day the insurgents are generally active, but please remain alert."*

Yeager and Meyers stood watch while Garrett and Mick tried to catch some sleep. After two hours, they shifted, and Garrett and Mick stood watch while Yeager and Meyers tried to sleep. The hard-and-fast rule of special ops was that you should grab sleep whenever you could get it.

But as soon as they entered the Congo the roads were so awful that sleep was out of the question. This was the sole main road through this region, but it was an unpaved dirt trail, too narrow to avoid all the terrible bumps and potholes. The truck jolted violently up and down, and occasionally Thomas had to climb out and lay down boards he'd stored in back in order to coax the truck over the massive holes and swaths of mud. It was a tiring job, but he did it all alone, without a word of complaint.

At 4:00 a.m., their journey was finally over. The truck, forced to move slowly, backed into a side road. Tree branches brushed against the canvas canopy, some of them snapping.

"We're here."

The four men stood up, stretching their stiff muscles. They took apart their bulwark of crates, picked up their gear, and alighted from the truck.

It was still dark out. The air was thick with the smell of foliage. It was cool, and they felt a slight chill in their long-sleeved shirts.

Yeager switched on his flashlight and was surprised at what he saw. The path the truck had stopped in was a sort of tunnel. The tree branches of the jungle on either side formed an archway that stretched off into the distance. Yeager, from a modern, developed country, was forced to readjust his perception. It wasn't so much that there was a forest on either side of the road, but that in the midst of a deep, massive, forest, insignificant little creatures called men had managed to carve out a primitive path that looked ready to be overwhelmed by the jungle bearing down on them.

The men broke down their combat equipment, stored it in their backpacks, and put on their photographers' vests with the GPS equipment inside. They all had on cotton shirts and cargo pants, and there was little chance that, from their outward appearance, at least, anyone would see through their disguise.

Yeager unfolded a map. "Let's check our position."

Thomas explained where they were, pointing at the map. "This main road running north and south is the dirt road we took from the border. Cars can't go any farther than this. The road is too rough, and the rebels have a headquarters in a town called Mambasa, at the end of the road. We're at this small path that branches off west from the main road."

The GPS coordinates confirmed this. They were just short of a village called Alafu. Yeager and his team would go into the jungle and proceed north, paralleling the main road. It was about seventy kilometers to the area where the Kanga band had its camp. If things went well Yeager figured they could take care of business in five days. Two days to reach the target area, one day to identify the camp the Kanga band was in, then two days for reconnaissance and carrying out the operation.

"The latest report is that the rebels and the Congolese army clashed a hundred kilometers northeast of here. The Congolese army lost sixty men, and tens of thousands of people in the area became refugees. Also, an antigovernment force ambushed PKO soldiers and killed some of them."

Normally unconventional warfare a hundred klicks away wouldn't be a problem, but in the Congo things were different. There was just the one road through the jungle connecting their location to the fighting zone. Plus every few kilometers there were villages along the road that were targeted by insurgents. If the insurgents began marching south they would definitely collide with them if they stayed on the main road. Thomas was right to let them out here.

"The rebels don't just attack towns along the main road; they also attack villages in the jungle. You need to be extremely careful."

To get to the Kanga band, Yeager thought, they would need to make their way through the deepest, thickest part of the jungle.

"Finally, here are the items you requested."

Thomas took down four long, machetelike hatchets from the truck. He'd thought of everything.

"Thank you, Thomas, for all you've done," Yeager said.

"You're quite welcome."

The other three men shook Thomas's hand, thanking him for his help.

"Well, I'm heading back to Uganda. Best of luck to you," Thomas said, and got back in the truck.

The canopied truck loaded with junk turned right, and when it disappeared through the trees everything around them turned pitch black. The men lowered their night vision goggles. When daylight came they would start their march, but before then they needed to get into the jungle and stay out of sight. They shouldered their forty kilograms of equipment, silently nodded to each other, and at a signal started forward. No one hesitated.

One after another the members of Operation Guardian were swallowed up by the dark, dense forest that covered the middle of the African continent.

11.

EVER SINCE THE woman calling herself Yuri Sakai had showed up, Kento had felt tense. Using his cell phone and e-mail made him anxious: he wondered if someone were spying on him, and when he was out walking at night he'd constantly glance around, fearful that he was being followed.

On this weekend evening, too, Kento slowed the pace of his experiments so he could go home later than usual. If he could leave with Nishioka, the lab chief, he'd be able to have someone walk with him as far as his apartment.

"Kento," a girl in his class called out to him, and he turned around.

"Yes?"

"You have a visitor."

"Really?"

"Down at the entrance."

Normally nobody visited the lab, so an alarm bell went off in Kento's head. From his station he couldn't see the entrance. "Who is it?"

"You should go see yourself."

"Is it an older woman?"

"No. A man."

"A man?" A different sort of anxiety came over him. Was this a new sort of threat? A thought flashed in his mind: he could take some of the chloroform they used as a solvent and, if need be, drug whoever it was. But that was a stupid idea. It might work in a TV drama, but in real life he might end up killing the person.

Kento hesitantly made his way down the hallway and peered over at the entrance. Right inside in the lab stood a neat and trim young man, looking a bit reserved. Of medium height and weight, he peered mildly in Kento's direction through his small-framed glasses. He seemed a soothing, calm type, not at all what Kento had been fearing. Kento relaxed a bit and went out into the hallway. "Hi. I'm Kento Koga," he said.

"Doi asked me to come," the man replied.

"Doi?" Kento repeated, and it finally dawned on him. "I see," he said with relief. "You're from the physical and chemical drug development department."

"That's right. My name's Jeong-hoon Lee."

Until he gave his name Kento had not detected any accent. "Nice to meet you."

Jeong-hoon smiled. "Are you busy now? Should I come back later?"

Kento glanced at his watch. It was 7:30 p.m. Luckily, today was Saturday. "Jeong-hoon, do you have any plans tonight?"

"No; no plans."

"Okay. Can I see you in about thirty minutes?"

"Sure."

Kento thought further. The two laptops he wanted Jeong-hoon to take a look at were back at the apartment. "I'm sorry, but would you mind coming to my place? It's a ten-minute walk from here."

"Can I park my motorcycle there?"

"No problem. Excuse me just a second." He went back into the lab, drew a map to his apartment on a memo pad someone had left behind, and came back. "It's apartment two oh four in this building. I'll see you there at eight."

"Sounds good."

"Okay. See you then."

After he said good-bye to Jeong-hoon Lee, Kento hurried back to the work he'd left half done. He set up one of his experiments so that the reaction could take place overnight, and then left the lab.

Kento felt a little strange about a foreigner coming to his tiny apartment. He remembered how bare his fridge was, stopped by a store that was about to close, and bought pastries and cans of juice. He was about to pick up some beer, but thought better of it. Offering alcohol to someone riding a motorcycle wasn't a great idea.

As he hurried along the road, a memory came back to him from junior high. He'd been at his father's parents' home and had gotten into an argument with his grandfather and uncle. The Koga household's men—his grandfather and the present head of the household, his uncle—had a visceral hatred of Chinese and Koreans.

"Never trust a Chink or a Korean," his uncle insisted while the men were drinking one night. Kento was frankly surprised. Could there be that many foreigners living in Kofu?

"Uncle, do you know any Chinese and Korean people?"

His uncle stared in amazement. "No," he said.

It was Kento's turn to be astonished. "How can you hate people you don't even know?"

His grandfather, shooting him a stern look, broke in. "When I was young, in Tokyo, I got into a fight with some Koreans. I got really hurt."

His grandfather had always been known for his physical strength. "Have you ever had a fight with Japanese?"

"Many times."

"So you hate Japanese, too?"

His uncle's jaw dropped. "Don't be an idiot. There's no reason for Japanese to hate other Japanese."

"But that's strange. You fought with both groups, but why hate only those who come from the Korean peninsula?" Kento deliberately used this way of referring to them rather than the term his grandfather had used—Chosenjin—because when his grandfather used this term to designate a particular race it had a derogatory tone. Kento sensed a foul sort of discrimination behind their words and wanted to dissociate himself from their stance. "Aren't both of you just forcing yourselves to come up with reasons to hate them?"

"Enough with the arguments, you fool!" his grandfather shouted, his face full of hatred. It was as if a deep-seated enmity within him was finally bursting forth.

"He's at that age when you say things like that," his uncle said in a sarcastic tone. "You're just like your father, Kento. Always argumentative."

Kento found it upsetting for them to berate him over something like this. Any love his grandfather and his uncle may have for their rela-

126

tives seemed trumped by the intensity of their hatred for *Chinks* and *Chosenjin*. They were narrow-minded people who knew only the small town they lived in and had decided that all foreigners were inferior. But what exactly did these words, *Chinks* and *Chosenjin*, mean? People they'd never once talked to? If so, they didn't even know what the words really designated. Their poor excuses for brains wouldn't allow them to see the contradictions in their own arguments. Kento, still just in junior high, was thoroughly disgusted with them.

Later Kento was horrified when he learned about the genocides that the Japanese had carried out. Right after the Great Kanto Earthquake of 1923, which leveled Tokyo, false rumors spread that Koreans were committing arson and poisoning wells. The government, police, and even newspapers spread these baseless accusations, and Japanese, stirred up by the rumors, massacred several thousand Koreans. They used guns, swords, and cudgels, and even tortured some people, tying them down faceup and repeatedly driving trucks over them. Japan at the time had conquered Korea and made it a colony, and a guilty conscience was at work, as well as the fear that the Koreans might exact revenge on them. The violence soon escalated to the point where even many Japanese were mistaken for Koreans and killed.

It was ordinary citizens who committed this barbarity. The thought sent a chill down Kento's spine. If his racist grandfather and uncle had been there at the time, they would have killed Koreans along with everybody else. People who had no qualms about expressing feelings of discrimination against other races could, without much provocation, let their brutality explode and slaughter others.

What evil spirit had possessed them? And what sort of fear and pain must the people who were killed have experienced? Japanese don't understand how frightening their own countrymen can be.

The only ray of hope within these horrifying visions was the venomous sentence his uncle had spit out: *You're just like your father.* Until junior high Kento had been oblivious to the discrimination lying hidden within Japanese society because of the home environment in which he'd been brought up. His father, Seiji, liked foreign exchange students. "Liu wrote a great paper," he'd say about one. And of another, "Kim did a great presentation at the conference," proud and pleased at each and every accomplishment of theirs. And his only son inherited this tendency. For Kento this was the sole virtue he was proud he shared with his father.

As Kento climbed the stairs to his apartment he thought about the way Korean-Japanese and Japanese had helped each other after the Great Hanshin Earthquake of 1995. Times had certainly changed. Kento could only pray that the guest who would be visiting in a few minutes held no grudge against the Japanese. When you had such foolish ancestors, difficulties followed you forever.

Inside his apartment, Kento hurriedly picked up his scattered clothes, making a space in the one-room apartment where a visitor could sit. Then he took the two laptops from under his bed and put them on his desk.

Right on time he heard a motorcycle roar up outside his building and come to a stop. He went out on his balcony, looked down at the alley below, and saw Jeong-hoon Lee get off his 750cc motorcycle and take his helmet off. Not many researchers rode such huge machines.

Kento went to the front door. "Come on in."

Jeong-hoon removed his shoes, stepped inside, and looked around the tiny apartment, grinning.

"Sorry to make you come all this way," Kento said.

"No—I'm the one who should apologize for dropping in like this."

After this polite exchange Kento had him sit down at the desk. "These are the two laptops I'd like you to take a look at."

"These two?"

"Yes, that's right." Kento noticed how stilted their conversation was, like a dialogue from a beginner's language textbook. "By the way, how old are you?"

"I'm twenty-four."

"Me, too," Kento said. "If you don't mind, maybe we could speak to each other more casually?" He hurriedly added, "You understand what I mean by *casually*, right?"

"Yep, sure do," Jeong-hoon said, immediately showing that he did.

Kento laughed. "You can call me Kento."

"Call me Jeong-hoon."

"Here. Have one of these whenever you like," Kento said, lining up the cans of juice he'd just bought on the tatami mat. "Now, the thing is, this smaller laptop won't boot up, and I was wondering if you could figure out what sort of data is on it."

Jeong-hoon opened up the black laptop and pushed the on button. As before, the screen remained a frozen blue. He tried the on button and the force quit function several times each, but was puzzled by the lack of response. Jeong-hoon took his own laptop out of its case, connected it with the small black laptop, and tried a number of operations. Kento didn't know much about computers and had no idea what he was doing.

After a half hour he turned to Kento, who was sitting on the floor. "This is a mystery," he said.

"Pretty tough to crack?"

Jeong-hoon nodded. "I thought it might be broken, but I can't say that for sure."

"So there's a chance it's not broken?"

"Yeah," Jeong-hoon said, and thought for a moment. His gentle eyes now looked sharp and focused—the face of a researcher. "If you can lend it to me for a week I could find out more. What do you think?"

"Hmm." It was Kento's turn to think. His father's final message had told him not to let anybody else have the computer. And then there was the incident with Yuri Sakai. Lending the laptop to Jeong-hoon might get him in trouble. "I'd like to, but the computer is somebody else's, not mine, so I can't lend it to you."

"Okay. Understood."

"Let's take a break," Kento said, offering Jeong-hoon a canned drink. As they relaxed Kento thought about the other laptop. The goal was to determine the true nature of the GIFT software, which should be Jeong-hoon's area of expertise, but Kento worried about how much of the background information he should reveal. Still, he did want to get Jeong-hoon's opinion of the task set before him: to create a drug that would treat a chronic disease, all in the space of a month.

Kento decided he could trust Jeong-hoon. "I'm going to tell you something now and I'd like you to keep it a secret, okay?"

Jeong-hoon frowned suspiciously and nodded.

"What I need to do is create a GPCR agonist in less than a month."

"Are you kidding? In a *month?*"

"That's right. That's why the GIFT software was created."

Kento briefly summarized the strange research his father had left behind. When Jeong-hoon heard that his father had passed away he expressed his deepest sympathy, but other than that, he listened in silence. At the end, as he explained the fact that several crucial steps were left out of his father's plan to create the new drug, Kento felt a little embarrassed. "It's impossible, right? I think it's just a bad idea my father came up with. A virologist in over his head."

Surprisingly, Jeong-hoon didn't automatically agree with him. He frowned, turning things over in his mind. "Let me think this through, logically, without any preconceptions."

"Sure."

"I know what your father was thinking when he planned this."

"Are you kidding?" Kento said in surprise, and leaned forward.

"There's only one condition that would allow an impossible plan like this to succeed. GIFT would have to be perfect."

"Perfect?"

Jeong-hoon nodded. "If the software models the form of the receptor and designs a chemical structure that will flawlessly bind with it, then the only issue remaining is what the people involved do with it."

"You mean the process of actually synthesizing the drug?"

"Right. Which is why in the steps your father outlined he included the minimal assay needed to determine if the synthesis worked or not."

Apart from the question of whether this was really possible, logically Jeong-hoon was entirely correct. As long as the drug design software created a perfect blueprint, all that would remain for the drug to be complete would be synthesizing the chemical compound.

The software you'll need for the research is in the white laptop, so use that.

His father's message had given him all the directions he needed. As Jeong-hoon had said, assuming that GIFT was perfect, they should be able to complete the task.

"But does perfect software like that really exist?"

"No," Jeong-hoon said simply.

Kento felt deflated. "So even considered logically, it's pointless?"

"But fathers' wishes should be respected," Jeong-hoon said, smiling, and reached out for the larger of the laptops. "Let's take a look at this GIFT."

They waited a moment as the software booted up, and when the computer-generated image of mutant GPR769 appeared on the screen, Jeong-hoon shouted in surprise. *"What the—?!"*

"So it looks weird? Even to an expert?"

"I've never seen such realistic graphics before, but it's—how should I put it? Very convincing." Jeong-hoon stared intently for a time at the model of the receptor, the ropelike structure that looped GIFT. He let out little interjections as he went along, punctuated with an occasional chuckle. When he finished checking it out, he turned to Kento. "This software shouldn't exist. It's fifty years ahead of present-day science. No human could create this kind of software."

"In other words, it goes beyond human intellect."

"That's exactly what it does. First of all, all you need to do is enter the gene sequence and you can see the three-dimensional structure of the protein. Plus you can design the structure of the drug that will bind with it de novo—from zero. It also predicts the complex structure after docking. And what's this?"

An item on the display menu said ADMET. Kento recognized that acronym. "It's an index for how a drug will react within the body. It stands for absorption, distribution, metabolism, excretion, and toxicity."

"Right." Jeong-hoon got it. "Pharmacokinetics and toxicity."

"Can you even investigate ADMET with this software?"

"It's not so unusual that it would have that function. There are other kinds of software that predict pharmacokinetics and toxicity. But GIFT allows you to determine this by species—human or mouse, for instance—and there's a column for inputting genome information so you could create custom-made treatment."

It finally dawned on Kento how extraordinary GIFT was. "If this software is perfect, then you wouldn't need to do clinical trials."

"Exactly. This software alone would allow you to run the entire drug-development process. All people would have to do is take care of the actual process of synthesizing the drug and checking it."

Kento and Jeong-hoon looked at each other and laughed.

"Okay, let's move on," Jeong-hoon said, and turned back to the laptop. He seemed to be enjoying playing with this unbelievable software. "Let's find proof that the software isn't perfect. There's got to be a good way."

"Would this help?" Kento asked, and pulled down a sheaf of print-outs from a shelf, the reports on PAECS that his friend Dr. Yoshihara had downloaded for him. "A Portuguese researcher has reported on the three-dimensional structure of that receptor."

Jeong-hoon looked through the report. "Homology modeling. Nice," he murmured, switching the display on the laptop a few times. The computer-generated graphics on the screen changed to an abstract model, a combination of spheres and ribbons. When he enlarged the active site of the receptor, the screen showed, at the atomic level, the part that bound with the ligand.

"Just as I thought," Jeong-hoon said. "The two models are quite different. The atomic coordinate values are different."

"So GIFT's a fake?"

Jeong-hoon frowned. "Too early to say. Logically, either the Portuguese researcher is correct or GIFT is correct, or both of them are wrong."

Kento was impressed by the fact that Jeong-hoon refused to give an easy answer. Tenacious logic was a researcher's sole weapon.

"Computer-aided drug design has run up against a wall, in fact," he went on. "Even using cutting-edge software it's difficult to predict the three-dimensional structure of membrane proteins. Most likely this Portuguese researcher is using an incorrect model."

Jeong-hoon booted up his own laptop, copied the DNA base sequence, and inputted it into GIFT. "Since we know the structure of the protein is accurate, let's compare the responses."

He hit the enter key and a message came on the screen, in English. PLEASE CONNECT TO THE INTERNET, it said.

"Why?" Jeong-hoon wondered.

Kento plugged the high-speed Internet line in his apartment into the white laptop. Once the machine was connected to cyberspace, the display on GIFT changed: REMAINING TIME: 00:03:11.

The numbers decreased with each passing second.

"Just three minutes?" Jeong-hoon muttered.

Three minutes later GIFT gave its response. On the screen was the three-dimensional structure of the protein Jeong-hoon had specified. As he checked various aspects of it, his face grew solemn. "This is really odd. This software has correctly depicted the structure of a protein that is made up of a hundred linked amino acids."

Kento was surprised. Didn't this mean that GIFT was indeed perfect?

But Jeong-hoon didn't rush to judgment. "The first thing we should consider is that this software is fake."

"Then how could it model the structure of the protein?"

"When it was calculating, it directed us to connect to the Internet, right?"

"Yeah."

"Maybe it searched out an existing structure on the Internet and made it appear as if it had calculated this itself. If you access the protein database you can find all sorts of information like that."

"I see," Kento said, but soon a new question occurred to him. "If that's true, though, then we can't decide whether GIFT is real or a fake."

"Exactly. We can't distinguish between a correct calculation GIFT's made on its own and a discovery that it's copied from somebody else. Because there's only one correct structure. And if we make it calculate an unknown structure, no one could tell which is correct—GIFT or some other model."

Kento felt taken in by a cunning trick. But if GIFT really were a hoax, who would have come up with such an elaborate prank? And why?

"Was your father familiar with programming?" Jeong-hoon asked.

"No. Not at all."

"Then where could he have gotten hold of this software?"

"I have no idea."

The name of the software—GIFT—was starting to take on an ominous tone.

"The other possibility is the hypothesis that GIFT is actually perfect. Though it's just a hypothesis," Jeong-hoon emphasized. "This program might have distributed computing software in it."

"Distributed computing?"

"That's the method used by the SETI-at-home project in their search for extraterrestrial life. By analyzing all the radio waves that reach Earth, they try to detect any artificial signals, all of which takes tremendous computing power. So what they did was connect the personal computers of volunteers and use part of their CPUs for the calculations. If you link tens of thousands of personal computers like that to do the calculations, you get more computing power than a supercomputer."

"Could I change the subject for a moment?"

"Sure."

"Did they find evidence of aliens?"

"Not yet."

Kento felt a bit let down.

"Six times, though, they've detected unknown radio waves coming from the center of the Milky Way. The waves remain a mystery to this day. Astronomers from all over the world have already decided on a protocol for announcing this news if they do find evidence of extraterrestrials."

"Wow."

"Let's get back on topic."

"Go ahead."

"Let's consider one of the functions of this program—to calculate the complex of receptors and ligands. There are two important factors that determine how well the software will perform this function: the machine's computing power and the algorithm."

"By algorithm you mean computational procedure?"

"Right. The method that will arrive at the correct answer through the least number of computational procedures, omitting any unnecessary calculations."

Kento tried his best to keep up. This was outside his area of expertise.

"First of all, if this computer is letting other computers do the calculations through distributed computing, it has plenty of computing power. But even if you link a hundred million computers together, it's impossible to do perfect molecular dynamics calculations."

Kento was aware of this, too. It was precisely because perfect calculations were impossible that after you made a drug you collected structure-activity relationship data and investigated a more optimal chemical structure. Technologically advanced nations competed so ruthlessly to develop supercomputers precisely because they were living in an age when computing power and science and technological advances were directly linked.

"And labor-saving computational procedures—algorithms, in other words—make up for the lack of computing power. Researchers have tried many different methods, but never found one that's perfect. No two algorithms will give you the same answer. That's the limit of present-day science. In other words, computing power is insufficient, and nobody's discovered a perfect computational procedure."

Kento said, "So GIFT can't be perfect is what you're saying."

"Logically, that's the case," Jeong-hoon replied. His expression remained unconvinced.

"Is there something else bothering you?"

"I'm not sure how to put it... Would you call it touch, maybe? Feeling?"

"You mean like a sense?"

"That's it. You get a strange sense when you use this software."

"What, exactly?"

"I don't know how to express it," Jeong-hoon said, scratching his head and trying to translate the sense of discomfort he felt into Japanese. "It's like, when you use it, you sense the program really *is* all-powerful."

This was a feeling that only Jeong-hoon, well versed in all sorts of software, could understand.

"Whatever researcher created this software is amazing. He made it appear to reveal tremendously complex biological activity down to the level of molecules and electrons. If you really can use this software, it deserves a Nobel Prize. A bunch of them."

Kento felt the same way.

"But I can't find any direct proof that it's fake. It's really an amazing program."

"Why would somebody create this software?"

"It's a mystery. A specialist would recognize right away it's impossible, while an amateur wouldn't know what kind of software it was."

Kento was startled. "So a researcher in another field might be fooled by it."

"What do you mean?"

"Someone like my father, who was in virology. He might have been told that it was a program that could do anything related to drug development and be totally taken in by it."

Yuri Sakai came to mind. It wasn't clear what sort of relationship she and his father had had, but maybe she was the one who brought him this program and suggested it could cure a chronic disease. She'd reeled him in with the promise of all the royalties he could earn. She planned to embezzle all the private research money his father had sunk into it and then disappear. The bank account under another person's name with the large amount of research funds in it had to be money Yuri was going to have him transfer to her.

But then why, after his father's death, did Yuri risk seeing Kento? It made sense if the small laptop she wanted to get back had some electronic data—e-mail exchanges, for instance—that might prove her fraudulent activities. She could ignore the computer with GIFT installed on it, because that alone wouldn't reveal where it originated.

"How gullible can you get?" Kento said angrily.

"But your father must have had some good points, too," Jeong-hoon said, trying to smooth things over.

The only thing that didn't fit this scenario, though, was the Heisman Report. What was in the fifth section? Kento still hadn't heard back from Mr. Sugai. Maybe he should ask him not just about the Heisman Report but also about this drug development fraud as well. Depending on how it played out, he had to be prepared for the police to get involved.

"Can I check out this laptop?" Jeong-hoon asked, pointing to the computer with GIFT installed. "I want to fool around with it a little more."

"Uh, sure."

"Thanks."

They talked for another hour, exchanged cell phone numbers, and Jeong-hoon left before midnight. During their visit Kento found out more about this Korean exchange student. He'd skipped a grade in high school and entered college at seventeen, so he must be unusually bright. His excellent Japanese was something he'd mastered just through lessons at school. And when he'd had to take time out from college to serve in the military, he'd worked at a US military base and had picked up English as well. Skipping grades, being drafted into the military—the situation with students in Korea certainly was different from that in Japan.

After Jeong-hoon left, Kento felt the special kind of joy that comes from making a new friend, someone he could really get along with. He took a shower in the tiny bathroom, brushed his teeth, and got ready to go to sleep. As he lay down in bed, he came to a final conclusion. Since he knew they couldn't use GIFT, he decided that the research his father had left him was impossible. He had to give up the idea of ever developing a drug to treat PAECS. Kento, used to disappointment, told himself that it was absurd, that trying to save the lives of one hundred thousand children had been totally beyond him from the beginning.

Still, he couldn't forget one tiny girl, fighting to breathe, her mouth bloody.

Maika Kobayashi.

The girl was only a twenty-minute walk from his apartment. Lying in a hospital bed, gasping for air, unable to get enough oxygen. The girl was alive now, but in a month she will have vanished from the face of the earth.

Dead.

There wasn't a single person in the world who could save her.

Damn it, Kento muttered, and switched off his bedside lamp to go to sleep.

He tossed and turned. In the narrow space between wakefulness and sleep, confused and chaotic images—neither thoughts nor dreams—came and went. A deserted laboratory. Confusion following a failed experiment. A sense of being blamed. Mice scurrying around in cages. An orphan receptor on the membrane of a cell in the dark, opening its huge mouth. An electronic sound. A light melody playing somewhere—

Kento gave a start and realized he'd been asleep. He reached out with his right hand from under the covers and picked up his cell phone from the floor beside him.

He blinked open his eyes and checked the screen. OUT OF AREA. It was 5:00 a.m. The room was still dark. Kento groaned and answered the call. "Hello."

"Kento Koga. Please listen carefully."

"What? Hello?"

The same high-pitched voice rang in his ear. "Kento Koga. Please listen carefully."

A computer-generated voice. A flat monotone.

"Who are you? And why are you calling at this hour?"

Kento was testy, but the other party continued, unruffled. "Within thirty minutes, you must be getting out of your apartment. Not remain where you are. Not remain where you are."

The Japanese was a little strange as the artificial voice repeated each sentence. Figuring it was a prank call, Kento was about to hang up when the voice said something new: "Do not give the small computer to anyone. Do not give the small computer to anyone."

It was talking about the black laptop, Kento realized. He shot up in bed and listened carefully to the mechanical voice.

"Within thirty minutes, you must be getting out of your apartment. Not remain where you are. Do not give the small computer to anyone." The artificial voice repeated the previous message. Then, at the end, it added, "Run away from your apartment quickly. Run away from your apartment quickly. Stop the power on your cell phone. Stop the power on your cell phone."

"Hello?" he asked again, but the call ended.

Kento slapped himself on the side of his head, trying to force himself awake. As he reviewed the weird message, he felt a chill—not from the cold air in the room but from the cold welling up from within him.

Do not give the small computer to anyone . . .

Within thirty minutes, you must be getting out of your apartment . . .

It was a clear warning. In thirty minutes someone was going to force his way in here and grab the laptop away.

Stop the power on your cell phone . . .

Kento hurriedly powered off his phone, though he wasn't sure whether he should take this warning seriously or not. The only person he could think of who might want to steal his laptop was Yuri Sakai. But then who was it who called him? The high-pitched computer-generated voice was probably just reproducing sentences that were typed in. It ignored his questions because the text of the message had been predetermined.

Not remain where you are . . .

The meaning was clear, but the Japanese was unnatural, like sentences composed by a foreigner. Jeong-hoon Lee's face came to him. No; Jeong-hoon's Japanese was much more fluent. Nearly perfect.

Kento got out of bed, switched on the light, and turned on the heater. His head was heavy from lack of sleep. If Yuri Sakai tried to force her way in, he wasn't too worried. He might be small himself, but he was strong enough to physically push her out.

Run away from your apartment quickly . . .

Still, the artificial voice had a strange urgency to it, as if it were telling him that if he didn't obey something horrific would happen.

As he went into the bathroom Kento again felt a chill. Yuri Sakai appearing in her van at the university at night. There'd been someone else in the car with her. He'd be dealing with more than one person.

"This is for your own good, too, Kento," she'd told him. Now he was able to read between the lines. It had been a threat: give me the laptop or else put yourself in danger.

As he dragged his feet, thinking it over, he'd already wasted ten minutes. But what should he do? He couldn't just be his usual indecisive self and give up. He had to do *something.* He used the toilet, and as he was washing up he decided on his next step. He didn't believe the telephoned warning, but he would leave the apartment and see how things developed. He'd go to a convenience store or somewhere else to kill time and come back after the sun was up.

He changed clothes and stuffed his wallet, apartment key, and the powered-off cell phone in his pocket. He was about to leave when he realized that in his flustered state he'd almost left the most important thing of all. The black laptop. But how to carry it? He took off his down jacket and rummaged through his closet until he found a lighter sports-type coat. The coat had a map pocket on the chest, just big enough for the laptop to fit in.

Just then he heard a car outside. It was 5:26. *I thought I had four more minutes!* He opened the curtains and sliding glass door and stealthily stepped out onto the balcony. It was still dark outside. He gazed down at the narrow, one-way alley below, lit only by the streetlights, and saw directly below him the roof of a van. It was similar to Yuri's van, but the color was different. It was clear, though, that it had deliberately parked in a spot that would block the entrance to the building.

Escape was cut off. If he were to get out of the building he'd have to slip past that van.

The passenger door opened, and a man emerged. He seemed about to look straight up, so Kento quickly pulled his head back. What was going on? Bent over, he went back to the door and crawled inside. His glasses had slipped down his nose, and he pushed them back up and paced the apartment. He'd made a fatal error. His light was still on, and the curtains and sliding door were open. The man from the van would know he was at home.

He heard several car doors opening and closing down below. There must be two or three of them, he was thinking, when he heard someone right outside his door, much sooner than he'd imagined. The intercom buzzed angrily, over and over. Kento started to tremble. It was too late to try to pretend he wasn't at home. He went over to the front door and peered out of the peephole. Just outside the flimsy door was a scowling middle-aged man. He had on a coat and looked like a businessman. Behind him were two more men, both wearing white surgical masks.

Kento was too frightened to respond, and he stood there, peering at the scene. The man in front turned and nodded to the other two. One of the masked men took out what looked like a cylindrical magnifying glass and held it over the peephole. Kento's vision suddenly grew blurry, and he couldn't see outside anymore.

He knew right away what they'd done. The magnifying glass compensated for the distortion of the fish-eye lens of the peephole, allowing them to see inside. The man with the mask could see him.

Kento instinctively stepped back. An angry voice suddenly yelled out. "Mr. Koga! Mr. Kento Koga! Metropolitan Police Department. Open up!"

Metro Police Department? Kento thought, totally confused.

"We know you're in there, so open the door!"

The police. Why would detectives show up at his door? He did know one thing: this wasn't a friendly house call. Shouting like this so early on a Sunday morning meant they were deliberately trying to draw the attention of the other residents.

Kento reluctantly unlocked the door and half opened it, the chain still fastened.

"Kento Koga?" the man with no mask said, thrusting an ID of some sort at him. "I'm Kadota from the Metro Police Department. Please let us in."

Kento was so tense his mouth had dried up. "Wh-what's this all about?"

Kadota looked even more stern. "It's about your father, Seiji."

"My father?"

"Unchain the door and let us in and I'll tell you the details."

A faint hope sprang up in Kento—maybe the police had started investigating this drug development fraud. But no matter how good a spin you put on it, banging on his door when he was barely awake wasn't exactly a friendly gesture. Kento looked out at the three grim-eyed men. "Can you show me your police ID one more time?"

Kadota made a sound of annoyance and flipped open the ID folder again.

"Doesn't a police ID have a black cover?" Kento asked.

"The old type did. We're using these now."

Kento read the division that this detective belonged to. "What does the Public Security Bureau do?"

Kadota closed the folder. "We're helping with an investigation. The police abroad asked us to look into the late Professor Seiji Koga."

"Abroad?" Kento tried to suppress his rising panic. What foreign countries had his father visited? He'd attended conferences in the United States and France. And he'd gone to Zaire, in Africa, to investigate the HIV virus. "From which country?"

"The United States."

"Which state?"

"It isn't from a state. The inquiry is from the Federal Bureau of Investigation. The FBI."

Another shock. "What does the FBI want to know?"

"Your father is a suspect in a crime. They think he stole some data from a research facility in the States."

Kento stared, dumbfounded, at Kadota. He might have had a low opinion of his father, but would the man resort to crime? He couldn't imagine it. Yet as soon as he thought this, his father's final, enigmatic message to him sprang to mind, and he suddenly felt like he was standing on a precipice.

If you get this message it means I've been away from you and your mother for more than five days.

Did he expect that he was going to be arrested?

"Your father has passed away, so of course he won't be prosecuted. But we have to ascertain the facts of the case."

Kento no longer knew what to believe. In a situation like this, what path should a researcher take? Logic. That's right—logic is the only choice. Don't rush to a conclusion. Be like Jeong-hoon was last night. What was the message his father left behind? What logical conclusion could be drawn from it?

But no need to worry. I should be back in a couple of days.

Kento looked down momentarily, away from the detective. His father was innocent. He was telling him that even if the police took him away he'd be cleared in a couple of days and be back.

"Do you have the laptop your father left behind?" Kadota asked.

"Laptop?" As he said this, Kento was surprised by the anger that welled up within him. *Stop seeing my father as such a fool!* he wanted to scream.

"The one he used in his research."

Do not give the small computer to anyone . . .

"Was it research data he supposedly stole? Not software?"

Kadota frowned suspiciously. "Research data," he asserted.

"One more thing," Kento insisted. "You're here because you suspect my father, correct? You don't suspect me, his son?"

"Of course not. We're just investigating all the parties involved."

Kento did a quick mental calculation. Even if he were to run away, he shouldn't be charged with a crime.

"We'd like to confiscate the computer. So we'd like you to let us in."

Trying to keep from shaking too much, Kento screwed up his courage. "I refuse," he said.

The detective's eyes turned icy. He took a document out of his coat pocket and thrust it in Kento's face. "We have a warrant. This is a raid, and we're coming in whether you like it or not."

Run away from your apartment quickly . . .

"All right. Let me get the chain off," Kento said, and Kadota pulled the toe of his shoe back from the crack in the door.

Kento quickly shut the door and slammed home the lock. Kadota started pounding on the door, and the bolt he'd just turned rotated back in the opposite direction. The detectives had gotten a master key from the owner. Kento hurriedly tried to slip on his sneakers, but his fingers got tangled and he couldn't tie the laces. The door opened a crack, and one of the detectives thrust in a huge bolt cutter and started to cut the chain.

Kento, finally able to get his shoes on, raced outside onto the balcony. Behind him he heard metal snapping. They'd cut the chain. From the corner of his eye he could see the detectives surge into his apartment. There was no time to shrink back. Kento climbed over the balcony railing, pressed one hand tightly against the coat pocket containing the laptop, and plunged over the edge onto the roof of the van. A 1.5-meter drop. The vehicle, impact resistant, gave way slightly and suffered little damage from this object slamming into it from above.

Kento rolled off the roof and onto the ground, and as he did, he was struck by how clumsy he must look, though this was no time to worry about appearances. He stood up, unhurt, and raced off in the opposite direction from which the van was facing.

He glanced back as he ran and saw a fourth detective stagger out of the driver's side of the vehicle, holding his head in both hands as if it hurt. The crown of his head must have gotten hit by the roof when it caved in. Now they'd have something to charge him with—assault and battery. The sudden, terrifying thought hit him, but he kept on running as fast as he could.

It was early Sunday morning, and the streets were deserted. In less than a minute he was out of breath. Kento was desperate, knowing he had to get away. These were pros when it came to pursuing people. The longer the chase went on, the less likely he was to get away.

He came out on a main street, two lanes in each direction. There was only a sprinkling of traffic, and he couldn't find a taxi. He slipped onto a side street, then turned left, deliberately switching directions, and came out onto another main street. This time he spotted a taxi. He waved both hands and climbed aboard when the taxi stopped. He glanced behind him but didn't see any sign of the detectives.

He was about to tell the driver where he wanted to go, but he stopped, uncertain. The taxi had pulled up to the curb facing in the direction of Ryogoku. The nearest station was too close to make it worth the driver's while, but he couldn't go too far, because he didn't have much cash.

"Take me to Akihabara," he finally said. The first trains of the day must be running by now.

"Akihabara it is," the driver said. He stepped on the accelerator and turned on his left turn signal.

In the backseat Kento tried to catch his breath and think. He was in deep trouble now. The police might already have contacted his parents' home in Atsugi. His mother would be frantic when she heard that her son had committed a crime. As soon as he'd reached somewhere safe he'd call her, but then he remembered the warning on the phone.

Stop the power on your cell phone . . .

Now he knew what this mechanical voice's message meant. If you triangulate the network towers for the phone you can isolate the location of its signal. Unless he wanted the police to find him, he had to keep his phone off. He'd have to use pay phones from now on.

The taxi pulled over at Akihabara station, the third station from Kinshi-cho. After he paid the fare he had only two thousand yen left. But fortunately he didn't have to worry about cash. In his wallet was the ATM card under the name Yoshinobu Suzuki.

He walked toward the station, wondering where he should go, when he suddenly realized he had a perfect place to hide. The dilapidated apartment building in Machida. So even if the police intercepted all his calls, they wouldn't know about the existence of this private lab. Solutions to all his problems had been worked out ahead of time, and Kento was impressed.

He stood in front of the ticket dispenser and glanced behind him.

Nobody seemed to be following him. He studied the map of the private rail lines, checking where he'd have to change trains, then headed for the turnstiles.

All he could do now was hide out in Machida and wait until he got hold of the final clue, the Heisman Report, and what it would reveal.

12.

IT WAS THE second morning after they'd begun their march through the Ituri jungle. Yeager woke from a shallow sleep and, lying in his hammock, looked at his watch. The backlit numbers showed five thirty, precisely when he'd planned to wake up. The sense of time he'd developed in the Special Forces hadn't left him.

He crawled out from under the mosquito net and waterproof sheet. The air in the forest was chilly. The dim predawn light was whitish, which surprised him until he looked closer and saw that he was surrounded by a thick fog.

Mick, rifle in hand, loomed out of the fog like the ghost of some dead soldier. On a two-hour sentry shift, Mick turned around and in a low voice said, "All's well."

Yeager nodded and looked at the other two hammocks. He could hear Garrett and Meyers breathing in their sleep. Mick pulled the waterproof sheets off them and started to wake them up.

Once all four of them were up they made preparations to set off. They rolled up their hammocks and took apart the frames they'd made for them out of branches. They only had two sets of clothes with them, and they exchanged the dry set they slept in for the damp clothes they wore on the march. They sprayed themselves with insect repellent, ate long-range reconnaissance rations—the taste was beside the point, since they needed the calories to keep going—and took their malaria pills. They relieved themselves and then covered over the hole they'd used for a toilet.

The conditions on this particular infiltration mission weren't so bad. If they were in a region where they were completely surrounded by the enemy, they would have to completely eliminate any trace of their presence, including taking all their excreta with them in plastic containers. They wouldn't even be allowed to use toilet paper. But surrounded as they were by hundreds of kilometers of jungle, they didn't have to be as cautious. The four members of the Guardian mission team were no more than tiny minnows swimming across a huge sea.

Yeager and Mick used their maps and GPS to pinpoint their route for the day and set several potential rendezvous points in case they ran into an unexpected skirmish and got separated.

They set out, heavy backpacks and weapons in hand, in single-file combat formation, with Mick taking point, followed by Yeager, Garrett, and Meyers. This formation allowed them to respond immediately to an attack from the front, the sides, and the rear. In the gloom of the jungle, though, they couldn't see very far, so they kept the distance between them tighter than normal.

After they walked for an hour the fog lifted. The sunshine filtering down from the tops of the trees beckoned them even farther into the jungle.

The endless sea of trees began to suck the spirit out of Yeager. The jungle had the power to unnerve a person. This was a world that stood apart from human reason, where bipedal, upright animals wearing clothes didn't belong. All kinds of creatures lived here, but only man was alienated from this space. And the farther he walked through it, the more a feeling akin to homesickness overcame him.

The best method to deal with the anxiety and fear the jungle engendered, his Special Forces instructor had taught him, was to one by one ascertain the threats it presented. The weather, the heat, the lack of food, the potential for losing your sense of direction, the poisonous creatures.

None of those threats applied here, Yeager reminded himself. The Ituri was different from Southeast Asia, where he'd done his jungle training. It was just below the equator, yet the elevation kept the temperature moderate. Whenever a gust of wind came, your sweat evaporated pleasantly. Insects and small animals were a threat, but there weren't many of them. Keep alert and there should be no problem. But what he was most thankful for were the numerous streams in which clean water ran. That water tasted even better than the bottled mineral water he'd drunk back on his last assignment.

And besides, the Pygmies had survived in this jungle for tens of thousands of years. If the Ituri jungle were such a harsh environment, they would have died out long ago. So there was nothing to be overly afraid of.

Mick came to a halt and signaled for them to come forward. Yeager and the others quietly joined him.

"What is that?" Mick asked, motioning with the barrel of his AK-47 at the base of a bush. "Is that the unknown creature?"

Yeager looked and saw a black creature, like a flattened worm, clinging to the trunk and squirming around.

"That's a kind of leech," Yeager said. "I've never seen this kind before, but I imagine that's what it is."

"Leave it be," Garrett said with a laugh. "What are we, naturalists?"

The slimy creature leaped at Meyers with unexpected speed. He jumped back abruptly, and the other three burst out laughing.

Something else moved in the brush nearby. The men swiftly aimed their rifles at it. An animal resembling a deer but about as big as a medium-size dog stood up and loped off into the jungle. It had been asleep, most likely, and the men's voices had awakened it.

It was a good time to take a break, so Yeager told them to take five. They put their backpacks down in a small open space between the trees, sat down on the undergrowth, and leaned back against the giant roots of the trees, which protruded from the ground and formed a perfect backrest.

Meyers took a swig from his canteen and asked, "What do you think this unknown creature is?"

"I have no idea," Garrett said.

"Maybe it's a flat snake," Mick said.

"What the heck is that?"

"It's a hypothetical creature in Japan. Whoever finds it will get some prize money."

"Maybe we should have gone to Japan, not the Congo."

Yeager wondered what kind of place Mick's home country, Japan, was. He pictured squalid hordes of people and a huge city filled with garish neon lights, but figured this was just a stereotype.

Meyers gazed around and, confirming how quiet the jungle was, lowered his voice. "Something's just not right about this mission."

"What do you mean?" Yeager asked.

"Think about it. We've been given two completely different targets. A group of people infected with a virus and a creature we've never seen before."

"I'm no specialist," Garrett said, "but maybe people infected by the virus turn into something like monsters."

"That's only in Hollywood movies. It's biologically impossible," Meyers declared. "Maybe the real goal of this operation is simply an assassination."

"Of the Pygmies?"

"No. Of Nigel Pierce, the anthropologist who's with the Mbuti."

"I had the same idea," Yeager said. "But if the point is just to kill Pierce, there have to be other ways to do it. There's no need to kill the Mbuti, too."

"Maybe they want us to silence them."

"If we attack at night there'd be no need to. Even if the Mbuti witnessed it, they wouldn't have any idea who we were."

"Then the point is actually to kill people infected by a virus."

"What worries me," Mick said, "is what happens after the mission. We're supposed to gather the organs of the dead bodies and bring them back, right? Their brains and sex organs and things."

Meyers frowned as he remembered this unpleasant duty.

"In other words we'll be bringing back a deadly virus. Isn't the real point of this mission to get hold of the virus so it can be made into a biological weapon?"

"The American military doesn't develop biological weapons anymore," Yeager said, defending his country. "At least that's what they say."

Meyers was about to reply but stopped. The other three fell silent and listened carefully. Faintly, something was moving through the brush upwind. Footsteps. And not just one set. More than five people. They weren't moving straight toward them but in a circle, as if to surround the mercenaries.

The men picked up their assault rifles and silently rose to their feet.

Mick pointed to himself, indicating he would take recon. Yeager nodded assent. Mick moved forward, rifle barrel held slightly down in combat readiness, while Yeager and Meyers covered the 180 degrees to the front of them and Garrett watched the sides and rear for any feint.

Mick moved cautiously through the jungle, his view obstructed for the most part by the thick growth. Yeager and Meyers followed close behind in single file so as not to lose sight of Mick and leave him cut off.

Finally Mick came to a halt, shielded behind the trunk of a large tree, and aimed his rifle at something ahead of him. But he didn't fire. The tension in his body relaxed, he lowered his rifle, and signaled for the others to join him.

One by one they came up beside him. They looked in the direction he was pointing and saw, five meters ahead, a group of large primates in a corner of the jungle where the trees were sparse. Seven chimpanzees. Seen this close, they were unexpectedly large. If they stood completely upright they'd be about the size of a small person.

These residents of unexplored regions didn't notice they were being observed by humans. The lead chimpanzee moved quietly, signaling, apparently, to the others strung out behind him. They crouched low and closed ranks. This was clearly a disciplined move, like a covert action, as though they were sneaking up on an enemy. It was such an intelligent, coordinated move that an observer might think it was done by humans dressed in chimp costumes.

"It's like they're imitating us, isn't it?" Garrett whispered, stifling a laugh. "Chimp Green Berets."

Yeager enjoyed watching them, too, but as he did he noticed movement in the sparse brush beyond them—another group of chimps. This second group was lounging around, grooming each other, taking it easy.

Yeager had an ominous feeling, and just as he was scanning the scene through his binoculars, the attack began. The second group of chimps, seven in all, snuck up on the first group, raised a crazed yell, and charged. Right then the branches around them began to move. The other chimps, shrieking, had run away. The group in the bushes soon scattered in all directions, with only one chimp remaining behind. That chimp crouched down defensively as the seven others, their hair standing on end, attacked.

The uproar was tremendous. The overwrought chimps shrieked crazily, at the top of their lungs.

Yeager figured it was a battle over territory, but he soon realized something was wrong. The battle was taking place in one spot only, in the middle of the bushes. That was where the seven chimps concentrated their violent attack. They surrounded the single chimp, grabbed it, and bit it, wounding it deeply. Yeager had no idea why they acted like this. He had the same awful feeling he had, deep in his heart, whenever he saw his fellow human beings engaged in acts of violence.

Two of the attacking primates grabbed the arms of the bleeding chimp and, at the same moment, lifted them up. They were a well-coordinated team. As the chimp was lifted to its feet, the leader chimp at the front grabbed something out of its arms. Yeager couldn't believe his eyes. It was a baby chimp. From its size he guessed it was still an infant. The chimp under attack tried desperately to protect its baby. Prey in his hands now, the boss chimp ran away, swung the baby chimp around by its legs, and smashed its head against a tree. The baby chimp's face writhed in agony, and it screamed out. The boss chimp didn't care, and it tore off one of the baby's arms and began eating it.

"What the hell?!" Meyers nearly yelled.

The chimps' bizarre agitation reached its climax. Hackles raised, they screamed uncontrollably. The feasting boss chimp gazed restlessly around, like some cunning old man, his hands nimbly stripping off meat from the baby, then leaves from the trees, as he ate them in turn. Watching this from afar, the other chimps edged closer, hoping to get a share, but the boss chimp ignored them. The boss put the baby's head in his mouth, ripping away the skin and muscles to get at the skull. The baby chimp, horribly, was still alive, its three remaining limbs weakly flailing about.

Mick, watching this silently, raised his AK-47 and aimed it at the boss.

"Don't," Yeager said, trying to stop him, but Mick pulled the trigger. The gun roared out, and the other chimps, frightened, instinctively scattered. Mick's shot had blown the baby chimp's head to bits, ending its agony, and the bullet had continued on through the boss chimp's throat, spraying the brush behind them with blood. The adult chimp and the baby, now corpses, collapsed into the vegetation.

"You goddamn monkey," Mick muttered.

Stunned, Meyers turned to look at his Japanese teammate. Garrett lowered his head and weakly shook it from side to side.

A strange emotion ran through the mercenaries. What the team had just witnessed was not just cannibalism among animals but a systematic massacre, a mix of reason and madness. In other words, war.

As he hefted the assault rifle, Yeager pondered the situation. Had humans been murdering each other even before they were actually human?

The men saw the wounded mother chimp race over to the corpse of her baby. This baby chimp, until a moment ago snug in its mother's arms, was now missing its head and an arm and had been cruelly tossed on the ground. What the mother chimp must be thinking as she gazed at the lifeless body of her child was something humans would never be able to guess.

"Show's over. Let's get out of here," Yeager said in a small voice. If by chance there were enemy forces in hiding nearby, they had to have heard the shot. "Mick, from now on no unnecessary shots."

The Japanese looked at him with a derisive sneer. Yeager's blood boiled, and he could barely contain his anger. Why had Mick shot the chimps? Was it a desire to save the baby chimp from further suffering, or was it hatred toward the boss chimp? In reality, wasn't it neither? Wasn't Mick instead trying to satisfy a crude vanity that wanted to show off to lower animals the kind of firepower he possessed?

"Let's head on out," Meyers said, and started walking. Garrett followed behind him, expressionless. Only Mick seemed in high spirits, which grated on Yeager's nerves all the more. It looked to him like all of them were trying, in their own way, to downplay the incident.

The four of them went back to where they'd left their backpacks. Yeager lifted his, and once they formed up in single file he motioned with his chin to Mick the direction they should take.

★   ★   ★

The photo that President Burns held in his hand showed an infant, its legs and arms ripped off. An Iraqi child. An ordinary citizen who had gotten caught up in the massive sweep against anti-American insurgents.

The president grimaced and pressed the photo into the hands of his vice president, Chamberlain. Chamberlain's expression remained fixed.

Across from them at the conference table, Secretary of State Ballard realized he'd have to adopt another tactic quickly if he were to persuade this pair of cold-hearted men.

"The number of civilian casualties has gone up, hasn't it?" Chamberlain said, trying to forestall him. "If the media sniffs this out it could cause problems."

Secretary of Defense Lattimer nodded slowly.

Ballard looked around the Cabinet Room table at each person in turn, trying to appeal to any remnants of conscience that might still lie hidden within the administration. "A hundred thousand civilians have already died in Iraq because of our attacks. Do you really think that's the way to gain the support of the Iraqi people?"

"That level of collateral damage is to be expected," Chamberlain asserted.

If a foreign military force were to kill Chamberlain's own family, would he repeat the same line? Ballard doubted it. But he put aside the sarcasm and innuendo and patiently continued. "With this much damage taking place, the enemy will be able to stir up even more hatred toward us and gain strength. If we want to maintain an acceptable level of security, we need to immediately send in reinforcements."

"That is not within your purview," Chamberlain said dismissively.

"I figured that when we decide military options we need to consider things from a diplomatic standpoint as well." Ballard had been, at one time, chairman of the Joint Chiefs of Staff.

"The decision's already made. We can't reverse it now."

As he looked at the men, all nodding, Ballard fell to wondering at what point the neocons had become so arrogant. Even among conservatives they were supposed to be just one small faction.

"So on this matter we're agreed, then?" Chief of Staff Acres said, checking that this was the president's intention before moving the meeting along. "Before we look at the last item on the agenda, those who are finished here may leave."

The assistant secretaries of state, with the exception of the one in charge of Africa, streamed out of the Cabinet Room. All that remained were the core cabinet members and those representing the intelligence community. Ballard gave up arguing with them.

"What's the final item?" Chamberlain asked.

"The special access program," the chief of staff said. "Code name Nemesis."

Once they heard this the mood in the room relaxed, as though it were time for dessert after a tough day of negotiations. Only Watkins, the director of national intelligence, and Holland, director of the CIA, tried not to let anyone sense the tension they were feeling. The special access program was entering a delicate phase.

The president's special adviser for science and technology, Dr. Melvin Gardner, entered, and the cabinet members greeted him warmly.

Dr. Gardner took his seat. "Let me brief you on where we are," he said matter-of-factly. "Operation Nemesis is proceeding smoothly. The first phase, in Africa, will be concluded in a few days. But there is one small issue that's arisen. According to reports from the NSA, there are some disturbing things occurring in Japan."

"Japan?" Burns asked, surprised. "Why Japan?"

"The details are still unclear. It's probably nothing, but we're taking steps to deal with it. As a precaution."

Sensing that the president wasn't satisfied with this explanation, Holland stepped in. "There's evidence that someone in Tokyo is trying to access Nemesis, and our investigation pinpointed a university professor named Seiji Koga and his son. A few days ago the professor died suddenly, and his son is continuing his activities."

"What does his son do?"

"His name is Kento Koga. He's a grad student."

"What's his field?" Chamberlain asked. "Journalism? Religion?"

"Pharmacology. His father was a virologist."

"But how could they have uncovered our black ops?"

"We're looking into that. The CIA recruited a local operative to get close to the young man. And the FBI is conducting its own operation through the local police antiterrorism unit."

"Naturally," Watkins added, "neither the Japanese operative nor the local police has been told anything about Nemesis. Everything is under our control."

"I see," said Secretary of Defense Lattimer, who would normally have been supervising manager of Nemesis. "The liaison from the Office of Special Plans asked me to get your opinion." By "your" he meant Secretary of State Ballard. "If, worst-case scenario, we have to take some harsh steps in Japan, can we count on the cooperation of their government?"

"What exactly do you mean by 'harsh steps'?"

"Indeed," Lattimer said. "I wonder if the head of the Office of Special Plans is considering the appropriate measures."

"The head of the office is that young fellow you were telling me about?" Burns asked.

"Correct. I understand he's a very capable person."

"If things don't go too far, I think the Japanese government will cooperate," Lattimer said, considering the balance of power between the two nations. Then, as might be expected of a moderate, he added, "I would, though, only like us to take harsh steps as a last resort."

As he listened to this exchange, Holland thought of the Grave, a stinking underground torture chamber in Syria. The place had a holding cell no bigger than a coffin, a variety of instruments of torture, and torturers who loved more than anything to inflict pain on anyone who visited. Burns had angrily denounced Syria for human rights violations, dubbing it an outlaw state, but this was a shameless lie directed at the world community. Ignoring the Geneva Convention stipulations on the treatment of prisoners, Burns continued to authorize the handover of terrorist suspects to the Syrian government for torture. And Syria wasn't the only country that carried out torture on America's behalf—enemy combatants had been handed over to Egypt, Morocco, and Uzbekistan as well. And the organization that carried out these lethal directives—called extraordinary renditions—was none other than the CIA, headed by Holland.

Holland, the president's accomplice in crime, gazed at Gregory S.

Burns with a gloomy feeling. A white man in the prime of life, president of the United States, greeted with a standing ovation every time he arrived somewhere to give a speech. The most powerful person on earth. But all it took was a word from this courtly looking man for people to be tortured and killed.

If he fell into the clutches of this evil man, this Japanese grad student would easily be crushed. Like a miserable bug.

13.

HE WOKE UP in pitch blackness. Kento thought it was still night and was going to go back to sleep, but then he felt how cramped his arms and legs were, and he remembered where he was. The private little lab his father had set up.

He extracted his arms from the sleeping bag and checked his watch. It was 9:00 a.m. He must have been exhausted, for he'd slept unexpectedly soundly. Yesterday, after the once-in-a-lifetime adventure of having leaped from his second-floor apartment to shake off the pursuing detectives, he'd taken a series of trains, finally reaching Machida. Upon arriving he used the ATM card issued in the name of Yoshinobu Suzuki and had withdrawn some cash and bought a change of clothes. Today was his second day on the run from the law.

Kento got up and was tempted to open the thick blackout curtains, but he wanted to avoid drawing any attention to himself, so he left them closed. If someone in the neighborhood found out about this mysterious laboratory, they very well might contact the police.

He turned the light on in the small room and washed his face in the kitchen sink. He had a lot to do today.

Breakfast consisted of a sweet roll he'd bought the night before at a convenience store. After eating he began taking care of the forty mice in the closet. As he started to clean out their cages he noticed a sheaf of documents in the back of the closet. They were in English, not Japanese.

The first page was a voucher issued by a foreign transport firm showing a shipment from the Lisbon University Medical Center in Portugal to the Tama Polytechnic University in Tokyo. The sender was Dr. Antonio Garrado.

Dr. Antonio Garrado.

Kento suddenly remembered this was the name of the world's leading expert on PAECS. Surprised, he looked through the rest of the documents.

There was a bill for 76,000 euros and a receipt with the number 40 written on it. This was the number of mice. His father must have paid this huge amount—equivalent to about ten million yen—for those forty mice in the closet, purchasing them from Dr. Garrado.

Another document stated that there were two types of mice: half of them were normal and healthy, while the second group displayed the pathology for PAECS.

There were four cages lined up, and Kento looked at the two cages on the right. These twenty weak-looking mice had had their genes artificially modified and were showing symptoms of the disease.

It made sense that his father, who hoped to create a cure for this intractable disease, had purchased the mice. In order to test in vivo the drug he hoped to synthesize, animal subjects that had the disease were a must.

Kento knew that raising transgenic mice like this in a run-down apartment was clearly illegal. Because animals whose genes had been modified did not exist in the natural world, the law required that they be kept under very strict supervision.

Even so, he couldn't bring himself to get rid of them. He went about cleaning their cages, careful to not let them get out. The genetically engineered mice, at any rate, didn't have much time left—assuming that Kento didn't come up with a drug that could treat their condition.

A sense of helplessness again reared its head, but Kento suppressed the feeling, silently going about the task of cleaning the mice's little abodes.

It was just before noon when he left the lab, heading toward Akihabara. There were a couple of places he needed to phone, but all the numbers were in his contacts list in his cell phone, which he had to keep turned off. Somehow he had to access them.

Kento changed trains at Shinjuku, doing what he could to take into account the possibility that the police might be trailing him. Akihabara station was where he'd run to the day before, and there was a risk that the police had it staked out. So he got off the train at the station before Akihabara and walked the rest of the way to the famous streets where all the stores were selling the latest electronic gadgets.

He made the rounds of a few stores, searching for a device an engineer friend had once had. In the fourth store he finally found it— a small, box-shaped device that fit in the palm of his hand. He went into a coffee shop, sat down in a corner, and turned the device on. The mechanism, which jammed radio waves from cell phones, immediately showed what it was capable of. A young woman at the counter, talking into her cell phone, suddenly said "Hello? Hello?" in a loud voice and stared at her now nonfunctioning phone.

Sorry, Kento silently said in apology. He took out his own cell phone and turned it on. The screen displayed the words NO SIGNAL. The base-station antenna was being jammed and couldn't catch the signal from his phone. No danger now of anyone tracing his position. Relieved, he opened his contacts list and copied down all the phone numbers he thought he might need.

As soon as he was done, he left the coffee shop and went into a phone booth along the main street. The first number he called was the one he didn't have to read his memo to remember—his home phone number.

"Hi, Mom."

"Kento?" Once she heard her son's voice, his mother came out with a burst of words. "I've called you so many times since last night. What is going on? We're having a major problem here."

Kento had a bad feeling. "What do you mean, a problem?"

"Someone from the police came and searched through your father's room and his belongings."

So the police had been to his house. His mother told him that they had used the same excuse they'd used with Kento, that they were seeking help with an FBI investigation.

"And one of the detectives asked me this strange thing," she went on. "He asked, 'Do you know about a book that has a Popsicle stain on it?'"

A chill went up Kento's spine.

Open the book you dropped a Popsicle on.

His father was right—his e-mails *were* being intercepted.

Consider all means of communication you use—landlines, cell phones, e-mail, and faxes—to be tapped.

His father hadn't been paranoid. Even this very moment he might be under surveillance. Kento felt an ominous feeling grip his chest. A huge, unseen power had him in its clutches and was trying to crush him.

"Do you have any idea what they're talking about?"

"No, I don't," Kento quickly replied. Following his father's instructions, he'd gotten rid of the book with the Popsicle stain and the memo hidden inside. But what in the world had his father been up to? It all seemed suspect to him now—both the inference he'd made about his father being swindled into funding the development of a new drug and the story the detective had given him about the FBI. There had to be an even bigger secret hidden in his father's actions while he was alive.

"They told me to tell them if you got in touch."

"The detectives?"

"Yes. You're not in some kind of trouble, are you?"

"I haven't done anything," Kento replied, and looked around him uneasily. If his home phone was tapped, then they could trace the location he was calling from. "Don't tell the detectives I called you, okay?"

"Why not?"

"It's too much trouble if I get involved. I'm too busy with experiments."

"But—"

"All right? And my cell phone is broken, so you can't call me. If something comes up, I'll get in touch."

"Kento?" his mother began, but he cut her off. He left the phone booth, hustling down the sidewalk, trying to put some distance between himself and the phone. He passed by some big-box electronics stores and stores selling video game software, and when he'd gotten about a block away he turned around. From far beyond the phone booth a uniformed policeman on a bicycle was heading in his direction. His heart began to pound. Was he looking for him?

Kento slipped into an alley and came out onto another main thoroughfare. The policeman didn't seem to be following him. He grabbed a taxi and went over to Jinbo-cho, another nearby shopping district. He went into another phone booth there and dialed his laboratory.

Professor Sonoda answered the phone, and when he realized it was Kento he gave a shout of surprise and then lowered his voice, as if not wanting to be overheard. "Kento! What in the world is going on?"

"Hmm?" Kento had officially asked for some time off, so his response took the wind right out of his sails. "What do you mean?"

"The police were here until a few minutes ago. They had a warrant for your arrest."

Kento was shocked. "*Arrest?* What did they say I did?"

"According to the detective you're charged with three crimes. Obstruction of justice, destruction of property, and negligent injury. Do you have any clue what this is all about?"

He certainly did. He'd obstructed the search of his apartment, had put a dent in the car when he'd run away, and the detective who'd been driving the car hit his head as a result.

"Yeah, but . . ." Kento stammered, trying to explain himself. "It's all a mistake. I'd never do anything like that."

"Then you should go to the police right away and explain the situation."

"All right. I'll do that." He had to keep his professor from worrying. "I might have to take a few more days off, but I hope that's all right."

"Don't worry about us. Take care of yourself first."

"Did the detectives say anything else?"

"That's all I heard. After that they barraged the staff with questions. About your relationships."

"Relationships?"

"They seem to suspect that you're hiding out in a friend's place."

He couldn't expect help from anyone else now. If he asked his friends in the lab for anything, they'd contact the police. Most of the phone numbers he'd gone to such trouble to write down were worthless.

"I suggest you go to the nearest police station and clear this up."

"I will," Kento replied. He apologized for all the worry he'd caused and hung up.

Things were going downhill faster than he'd expected. If the police caught him now, he wouldn't get away scot-free. He'd probably be forced to quit grad school and might even wind up in jail.

He pictured how upset everyone at his lab must be and fell into a dark funk. Bad rumors get around quickly. The lab was always his one refuge, a place where he felt he belonged, and now that it had been breached, the humiliation and sense of helplessness had him on the verge of tears.

He took the subway, unsure of his destination, and sat there, tortured by the uncertainty of his future. He couldn't run from the police forever. The most realistic choice, certainly, was to give himself up to the Public Security Bureau. But beyond the fear of being put in handcuffs and treated as a criminal, an unfocused apprehension held him back. Why would the FBI have falsely accused his father? And why were the Japanese police accusing him of wrongdoing—even trying to arrest him? He had the eerie sense of a larger force that lay behind them, reaching out of the darkness to grab him in its clutches. Something was happening out there, hidden from him, and he had to find out what it was.

The subway train arrived in Shibuya, and Kento got off. As he walked around on the street, he concluded that the only thing he could do was try to maintain the status quo. As he'd decided from the beginning, he needed to answer the final riddle—he needed to ascertain the contents of the Heisman Report.

He went into a phone booth and lifted the receiver. He checked the list of phone numbers he'd written and dialed Sugai's office. The reporter answered his cell phone on the third ring.

"Oh, Kento."

Kento was relieved that he sounded so calm. The police had clearly not yet visited his office.

"Did you listen to the message I left on your cell phone?" Sugai asked.

"No—I'm sorry, but I haven't. My cell isn't working."

"Then I'll repeat it. I got an e-mail this morning from a colleague at our Washington bureau."

"Did he find out anything about the Heisman Report?"

"Yes, and it was pretty surprising. Three months ago there was a withdrawal notice sent out on the Heisman Report, so it's impossible to get a copy of it. In other words, it's been classified."

"Classified?"

"Right. US documents that can cause problems are kept from the public for national security reasons."

National security reasons. For a grad student in Japan, the phrase was like something from a different world. Still, he was sure it had something to do with what he'd gotten himself mixed up in. The oppressive feeling he'd been having got even stronger, overwhelming him. It was as though his father's final message to him had predicted everything that would happen.

I'd like you to do the research alone. Don't tell anybody. But if you find yourself in danger, give it all up right away.

"But why would it be classified now?"

"I have no way of knowing. But if you really want to find out what's in the report there is a way. As I mentioned before, you could search through magazines from thirty years ago. Back then the report wasn't secret at all."

"How would I find old magazines?"

"The National Diet Library should have them."

Kento had used the Diet Library in the past, but was reluctant to follow the suggestion. When you entered the library you had to fill out a form giving your name and address. He wasn't sure if the police dragnet extended that far, but it was best to play it safe.

"I'm sorry I couldn't be of much help. Is that okay?"

"Sure," Kento began, and then remembered he still had something he wanted ask Sugai. "But there's one more thing. What's the best way of investigating a person's background?"

"A background check? I'd have to ask the reporters on the city desk. There's somebody you want to look into?"

Holding out a faint hope that Sugai would undertake it for him, Kento described what he knew about this mystery woman, Yuri Sakai, including her looks and her age. Sure enough, this seemed to spark Sugai's interest. "And she wanted your father's laptop? Do you have any other leads?"

"Only that I think she must be a science researcher."

"The chances are pretty slim I'll find anything, but I'll give it a go. If your cell phone's dead, how can I get in touch with you?"

"I'll call you, if you don't mind."

"Sure, that's fine. Call anytime."

"Thank you for everything," Kento said, and hung up. He felt a little better now that he could see what had to be done. Namely, grappling with stacks of old magazines to find out what was in the Heisman Report.

Kento walked over to the main shopping street in Shibuya, found an Internet café, and went in. Using the computer in one of the small private cubicles, he discovered that the largest library specializing in magazines in Japan was located in Tokyo. The library had seven hundred thousand magazines ranging back to the Meiji period that one could freely read—and, best of all, the place was privately operated.

Kento estimated that by tomorrow evening he'd finally understand what this adventure his father had handed down to him was all about. Because lying untapped in the holdings of that library was the report he was looking for. The one that traced the extinction of the human race.

14.

A FEROCIOUS RAIN continued to fall, so intense it felt like the dense forest would be swept away. A veritable flood from the sky. Huge drops of rain ceaselessly pelted the tops of the trees, and the entire forest gave off a deep rumbling sound as the trees shook from side to side.

This unusual storm in the middle of the dry season actually was a lucky break for Yeager and his team, for it gave them a chance to close the distance between them and their target. When it rained the Mbuti didn't go hunting and stayed close to their camp. The team could search out where they were without worrying about keeping quiet as they went or accidentally running across their prey.

The forty-member Kanga band had a permanent camp near the main road, but they moved about among the eight hunting camps they kept deep in the jungle. Their territory stretched some thirty-five kilometers from east to west. Yeager and the team were getting close to the most remote camp, the one deepest in the jungle.

One kilometer from their target they stopped at a dense stand of trees, spread out a waterproof sheet as a shelter, and changed into jungle camouflage. They put on their full array of gear, including tactical vests bulging with extra cartridges. Then they proceeded six hundred meters ahead and put their backpacks down in a spot in the thick brush. This would be their rendezvous point. They inputted their present location into their GPS devices, for going just ten meters into the jungle was far enough to get lost.

"We'll approach their camp from two directions, north and south," Yeager instructed the team. They all had on face paint, and in their dark camouflage only the whites of their eyes shone. "Garrett and Mick will approach from the north, and Meyers and I will come in from the south. We'll check that Nigel Pierce is in the camp and that there are the right number of people."

The other three nodded, serious looks on their faces, and Yeager was satisfied. Ever since Mick killed those two chimpanzees the atmosphere among the team had shifted. The men no longer tried to get to know each other better, and they became a taciturn group of men simply intent on carrying out their mission. Yeager, as team leader, was anxious about whether there was any outward antagonism among the members, but this fear turned out to be baseless. Professional soldiers knew that any strife among the team would put them all in danger. Bringing emotional conflict out in the open would increase the risk that they'd die. Yeager himself had intentionally put aside the antipathy he felt for the cheerless Japanese man.

"Let's run down the checklist," Garrett said. "The UN peacekeeping force is intercepting the insurgents' radio transmissions. We don't want to get caught in their surveillance network, so the output on our field radios is limited. They only can transmit up to two hundred meters. Keep any transmissions to an absolute minimum. The signal to return to the rendezvous point will be five buzzes."

Yeager added a few words about the inscrutable order they'd been given. "Finally, there's the living creature you've never seen before. If you run across this mysterious being, remember to kill it right away and recover the body."

The three men nodded, bemused smiles on their faces. Yeager smiled, too, unable to keep a straight face.

The Guardian members split into two groups, each carefully walking along its appointed route. Yeager was apprehensive about the Mbuti. For tens of thousands of years they'd lived in the jungle, adapting to the environment. Even an experienced Special Forces soldier was no match for them on their home turf.

In ten minutes they came upon a clearing. The latitude and longitude matched the figures given to them at the briefing at the Zeta Security headquarters. Yeager and Meyers hid behind a large tree trunk, took out their binoculars, and scanned the hunting tribe's camp.

The clearing was much smaller than the mock-up village they'd practiced on. It was about twenty meters on each side. In the middle were wooden benches, and surrounding these were the small, semispherical huts. But through the haze of the rain there was no sign of anyone in the camp, and half the huts were falling apart.

With Glocks, silencers attached, in hand, Yeager and Meyers made their way through the muddy ground and slowly entered the clearing. They used hand signals, deciding who would check which huts, and went to work.

Yeager looked into the hut at the end of the row before him. It was obvious how they'd constructed these huts, which were about two meters in diameter. Long tree branches had been bent in a semicircle, the ends thrust in the ground to anchor a framework, and large leaves laid on top. A primitive construction.

As he checked one hut after another, Yeager kept an eye out for anything nonhuman. This "living creature" he'd "never seen before" might be lurking in the corner of a deserted hut. But all he ran across were small insects.

Once they figured out that no one was in the camp, Yeager signaled to Garrett and Mick, still watching from the jungle, to assemble.

"There're traces of a campfire," Meyers reported in a low voice. "The ashes are recent. People were here not long ago. The band must have moved on to the next camp."

Yeager nodded. The silence around him was so deep it made him shudder. The campground shone white in the dimness.

He and Meyers looked up at the sky. The rain that had been falling since morning had let up, and the dark clouds had quickly dissipated. This was the first time since entering the jungle that they had such an expansive view of the sky. It felt as if they'd floated up from the dark depths of the ocean, their faces breaking the surface.

Garrett and Mick emerged from the shadows of the huts. "Let's head to the next campsite," Yeager directed them. "Five klicks east."

It was still only 2:00 p.m. They should arrive before dark.

The men went back to where they'd left their backpacks and set out again. The route they took was deep into Kanga band territory. Now that the rain had stopped they had to be cautious about making noise.

An hour later, the returning sunlight must have made the raindrops on the forest floor start to evaporate, because a powerful odor of the jungle rose up from the ground. The smell was a thick brew of trees and leaf mulch, the air surrounding them heavy and oppressive.

They'd waded through several rain-swollen streams when Yeager thought he heard a person's voice. At first he thought he was hearing things. But when he stopped and listened carefully he realized it wasn't the voice of a bird or animal but a person yelling out. Yeager quickly checked their position on the GPS. They were about a kilometer from the Kanga band's next camp.

Mick, taking point, noticed the voice, too, signaled for them to stop, and turned around. Each of them silently dropped to one knee where they were, checking to front and back, left and right. This whole time the man's voice continued to yell out faintly. It wasn't a scream. They couldn't make out the individual words, but whatever language it was had a special kind of intonation.

The yells suddenly stopped, echoing for a short moment. The four mercenaries spent a few minutes in place, checking out their surroundings, and when they understood there was no threat nearby they gathered around Yeager.

"What was he yelling?" Meyers whispered. "Did anybody understand it?"

"I think it was English," Garrett replied. "But I didn't catch what he said."

The men exchanged looks. The Mbuti spoke the same language as the local farmers. The other lingua francas of this region were Swahili and French. But not English. The worst-case scenario came to mind— that the antigovernment forces had already attacked the Kanga band. The Ugandan and Rwandan forces that had invaded the eastern part of the Congo used English as their common tongue.

"Was he calling for help?" Meyers asked.

"No. There was just one voice, and I didn't hear any other screams," Yeager said. "I don't think it was an attack."

"Then who was yelling? That anthropologist? Nigel Pierce?"

Speculation would get them nowhere, so Yeager decided they should move out. "Leave your packs here," he said. "This will be our rendezvous point. Mick, take your grenade launcher with you." Yeager and Mick took the HK69 grenade launchers from their backpacks and stuffed 40mm grenades in their pouches. They handed out five hand grenades each to Garrett and Meyers.

They checked their equipment and fanned out again in two groups to the north and south as they approached the camp, a kilometer away.

Yeager, who'd had reconnoitering training, soon noticed a path. The thick vegetation had been pushed away on both sides. It must be a hunting path the Mbuti used. He checked the ground but found no trace of any armed military force having passed by.

After a half hour Yeager heard chickens up ahead and people's voices. The Mbuti. Their voices sounded relaxed and peaceful. At least they weren't under threat of attack.

Yeager came to the edge of the camp, picked an old tree nearby, and began to climb it, trying to keep as quiet as he could. Meyers stayed below, standing guard.

Holding on to a branch about three meters off the ground, Yeager looked out from behind the trunk and trained his binoculars on the clearing up ahead. And for the first time in his life he saw Pygmies.

Even from far off he could tell how small they were. From a Western perspective they looked like a group of grade-school children. They were muscular, but for some reason many of them had swollen abdomens. Their skin color was relatively pale, probably the result of living in the jungle, where little sunlight penetrated the foliage. The men had on well-worn shorts, and the women wore cloths of many colors wrapped around them. Some of the women were naked from the waist up, but their pendulous breasts hung straight down, and there was nothing erotic about it. In fact, the whole tableau was like a picture of human beings stripped to their essence. If you took away their minimal clothes and the pots and knives they used for cooking, it was the same primitive existence they'd been living for tens of thousands of years. They might be far from civilization, yet when he looked carefully at the faces of the young and old, males and females, before him, Yeager could make out all the same expressions you'd find in modern man—some innocent and tranquil, others intelligent, silly, or thoughtful.

It was still some time before sunset, but the sunlight shining down on the clearing was already being blocked by the trees. This tract of land would soon be covered in darkness. Yeager began collecting all the intel he would need for their operation.

The camp had eleven dwellings, each a few meters apart, arranged in a U shape. Yeager was observing the camp from one side, so he didn't know how many people might be hidden behind the huts in front of him. But this blind spot would be covered by Mick and Garrett, who were on the opposite side of the camp.

Most of the adult males occupied the central part of the clearing, a kind of meeting place, by the look of it. There were fifteen of them. They were sitting on wooden benches, smoking cigarettes and chatting. Women were outside their huts, getting dinner ready. Starting up cooking fires, seated on the ground, assembling a meal out of some kind of fruit that resembled a potato. From where Yeager was he could count five women. There were children as well. Five boys had rolled a vinelike plant into a ball and were playing soccer with it. And there were six girls, some decorating their hair with flowers, some looking after the smaller children, others helping their mothers with cooking.

Yeager continued to observe the people he would be killing, trying hard to detect any trace of illness. If he could make sure they were infected with this lethal virus he could dispel his guilty conscience. Putting bullets in their heads would be that much easier if it were a mercy killing, saving them from an even more horrific death. But they all looked perfectly healthy.

In the narrow field of vision through his binoculars, an odd-looking person suddenly appeared, a middle-aged white man, tall and thin. A scraggly beard covered the lower half of his face. This had to be Nigel Pierce. Pierce had emerged from the hut at the very end, and he was dressed as the Mbuti were, in a worn-out T-shirt and shorts. Next to them, Pierce indeed looked like a giant.

It was clear now that this was the Kanga band camp. None of them showed any symptoms, so the virus must still be in its incubation period. Yeager brushed aside the pressure that had been bearing down on him and began considering whether they should carry out the attack that night. Wiping out every single one of them meant annihilating a virus that could destroy the human race. When Yeager saw the scrawny dog romping around at Pierce's feet, he knew he'd have to get rid of it first so it didn't raise the alarm.

Pierce stood up and looked out at the jungle. Thinking he'd be noticed more if he made a move to hide, Yeager kept stock-still.

Pierce leaned back, filled his lungs with air, and suddenly yelled out in English. "Listen carefully! I know you can hear me! I know you're nearby!"

Below him, Meyers, startled by the shouts in English, turned and stared, wide-eyed, in the direction of the camp.

The timbre and inflection of the voice were the same as the one they'd heard a while ago. But who could this anthropologist be yelling at? Yeager swept the camp with his eyes, but the Pygmies were going about their business, unconcerned.

"I'm talking to you! Jonathan Yeager, Warren Garrett, Scott Meyers, and Mikihiko Kashiwabara. The four operatives in Operation Guardian!"

Garrett's voice crackled through Yeager's radio. "Gang two here. Our operation's been compromised."

Yeager pressed the button once to respond with the yes signal, then studied Pierce through his binoculars.

"Nobody here is infected with a virus! Operation Guardian is a sham! You're going to be killed! All of you will be killed by the president's administration!"

Stunned, Meyers looked up at Yeager from the base of the tree.

"You know what I'm talking about, Garrett! Your disloyalty has been exposed! There's nowhere to run!"

What was Pierce talking about? And how had Garrett been disloyal? Yeager, totally confused, tried to sort it all out, but now it was his name being yelled out.

"Yeager, listen to me! Your son can be saved! There's a way to treat that disease! We're preparing a method to treat Justin!"

Yeager felt like he'd been punched in the head. He understood Pierce's message loud and clear.

Justin's life could be saved.

Jolted by this unforeseen development, Yeager waited for the next words. But Pierce stopped yelling, and, just as he did when he'd first appeared, he gazed at the jungle around him and then went back inside the hut, which was about chest-high for him.

Yeager and Meyers stayed still, unmoving. An hour passed, and when the entire camp was swallowed up in darkness Yeager pushed the radio call button five times to signal the team to withdraw.

Garrett and Mick were already waiting at the rendezvous point. When Yeager and Meyers arrived Mick said in a low voice, "All clear."

The members, night vision gear in place, turned toward Yeager. They were silent, waiting for their leader to speak. Yeager was pondering whether he should order Garrett, their communications specialist, to contact their employer, Zeta Security, for instructions. But what if what Nigel Pierce said was true—that they'd fallen into a trap set by the White House? And it was true what he said about Justin?

Growing impatient at Yeager's silence, Mick spoke up, his voice angry. "Who told about our operation?"

"How can we know that?" Meyers said. "We're just at the tip of the operation. There're lots of other people involved."

"No. Pierce was clear. He said Garrett had been disloyal."

Garrett spun toward Mick. "You're saying I betrayed the operation?"

"That's right."

Garrett snorted. "You've got quite an imagination."

"Don't play dumb. You're a liar. I know you never were in the marines. You're hiding something."

"Hold on! All of you!" Yeager broke in. "Everybody put your rifles down."

The three of them didn't follow his order, so Yeager slowly laid his rifle on the ground. Meyers soon followed suit, and then Garrett and Mick reluctantly let go of their rifles.

"Let's think things through here," Yeager said. "Nigel Pierce has caught on to our operation. He said Operation Guardian is a sham. There's no viral infection, and we're all going to be killed. According to him."

"But that can't be true, can it?" Mick said. "He's trying to confuse us so we stop the mission. Cause if he doesn't do something, he'll be killed."

"But his information is correct. And he knows our real names, not our aliases. And also he . . ." Yeager hesitated. "He knows I have a sick child."

"So what? So you believe him? Tell me you're not thinking of halting the mission."

"Take it easy, Mick," Meyers said. "We have to think this through carefully, or else it could cost us our lives."

Yeager was upset. Pierce had said there was a way to save his son. It was like he was taking Justin hostage.

Garrett suddenly broke in. "I think what Pierce is saying must be true."

The other three turned to face him.

"At least there's a reason for someone to want to take my life."

"Who's trying to take your life?"

"The White House," Garrett replied, and held up a hand to cut off Mick, who was about to interrupt. "Can we talk alone?" he asked Yeager.

"Okay."

"We have a right to hear this, too," Mick said, pressing closer, and Meyers grabbed him by the shoulders and pulled him back.

"Knock it off. This is a military operation. We follow what our leader tells us."

Mick was about to argue, but when he saw Meyers's hand go to his leg holster he stepped back. "All right. I get it."

Yeager picked up his rifle, and he and Garrett went off into a grove of trees.

When they were far enough away, Garrett said, "It's no secret anymore that I never was in the marines. I'm an active duty Blue Badger."

A CIA operative. "So you're with the Agency?"

"Yes. Paramilitary personnel. The Agency sent me to observe Operation Guardian."

"Sort of like guard duty over us?"

"Exactly. I'm sorry I had to lie to all of you."

"Is that what he meant by you being disloyal?"

After a moment of hesitation Garrett said, "No. That's something else. Pierce is referring to extraordinary renditions. The administration is torturing Islamic extremists. I'm not talking about obvious things like waterboarding or sexual abuse. They secretly send detainees to third-party countries like Syria and have them undergo even more horrible forms of torture. Nobody comes back alive. As we speak someone is strapped down to a folding steel bed frame somewhere and being bent in two until he dies." Garrett became emotional as he went on, which was unusual for him. "These are war crimes. Plain and simple. I secretly got in touch with an NGO, a human rights watchdog organization, and became a double agent. The goal was to gather enough proof to bring Burns in front of an international tribunal for war crimes."

"The president of the United States?" Yeager asked in disbelief. "That'll never happen."

"I know. It's impossible. But it will intimidate him. If a suit is actually taken up by the International Criminal Court, at least it'll put a stop to US-led torture." Garrett was calm again and seemed resigned. "What I'm saying is, I became a traitor to save my country's honor. If the Burns administration wants to kill me, there's not much I can do about it."

Yeager looked down, wondering how much of Garrett's story to believe. "But why would Nigel Pierce know all this?"

"That I don't know."

"One more question. If they just want to kill you, then what's the need for a complicated operation like this?"

"I think Operation Guardian came first, with the plan to kill all the operatives. And then they just included me in it."

"But why kill the other operatives—the three of us?"

"To silence you? Because we're going to slaughter these innocent Pygmies."

"But that doesn't make any sense. If you believe Pierce, there's no lethal virus. So there's no reason to kill the Mbuti."

The two of them exchanged a meaningful glance.

"But consider our highest-priority target," Garrett said. "This 'creature' we've never seen before."

What had been the butt of jokes up until now suddenly threw a dark shadow over Yeager's mind. "You have any idea what this creature is all about?"

"Not a clue," Garrett said, shaking his head and looking straight at Yeager. "I've told you everything I know. It's up to you whether you believe me or not."

Yeager sat in silence for a time, and then made his decision. "Okay, we're going to change part of the plan. Follow me."

The two of them went back to the rendezvous point. Mick, obviously irritated, asked, "So have you come to a conclusion?"

"Yeah. Tonight we're going to attack the Kanga band. But our goal isn't annihilating the Mbuti. We'll kidnap Nigel Pierce and interrogate him. We'll hear straight from him what this is all about. Any objection?"

Meyers and Mick shook their heads. For the time being they seemed convinced.

"What do we do about contacting Zeta?" Garrett, in charge of communications, asked. "Should we send the call sign that we're starting the attack?"

"Forget about them."

"What if we get ambushed?" Mick asked. "The Pygmies know we're nearby."

"Then we defend ourselves. But try not to kill anybody. If we threaten them with our guns we should be able to keep them under control. Then we take Pierce away and interrogate him. Get your gear ready. We move out in fifteen minutes. Understood?"

The others nodded and picked up the AK-47s at their feet.

The magazine specialty library was in the middle of a residential area in the Setagaya district of Tokyo. It was a smallish, two-story cement building, and it was hard to believe that it housed seven hundred thousand magazines.

When Kento arrived a little before 9:00 a.m. there were already five people waiting outside for the place to open. He'd read on the Internet that most of the people who used the facility worked in the media, and he figured these people must be journalists.

A staff member appeared at the glass front doors and opened them right on time. Kento followed the others to the counter, staying at the back of the line, and filled out the form to use the library.

"Please write your name and address here," Kento was told as a staff member held out the form to him, and he hesitated for a moment. Finally he wrote in an alias, Daisuke Tamura, and a phony address. Probably breaking the law again, he thought.

He paid the five-hundred-yen entrance fee and went over to the reference corner. There all you needed to do was type in the keyword you were searching for in one of the computers and it would list all the magazines that had articles containing the term. Kento sat down at an open computer and typed in "Heisman Report."

The screen listed twenty-five magazines, most of them published in 1975. Just as Sugai had told him, these were articles from thirty years ago.

It had been all too easy, and Kento felt a bit deflated. He went ahead and filled in a reading request form for all the magazines and took it to the counter.

They told him he could read the magazines on the second floor, and he walked upstairs to the reading room. The room was a bright sunny space surrounded by glass picture windows and furnished with oversized reading tables. Several of the people he'd entered the library with at the same time were already seated, combing through various journals.

"Mr. Tamura, please come to the loan counter," the PA announced, and it took Kento a moment to realize they meant him. He hurried off to collect the magazines.

Twenty-five magazines made quite a stack. He made two trips over to a reading table and sat down, wondering where he should start. The magazines were of all types, from raunchy men's magazines to heavy political journals. He decided to begin with the lighter type of magazine and picked up the copy of *Heibon Pinch*.

The nude photos from thirty years ago amused him, with their whited-out genital areas. Kento reflexively grinned, then, worried about the impression he was making on others around him, cautioned himself that he should look more serious. He scanned the table of contents and soon found the article about the Heisman Report.

Top Secret Report to the US Government! Research into the End of Mankind Reveals the Horror of an All-Out Nuclear War!!

It was a five-page special report, and Kento read every word.

The story detailed what would happen to the world in the event of a nuclear war. The number of nuclear warheads the United States and the Soviet Union had contained enough destructive power to wipe out mankind twenty times over. Fifty thousand nuclear missiles were aimed at fifteen thousand targets, so there was no place on earth to run. The article said that the average missile was two megatons, equivalent to the entire amount of bombs dropped in all the air raids in World War II. The silos housing the nuclear missiles were designed to be impervious to nuclear attack, so even after the first wave of attacks, when all mankind had been wiped out, an automatic retaliation system would continue to operate, and tens of thousands of missiles would continue to fly over the deserted planet. Even if some people survived in fallout shelters, their food stores would soon be depleted and they'd die, because the soil of the entire earth would be contaminated with radiation and most animals and plants would go extinct. Any living thing that happened to survive would suffer mutations from the radiation and become monstrously deformed.

The report clearly underscored the incredible stupidity of the human race. Kento was shocked to learn what idiotic beings humans really are. Maybe not all mankind—but at least those countries that possessed nuclear weapons. The number of missiles listed in the report was from thirty years ago, and he wondered how many missiles existed today and how many times the present-day nuclear countries would be able to destroy the human race.

The report was fascinating, but it had nothing to do with the research his father had entrusted him with. The Heisman Report was supposed to discuss several possible reasons for the extinction of mankind, but this article dealt solely with the threat of nuclear war. It didn't touch at all on any of the other sections of the original report.

Kento picked up the second magazine, the June 1975 issue of *GORON*.

Nuclear Winter Will Come? The Startling Warning of a Secret American Report!!

This one was also about the terror of a nuclear war. As Mr. Sugai had told him, in the last half of the twentieth century the extinction of mankind by nuclear war was a hot topic. I get it, I really get it, Kento thought, eyeing the heap of magazines.

It looked like it would be quite a task to unearth some useful information.

★   ★   ★

More than six hours had passed since they'd reassembled at their observation post, as Yeager and the others waited for the right opportunity to put the kidnapping plan into operation.

The Pygmy hunting camp was enveloped in darkness. People's faces flitted into view in the campfires before each hut, moving in and out of the shadows.

Fires like this in the midst of deep jungles were themselves an astounding thing. No wonder wild animals didn't come near, Yeager thought. Fire was the sign of living creatures who had taken one step beyond the world of nature. It was a heartwarming scene, one that called up tender, nostalgic emotions.

Once the Mbuti had finished eating, they took out homemade musical instruments and began singing and dancing. They had an amazing talent for music. Singers' voices layered over the sounds of flutes, drums, and primitive harps, with multiple melody lines intertwining to form a wonderful harmony. These joyful voices asserted the existence, in the midst of the dark, wild jungle, of creatures called human beings.

Yeager watched carefully to see if there was anything to suggest they were on their guard, but all these tiny people were just enjoying singing and dancing, with no indication whatsoever that they were preparing to do battle. At one point children who were dancing pointed up to the sky and started to say something. Yeager looked in the direction they were pointing and saw a star in the night sky speed from south to north. He wondered how this artificial satellite orbiting the globe appeared in their eyes.

Nigel Pierce, the target of their kidnapping, went into his dwelling while the dancing and singing was still in full swing and didn't reappear. They tried looking in with infrared imaging equipment, but boxes stacked up inside interfered and they couldn't get a bead on Pierce.

At 2300 hours the lively party ended, and the women and children went back to their huts. The only ones left were eight men who stayed behind, talking in the open gathering space in the middle of the compound.

A new day came, and it was 0200 hours when the men finally went to bed. The mercenaries waited another hour, until all forty of the Kanga band were asleep. Yeager made a final check before they swung into action. With their night vision equipment they would have a decisive upper hand if they needed to fight in the darkness. They checked where the two dogs were sleeping, but the animals were such scrawny specimens it was hard to envision them being effective watchdogs.

Yeager stealthily climbed down to ground level from the treetop. He nodded to Meyers, on guard duty, then pushed the button on his radio twice to signal the other two to start approaching the camp.

Yeager and Meyers circled the camp from the south side to the east side, then stood still and removed the headsets from their ears. From several spots along the U-shaped line of huts they could hear snoring and the sounds of people sleeping. Good, Yeager decided. Most everyone's asleep. He turned his night vision goggles to Pierce's hut, the one on the far end, and saw Garrett and Mick coming up from the rear.

Yeager lowered his AK-47, attached it to a sling hanging from his shoulder, and picked up the Glock with the silencer. He had a towel stuck in the front pocket of his tactical vest, which he intended to stuff in Pierce's mouth so he didn't make any noise.

Yeager signaled everyone to take their positions. The other three moved into position, taking up a defensive circle, backs to the hut. The sleeping dogs on the other side of the clearing didn't move.

Yeager slowly made his way to the side of the hut. He listened carefully but couldn't hear anyone asleep. Pierce might still be up. But they'd planned for this eventuality. Point a pistol at him, and he wouldn't resist.

Yeager crouched over, checked his grip on the pistol, and slipped to the front of the hut. The entrance was open, and the electronic image in the night vision goggles showed the inside of the dwelling. No need to search for their target: he was right there. Nigel Pierce, beard and all, was straight in front of him. Pierce was seated on the dirt floor, staring right at Yeager. Yeager didn't flinch but aimed his pistol right between Pierce's eyes. "Don't move," he ordered in a low voice and began to step inside the hut. But in that instant he froze.

A weird sight appeared in his night vision goggles, and the hair stood up on the back of Yeager's neck. In Pierce's arms was a kind of creature he'd never seen before.

The most striking characteristic of this creature is that you'll know as soon as you spot it that it's a totally unknown type of being.

This unknown creature stared back at him. Its hairless body and short arms and legs made it look like a human child. But that just made the strangeness of its head stand out all the more.

It might confuse you when you see it, but the point is not to think about it.

This creature, so like a human child, had a disproportionately large head. The front of it was a large round protuberance, and the rest of it tapered off sharply from the forehead down to the chin, like an inverted triangle. Its body was like that of a three-year-old child, but its facial features were even more infantile. Its face was slender, like a newborn baby whose skull had not yet hardened, and only its body, from the neck down, was developed.

Don't ask yourself what sort of creature it is.

But there was something in its face—with its large eyes slanting upward—that set it far apart from a human infant. In these upturned eyes fixed on him Yeager could sense a clear awareness and intelligence. But what was the sharp light from those eyes trying to convey? Caution? Curiosity? Madness? Maliciousness? In the face of this enigmatic being Yeager felt fear. This was like a human, but it wasn't human.

Once you see it, just shoot it.

Coming to his senses, Yeager pointed his pistol at the creature. "What the hell *is* that?" he asked.

Trying to avoid being tempted by the sweetly smiling beauties in the slick periodicals, Kento took up the eighteenth magazine and at last found the article he was looking for.

Contemporary Politics Quarterly, the summer 1975 issue. A small magazine, more like a pamphlet. The opening pages consisted of a special report entitled "Research at US Think Tanks."

About halfway through the article he read, "Below is the entire text of a report from the Schneider Institute to the White House entitled the Heisman Report." Kento sat up in his chair and eagerly began turning the pages.

A title leaped out at him: *Research into Factors Leading to the Extinction of the Human Race, and Policy Proposals.* This was the formal title of the

Heisman Report. The author was Joseph R. Heisman, PhD, senior researcher at the Schneider Institute.

After a short introduction was an explanation of the report's aims and an explanatory note.

"This report does not refer to factors for extinction on an astronomical or geological time scale—for example, the end of the earth in five billion years, when the sun burns itself out, or the disappearance of the human Y chromosome tens of thousands of years in the future, which will make reproduction impossible."

Makes sense, Kento said to himself, and went on to read the main part of the text.

1. Disaster on a Cosmic Scale

The first section discussed the collision of an asteroid with earth and the collateral damage this would cause. What Kento found unexpected was the fact that Dr. Heisman called attention to what was, thirty years ago, an issue seen as lying on the border between science and science fiction. In his words, it was "an event that could occur in the near future, one we must not overlook." Heisman went on to say, "Recent geological investigations have revealed that other cosmic bodies have collided with the earth much more often than previously imagined."

Dr. Heisman was nothing short of a visionary. Nowadays countries all over the world keep a close watch on near-earth objects, and there had been several near misses involving asteroids big enough to destroy a city.

2. Environmental Fluctuations on a Global Scale

The second section dealt with issues Kento hadn't been aware of, i.e., the reversal of the north and south magnetic poles. Evidence pointed to a reversal of these north and south poles several times in the earth's past; one theory held that the extinction of the dinosaurs occurred because of such a reversal. At first glance this seemed like an issue in the distant future, a problem on the scale of geologic time, but the Heisman Report had the following warning: "In the past two hundred years terrestrial magnetism has weakened considerably, and it is believed that it will disappear completely in a thousand years. Afterward there will most likely be a reversal of the magnetic poles, but before this occurs, when terrestrial magnetism has disappeared, the magnetosphere protecting the earth will be lost, and solar rays and other harmful cosmic rays will fall on the unprotected earth, leading to the extinction not just of mankind but of most other forms of life as well."

Would scientists in the thirtieth century have developed technology to avoid this crisis? Do your best, Kento thought, sending out a word of encouragement to his descendants a thousand years from now.

3. Nuclear War

This section took up most of the pages of the report. The report warned that all kinds of nuclear war—limited nuclear war, all-out nuclear war, and accidental nuclear war, in which missiles are fired by mistake—would lead to the destruction of the human race. "Once a nuclear attack occurs, the balance that has been maintained through the nuclear deterrent will collapse, inevitably leading to a series of retaliatory strikes." The report went on: "Even a limited use of nuclear weapons will create a deadly layer of ash covering the entire earth, which will damage the ecology, or it will increase the density of nitric oxide, damaging the ozone layer and leading mankind to the edge of extinction. Further, food resources will be dealt a serious blow, which will lead to mass starvation and the outbreak of a new war. Then a Third World War will be unavoidable, and this conflict will quickly become mankind's final war."

Joseph Heisman did a thorough job of arguing against nuclear war. Perhaps a bit of self-recrimination was included in this, given the fact that it was scientists themselves who had developed these very nuclear weapons.

4. Epidemics: The Threat of Viruses and Biological Weapons

This section was right in Kento's father's field, and he found this unexpected. His father had been most interested in section 5 of the

Heisman Report, and Kento had been expecting that section to contain a discussion of the threat of viruses.

"We conclude that it is not possible for naturally occurring epidemics to wipe out society. The Black Plague and Spanish influenza brought massive numbers of deaths, but they did not lead to our extinction. It is still unclear how the limited number of genes within human beings counter the countless number of antigens in the world, yet it is clear that we have obtained sufficient genetic diversity to resist many kinds of pathogens."

Didn't a Japanese scientist win the Nobel Prize for solving this riddle? Kento tried to recall.

"No matter how dangerous the epidemic, there will be individuals whose immune systems can defeat the disease. Those of us alive now are living proof that over the last two hundred thousand years *no* epidemic has arisen that can wipe out mankind.

"But the one remaining worry is the appearance of a virus that will directly attack the immune system."

Kento instinctively leaned forward. That virus had already appeared. The HIV virus that causes AIDS.

"According to congressional testimony given in June of 1969 by the assistant head of research and development at the Defense Department, 'In five to ten years we will create a pathogenic microorganism unaffected by the immune process.' If such a biological weapon is used in a regional conflict or escapes from a research facility, and if the infection spreads, the continuation of human beings as a species will be at risk."

Dumbfounded, Kento tried to recall what he knew about AIDS. The disease was first identified in the United States in the early 1980s. If plans had progressed as the person from the Defense Department testified, this "pathogenic microorganism unaffected by the immune process" would have been developed in the 1970s. Allowing for a latency period for the virus, the development of biological weapons and the appearance of AIDS overlapped exactly in terms of time period.

Was the AIDS virus a biological weapon developed by the United States?

There was one more reason this possibility occurred to Kento. Ten years ago, his father had gone to Zaire, as it was then called, where the

AIDS epidemic was becoming ever more serious. He was part of an epidemiology investigation team funded by the Ministry of Education, Culture, Sports, Science, and Technology that was charged with determining whether the HIV virus had spread to the Pygmy tribes. But as soon as they got to Zaire a civil war broke out, and Seiji barely escaped with his life back to Japan.

His father. An epidemiologist. The Heisman Report. An FBI investigation. Put them all together and the outlines of what was going on became clear. Seiji had gotten hold of proof that the HIV virus had been developed as a biological weapon and that the US government was trying to cover this up.

Wait a second, Kento told himself. He leaned back in his chair and stared up at the ceiling. No good to blame everything on a plot devised by the United States. There have been many investigations into the HIV virus by specialists, and most of them concluded that the virus originated in Africa. Plus, when Seiji went to Zaire—which became the Democratic Republic of the Congo after a change of government— he didn't come back empty-handed. He was able to collect blood samples from one Pygmy tribe, the Mbuti, and determined that not only weren't they infected by the HIV virus, they weren't infected by any type of virus at all. The virus that would have helped show that HIV was a biological weapon was missing.

He had seemed to be on the right track, but now Kento felt he had to discard that hypothesis. He took a rumpled handkerchief from his pocket and polished his glasses.

The time had come to read through section 5. If he struck out here, he'd have no more clues. His great adventure taking on the FBI would be over. He pictured how miserable he'd look turning himself in to the police, a thought that put him in a dark mood. He turned the pages of *Contemporary Politics Quarterly*. The section he was looking for began in the upper left-hand of the open page.

5. Human Evolution

"We find problematic the statement that biological evolution occurs only when there is a sudden modification in genes. The fossil record shows that biological evolution is both gradual and intermittent. In the phenomenon of evolution lies an unknown, hidden mechanism that both gradually and intermittently transforms species. Organisms accumulate subtle changes over long periods of time, but also at certain times can display sudden transformations. And this applies to us primates as well.

"In the book *Humans and Evolution*, Professor Georges Olivier of the University of Paris discusses human evolution from the standpoint of physical anthropology. In his words, 'Soon future human beings will suddenly appear.' Approximately six million years ago creatures branched off from ancestors they share with chimpanzees. They evolved first as *Pithecanthropus*, then as hominids, Neanderthals, and Cro-Magnons, and this process clearly reveals that evolution is speeding up. The further evolution of mankind could take place tomorrow.

"The next generation of humans that evolve from present-day man will have an enlarged cerebral neocortex and possess an intelligence that vastly surpasses ours. Olivier imagined their intellectual abilities in the following way: 'They will have the ability to perceive a fourth dimension, to immediately grasp complex wholes; they will have a sixth sense, an infinitely developed moral consciousness—mental qualities that are incomprehensible to us.'

"It is less likely that this next generation of humans will appear in developed countries than in undeveloped areas cut off from their surroundings. It is easier for individual genetic mutations to be established among the kinds of small groups that dwell there.

"What sort of action will these new humans take? One thing we can say with certainty is that they will try to destroy us. Unless they eliminate us, they will not be able to secure their own habitat. They will view us as extremely dangerous lower animals that spend their time killing their own species and who possess the scientific technology to destroy the earth's environment. Creatures with lower intelligence and moral capacity will be obliterated by those of higher intelligence.

"When human evolution occurs, we will soon vanish from the face of the earth. We will suffer the same fate that befell Peking man and the Neanderthals."

PART 2

NEMESIS

1.

RIGHT AFTER ARTHUR Rubens took the test to enter kindergarten, his parents were called into the principal's office and told that their son's IQ was off the charts. "Off the charts" was meant in a good way, and Rubens's parents—his father, who ran a small chain of restaurants in Maryland, and his housewife mother—were ecstatic.

When Rubens reached his teens his IQ was within measurable limits but still continued to be at the upper reaches of the normal distribution curve. The graph of this curve told the story—only one in every ten thousand people possessed his level of intelligence. Assemble all the people in America who had the same IQ level or higher and they wouldn't even fill a baseball stadium.

Contrary to the expectations of those around him, though, Rubens himself soon gave up on his ability. By the time he was in his midteens he already knew he was not very creative. Assimilating the academic achievements of his predecessors was no problem, but he couldn't add anything innovative to the pool of existing knowledge. In the history of mankind flashes of inspiration from geniuses have built science and civilization, and from an early age Rubens knew he lacked the kind of antennae that could pick up those kinds of divinely inspired revelations.

So when he entered Georgetown University at age fourteen, he no longer saw himself as a child prodigy but merely as a brilliant person. He wasn't interested in money or power. The only desire that set him apart was a burning zeal for knowledge, which led him to sit in on a wide variety of classes. What interested him most was the history of science. For him, tracing this history, from natural philosophers of the sixth century BCE to developments in theoretical physics in the twentieth century— the entire journey down the paths of human knowledge—was a kind of pleasure that nothing else could match. From a scientific perspective, the most regrettable period in human history had to be the Dark Ages, when Europeans put a halt to this march of knowledge. If this period hadn't happened, mankind would have made it to the moon in the nineteenth century at the latest.

Rubens enjoyed his studies, but the rest of his student life was awful. His youth and intelligence, and his blond hair and handsome features, were more than enough to rouse the jealousy of older students. When his classmates bullied him their eyes were full of malice, but what really annoyed him was how they kept bringing up the fact that he was a virgin. As he saw the ugly faces of these jealous men jokingly—but, deep down, seriously—show their contempt for him, Rubens noticed a certain trend: the less intelligent men were, the more superior they acted when it came to sex. Whenever Rubens tried to be friendly with any coeds, the harassment would get even more intense. The idiots around him reminded him of male animals butting their huge horns together in a battle over females.

The experience turned Rubens into a cold observer. If he played dumb and pretended not to notice the spitefulness of others, they got carried away and revealed their brutish nature all the more. Without realizing they were like an open book to him, they showed themselves for what they truly were—nothing but animals.

Competition in society, he concluded, came down to two things: food and sex. In order to eat more than other people, to store away more goods for themselves, to grab the most attractive members of the opposite sex, people easily grew contemptuous of others and abused them. People who maintained this animal brutishness used intimidation and intrigue to rise to leadership positions. The free competition that capitalism guaranteed was a clever system to sublimate this violence and direct it instead into the energy behind economic activity. Without laws or the welfare state, the animal appetites of capitalism would never be held in check. At any rate, the animals called human beings were, he concluded, deceitful, using intellect to prettify and conceal their primitive desires and justify their actions.

Six years after entering the university Rubens obtained a PhD in foundational mathematics and experienced for the first time, physically, the beauty and grace of a woman. Then he left Georgetown behind. He got a postdoc at the Los Alamos National Laboratory and then a position at a research facility in Santa Fe in order to study the new field of complex systems. At a café there he happened to run across a psychologist who told him an interesting story, one that determined the course his life would take. The story was about research into the firing rate of American soldiers.

"During the Second World War, when US soldiers came face-to-face with enemy troops, at what rate do you think they actually pulled the trigger and fired?"

The question was asked casually, over coffee, and Rubens answered without giving it much thought. "About seventy percent?"

"No. Only twenty percent."

The psychologist, seeing the surprise and doubt in Rubens's face, went on. "The other eighty percent said they ran out of ammo, or made up some other excuse, to avoid killing. This percentage didn't change even in the face of banzai charges by Japanese troops. For soldiers on the front lines, the stress of killing someone else was evidently greater than the fear of being killed themselves."

"That's surprising. I always figured human beings were more savage."

The psychologist grinned. "There's more," he said. "This report confounded the military. Can't have the troops becoming moralistic, right? So they conducted psychological research to see how they could raise the firing rate. By the time of the Vietnam War they'd gotten it up to ninety-five percent."

"What did they do?"

"It was simple, really. They replaced the round targets on the shooting ranges with targets in the shape of humans and had them pop up like real people. And they instituted a system of rewards and punishment based on how well soldiers did at the range."

"Operant conditioning?"

"Exactly. Like training mice to push the lever that provides them food. However," the psychologist said, his expression turning a little downcast, "this reflexively-shoot-the-enemy-when-you-see-him method of training had a huge defect. They'd removed the psychological obstacles for the soldiers up to the point of shooting, but they hadn't considered post-shooting trauma at all. The result was massive numbers of returning Vietnam vets with PTSD."

"Okay," Rubens said doubtfully. "But if human beings hate murdering that much, why don't wars disappear? And how could the United States win the Second World War with a firing rate of only twenty percent?"

"First of all, two percent of all male soldiers are what you'd call born killers. Psychopaths, people with no psychological compunction about killing. Most of them, though, when they return to civilian life, lead normal lives. Only when they're in the military are they 'ideal soldiers' who kill without regret or a guilty conscience."

"But you can't win a war with just two percent, can you?"

"They discovered it's easy to make the remaining ninety-eight percent into killers, too. You start by training them to obey authority figures and identify completely with the group in order to wrest away their individuality. Then you work to put a distance between them and the people they kill."

"A distance?"

"Right. In two senses of the word. A psychological distance and a physical distance.

"If the enemy is from a different race," he explained, "with a different language, religion, and ideology, then there's already a psychological distance, which makes it all the easier to kill them. In wartime it's easy to change people into killers if they're the kind of people who ordinarily put a psychological distance between themselves and other races, who see their race as superior and other races as inferior. Look around and I'm sure you'll find a couple of people who fit that description. Teach people that their opponents are morally inferior brutes and you wind up with slaughter in the name of justice. This sort of brainwashing takes place both in peacetime and wartime. Calling the enemy derogatory terms like Jap and Dink is the first step.

"To maintain a physical distance," the psychologist went on, "you need advanced weapons technology.

"Even soldiers who hesitate to shoot the enemy close up don't hesitate when they can't see the enemy directly and are given ever more destructive weapons that allow distance killing—trench mortars, naval artillery, bombs dropped from planes. Soldiers who are traumatized for life by shooting the enemy right in front of them can kill hundreds of people in bombing raids with no lasting scars.

"Some scholars say that what separates humans from animals is the power of imagination. But when people use weapons like these, any imagination they might possess is paralyzed. They drop bombs on people but can't see the horrible deaths of those below them trying to escape. And this sort of perversion is not limited to soldiers. It's a universal psychology found in ordinary citizens. Do you see my point?"

Rubens nodded. People look askance at a soldier who bayonets an enemy but treat a pilot who shoots down ten enemy aircraft as a hero.

"Weapons of mass destruction try to distance the enemy and create as many victims in the easiest way possible. Instead of beating a person to death with your fists we've moved to using a knife, then a gun, then a cannon, a bomber, and finally nuclear intercontinental ballistic missiles. In the United States, creating these weapons has become one of our key industries. That's why war will always be with us."

As he got more into this kind of research, Rubens realized all modern wars share a common structure. Those involved in war are the people with the cruelest wills. In other words, the leaders who decide to go to war are the ones farthest from the actual war, psychologically and physically. The president of the United States attending a banquet in the White House hardly has enemy blood spurt over him and never hears the gut-wrenching battlefield cries of a buddy whose body is torn apart and is dying in agony. The president is swathed in a protective cocoon, where he feels almost none of the psychological guilt associated with murder and can give free rein to his innate brutality. As military organizations have evolved into this sort of structure, and as science and technology have further refined weapons, the slaughter of human life in modern warfare has intensified. The decision makers in war can, without a twinge of a guilty conscience, order massive air raids that kill untold thousands.

Are a country's leaders, who order wars knowing they will lead to the deaths of tens of thousands of people, normal persons in terms of cruelty? Or are they rather abnormal, hiding their excessive aggressiveness behind a pleasant smile?

Rubens decided it must be the latter. People who are obsessed with power, who have survived the political battles that got them into their current positions, have to have a belligerent, combative quality far beyond the norm. Still, since in a democracy the will of the people determines the system by which the leader is chosen, any leader emerging from it must embody the will of the majority. That being the case, it is possible to replace war psychology with the psychology of those in power. In order to answer the question of why people fight wars, Rubens found it essential to throw light on the psychopathology of the person who orders a nation to go to war.

As he deepened his insight into complex adaptive systems at the Santa Fe lab, in his spare time he enjoyed pursuing this line of reasoning. Even after he returned to the Los Alamos facility, where he worked, his desire to inquire further into the war psychology of leaders never lessened. He quickly mastered psychopathology and clinical psychology and, using these and the methods of pathography, analyzed the personalities of the two main US presidential candidates. He concluded that the election of Gregory S. Burns would lead to a higher chance of war. Half a year later, when Burns won the presidential election, Rubens decided that human history was moving in a bad direction and that he wanted to see this process from the inside. He was in his late twenties by then and had opted out of the scholarly life. The time had come for him to leave the ivory tower and get out in the open sea of the world at large, filled, as it were, with the living creatures called humans.

He started by using connections he had at the Los Alamos lab to look for a job that would place him close to the White House. Rubens's exceptional intellect was highly attractive to government agencies. Both military intelligence and DARPA, the Defense Advanced Research Projects Agency, tried to recruit him, but just then he learned about a think tank he'd never heard of before. The Schneider Institute, headquartered in Washington, DC. It was one of many think tanks established in the wake of World War II, and while other think tanks focused on such areas as economics, diplomacy, and military strategy, the Schneider Institute worked on information strategy. Officially they were a private PR firm, but their biggest clients were the CIA and the

Defense Department. The institute did its best to keep a low profile and was much less known than think tanks such as the RAND Corporation.

The Schneider Institute maintained a neutral position, neither conservative nor liberal, and thus had good relations with every administration. Rubens decided it was the perfect place for him, and he went for an interview and was hired.

Rubens was given his own office and the title of researcher at the institute, which occupied an unassuming six-story building near the Potomac. Other than the miscellaneous work he was compelled to do, he was told he could pursue any sort of research he wanted to. He found out later that this was a probationary period. He was given a battery of psychological tests and lie detector tests and underwent a thorough background check by the FBI, during which agents visited his former places of residence. A year later, after they'd determined he had no financial difficulties, no foreign relatives, didn't participate in any antigovernment movements, had no criminal record, and had no perverted sexual inclinations, he was granted TS/SCI-level security clearance. And he immediately became much busier. He was promoted to analyst and was dispatched to the front lines of the information war the Pentagon was leading.

The top-secret operation in which he was placed was directed not at enemy countries but was psychological warfare aimed at the American people. The Burns administration was in the midst of planning an attack on Iraq and needed to persuade the public to support the impending war effort. They selected some eighty retired military officers who would do what the Pentagon told them to and dispatched them to the media as supposedly independent military analysts supporting the invasion of Iraq. It is all too easy to use the media to manipulate public opinion. As the commentators on TV repeated the line that Iraq was an imminent threat, President Burns's public support quickly shot up.

At the same time, the CIA snuck thirty Iraqi Americans into Iraq, and they determined that Iraq had abandoned the development of weapons of mass destruction. The only proof that Iraq still was developing these weapons—documents that purported to show that Niger had exported uranium to Iraq—turned out to be fake. The nuclear material in question had already been purchased as futures a few years in advance by several countries in Europe and by Japanese corporations. But the Burns administration ignored these reports and went ahead with its war plans.

After he took care of the assignments he was given, Rubens was free to closely observe events, and he quickly concluded that this was a war of aggression aimed at securing Iraq's oil resources. An unjust war, but one that profits the country. Rubens paid particular attention not to abstract concepts like the nation or the military-industrial complex but to actual people. The personality of the nation was none other than the personalities of the decision makers involved.

The key leaders of the invasion were those lining their pockets through the war. Chamberlain, a former secretary of defense who had supported outsourcing some military duties to private contractors, stepped down with the change in administrations to become head of a private enterprise doing business with the government, a move that made him huge profits. Under the Burns administration he made a comeback, returning to the White House as vice president, and was at the forefront of pushing for the attack on Iraq. Before the invasion even took place he had begun to outline plans for the postwar reconstruction effort. Naturally, after the war, the company that contracted to rebuild the Iraqi infrastructure was none other than the energy company he had led. Since then he'd increased his private wealth by tens of millions of dollars.

There were any number of politicians within the administration who used the neoconservative philosophy to gloss over their own greed. Even Lattimer, the secretary of defense, had deep connections with munitions companies.

The most difficult thing for Rubens to fathom was President Burns himself. From his public comments it was clear that he had a deep hatred for the Iraqi dictator, but Rubens couldn't figure out why he loathed him so much he would kill him. This wasn't just to profit the country or to push pork-barrel projects for the military-industrial complex. There might even be an unconscious motivation that Burns himself was unaware of. Here Rubens followed the limited reports in the media on the president's upbringing and constructed a hypothesis. Burns saw his autocratic father reflected in the Iraqi dictator and wanted to overthrow him. Rubens mocked his own analysis as simplistic, based on insufficient data, but if this insight were indeed true it was a frightening prospect. More than a hundred thousand people died, all because of one man's relationship to his father. And once he reached his goal and had overthrown the enemy, Burns must feel a sense of emptiness, because this wasn't his real enemy. All he'd done was kill the opponent he'd fabricated deep in his psyche.

At any rate, the war began, and while the killing was still going on all over Iraq, Burns declared victory. Several hyenalike nations, under the pretext of helping the reconstruction efforts, established themselves in the defeated country. Governments didn't like the idea of their troops continuing to die after victory had been declared, and a black comedy ensued, in which private mercenaries were hired to guard regular troops. Other nations that showed themselves willing to follow the intentions of the United States in this pathetic enterprise were given a small portion of the leftover spoils of war—partial rights to some of the oil fields. Blinded by the inhumanely acquired profit their countries could reap, the leaders of these nations used the excuse of weapons of mass destruction to deceive their citizens, or else the citizens pretended to be deceived, and they indirectly contributed to killing the Iraqi people. Behind this, the energy industry made enormous profits, and citizens were able to enjoy a better lifestyle, while many of the troops at the front lines were deeply wounded physically and emotionally.

The American leaders who spearheaded this, one of the most idiotic wars in human history, would, when their lives were over, no doubt be thrown into the pits of hell by the God they professed to believe in.

Around the time the postwar reconstruction was getting bogged down, Rubens, by then promoted to senior analyst, decided to leave the Schneider Institute. He'd seen everything he could see at the think tank. The next thing he wanted to observe was the regenerative power of the United States. The American people weren't stupid. Pushback against the lunacy of the Burns administration was bound to come. It was even possible that in the next election America would elect the first African American or woman president. If he joined the staff at the headquarters of the leading candidate he'd be able to observe even more closely the mentality and brutality of someone seeking to become the most powerful person in the land.

Around this time Rubens was called to a meeting by another section of the institute. Waiting for him in the secure conference room was the external affairs section chief, the liaison between the institute and the CIA and NSA and the rest of the intelligence community.

"I'd like you to read this," Rubens was told and handed a copy of a report entitled *Research into Factors Leading to the Extinction of the Human Race, and Policy Proposals*. He was surprised to find that the author was listed as Joseph R. Heisman, PhD, senior researcher at the Schneider Institute. Dr. Heisman's field was theoretical physics, but he was well known, a prominent scholar well versed in all scientific fields. He was a particular authority on the history of science, and Rubens had read several of his books. Rubens had no idea that Heisman had been on the staff of the Schneider Institute thirty years earlier.

Rubens read the Heisman Report with great interest. What really impressed him was how much of a complete pacifist its author was. It must have taken a lot of courage to submit a report like this during the height of the Cold War. Rubens's admiration for Heisman grew all the more.

"What's your take on the report?" the external affairs section chief asked.

"He makes a lot of sense," Rubens said briefly.

"Take a look at this," the chief said, and handed him another document. "The Africa bureau of the NSA intercepted this e-mail out of the Democratic Republic of the Congo. It was sent by an anthropologist named Nigel Pierce to a fellow researcher. I'd like you to examine the contents, evaluate it, and submit a report within a week. The main thing is the message's credibility—whether this kind of thing could really happen or whether it's a misconception on Professor Pierce's part."

"Mind if I clarify two points?"

"Go ahead."

"Why me? Isn't this a job for analysts at the NSA or CIA?"

The chief smiled faintly. "They can't handle it. You're the only person qualified for the job. The warnings in the Heisman Report seem much more real now, and they turned to our institute to take care of it again."

Rubens nodded and asked his second question. "Don't I need to know some background on Nigel Pierce?"

"You can refer to this," the chief said, taking a report out of a folder.

Rubens looked through the report. According to a background investigation done on Pierce by the CIA, he was a forty-seven-year-old Caucasian male, the heir to a large import-export firm, Pierce Shipping. But Pierce himself was a scholarly type, so he gave over the family business to his younger brother and received a doctorate in anthropology at age twenty-seven. He spent his time after this mainly doing fieldwork, and at forty-one he was appointed professor of anthropology at Roslyn University.

Pierce didn't have much of a reputation as a scholar. His thesis on the Mbuti Pygmies was sharply criticized as "fascinating as travelogue but lacking in scholarly value." In fact, Pierce was only able to continue as a professor through the generous research funds provided by the Pierce Foundation, run by his family. The CIA report included a personality profile that said he was "quite sound psychologically. He has little sense of competitiveness and ambition in regard to scholarship and pursues it more as an avocation." He seemed like a frank, laid-back sort of person, the complete opposite of a typical politician.

A photo was attached to the report. Rubens studied the tanned, bearded face, then turned to the intercepted e-mail. TOP SECRET was stamped on the pages. Expecting it to be a report on the lethal virus, Rubens was nothing less than astounded by what he read.

Dear Dennis,

As you know, I trusted the cease-fire between the Congolese government and the antigovernment forces and came back to Ituri Forest. I was able to meet my good friends the Mbuti again but ran into a surprising situation and wanted to tell you about it. Please keep what I am about to say confidential. I'm sending this e-mail to you to serve as proof that I'm the first person to observe a new stage in human history.

Soon after I arrived at the Kanga band's camp I saw a creature I'd never seen before. It's difficult to describe it in words. It has the body and limbs of a human infant, but its head is very different. Especially if you look at its eyes you can see it belongs in a different category from human beings. I think we possess an innate ability to distinguish different species. The moment I laid eyes on this different species of human I couldn't think straight. All sorts of questions swirled around in my mind, and my whole body froze. I literally could not move.

After a while I was able to think rationally again, and though I don't like to use the term, I thought I was looking at a deformed child. I learned that the child was born three years before to a Mbuti couple. As I observed the child I saw that, while its physical body functioned normally, it has an intelligence far exceeding its age.

For several months after that I was able to see the startling intellectual powers of this child. It's nothing other than superhuman. I'll provide all the details after I'm back home, but here let me just give a couple of examples.

I taught the child English, and it mastered everything, including reading and writing, in two weeks. It can argue now on politics, economics, and other complex issues. Though it's three years old, its pharynx isn't developed yet and it can't converse using sound. Instead it uses the keyboard of a laptop computer.

Its abstract mathematical reasoning really stands out, and I was astounded by how easily it could do prime factorization. I used my computer to give it forty-digit composite numbers, and it was able to break these down into two prime numbers in five seconds. Imagine—a three-year-old child has insight into mathematical theorems on prime numbers that mankind has never been able to solve! If the American government, especially the Defense Department, found out that a Pygmy child can break the highest-level RSA code, it'll be quite a shock. Who knows? It might even be possible to find a proof for the Riemann hypothesis.

I think by now you've figured out what I'm trying to say. Considering the hyperdeveloped forehead—anatomical observation suggests neoteny—this is a different race of human being, resulting from a sudden mutation in the cerebral neocortex. There's a high possibility that what we're looking at is an instance of human evolution. We can determine where in the DNA the mutation has occurred, and whether crossbreeding with modern man is possible, only if the child is taken to a developed country.

For your information, the child's father is an ordinary Pygmy. Its mother died of illness, but apparently nothing about her was out of the ordinary, either. I went to other bands to check, but this is the only child who's like this. A sudden mutation must have taken place in the reproductive cells of one of these parents from the Kanga band.

Fighting has broken out again in the eastern Congo, so I won't be able to leave the Ituri Forest until it subsides. Both the government forces and the rebels are vicious, and I'm very afraid we'll be attacked. I plan to figure out a way to get the child out of the country when the time is right.

My computer and satellite phone aren't working very well, so I might not be able to send any more e-mails. But don't worry. As soon as we're somewhere safe I'll get in touch. As I said, please keep all this confidential.

Looking forward to the day we can meet again.

Nigel Pierce

After he finished reading the e-mail, Rubens had to be careful not to let his excitement show. His workplace didn't welcome anyone who got emotional. "I'll have the evaluation ready in a week," he said simply, and left the conference room.

Rubens was once again amazed at the surveillance capabilities of the

United States. The world's largest intelligence organization, the NSA, which far exceeded the CIA in size, operated a worldwide wiretapping network called Echelon with four other English-speaking countries. The system was able to intercept and listen in on all means of communication—landlines, cell phones, faxes, e-mails. But since it couldn't handle all the data collected, the computers had a program that automatically extracted messages that touched on national security. This dictionary program had no doubt flagged some of the words used in Pierce's e-mail—probably, in this case, keywords such as *rebel forces, prime factorization, highest-level, RSA code, American government, Defense Department, shock,* and *fighting.*

It was obvious why the NSA had viewed Pierce's e-mail as a problem: the ability of this Mbuti child to perform prime factorization. An ability like that would disable modern codes. This could pose a major national security threat.

But for Rubens this risk assessment was shortsighted. The question was what would happen to the whole world if an intelligence surpassing that of humans appeared. The precarious order that mankind had, after great pains, managed to maintain would collapse at a single stroke.

On the same day that he read the intercepted e-mail Rubens spent a good many hours in the library at his alma mater, Georgetown. He needed to dig into this question of whether it was possible for mankind to continue to evolve.

Charles Darwin and Alfred Russel Wallace came up with the idea of natural selection almost simultaneously, and in the 150 years since then it has kept its place as the central hypothesis of biological evolution. Sudden mutations change the traits of organisms, and if these changes are a disadvantage in terms of survival, the line dies out. If they are an advantage for survival, then the organism survives and leaves behind descendants. This process continues through generations, with the accumulation of subtle variations finally changing the species itself. Neither of these two scientists knew about Mendelian genetics, let alone the existence of DNA, and arriving at this theory solely on the basis of observation of nature revealed amazing powers of insight. But because of this their theory has been criticized as only telling half the story of the phenomenon of evolution. Darwinian theory only considers what happens after sudden mutation takes place and doesn't touch on the mechanism by which such mutation occurs. Their theory does not explain the whole process.

Later advances in molecular biology led to increased understanding of evolution. Outside factors such as radiation, or mistakes in DNA replication when reproductive cells are created, can lead to variation in the genetic information in organisms. In reality, of the three billion base pairs in the human genome, an average of one DNA base every two years changes into a different base. Most of these random changes, however, are neutral and do not affect survival one way or the other, and it is a matter of pure chance whether they become fixed in the entire species.

Rubens learned that there had been further major discoveries in molecular biology in the previous few decades that rewrote many accepted theories. Sudden mutation not only causes single-base substitution but changes the genome. In the history of biological evolution one gene can be copied, or move to a different position, or the entire DNA can be copied whole and doubled. There is no doubt that these dynamic changes in base sequence are the driving force behind biological evolution. Also, at the end of the last century the surprising discovery was made that even without a change in DNA, organisms can change their traits. The methyl group and acetyl group of chemicals can promote or suppress the expression of genes. Moreover, these chemical modifications are accurately transmitted from parent to child, so once these changes occur the next generation inherits them.

The more Rubens learned about the mechanism behind changes in DNA, the more he decided that biological evolution takes place much more rapidly than previously thought—in other words, on a much shorter time scale than geologic time.

As the Heisman Report indicated, "Organisms accumulate subtle changes over long periods of time, but also at certain times can display sudden transformations."

What if we focus on human evolution? Six million years ago a species of primates branched off into two lines. One line became chimpanzees, the other humans. But oddly enough, while in the intervening six million years chimpanzees have hardly changed at all, the other line evolved from *Ardipithecus* to humans, producing at least twenty different varieties of human beings until arriving at present-day Homo sapiens. This wasn't a straight line but branched off numerous times, and in ancient days it was common for multiple species of humans to coexist on the earth. Modern man, who left Africa fifty thousand years ago and spread over the entire planet, must have encountered hominids and Neanderthals. And the answer was becoming clearer as to why, compared to chimpanzees, human evolution was so accelerated.

Several genes were discovered in the human brain that sped up the rate of evolution. One is the HAR1 gene (human accelerated regions), which is involved in the development of the cerebral cortex. In the three hundred million years of biological evolution since this gene appeared, it made only two base substitutions, but in the six million years of human evolution eighteen of these base substitutions have taken place. So among all the subfamilies on earth, only Homininae have changed the direction of evolution and shown an explosive development in intellect.

Rubens also turned his attention to the FOXP2 gene. Chimpanzees share this gene with humans, and the genetic difference between them and humans is slight, but despite this there is a tremendous difference in language ability between the two species. FOXP2 is a transcription-factor type of gene. While it accelerates the expression of sixty-one genes, it suppresses fifty-five other genes. A change in just this one gene thus can affect the function of more than a hundred other genes. The result is that humans have the ability to acquire advanced language skills.

In light of the accelerated regions in human DNA, and the great influence subtle changes in genes can have, Rubens couldn't dismiss Professor Pierce's report of human evolution as mere nonsense. Also, just before he was about to write his assessment, Rubens ran across some additional crucial research. Modern man, who appeared two hundred thousand years ago, continued living a primitive life for 190,000 years. Why did mankind suddenly start building civilizations? The answer to this riddle is found in the human genome. A gene called ASPM, which appeared six thousand years ago, left evidence of having transformed the human brain. After this it is believed that divergent evolution took place, meaning that geographically separated groups acquired the same functions and civilizations sprang up one after another. If this hypothesis is correct, then modern man has already experienced the evolution of the brain, albeit on a small scale. Rubens realized that before arguing about whether this kind of human evolution is possible, it was crucial to understand that it had already taken place.

After he left the library Rubens went back to his town house in Georgetown, sat down at his computer, and wrote up his assessment in a single sitting. He tried to use a cautious tone in the conclusion:

> Regarding the Mbuti infant mentioned in Professor Pierce's e-mail, we are unable to conclude whether it is a new species of organism. Strictly speaking, it is reasonable to assume that the person has a deformity of the cranial structure. But if this deformity is the result of mutation in a base sequence, far from harming the person, it will rather work to accelerate his intellect. In this sense it may be appropriate to label this an "evolved human being" or a "new species of being."

On the appointed day Rubens turned in his assessment to the chief of external affairs. He was immediately given another assignment.

"This incident will be in the president's daily briefing," he was told. "They'll ask us for a contingency plan, so I'd like you to get a head start on that."

"By contingency plan you mean—"

"What we should do with the creature."

This put Rubens in a tough spot. They didn't want a plan based on biology but simply a way to get rid of a national security threat. Three choices immediately sprang to mind—leaving the creature alone, taking it captive, or killing it—though he felt none of these was a perfect solution.

Rubens went back to the library to gather information for the contingency plan. A basic question still lay untouched, namely, why had the Pygmy child's genes mutated? Or, to take it back farther, what had happened with the parents' reproductive cells?

He read through various documents and came up with three hypotheses he thought might help in formulating a contingency plan. And he painstakingly investigated each one.

The first item that caught his eye was research into the structure of DNA nucleosomes. The document discussed the discovery that there is periodic base substitution in medaka, a type of fish. DNA, a long, stringy double helix, does not sit inside a cell as is but is wrapped around a spherical protein called a histone, much as a thread is wrapped around a spool. Compared to the length of DNA, a histone is small, so once DNA is wrapped around one histone it then neatly wraps around the next to form a line of countless spools. The mutation observed in medaka DNA, as if corresponding to the periodicity of this spool structure, occurs at an interval of every two hundred bases. When this research is applied to the nature of human evolution, it becomes evident that there are places where it is easier for base substitution to occur, and the genes involved in the growth of the brain in Homininae just happen to coincide with those regions. Random base substitution takes place over and over, but most of the fertilized eggs are naturally miscarried because of genetic errors. But now, among the Mbuti people in jungles of the Congo, an individual was born whose brain had evolved. If this conjecture were correct, the mutation in reproductive cells would not have taken place among all the members of the Kanga band but only in one of the parents of the child. So the response plan should focus on the parent and child only.

The second hypothesis dealt with the Tunguska event. In 1908 a massive, mysterious explosion took place deep in Siberia, in the Tunguska region. A huge ball of fire in the sky flattened some eighty million trees and blew people off their feet as far as sixty kilometers from the hypocenter. In terms of TNT explosive power, the explosion was fifteen megatons, equivalent to the energy of a thousand Hiroshima-size bombs. It was still unclear what, exactly, exploded, though speculation centered on a comet or asteroid exploding in the atmosphere. What drew Rubens's attention were the abnormal changes in plants afterward. Plants near the hypocenter grew three times faster than normal and in some cases transformed into different shapes, showing a clear genetic abnormality. The same phenomenon was seen after nuclear explosions, although, oddly enough, no residual radiation was detected near the Tunguska site. Still, the mutation rate for plants was much higher than it was after nuclear contamination.

Rubens next asked, through the external affairs chief, for military reconnaissance data from the NRO, the National Reconnaissance Office. He discovered that every year reconnaissance satellites detect an average of seven explosions of small celestial bodies in the atmosphere. These are far smaller than the explosion in Tunguska, though still about the size of the Nagasaki atomic bomb—twenty kilotons. If these astronomical phenomena produced genetic changes in organisms, and if one had taken place in the sky above the Ituri jungle, where the Mbuti live, it's possible it affected all the people who live in the vicinity. But multiple checks of the NRO database showed no such explosions over the skies of the Congo in the last twenty years. Most of these astronomical phenomena take place over the ocean, far from any humans. So Rubens rejected this second hypothesis.

The final hypothesis was the one that ultimately determined the direction of the response plan, namely, the virus evolution theory. It was simply one of the hypotheses concerning biological evolution, but it contained an idea that Rubens couldn't ignore. Because viruses cannot replicate on their own, they do so using the cells they've infected. They inject their own DNA into the DNA of the host cell and then replicate. But for some reason, in certain cases once the DNA has been inserted the virus becomes inactive. When that happens the base sequence of the virus is included in the host cell, and that mutation is transferred to the daughter cells each time there is cell division. The genome is transformed. In some cases the infecting virus takes in part of the host cell's genes and replicates. This virus in turn infects a new individual, and once it becomes inactive the original host's DNA is incorporated into the next host's DNA. This phenomenon takes place in the reproductive cells, becomes a fertilized egg, and if the added base sequence acquires a new function, that becomes a part of evolution. If the virus evolution theory were correct, it would be possible for biological evolution to take place multiple times and simultaneously through viral infection.

Applied to the issue at hand, the theory would enable a scenario in which a new type of virus appeared in the jungles of the Congo, infecting the Mbuti and leading to an evolutionary transformation.

Rubens looked into whether there had been any epidemiological investigations of a viral infection among the Mbuti and found that a Japanese virologist, Seiji Koga, had conducted onsite fieldwork into HIV infections. Happily for Rubens, the fieldwork included the forty members of the Kanga band. Maybe Koga had unwittingly detected an unknown virus that would produce evolutionary changes in humans.

His scholarly interest aroused, Rubens immediately ordered the original Japanese paper and had the NSA translate it. Unfortunately, this proved fruitless. The investigation had taken place ten years ago, well before the time the three-year-old Mbuti child was born. And the Mbuti were found to not be infected by any virus whatsoever.

It was conceivable that the new virus appeared after Dr. Koga's investigation, so as far as the response plan was concerned the possibility remained that the evolutionary change could take place simultaneously among multiple individuals.

Rubens had pushed himself hard doing the research and was relieved at what he'd found, because it meant that they should be able to avoid the worst choice of the three, the one that involved killing. Since it was possible that the viral infection had led to the birth of multiple superhumans, the entire Kanga band would have to be killed to eliminate the threat. But Rubens found it hard to imagine his superiors authorizing a massacre on that scale.

Of the two remaining choices—leaving the creature alone or capturing it—Rubens had to eliminate the first. There was a danger that this amazing intellect could potentially break the most secure codes, which might fall into the hands of a potential enemy.

But capture also was worrisome. According to the Heisman Report, this superhuman possessed "mental qualities that are incomprehensible to us." It was impossible to predict how it would react to the attempt to capture it. To avoid the unexpected, they had to be cautious and not take extreme hostile action against it.

This was phase 1 of the investigation. A team of specialists, guarded by Special Forces troops, had to be sent to the site to check out the veracity of Pierce's information.

Once they established the facts they would proceed to phase 2, isolating all members of the Kanga band and all participants in the operation. The participants would need to be quarantined because of the possibility that they'd been infected at the site. A certain amount of deception was necessary, and they would need to fabricate a story about the spread of Ebola or some other lethal virus in order to justify the quarantine.

In phase 3 all the people in quarantine would be subjected to biochemical testing so they could determine whether a virus that could produce an evolutionary change really existed. If they did detect the virus, then the steps after that were up to the politicians. Most likely they would push to develop an antiviral drug to nip this evolutionary change in the bud. And if it turned out that the viral threat was a false alarm, then the people in quarantine could be released.

Concerning the three-year-old child with the mutated brain, it and its parent could be given United States citizenship, financial support, and be put under a not-so-stringent watch. The major premise would be respect for their individual rights as people, avoiding extreme measures such as imprisonment. They needed to impress upon the creature that modern man was not an enemy and then use the intellect of this superhuman to benefit the United States.

Rubens's plan, however, was rejected the day after he turned it in.

"The higher-ups think it's too soft," the external affairs chief told him when they met in the conference room at the Schneider Institute. "We have to quickly eliminate this threat to the United States."

"Eliminate?" Rubens realized immediately what this meant. Killing them.

"Also, financing your plan and implementing it are both problematic. We have our hands full fighting two wars in the Middle East. And it's impossible to quarantine forty Pygmies in a war zone."

"It should be doable if you use civilians, not the military. If you put out the story that the effort is intended to defeat a lethal virus, you can disguise it as humanitarian aid. None of the factions fighting in the Congo wants to make enemies of America."

"Listen, Arthur," the chief said mildly as he corrected this rash analyst. "You still don't get it about this administration, do you? You can convince me, but that's not going to change their opinion. They'll just find another think tank that'll do as it's told."

It was a beginner's oversight, and Rubens felt embarrassed by his naïveté. True enough, that's how they operated. They'd pick apart any opposing opinion, exclude it, and surround themselves with yes men. An autocratic approach to decision making dressed up as democratic. This was how the Burns administration spearheaded the slaughter of so many Iraqi civilians.

"Their decision isn't based on an examination of the plan's validity. It's simply how they like to do things. This administration has a typical cowboy approach, and they don't like roundabout methods. If there's somebody who can break their most secure codes, they want to remove him right away. Before an enemy country can find out."

"But let's say they kill the Pygmy child. The potential threat remains. If a virus caused the mutation, another child like him might be born in the Kanga band."

"They took that into account when they made their decision."

Shocked, Rubens stared at the chief across the table. He thought he had a good grasp of the psychopathology of the Burns administration, but he'd vastly underestimated their viciousness. The conference room was secure, but still Rubens lowered his voice. "You're saying that they plan to liquidate the entire Kanga band, including Nigel Pierce?"

The chief grimaced and nodded. "If you're going to survive here in Washington you need to be careful with the words you use. Not *liquidate*, but *eliminate*. As long as there's a possibility of viral infection, we'll have to eliminate more than those forty-one. The troops who carry out the operation will have to go, too."

As he vigorously argued against this, Rubens was surprised to find an unexpected moralist within him. "But the military won't accept that. These will be Special Forces–type troops, people they've spent millions of tax dollars training. You really plan to *eliminate* crack troops like those?"

"That's why we have private defense contractors. We just send in mercenaries. Plus, if this plan really comes to fruition, it will be an assassination led by the White House. Safer to outsource it."

This wasn't murder, Rubens thought. It was genocide. The target was an individual who made up an entire race. A genocide of one. "But what's the plan if the viral infection has spread beyond the Kanga band? You'll eliminate all the people who live in the area?"

"I'm sure they'll discuss that when the time comes. Submit a new plan by tomorrow," the chief ordered. As he was leaving the conference room he turned around. "Watch your back, Arthur," he said.

This wasn't a threat, Rubens decided, but a piece of friendly advice.

Rubens left the institute while it was still light out and walked back home down M Street, the one street he most enjoyed strolling in all DC. The street was filled with small, elegant shops, and the crowd on the street was lively, as if regretting the waning sun. What Rubens saw, however, was people living lives as well-intentioned citizens, people who had come to terms with the savage desires deep within them. This is America. And the Burns administration was humiliating this country.

Rubens came to the steep steps at Prospect Street and stood there, deep in thought. There was one thing he understood about the decision to liquidate this newly evolved species of human. Just as chimpanzees can't manipulate humans, humans would not be able to control this new species of superhuman. If allowed to live, it could pose a threat to human society. The problem was the forty-some innocents caught up in it. If he didn't think of a way to save their lives, he would be the ringleader in their massacre.

He could resign, but quitting his job wouldn't change anything. Somebody else eager to go along with Burns's ideas would just take his place, and the massacre would proceed. He, Rubens, was the only one who could reduce the number of victims.

He could send a warning to Nigel Pierce, but that meant sending an e-mail through Pierce's satellite phone, which was out of the question—Echelon would immediately catch the message and trace it back to him.

Watch your back, Arthur.

Rubens sensed the danger he was in. He felt like he'd been slowly, unknowingly, dragged into a criminal organization, threatened, and forced to become a hit man. Actually, the White House *was* a lot like the Mafia. When they had a problem, murder was one of the options they considered as a solution.

211

After giving it a lot of thought, Rubens decided which path he should take.

He returned to the town house he rented near Georgetown University, went into the small room he used as a study, and began composing a new plan.

First of all, in order to get those involved in the operation to commit mass murder, he appropriated the notion of an explosive outbreak of a lethal virus. And he named this fraudulent operation to save humanity from the risk of extinction Guardian.

Unlike his earlier report, his new plan included a great number of specialized terms and difficult concepts without any explanation. He also hinted that the operation would be quite risky and that there was a high chance of failure.

Rubens implied that the person who could best manage the mission had to possess certain qualities. He had to be grounded in politics and military matters but also needed academic training in biology. He should be the kind of person who, if and when the upper levels of the administration gave the order, could be easily sacked. There couldn't be many people who would fit the bill—other than the young analyst from the Schneider Institute.

Rubens was staking everything on this. Well before the Iraq War think tanks had become a vital part of the military-industrial complex and civilians who worked at some of them had set up the Office of Special Plans and became prime movers in the war. It was perfectly conceivable that Rubens would be involved in this secret operation, including its execution.

It was past midnight when he finished writing his proposal, and he turned to the blanks he'd left for the code names. The target, the three-year-old child, he code-named Nous, a Greek term that meant superior intelligence and was the origin of the term noosphere, coined by the Jesuit philosopher Pierre Teilhard de Chardin to refer to what he saw as the third stage in biological evolution. And Rubens named the operation to murder the three-year-old child after the Greek goddess Nemesis, the goddess of divine retribution, the name given to the massive meteorite that brought about the extinction of the dinosaurs.

★   ★   ★

A month later Operation Nemesis, classified as a special access program, was approved by President Burns and set in motion. A combat operations center was established in the basement of the Pentagon, in corridor 3. OFFICE OF SPECIAL PLANS, SECTION 2, the sign on the door read, and to get inside one needed to show a security badge and ID card and undergo biometric scans. Rubens was, naturally, given access, for the White House had, as he had hoped, named him operations manager.

Everything had gone as planned. He was given authority to change the operation if he deemed it necessary, right before the four operators selected from private defense contractors were to kill the Pygmies. Rubens had decided he would use the sole weapon at his disposal, his extraordinary intellect, to save the lives of those forty people.

There were eleven staff members in the operations center, including the deputy assistant secretary of defense for African affairs, designated the overall supervisor; one military adviser and one science adviser; and below them Rubens and six staff members under his direct supervision, including some from the Defense Intelligence Agency and CIA strategic planning headquarters. These staff members were go-betweens, ready to liaise with staff members from their respective organizations who were standing by.

Rubens was especially thankful that the science adviser was Dr. Melvin Gardner. Gardner had begun his career in quantum mechanics, then moved into physical chemistry and later molecular biology. He had made major contributions to these fields, earning him a National Medal of Science. He had the perfect background to advise the operation, and his calm demeanor did much to soften the often ruthless atmosphere in the operations center. In contrast, the military adviser, Colonel Glenn Stokes, assigned from the Office of Special Plans, was a difficult character, and the other members enjoyed listening to the clash of opinions between him and Gardner.

Rubens was able to talk with Gardner one-on-one just before the operation commenced to go over some basic procedures.

"Professor, do you support killing Nous?" Rubens asked pointblank.

Gardner answered calmly. "I think it's probably unavoidable. Say that three-year-old grows up and successfully conducts cold nuclear fusion. It will change power relationships worldwide. He'll control mankind in every field—not just in energy but also in science and technology—weapons development included—medicine, and economics. If it came to that, all wealth and power would accrue to Nous."

Gardner seemed to have a correct grasp of the nature of this biological threat in the jungle of the Congo, and in this he and Rubens were on the same page. *Power* was the threat. Not the destructive power of nuclear weapons or the power of cutting-edge technology but the intellect that gives rise to them.

"Unfortunately," Gardner went on, "we're intolerant. We can't stand beings more intelligent than we are. Personally, though, I'd love to meet Nous."

Rubens felt the same way. "I wonder what he'd look like if he grew up."

"Considering the possibility of neoteny, his face would probably look like that of human children. Even though he looks odd as an infant, eventually he'd be indistinguishable from human children."

"I see."

Modern man was said to be the neotenic incarnation of its ancestors, the anthropoid apes. The skulls of a chimpanzee infant and an adult human are basically identical. If Nous grew up you wouldn't be able to tell him apart from a human child—except that he would be small in stature, like the Pygmies.

"Now, about the most critical element of this operation—"

"Nous's present intellectual ability?"

"Exactly. Judging from the intercepted e-mail sent by Pierce, it's reasonable to assume that his increase in brain capacity was limited to the cerebral neocortex."

"There's a lot we don't know about the robustness of brain development," Gardner said, and sighed. "Didn't it say that his forehead was particularly developed?"

"Yes."

"Since higher-order psychological activity is concentrated in the frontal lobes, it's best not to underestimate what he's capable of."

"So we should assume the maximum."

"That would be my advice."

They ended up using the difference between human intelligence and chimpanzee intelligence as the standard. Because Nous was three years old, the assumption was that he was as intelligent as an adult human.

"In that case it's going to be a well-matched contest," Gardner said, as if he had found a worthy chess opponent.

Once the operation was actually up and running, Rubens immediately set out controlling access to the information related to it. Through the Information Security Oversight Office, he had the Heisman Report in the National Archives classified as secret. He then had all websites that mentioned the report erased and ordered the NSA to tamper with search engines so they wouldn't pull up the term.

Operation Nemesis started out smoothly, but as preparations went ahead a disquieting mood settled over the command center. The greatest difficulty facing them was the selection of the operatives to be sent to the Congo jungle.

Harry Eldridge, assistant secretary of defense and official director of the operation, relayed the wishes of the White House to Rubens. "Include Warren Garrett, a CIA paramilitary operative. He'll monitor the operation on the ground."

Rubens was surprised. "You want an OGA employee in the operation?"

"That's right."

"You're sure it's okay?"

Eldridge frowned. "That's what the higher-ups tell me."

The reason for this was only given on a need-to-know basis, so Rubens didn't find out, though it was clear that the Burns administration wanted to eliminate this Garrett.

For the remaining three operatives Eldridge used his connections with private defense contractors to come up with a list of likely people. But one after another, these candidates, who were operating in Iraq, were killed in enemy attacks. Each time, the list was revised, until finally they came up with a mixed bag of candidates—one former army Special Forces, one former air force pararescue, and a Japanese who had served in the French Foreign Legion. The men were technically competent enough, but Rubens had questions about the disposition of Jonathan Yeager, the former Green Beret. The background check showed he had a son who was suffering from a chronic disease and didn't have much time left to live. In unfortunate cases like this close relatives often had inner self-destructive urges, and Rubens was afraid that under the strains of a physically demanding assignment he might fall apart.

Afterward a totally unexpected situation developed regarding the problem of Yeager's child. The NSA was the first to give them the information. A computer in Japan had run a search on the term *Heisman Report*. When Rubens saw the name of the person the NSA identified as initiating the search, he couldn't believe his eyes.

Seiji Koga.

The same scholar who had been on the epidemiology investigation looking into viral infections among the Mbuti. But why would he be interested in the Heisman Report? It had to be more than a coincidence. The warning in the Heisman Report was, after all, the basis for Operation Nemesis and the plan to murder all forty members of the Kanga band.

In the worst-case scenario, the secret was leaked. They did a follow-up investigation and found something quite unexpected. At the same time Dr. Koga visited Zaire, in 1996, Nigel Pierce was staying at the Mbuti camp. It was very likely they knew each other. But there was no proof that they kept in touch after the civil war broke out and they both returned home.

The CIA and NSA monitored Seiji Koga. NSA intercepted all his communications. Though they didn't find anything that confirmed their suspicions, their report to Rubens did perplex him. It turned out that encrypted e-mails were being sent back and forth between the eastern Congo and Japan.

When Rubens was told, "We don't know the sender or recipient, and it's impossible to decrypt the messages," he questioned the NSA liaison. "You can intercept the e-mails but can't tell who sent them?"

"Correct. This correspondence uses a unique transmission protocol. They've made their own private communications network."

"But wouldn't they still need an IP address? If you check with the Japanese providers you should be able to find out."

"Already done. But the person who made the contract with the provider is missing."

"What do you mean?"

The liaison gave him a report from the Japanese domestic antiterrorism unit, section 3 of the Metropolitan Police Department Public Security Bureau. "The person who made the contract is someone who had huge debts and disappeared more than ten years ago. Local police believe someone bought this missing person's *koseki*—official family record—and, posing as that person, obtained the IP address. Apparently criminals involved in fraud often buy and sell these *koseki*."

"The address given in the contract was an apartment in a cheap building in northern Tokyo, but there was no sign that anyone lived there. The lease for the apartment was in the same name as the one who contracted with the Internet provider, and it's impossible to know who's really behind it."

"What about the Congo? Who contracted with the satellite communications service they used to send the messages?"

"It's the same Japanese name."

Rubens considered this. Were these encrypted messages between Seiji Koga and Nigel Pierce? If so, what was the purpose? "The NSA doesn't know what the content of the message is, either?"

"We don't. The encryption technology is neither RSA nor AES. There's a high possibility it's a one-time pad code."

Rubens knew what he meant. The unciphered text was encoded, one letter at a time, using a one-time pad, or key, based on a preset random number sequence. It had been proven mathematically that this type of encryption was impossible to break. This method wasn't often used because of a practical problem—both the sender and receiver needed to share a common, huge random number sequence beforehand. These days one-time pad encryption was used only in the hot line linking the United States with Russian presidents. The computers used for the encrypted messages between the Congo and Japan must already have the encoding system integrated into them. The random number sequences used to both encrypt and decrypt the messages must have already been stored in the hard drives. The only way to break them was to get hold of those random number sequences.

"Can't you hack into the computers?"

"We tried, but it was no go."

There are computers the NSA can't hack into? Rubens was startled to learn this.

"I'd like to add one more task for Operation Guardian," the liaison said. "I want them to confiscate Pierce's computer. Once we extract the random number sequence from the computer, we can read any message sent on it."

"Sounds good," Rubens said, approving the addition to the mission. It didn't matter much, for he knew that Operation Guardian was destined to be halted at the last minute.

The operation had already experienced a series of unfortunate setbacks, and he was beginning to suspect that Nous's intellect was behind it all. Though at this point he couldn't say for sure. The enemy's methods were ingenious, but a person with the right background should be able to plan for them.

"To get back to what we were talking about," the liaison said. "If we have the FBI mobilize the Japanese police, we can get the contract with the provider canceled. What should we do?"

Rubens agreed. Unless they eliminated any uncertainties, the mission could spin out of control. "Do it," he said.

A few days later Rubens received an update. Soon after they took away the IP address that had been assigned to the missing person, the coded messages between the Congo and Japan started up again. They were using an IP address under another name now. Rubens understood how they'd blown it. Not only had they failed to stop the transmissions, they'd also alerted their opponent to their presence.

"Should we try again?"

"No; it'll just be a repeat. Continue intercepting the messages and do your best to decipher them."

What could be happening in the Congo and Japan? To grasp the big picture, Rubens initiated not just SIGINT—signals intelligence—but HUMINT, human intelligence. He ordered the CIA's Tokyo office, part of the US embassy, to recruit a local covert operative. He wanted to know everything there was to know about the background of this virologist, Seiji Koga. The CIA compiled a list of everyone connected with Dr. Koga, and the NSA wiretapped all their communications and selected one person who was having an extramarital affair. Using a carrot-and-stick approach—money as the carrot and proof of the affair as the stick—they persuaded this individual to cooperate. The code name of the operation was based on the profession of the operative, Scientist.

But as soon as Scientist set out to investigate, Dr. Koga died suddenly of an aneurysm. There was no question it was a natural death. The only task left was to confiscate the computers he left behind. The random number sequence that could decipher the messages he and Pierce had exchanged should still be in the hard drive.

Right then the Echelon wiretap network had a new catch. Another person was searching for the term *Heisman Report* online. That person was Seiji Koga's son, Kento Koga. And this young grad student's actions were even more suspect. He'd started searching online for information on the incurable disease known as pulmonary alveolar epithelial cell sclerosis—none other than the genetic disease that Jonathan Yeager's son was suffering from.

The connection between the Congo and Japan that was about to be severed by Dr. Koga's death seemed to have been passed down to his son. The intel that the NSA had intercepted under its GAMMA classification level told this story.

Open the book you dropped a Popsicle on.

This was a message that Seiji Koga sent to his son via an automated program after his death. Dr. Koga must have anticipated a situation in which the Japanese police would stop one of the servers and take him into custody. The key to this short instruction could be found in a book that only this father and son knew about and in the message no doubt hidden inside it. Dr. Koga had foreseen the risk of electronic eavesdropping and had resorted to a simple but effective counterespionage method.

What Rubens couldn't understand were the son's actions. He'd blithely accessed the Internet, totally ignoring the possibility that he might be under surveillance by the NSA. And when Scientist was sent to approach him, the report came back that the son probably didn't know anything about his father's activities while he was still alive.

Rubens accepted this, which led him to make his second mistake. The goals of the operatives in Japan now centered on the computers Dr. Koga had left behind, and local police were sent to confiscate them, but just before they could someone had called Kento's phone to warn him. Surprisingly, this was a computer-generated voice sent from a public phone in New York. So there was someone helping Kento in America as well. The upshot was that Kento Koga shook off the police and escaped.

At this point Rubens was sure of one thing. Secret information on Operation Nemesis was being leaked, and some unidentified group linking the three countries—the Congo, the United States, and Japan—was, for reasons unknown, illegally accessing the intel. But he still couldn't fathom the group's motive. Maybe they wanted to save the lives of Nigel Pierce and Nous, but they'd done nothing to prevent the attack by the four mercenaries. Pygmies, with their primitive hunting weapons, were no match for the firepower of four former elite troops. Even if they were to escape, the Ituri region was filled with armed insurgents lying in wait. Survival was out of the question.

While all this was going on, Operation Guardian was steadily under way in Africa. The four operatives had completed their training, infiltrated the war zone in eastern Congo, and closed in on the area near the Kanga band's camp.

Despite these security concerns, Rubens believed the operation was still under control. The plan to assassinate Nous would succeed. Then all that would be left was, at the last minute, to change part of the strategy so that all the other people would not be eliminated, too.

And now . . .

It was 9:00 p.m. EST in the United States, 3:00 a.m. in the Democratic Republic of the Congo.

Operation Guardian was entering its final phase.

Along with the other six staff members still in the Office of Special Planning, Rubens was staring at the large screen that covered one wall. On it was a live feed from the military reconnaissance satellite in orbit over the Congo. The superzoom lens flattened out the image of the Kanga band camp as though it were a monochrome floor plan. Infrared sensors picked up body heat from whatever it photographed, and the objects appeared in gradations of white and black.

Eleven huts were arranged in a U shape. Some of the leaves covering the roofs were sparse, and the interiors were visible. Because of their body heat, the silhouettes of the people sleeping inside rose up whitely.

What made the images from this highest-security feed look kind of silly were that the images of the four Operation Guardian operatives running surveillance on their targets were on the same screen. There were two each on the north and south sides of the camp. These bodies, radiating their 98.6-degree heat, had not moved for hours as they watched the Mbuti. Rubens felt as though he were watching children intent on a game of hide-and-seek.

In the temporary lull before the operation began, Rubens pondered the leak of classified information.

The warning call from New York to Kento Koga. There was definitely a spy among them. When and how did the enemy find out about the existence of the special access program, not to mention the unknown mole? Rubens had investigated the chain of command below the president, but unless someone had hacked into the US secret communications network, it was impossible for anyone to know the outlines of Operation Nemesis.

Which meant an even more imminent threat.

Nous may have already broken their codes.

In his talk with Dr. Gardner they'd estimated the intelligence of the three-year-old to be that of an adult human. According to the intercepted message from Pierce, the child had an ability far beyond that of humans when it came to prime factorization. If he brought that mathematical genius into full play, he'd be able to decrypt not only RSA codes but one-way functions as well. Pierce, who was with Nous, had his laptop in the jungle. Even from the middle of the African continent he was able to access cyberspace.

A secure outside phone line rang from the front of the three rows of worktables. The regular check-in call from Zeta Security. Avery, the DIA rep, took the call, and he turned to Rubens, who was in the last row. "Still no go sign for the attack," he said.

Jonathan Yeager and the others must have decided to do reconnaissance on their target tonight and postpone the attack until tomorrow or later.

Thinking this was the perfect chance, Rubens printed out the document he had ready to go on his computer—Seiji Koga's monograph stating that the forty members of the Kanga band weren't infected with any kind of virus. Rubens had secretly changed the dates on the fieldwork in the report. He took the sheaf of printouts over to Eldridge's desk.

"There's still room to change the operation," he said, and Eldridge, about to leave, halted.

"An epidemiological study after Nous was born denies that the Mbuti are infected with any virus."

Eldridge looked through the report and scowled. He might hold the post of assistant secretary of defense, but he couldn't make heads or tails of the Western blot technique used in the report.

"So what are we talking about here?" he asked. "Give me the highlights."

Rubens was relieved that his reaction was what he'd expected. There was no risk now that he would scrutinize the tampered report very closely. "It shows that the genetic mutation took place in an individual, not in the group. Based on this, there's no need to eliminate the other members of the Kanga band, Nigel Pierce, or the four Guardian operatives."

"We only need to worry about Nous and his parent?"

"Correct."

Eldridge frowned as he considered this, his expression that of a politician who calculated every move he made. He rested a hand on Rubens's shoulder and guided him over to a corner of the operations center. "I'm very happy if we can avoid unnecessary bloodshed," he said. "But the only ones we can exclude from being a target are the thirty-eight remaining Pygmies. For security's sake we can't let Pierce survive. And that goes for the four operatives as well."

"But all of them have security clearances."

"The decision is final," Eldridge said, his tone uncompromising. "There's no changing it. I want all seven of them—Nous and his father, Nigel Pierce, and the others—dealt with as planned."

Rubens couldn't fathom why they insisted on killing the four operatives, though he did sense it had something to do with Warren Garrett. In the end they'd have to kill seven people. Okay, he decided. That much he was willing to accept. But that and no more. Rubens wasn't sure if he should blame himself for participating in the assassination plan or take some measure of pride in having saved the lives of thirty-eight people. Either way, he and Eldridge were able to make this decision because, obviously, they weren't the ones who would kill the operatives themselves.

Eldridge smiled to break the tension. "Tell the people on the ground there's no need to kill all the Pygmies."

Now that he'd gotten official approval from his superior Rubens wove his way through the tables to Avery's desk to let him know.

"Arthur!" someone shouted, and he turned. One of his subordinates was pointing at the screen. The four operatives were on the move. They weren't withdrawing: instead, crouched down, they were slowly and steadily closing in on the camp. At first Rubens thought it was just part of their reconnaissance, but it didn't make sense that they were all moving in tandem. This was the wrong formation for a sudden attack. As he watched for a while he realized that they were approaching the last hut from two sides. Something was wrong.

"Make sure our line to Zeta is open," Rubens commanded. "And check again whether the call sign's gone out. However they respond, command Gang two to stand down." He'd gone to all the trouble to get the mission changed, and now what were these soldiers doing?

"Roger that," Avery said, and picked up the phone.

The reconnaissance satellite transmitted real-time images of the men's movements on another continent to the command center. The figure whom Rubens judged to be Yeager lowered his assault rifle and changed to a pistol. The other three men formed a defensive circle at the front of the hut. The leaves covering the roof of the hut were too thick for the infrared sensors to see inside.

Avery pulled the receiver away from his ear and raised his voice. "Communication with Gang two has been cut off."

"What!?" As Rubens said this Yeager smoothly slipped around from the side of the hut to the front, his pistol, held in both hands, pointing toward the inside.

Rubens, stunned into silence, watched the images. If the assault had already begun it was too late to stop it. All forty people in the Kanga band were doomed.

But right then the subjects on the screen froze, as if a moving picture had become a still image.

After a few moments, Rubens could imagine the scene.

Jonathan Yeager was coming face-to-face with an intelligence that was not of this world.

He'd seen Nous.

2.

"PLEASE STAY CALM. We are not going to resist."

Nigel Pierce, holding this creature, the likes of which Yeager had never seen, pronounced each word slowly, as if whispering.

Yeager, in firing position, didn't move. He stared at this inhuman-looking creature. The breeze blowing through the night jungle silently brushed his neck.

"Would you take a look at the computer over there, in the right-hand corner?"

Yeager quickly shifted his gaze. In a corner of the bare dirt floor was a laptop. One glance told him what was on the screen—the monitoring image feed from the military reconnaissance satellite. A clear image of them surrounding the hut.

"You're being watched by the Pentagon. I want you to go back into the jungle as if nothing had happened."

Yeager looked again at the creature that had made him freeze. With its large eyes shining below its bulging forehead, the child reminded him of some goblin living in a forest.

"In two minutes the satellite will be out of range. Once that happens I'll go out to you."

Behind him Yeager heard Mick hiss, "What are you waiting for? Do it!"

"Believe me," Pierce said. "In two minutes you'll see all the proof you need."

"Proof? Proof of *what*?"

"That you'll all be killed. That the Pentagon means to wipe out all the Operation Guardian operatives."

Yeager hesitated and in that instant saw, out of the corner of his eye, Mick move into the hut. Mick raised his Glock, but Yeager instinctively knocked it away. The pistol fired, the sound a low grumble as the silencer attenuated the treble frequency. The whole thatched hut shook. The bullet passed right above Pierce's and the child's heads and into the jungle outside.

Yeager wasn't sure if Mick had meant to kill Pierce and this unknown creature or whether his grabbing for the pistol had made it go off. Either way there'd been no time to argue. Still holding on to Mick's arm, Yeager said, "Holster your weapon."

"What?"

"The satellite's watching us. It'll pick up the heat from the muzzle."

"Yeah, but . . ." Mick began, but soon fell silent.

Yeager heard loud crying. Startled, he turned his night vision goggles to the inhuman creature.

The child was crying. It clung to Pierce and was sobbing. It seemed to be afraid of the shot. It might look strange, but inside it was like any other child. Dispirited by this, Yeager was still able to analyze the situation calmly. If Pierce was going to give himself up there was no need to kidnap him.

"Fall back," Yeager commanded his team, but before he withdrew he turned to Pierce. "We'll wait thirty meters to the south. Do anything suspicious and we'll shoot."

Pierce nodded his whiskered face.

Yeager backed out of the hut, facing it, and began the pullback. Mick had stuffed the pistol in his belt and covered it with his tactical vest. Garrett and Meyers, still in contact formation, rifles at the ready, accompanied Yeager.

They moved off into the jungle, across from the clearing, to a spot where the trees covered the sky, where they wouldn't have to worry about the satellite capturing their image. Yeager ordered Garrett to initiate a diversionary tactic. "Contact Zeta," he said. "Tell them we searched for the creature we'd never seen before but didn't find it."

"Roger that."

"And tell them we plan to initiate Angel in twenty-four hours"— Angel being the call sign that the attack had begun.

Garrett lowered his backpack, took out a mil-spec laptop, and began typing in the message.

"What was inside?" Meyers asked.

"The kind of creature you've never seen before."

"What?" Meyers blurted out. "You saw it? What was it? Some kind of reptile?"

Yeager was hard put to respond, and Mick broke in. "That thing was an alien."

"What are you talking about?"

A beam of light shone out from the hut, and Nigel Pierce emerged, carrying a penlight. In his other arm he held the child. Mick held his AK–47 at the ready, prepared to fire.

"That's it there," Yeager told Meyers, though from this distance the night vision image looked no different from that of a normal child.

As the men focused on them, Pierce peered inside the hut next door, put the child inside, then gave a short whistle. From the other side of the clearing one of the dogs stood up and ran over to the tall Caucasian man. Pulling the dog along with him, Pierce, as promised, showed up at the spot where Yeager and the others were waiting.

"Why did you bring a dog?" Mick asked, clearly on his guard.

"It's a guinea pig," Pierce answered. "I'm going to pick up where I left off."

"Hold on," Yeager broke in. "Let me ask a question first. Take a seat."

Pierce looked at each of the armed men in turn, then sat his lanky frame down on the ground.

"What *is* that child? It doesn't look human."

Pierce, ever the scholar, answered crisply. "The child's brain has undergone a mutation. But it's not handicapped. A genetic mutation took place, and it has a brain superior to ours."

"Superior to ours?"

"Superior to that of anybody else on earth. The White House is afraid of the child's intellect because it can break any code, including military encryption. That's why they hired you to kill it."

"Hold on a minute," Meyers said. "A mutation caused it to have superior brainpower?"

"That's right."

"If that's true, then it's not just a child with a genetic defect. It means mankind has evolved."

"Exactly. The evolution of Homo sapiens has occurred right here, in this very region."

Meyers shook his head in apparent disbelief and was silent.

For his part, Yeager couldn't deny what the anthropologist was saying. He'd already seen part of the proof. "How did you get hold of that satellite imagery?"

"This child hacked into the system. Using my computer."

"That's impossible," Garrett interjected. "You can't hack into it that easily."

"You can. The programming language people create is vulnerable. And the child penetrated it."

"But even if he were able to access the transmissions, the information's all encrypted..." Garrett began, and stopped. "Wait. Are you telling me he broke the encryption?"

"I am. The child came up with an algorithm that can break any one-way function. I had access to US secret plans, so I was able to know all about your mission ahead of time."

"Okay," Yeager said, leading into his most important question. "But why do we have to be killed?"

"Because of why the genetic mutation occurred. The person who planned Operation Guardian took into account the possibility of viral infection. The risk that whoever came into this region would be infected with a virus that would change the brains of their descendants. In other words, the White House feared that you would become infected and that the children born to you might have genetic defects."

Children with genetic defects—Yeager frowned at the expression. That's exactly what had happened to him already.

"But this virus doesn't exist. And neither does the lethal virus that's being used as an excuse for Operation Guardian. The operation is a complete fraud. The real mission, the one that includes all of you, is code-named Nemesis."

"You said you had proof that we were going to be killed?"

Pierce nodded. "You were ordered to take some medicine after the operation," he said confidently. "You must have been issued a drug to take to combat the virus."

He was talking about the white capsules they were handed at Zeta Security. Pierce really did seem to know everything.

"Show them to me," he said.

The others hesitated, but Meyers quickly took out his waterproof case. Inside were four capsules, one for each of them.

Pierce took one. "I'm taking out an army knife, so don't shoot me, okay?" He started slicing open the end of the capsule. Amazingly, the clear capsule was actually in four layers. Inside was a smaller capsule with a minute amount of white powder packed into the cavity.

"They fixed it so it's digested slowly," Pierce explained as he took out a piece of smoked meat from his pocket and sprinkled the white powder on it. He offered it to the dog beside him, who grabbed it, chewed, and gulped it down. Immediately the dog's eyes lost their luster. It became a standing corpse: blood dribbled out of the side of its mouth, and it collapsed in a heap.

"If you'd taken the capsule, this is how you'd all end up."

The corpse of the dog lay there, unmoving. Faced with the vicious animus aimed at them, the four mercenaries were speechless.

"Cyanide?" Meyers finally asked.

"Yes. Each capsule has ten times the lethal amount."

Yeager looked up at the paramilitary CIA member. Garrett returned his gaze, and below the night vision goggles his mouth grimaced and then smiled. "You understand now how much the White House hates me."

Garrett finally believed Pierce's story. Even Yeager, with such clear evidence right in front of him, no longer trusted his country. If they'd followed orders they would have been killed. "Is our enemy America, then?"

"I'd say so," Garrett said, nodding bitterly.

The gloom lasted just a moment, replaced in Yeager by rage at how they'd been betrayed. "So what country do we belong to now?"

"None. You're just individuals now."

"Wait a second," Mick said. "Do you guys really believe him?"

"If you're saying you don't, then go ahead and take the capsule."

Mick looked down at the dead body of the dog and was silent, unable to counter.

Yeager turned to Pierce. He still had a slight doubt. "So what is your goal here?"

"For me and the child, and all of you, to get out of Africa."

The four mercenaries exchanged glances. Their focus shifted back to the reality of the tall order that was facing them.

"I assume you have a plan?"

"I have some ideas, but they're not a hundred percent sure. The White House isn't our only enemy. It's hard to predict the movements of all the armed groups swarming over this region."

"Hold on," Mick cut in again. "I can understand why we've been targeted. But if we try to escape, won't this kid and the old guy just get in the way?"

Pierce ignored the Japanese and fixed his gaze on Yeager. "If you abandon the two of us, you won't be able to save Justin."

All of them turned to look at Yeager. Yeager was angry that his son's life was being used as a bargaining chip, but he managed to appear calm. "You said there's a way to save him?"

"Yes. A friend of mine is developing a drug to treat PAECS. He should be done within a month. If Justin takes the drug he'll make a complete recovery."

If he were to be believed, then Justin would be pulled back from the very brink of death. Yeager had no other choice but to believe him. Doing nothing meant his son would die for sure. The question was whether they could get out of this region alive. As Pierce said, the White House wasn't their only enemy. Even a low estimate would put the number of armed troops operating in the Ituri region at seventy thousand. How could four soldiers break out of an encirclement like that?

"Plus," Pierce said, looking at Mick this time, "this child and I can help you. We can figure out what the Pentagon is up to. Not a bad bargain, I'd say."

The men stood there for a time, in the stillness of the jungle, about to lay their lives on the line.

Yeager had one more question for Pierce. "Do you have a secure means of communication? Can you contact other countries without being intercepted by Echelon?"

"I think so, but there are limits. We can't always pick and choose the time."

"What I want are updates on Justin's condition."

"Updates every couple of days should be no problem."

"All right," Yeager said, and turned to face the other three. "Under one condition, I'm with Pierce."

"Condition?" Pierce asked dubiously.

"I'll stay with you as long as my son's alive. If Justin dies, and I think you're a burden, then you're on your own."

Pierce apparently hadn't counted on this. For a moment he looked taken aback, but then regained his confident tone. "Sounds good. I have no problem with that. Your son will surely live."

With these words Yeager felt a warmth toward Pierce. *Your son will surely live.* In the five years he and Lydia had longed to hear this, no one had ever said it to them.

Yeager finally had found a cause he could fight for. Not a fight for country, ideology, or money. But a battle to save his son.

"I'm not going to force you to follow me," he said to the others. "Each of you should decide what's best for you."

Garrett quickly replied. "I'm with Yeager."

"Me, too," Meyers said.

Mick shrugged. "It's safer if we all go together."

Yeager nodded, happy at their decision. He turned to Pierce. "Does the child have a name?"

"Akili."

"And where are we headed?"

"To the far side of the world. It's a long trip to get out of Africa," Pierce replied. "But our final destination is Japan."

After leaving the magazine specialty library Kento followed signs to the local public library and went inside. The Heisman Report explained nothing about what his father had been up to while he was still alive. Still, he had a vague notion that he had grasped some decisive clue, as if, in the foggy distance, he could barely discern the outlines of what he was searching for.

He went through the narrow stacks to the anthropology section, where he selected a few books and took them over to the reading room. The fifth section of the Heisman Report touched on human evolution, a field Kento wasn't familiar with.

He read quickly through an introductory text on the subject and learned how human history developed after humans and chimps split off from a common ancestor. In the six million years since, many species of humans had appeared and then died out. Present-day man had first appeared some two hundred thousand years ago. At the time, other species—early man and Neanderthals—were still alive.

On the Indonesian island of Flores, until only twelve thousand years ago, there was a species of human called *Homo floresiensis*, or Flores man. These individuals were only a meter tall. Their cranial capacity was only a third of modern man's, but they were intelligent, able to use fire, make stone implements, and hunt. Kento found it surprising that modern humans had lived on the same island with *Homo floresiensis* for tens of thousands of years. In other words, for tens of thousands of years, the two species had coexisted on one island. It wasn't clear whether they had much contact with each other, but even now in Flores there were legends told of tiny people who lived in caves. But like so many species before them, Flores man died out.

Whether it was Flores man, Neanderthals, or Peking man, when all these species of humans went extinct there must have been one final survivor. This person had a mind, had feelings, and could grasp the situation he was in. He—or she—must have understood that no one else of the species remained, that he was the last and completely and utterly alone. The loneliness and despair must have been overwhelming. Kento felt his chest tighten at how miserable the person must have felt.

If even one of the warnings in the Heisman Report proved to be true, mankind would suffer the same fate. Kento returned the books to the shelves and left the library, pondering again section 5. It made sense to think that mankind was still evolving. There was no biological proof whatsoever that evolution stopped with present-day human beings.

As he walked down the streets of Setagaya, Kento pulled his copy of the Heisman Report out of his pocket. The report said that when these "superhumans" appeared they would "possess an intelligence that vastly surpasses ours." Regarding the properties of this intelligence, the report had stated, "They will have the ability to perceive a fourth dimension, to immediately grasp complex wholes; they will have a sixth sense, an infinitely developed moral consciousness—mental qualities that are incomprehensible to us."

Kento was especially struck by the fact they would be able to *grasp complex wholes*. For a scientist, such an ability was a kind of dream. Within a cell, for example, there are many signal transmissions connected to the mechanism that produces PAECS. The thousands of interconnected biochemical reactions were so complex that it was impossible for humans to grasp even the entire workings of a single cell. It was beyond human intellect.

But what if it *were* possible?

Kento suddenly came to a halt, the people behind him almost bumping into him. He stood stock-still in the middle of the street in this busy shopping district as all the clamor and noise around him faded away.

Beyond human intellect.

The words swirled around in his head. And he could hear Jeonghoon Lee's voice.

No human could create this kind of software.

If an evolved species did appear, though, wouldn't it be possible for it to create a perfect software that designed new drugs? Software that could make a three-dimensional model of the protein, design the material that would bond with it, and even correctly predict the pharmacokinetics of the drug?

He made it appear to reveal tremendously complex biological activity down to the level of molecules and electrons.

But what if GIFT didn't *appear* to show this, but actually *did* reveal this complex biological activity? Didn't this mean that the kind of evolution the Heisman Report warned about was already taking place on the earth?

Kento looked down, pushed his glasses back up his nose, and continued to ponder this. If an intellect that surpasses that of humans appeared in this world, how would a superpower like the United States cope with it? Wouldn't they try to kill it? Even if they attempted to use this superhuman intellect for their own benefit, they couldn't handle it. Not only would they be unable to control it, they risked being controlled themselves.

And what sort of actions would this "super race" take? The Heisman Report predicted that it would try to destroy the human race, but Kento wasn't convinced. First of all, our inferior intellect couldn't predict what sort of judgment this superintellectual species would make. After all, the individuals possess *mental qualities that are incomprehensible to us*. Also there was the one clue that suggested their intentions—namely, GIFT. If this truly was a complete software system created to design drugs, then it was indeed a gift to the human race. Far from destroying us, the super race would have given a boon to mankind, an invention that would save us from countless diseases. Creating this software could be their message to us that they were not our enemy.

Kento felt he was getting a little ahead of himself, so he returned to the starting point. Directly or indirectly his father must have come into contact with this superhuman intelligence and gotten hold of GIFT. And if the United States had then gotten wise to this and moved to stop it, everything that had happened would make perfect sense. But in order to prove his hypothesis Kento would need to get evidence that this super race actually existed.

But how?

Kento racked his brains and finally came up with an answer. If he used GIFT and actually produced a drug that would cure pulmonary alveolar epithelial cell sclerosis, this would be at least indirect corroboration that this new species actually existed. Human beings, at their present state of knowledge, weren't capable of creating software like that—software that was perfect.

But to produce this drug he would need reinforcements. He'd have to get that brilliant Korean exchange student to help out. As he tried to figure out a way to get in touch with Jeong-hoon Lee, Kento realized he still was in luck.

"Kento? What's up?" Doi's relaxed voice on the other end of the line gave Kento a touch of hope. "The caller ID said 'unavailable,' so I was wondering who it was."

"My cell phone's broken. I wanted to ask you—have you been hearing any strange rumors?"

"Strange rumors? What do you mean?"

"It's okay. If you don't have any idea what I'm talking about, that's fine."

Doi still hadn't heard about the police investigation. The police hadn't traced who among the other grad students were Kento's friends, so they wouldn't have found out yet about Jeong-hoon Lee.

"Oh—you're calling about that, huh?" Doi suddenly said, startling Kento.

"That?"

"That girl in the humanities."

He meant Marina Kawai. "I wish I were, but no."

"If you buy me lunch I'll let her know you'd like to go on a date."

Set up a date? This was hardly the time. He was on the run from the law, for God's sake. "No, that won't work."

"Really? If not lunch, how about a coffee?"

"No. I'm really busy now and can't take the time. Okay, I'll see you."

"Hold on. Is that all you called about?"

"Yeah." Doi seemed less than convinced, so Kento added, "Don't tell anybody I called, okay? I'll fill you in on everything pretty soon."

"Got it," Doi said, his tone showing he didn't get it at all. "Whenever you feel like buying me lunch, give me a call."

"Okay."

Kento hung up, shook off the mental picture of Marina Kawai, and looked back at the list of phone numbers he'd written down. He punched in a number, hoping the call would go through, and heard the voice he'd been waiting for.

"Hello?"

"Jeong-hoon? This is Kento Koga."

"Oh!" Jeong-hoon exclaimed, which put Kento on his guard. Had something bad happened?

"Did you hear the message I left you?" Jeong-hoon said excitedly.

"No. Did something happen?"

"It's about GIFT. I tested the program. Pretty thoroughly."

"And?"

Jeong-hoon hesitated a moment. "Don't laugh when I say this, but that program is for real."

Though he'd expected this, Kento still couldn't help but be surprised. He paused to take a breath. "How did you verify that?"

"Our lab is doing joint research now with a pharmaceuticals company. I inputted the chemical structure of the new drug we're working on into GIFT so it could predict the results. And it got everything absolutely correct, including the side effects. We haven't published this data anywhere, so GIFT calculated this all on its own. It's the same as if we'd experimentally verified GIFT's predictions."

"Did you just try one compound?"

"No. I tried two lead compounds and ten derivatives, and all the data on structure-activity relationship was within the margin of error. It can't just be a coincidence."

"Jeong-hoon," Kento said, trying to keep his voice from rising in pitch. "What's your schedule tonight?"

"I can leave the lab at six."

"It's a little far, but could you come to Machida?"

"Machida? Where's that?"

Kento told him where it was, on the other side of Tokyo. "I have my motorcycle," Jeong-hoon said, "so it shouldn't be a problem."

"Just be careful you're not being tailed."

"Tailed?"

"That nobody's following you." Kento decided it was only fair to let Jeong-hoon know of the risk he was taking. "I have to apologize in advance, but we're getting into something pretty risky here."

"What do you mean?"

"Worst-case scenario, the police will grab you and kick you out of Japan."

On the other end of the line Jeong-hoon was speechless.

"If you don't mind the risk, then I'd really like you to come over."

After a moment Jeong-hoon asked, "That's the worst case?"

"Yeah."

"And the best case?"

"We save the lives of one hundred thousand children."

"I see," Jeong-hoon said, his voice upbeat again. "I'll be there."

3.

WHILE HE WAS waiting for his superiors to arrive, Rubens stayed in the little conference room off the main operations center and reviewed the material they had on the mission.

First was the NSA intercept of Kento Koga's communications. Kento had accessed an online protein data bank and done a BLAST search for "mutant GPR769." Next he'd phoned someone named Yoshihara and asked to see him. His goal was to gather information on pulmonary alveolar epithelial cell sclerosis. According to the CIA, Yoshihara was an intern at a university hospital.

Then there was the call from a public phone in New York, the warning call to Kento. The NSA had scrutinized the synthetic message, which used an artificial voice, and concluded that the Japanese was unnatural. The meaning was clear enough, but the sentences sounded odd to a native speaker. NSA linguists soon cleared up this mystery. They inputted English sentences into commercial translation software and came up with exactly the same Japanese sentences. Most likely the person who sent the warning to Kento Koga didn't know Japanese and had the software translate some simple sentences. The question was, who was this person? And why had he accessed Operation Nemesis?

Rubens looked through the last report, a list of private defense contractors killed by insurgents in Iraq. Included in the list were fifteen operatives who should have been chosen for Operation Guardian. Since the candidates had, one after another, been killed, the other members—other than Warren Garrett, who'd been at the bottom of the list—moved up. Three of them had reached the top: Jonathan Yeager, Mikihiko Kashiwabara, and Scott Meyers.

The White House had begun to view these precise attacks by Iraqi

237

insurgents with some alarm. The enemy lay in wait along the routes the military contractors took. But how were they getting hold of the details of top-secret operations? Could someone be intercepting and decrypting American military communications?

For a while Rubens turned his attention to these attacks in Iraq—to one incident in particular, in which four military contractors were slaughtered in a provincial city. These former Special Forces ops were ambushed in the street and shot and killed at close range. People nearby, ordinary Iraqis whose worsening feelings for Americans exploded into rage, had shouted out a chorus of *Allahu akbar!* Military contractors operated outside the bounds of law, so they could, and did, kill ordinary Iraqi citizens with impunity. And this domineering attitude helped spur anti-US sentiment. The corpse of one of the Americans was kicked so badly the head was wrenched off, while another was hung from a bridge on the main highway.

The United States was merciless in its response to this atrocity. Along with the Iraqi army, they formed a joint strike force of eight thousand troops and conducted a general attack on this city, which was a hotbed of insurgent activity. A fierce urban battle ensued, in which eighteen hundred soldiers and civilians died to avenge the death of the four contractors. On top of this, the United States used several depleted uranium bombs, the radiation from which would no doubt produce a sharp rise in cancer and deformities in children. All this was done by creatures who boasted that they possessed the highest intelligence on the planet.

"Did something happen?" Rubens turned at the sound of the calm voice and saw Dr. Gardner standing at the door. He'd been called to the operations center in the middle of the night and was dressed casually, without a tie.

Rubens waited until the science adviser had seated himself across the table. "Are we maybe underestimating Nous's intelligence?"

From the question, Gardner knew a critical problem had arisen. His gentle eyes stiffened. "It's not beyond the realm of possibility. At this point we can't say anything definite about Nous's intelligence. It's all speculation."

"So you wouldn't deny the possibility that his intelligence already exceeds that of modern man?"

Gardner nodded. "Or that he shows an extraordinary ability in a particular area. As with total factorization."

"How about other areas?"

"We should go back to the Heisman Report," Gardner said, linking his hands behind his head and gazing up at the ceiling. "The hypothetical abilities quoted for this super race in the report—the *ability to perceive a fourth dimension* and *a sixth sense*—these are all nonsense. If Nous tries to think about the fourth dimension and beyond he'll still have to depend on mathematical abstractions. And a sixth sense is the realm of the occult. As a scientist I have nothing to say about that."

Rubens felt the same way.

"And about this *infinitely developed moral consciousness*, anyone with that would be like God. This isn't an issue scientists debate."

Again, Rubens agreed.

"What is correct, though, are the two remaining points. First, *mental qualities that are incomprehensible to us*. It's natural that humans won't be able to understand Nous's thought process and emotions. If the shape of the brain changes, so, too, does mentality and thoughts. And then..."

Gardner shifted in his chair and leaned forward over the table. "The last point is the one we really need to watch out for."

Rubens was happy to know that he and the science adviser saw things the same way. "The ability to *immediately grasp complex wholes*?" he asked.

"Exactly. This short phrase says a lot. Skepticism about reductionism, the ability to foresee people's confusion in the face of chaos. The kind of ability scientists of the second half of the last century hoped the next generation would have. But didn't you study this field?"

"At the Santa Fe institute I did research on complex adaptive systems, so I'm familiar with the subject."

"If Nous has the ability to *immediately grasp complex wholes*, what, precisely, would he be capable of?"

"He might be able to predict conditions that we see as unpredictable—what we label chaos. In other words, there would be a further paradigm shift in the field of complex systems." As he spoke Rubens became acutely aware of how markedly different this next generation of human was from present-day man. "If so, he could construct accurate simulation models for all kinds of things, not just natural phenomena but psychological and social phenomena. Specifically, there would be a dramatic leap in understanding of biological phenomena and much more accurate forecasts of economic trends, earthquakes, long-range weather predictions, and the like."

"So as we speak Nous might be able to tell us accurately what the weather will be like ten years from now."

"That's one example, yes."

"If Nous were to acquire those kinds of abilities, would we be able to understand his thinking? Say he were to write an explanation of weather forecasts; would we be able to follow it?"

Though caught off guard by this sharp question, Rubens didn't hesitate. "I think it would be impossible. Nous goes beyond human intellect. Humans could never follow his thought process."

"I suppose so," Gardner said, smiling faintly. "I suppose you're correct, Arthur."

Silence settled over the small conference room. To Rubens, Gardner's smile was a mix of helplessness and liberation. Accepting the possibility of human intellectual evolution meant recognizing the limits of present-day man's intelligence. And not just intelligence. The qualities of this super race, as specified in the Heisman Report, were exactly what present-day humans lacked. Just as we are unable to *immediately grasp complex wholes*, so, too, do we not possess an *infinitely developed moral consciousness*. This isn't a question of reason but of our behavior as living beings. Only people who have satisfied their appetites for food and sex talk about world peace. But put them in a situation where they're starving, and their hidden, true selves will come to the fore. As the Chinese philosopher Xunzi proclaimed in the third century BCE, we are creatures who "will always fight when we lack something."

As long as human history continues, the longing for peace will be delayed. There is always conflict somewhere in the world between peoples. The only way to eradicate atrocities is to eradicate humans and leave what follows to the next generation of beings.

A question arose in Rubens's mind. Was Nous more moral than humans? Or more cruel? Would he permit an intellectually inferior race to coexist with him, or would he set out to wipe us out? Even if he allowed us to coexist, we would still be under his control. Just as people now protect endangered animal species, these superhumans would keep a few of us around, under their watchful eye.

There was a knock at the door, and Eldridge, director of the operation, came in, along with the military adviser, Colonel Stokes. Eldridge had on casual clothes, a jacket over a turtleneck sweater, but Stokes was in full military uniform.

"I already updated Colonel Stokes on the situation," Eldridge said.

Stokes acknowledged that. "So the operatives have deviated from the plan."

"Correct."

"I don't think that's anything to get upset about. Special Forces troops are trained to adjust to the situation on the ground where needed. That's what they're doing."

Rubens debated whether he should announce his hypothesis, which was sure to shake them up, but decided to wait a little longer. "The CIA satellite imagery analyst is on his way here. We'll know more once he arrives."

Eldridge nodded. "We need to base our actions on objective evidence. We have that coded communication between the Congo and Japan. At this point we don't know its purpose. If it's done to interfere with Operation Nemesis, then it's possible our four operatives have run into something unforeseen."

"Any progress on the investigation in Japan?" Stokes asked Rubens.

"We've narrowed down the area where Kento Koga could be. He seems to be hiding in a district called Machida, and starting tomorrow we'll be watching the local train station. Our assets in Japan, though, are limited, and other investigations are not going as well as we'd hoped."

"How many assets do you have?"

"We have ten full-time police officers on the ground. But they've got their hands full checking Koga's home, the university, and other possible hideouts. And we have the Tokyo CIA station chief and a local asset he's recruited."

"By local asset," Gardner asked, "do you mean the one code-named Scientist?"

"Correct."

"What's the person's background? And his relationship with Seiji Koga?"

"I don't know," Rubens replied, looking at the military adviser. "I'm leaving that up to the CIA, so I can't really say."

"To sum up, we have to be prepared if things go south," Eldridge said. "If the operation starts to get out of control, we need to move into the emergency response phase."

"What is that?" Gardner asked.

"We treat the four operatives, Nigel Pierce, and Kento Koga as terrorists. Authorities in each country take them into custody, and we place them in extraordinary rendition."

"Extraordinary rendition? Meaning..."

"Nothing you need to worry about, Professor," Eldridge said evasively.

"So-called extreme measures?"

The government official responded brusquely to Gardner's expression of simple curiosity. "These are administrative measures based on presidential policy guidelines NSD seventy-seven and PDD sixty-two. The guidelines themselves are classified. Once a memorandum of notification signed by the president arrives, the CIA takes over. Is that sufficient?"

In other words: *Don't dig any deeper.* Wisely, Gardner backed down. "Understood," he said.

For Rubens the biggest miscalculation was Kento Koga's actions. He hadn't believed a mere grad student could evade the law and successfully remain off the grid. If he had given himself up to the authorities and let them interrogate him, there was room to go easy on him. But now Eldridge was considering drastic measures. Like other DC officials, Eldridge was only worried about not blemishing his career, and he aligned himself totally with the Burns administration's way of thinking. If Kento Koga were arrested now, he'd be whisked off to one of the countries that conducted torture for the United States and would never see his family again. Rubens wanted to save him if he could, but unfortunately he wasn't in charge of secret ops in Japan. Eldridge was.

"We've covered Japan, but how about the emergency response phase in the Congo?" Gardner asked.

"If the operatives start taking unexpected action, we need to wipe them out immediately, Nigel Pierce included. We'll use the local military forces to stamp them out."

Gardner's eyes went wide. "Will these outlaws cooperate with us?"

"There's an arms dealer who operates in the area, and we'll use him to persuade them they can make a profit on this. Tell them there are five white terrorists in the Ituri jungle with a huge bounty on their heads. The military power of tens of thousands, led by their greed for money, will take care of the rest."

"But what if there really is an evolved virus? Won't the insurgents risk getting infected?"

"Rubens's report shoots down the virus theory."

Rubens could have kicked himself. The phony report he'd concocted to save Yeager and the others had backfired.

The phone on the table rang, and Rubens heard the voice of a subordinate seeking entrance to the operations center.

"Come in," Rubens said, and Diaz, a CIA agent working with Operation Nemesis, entered the room with a colleague.

"This is Frank Hewitt, who's been running imagery analysis."

The lanky young man Diaz introduced was carrying a laptop. After the usual greetings Hewitt plugged his laptop into the projector and showed an image on the main briefing screen.

"This is the most recent satellite imagery taken over the Congo," he said.

Eldridge, Stokes, and Gardner stared intently at the image. It was from inside the jungle, a monochrome scene that could have been shot during the day or night. The Operation Guardian personnel were approaching the end of the U-shaped line of huts.

"We believe this hut is Nigel Pierce's."

"Based on what?" Rubens asked.

Hewitt enlarged one section of the image. "There's a geometrical structure concealed in the hut. A solar electricity panel."

"I see." In the Congo jungle, where there was no electricity, Pierce was using solar energy to power his computer.

Using a laser pointer, Diaz highlighted the four operatives one by one. "The one with the medical kit is Meyers; Garrett's the one with the communications gear. And of the remaining two, the taller one is Yeager."

Rubens turned to the military adviser. "Colonel, what do you make of their movements?"

Stokes frowned. "They look like they're going to kidnap him rather than kill him."

As the soldiers maintained a defensive circle, Yeager half leaned inside the hut. And then all movement ceased. Ten seconds elapsed, during which nothing happened, then Kashiwabara switched to a pistol and came in beside Yeager. The two of them moved violently, as if reacting to something, but because the upper halves of their bodies were inside the huts the details weren't clear.

"Here," Hewitt said, rewinding and playing the scene over and over. "A corner of the image gives us a clue what was happening."

The view switched to the rear of the hut, where a tree was enlarged. The image was enlarged further, down to individual pixels, and the screen became a gray rectangle. "If you play this scene in slow motion, you'll see this."

It was at first a black square, then one frame glowed gray and slowly resolved itself back to black.

"The temperature of one part of the tree trunk went up for an instant. This isn't a natural phenomenon. A red-hot flying object bored into the trunk."

"Meaning?" Eldridge said impatiently.

"From the movements of the two men in the hut, it appears that Kashiwabara fired his weapon, Yeager interfered, and the shot missed its intended target. I can't determine the precise path of the bullet, but I would estimate a thirty-degree upward angle. Also, when Kashiwabara exited the hut, his pistol was not in his holster but hidden away. I think he did this because they realized they were being observed by infrared satellite."

"Why did they realize they were being observed?" Stokes asked dubiously.

Eldridge looked flustered and glanced over at the brilliant person who'd come up with the operation.

Rubens knew the situation was spiraling out of control. The satellite imagery was being hacked. The United States was already facing a huge national security threat. And that was not all. The Burns administration had fallen right into the trap. They weren't the ones controlling this top-secret operation. Nous was. Rubens ordered Diaz and Hewitt out of the room and sat there in silent contemplation, elbows on the table, his head in his hands.

Operation Nemesis had begun with Nigel Pierce's e-mail. When he sent it he must have known that it would be intercepted by Echelon. The point was to see how the White House would react to news of the next stage in human evolution. Pierce and Nous, surrounded as they were by hostile armed forces in the depths of the Congo jungle, must have held out hope that the American government would try to protect them.

But the Burns administration had chosen to wipe out this superhuman race, leaving Pierce and Nous with only one choice: to escape to the outside world. They had to obtain military power. But even if they wanted to hire mercenaries, the Pentagon kept watch on the activities of private defense contractors. That would be impossible. So they decided to turn to the assassins sent out on Operation Guardian.

It wouldn't be hard to persuade Warren Garrett to join them. Garrett must have already sensed that the White House wanted to get rid of him. The only way for him to survive was by betraying his employer.

There must have been a selection process at work to pick the remaining three. Candidates who didn't meet the standards were killed in Iraq, one after another. Secret US information was hacked and leaked to Muslim extremists, who then attacked the US contractors. And Yeager, Meyers, and Kashiwabara moved to the top of the list.

Rubens still couldn't fathom why a former US pararescue soldier and a Japanese mercenary were chosen. Yeager, however, was easy to figure out. Kento Koga's actions made it clear: the former Green Beret member was told there was a cure for PAECS. In exchange for saving his son from the disease, Yeager turned against his own country.

Behind this plan lay a network linking Pierce in the Congo with Japan and America. Seiji Koga had met Pierce while conducting virology fieldwork in Zaire and was drawn into the plan. After his death, his son, Kento, carried on the work developing a drug to treat the disease. But no matter how much Nous's intellect was involved in this, it was debatable whether a cure for PAECS could be found. There just wasn't enough time.

Unable to stand the silence any longer, Eldridge spoke up. "What are you thinking about?"

Rubens hesitated. What should he tell him, and what should he hide? What should he do to minimize the casualties? With the mercenaries now won over to Nous's side, helping rescue them meant letting Nous survive. But wouldn't that put the United States, and all mankind, in danger?

Dawn in the jungle was chilly.

Voices filtered out from the line of huts in the fog-shrouded Kanga camp, but no one was outside yet. The Pygmies must be warming themselves inside, for lines of smoke drifted up from the thatched roofs.

While it was still dark, the soldiers of Operation Nemesis had gone back deep into the jungle to retrieve their backpacks, so they had only been able to nap a short time. But for Yeager something else besides the lack of sleep kept his body chilled—concern about his son. A week had passed since he'd last had news from Lydia.

"Guardian sure is the perfect name for this operation," Garrett said as he laid his equipment down under a tree. "We've definitely become guardians. Of that anthropologist and that Akili kid."

And guardians of my child, too, Yeager thought.

"I can't wait to meet Akili," Meyers said innocently.

"You'll be disappointed," Mick replied coldly. "He's creepy."

"What—do you hate kids or something?" Yeager said, teasing him.

"That thing's not human."

"No; I'm talking about human children."

Mick stared at Yeager, trying to discern the reason behind the question. "I hate weak people. People who get hit and don't hit back and just cry. They make me sick."

"I bet you were like that when you were a kid."

Mick's eyes flashed hatred for an instant before his usual thin smile returned. "No. I got back at them real good. After I became an adult, I mean."

Yeager understood now about this dark shadow that possessed Mick. In order to not cry when he was beaten, to be able to hit those who abused him, Mick must have turned to steroids to bulk up and then later gone overseas to train as a soldier. Only someone who had been terribly abused and hurt as a child would go to such extremes.

Footsteps sounded, and a tall man's silhouette loomed out of the fog, coming toward them. But the mercenaries' eyes were drawn to the tiny figure walking beside Pierce. All Akili wore was a pair of makeshift shorts, so they could see his whole body. From the neck down he was a typical three-year-old child. But his eyes and that massive, swollen forehead were not human. Those eyes that had frozen Yeager with their piercing look the night before were still, even first thing in the morning, as forceful as ever. This grotesque child, holding Pierce's hand, its head swaying back and forth as it walked, looked unreal, like some monster from the movies.

"Cuter than I expected," Meyers said.

The other three looked at him. "You're kidding, right?"

"No, I'm not. His eyes are like a cat's."

They were catlike, come to think of it, but Yeager didn't see anything cute about it. In front of Akili he felt the same discomfort he experienced when shown some grandiose religious painting and forced to feel awe in front of it. "Give me dogs any day."

"Yeah, you're right. He does sort of remind me of a cat," Garrett said. "He seems like he's seeing right through me. Maybe he's more like a lion than a cat."

"Definitely a lion," Mick said in a low voice. "That kid is dangerous. We should get rid of him."

"Don't get any ideas," Yeager cautioned.

"Good morning," Pierce said cheerfully as he came up to the group. "Gentlemen, let me introduce Akili."

The men crouched down and peered at the boy, who stared back with upturned eyes and a stern expression. Pierce told him the names of his new guardians, the mercenaries, one by one, but Akili's expression didn't soften.

"Does he know English?" Garrett asked.

"He understands it, but his pharynx hasn't fully developed, so he can't speak yet." Pierce showed them the laptop he had tucked under his arm. "When he wants to say something he types it out on the keyboard."

This form of communication seemed particularly out of place where they were—deep in the jungle, in essentially uncharted territory. "Akili," Yeager said, speaking directly to him. "Is what Pierce says true?"

Akili immediately nodded. The other men, taken by surprise, called out in amazement.

"Can you really break codes?" Garrett asked.

Again Akili nodded.

"How?"

Akili looked up at Pierce and motioned for the laptop. The anthropologist handed it to him, and Akili's tiny hands began to move. As he typed, using two fingers, letters appeared on the display.

Even if I explained how I break codes you wouldn't be able to understand.

A wry smile came to Garrett's face. "Doesn't give us much credit, does he?"

As he watched Akili's movements, Yeager felt a vague doubt rise in his mind. The boy's typing was so slow. In addition to the question of whether the child had the intellect to hack the military communications network, these dull, sluggish movements raised doubts about whether it was physically possible. "Can you cure PAECS?"

Akili nodded.

"How do you treat it?"

Akili answered using the laptop screen. First I create software to develop a drug, use that software to design the drug, and then actually synthesize the compound.

"Who made the software?"

I did.

Yeager considered this. Was it possible that Akili had been drilled to just type in preset responses, a series of letters, to certain questions and answers?

"There's one last thing I'd like to confirm," Garrett asked, seeking Yeager's permission. "I want to corroborate what Pierce is saying."

"What do you have in mind?" Pierce asked.

"Can you get all the people together?"

"What for?"

"If you want us to protect you, just do what I say."

Pierce looked none too happy, but he turned toward the camp and yelled out something in the local language.

People began to come out, looking toward them to see what was going on.

Yeager and the others went over to the middle of the central clearing of the camp to wait for the Pygmies. The forty-some people approached, seemingly not on their guard. The Pygmies, who only came up to the mercenaries' chests, smiled bashfully.

Karibu, many of them said, and when Meyers, not knowing what it meant, repeated the word, they burst out laughing.

"*Karibu* means 'welcome,'" Pierce explained. "*Habari* means 'hello.'"

When Yeager and the men said *habari*, the Mbuti faces grew even more cheerful, and they repeated the greeting back.

"I told them you're friends."

Garrett looked around the assembled group and slowly began speaking to them in what sounded like Swahili. The CIA agent had been the first to be selected for Operation Guardian and had apparently drilled himself in the lingua franca of the region.

"Does anyone speak Swahili?" he seemed to be asking. Half the people raised their hands. Garrett continued questioning them, then beckoned to one man. The man, who looked to be about thirty, had a sad expression. He was wearing a worn-out T-shirt and shorts and was just over 140 centimeters tall, about average size for an Mbuti.

"His name is Esimo. He says he's Akili's father."

After Garrett's explanation, Yeager and the others looked intently at the little man. Other than the fact that he was far shorter than Westerners, he looked like an ordinary person.

"I have something I want to ask, too," Meyers said. "Can you ask him if Akili has any siblings?"

Garrett nodded and asked Esimo in Swahili. Accompanied by various gestures, Esimo began relating his story—a sad one, judging by the expression on his face. Garrett seemed to have trouble completely following him, and after much back and forth was finally able to translate.

"He doesn't have any siblings. Esimo's first wife got sick when she was pregnant. He asked the *mzungu*—white doctors—to cure her, and they took her to a hospital far away. But she never came back. She apparently died."

"Mzungu, mzungu," Esimo repeated, pointing at Mick. To him Asians and Caucasians were apparently in the same category.

"Then Esimo's younger brother was bitten by a poisonous snake and died, so he took his brother's wife as his own. That was Akili's mother. But right after Akili was born she had terrible hemorrhaging, and she died."

Esimo's melancholy expression must be the product of the cruel reality his primitive society had exposed him to. Without access to medical care he'd lost two wives and his younger brother as well as what would have been his first child.

"After that Esimo remained without a wife. Akili is his only child."

"I wonder if both wives died because of the fetus," Meyers said. "If that's true then the chances are high that the brain mutation must be from the father's genetic background. There was a mutation in Esimo's reproductive cells, and this was passed along to his child."

Mick smiled coldly. "A child who has an abnormal father will suffer."

"Listen. This is important. If the mutation is really from the father's genes, then Akili won't be the only one they're after. They'll try to eliminate his father, too. Because if he had any more children they might have the same mutation."

"No need to worry about that," Pierce said. "When we leave here the Kanga band will vanish. The forty people here will scatter and join other bands. They don't have to register their residence, so there's no need to worry about Akili's father."

Esimo broke in in a loud voice, urgently repeating two words, *kuweri* and *ekoni*. Garrett had to ask him several times what he meant and finally was able to translate.

"He insists that Akili was born that way because of food. He said that when his wife was pregnant she ate an animal she shouldn't have."

"That's impossible," Meyers said.

Garrett looked up and addressed the Pygmies in Swahili. When this message was translated into their local language, people began talking loudly. The circle around Garrett grew tighter as people pressed in closer. Yeager didn't know what they were saying, but to him the Pygmies' facial expressions seemed exaggerated.

Garrett listened to each in turn and explained what they were saying. "I asked them about Akili. All of them feel he's not an ordinary human. Not just his looks, but his abilities."

"Like what, for instance?" Yeager asked.

"He learns languages really fast. Not just Kimbuti, their language, but Swahili and Kingwana, a dialect of Swahili. And he understands English, too. And during the rainy season, when the band lives close to a farming village, that was all it took for him to master arithmetic. Thanks to which the band is no longer cheated when they sell meat to the farmers, the Bila people."

"Wouldn't any bright child be able to do that?"

"There's more. It's kind of strange . . ." Garrett paused, unsure how to continue. "Akili has a weird ability to manipulate tree leaves."

"Tree leaves? What are you talking about?"

"I don't know."

"Why don't we ask him?" Meyers said. He knelt down in front of Akili. "Did you hear what we were talking about?"

Akili nodded.

"What is this about manipulating leaves? Can you show us?"

Akili's expression changed. His eyelids narrowed, and the corners of his tiny mouth tightened. He's smiling, Yeager noticed. Like a child who's having fun playing.

Akili drew a small circle in the dirt at his feet, picked up a fallen leaf, and stood up. He held the leaf out at arm's length, moved around the circle as if calculating something, then opened his hand and let the leaf fall. The leaf fluttered in the air and came to rest in the exact middle of the circle he'd drawn.

It took Yeager and the others a moment to realize how mysterious the phenomenon they had just witnessed really was. Meyers picked up the leaf and tried dropping it. The leaf was tossed about in the unpredictable currents of air and wound up a good meter away from the target.

"How can you do that?" Meyers asked incredulously.

Akili typed in his answer on the keyboard. I understand the movements of the leaf.

All I can say is I understand.

Not a convincing explanation, but it was clear that Akili possessed a strange ability unlike anything they'd ever known. Humans had sent men to the moon but couldn't predict the flight of a falling leaf.

"Gentlemen, can we wrap this up?" Pierce asked, switching screens on his computer. "The reconnaissance satellite will be in range in five minutes."

The mercenaries, not completely satisfied, exchanged glances.

"I think we have to trust you," Garrett said. "If we'd taken that medicine we'd all be dead."

The others had to agree with that, and they set off toward the jungle.

Pierce stayed behind, giving instructions to the Pygmies, probably telling them to just act normally. The Mbuti went back to their huts and soon started fires outside so that they could cook breakfast.

In the jungle, out of sight of the satellite, the four operatives met up with Pierce, Esimo, and Akili.

"I'd like to set off right after breakfast," Pierce said. "Can you show me your map?"

Yeager took out his map and laid it in front of them. "Here's what I suggest. Operation Nemesis has been meticulously planned, but they've only devised an emergency plan for inside the Congo. If we can get over the border—that's like the end zone in football. We'll try to break through, to get out of the country. Of course the enemy will do everything it can to prevent us from escaping."

Their present position was in the eastern region of the Congo, only 130 kilometers from the Ugandan border, a distance they should be able to traverse in four days. The problem was the twenty-some armed groups stationed at all points along the border. It would be a fierce struggle from the five-yard line, as it were, to the end zone.

"Have you decided on a route to the border?" Yeager asked.

"Several," Pierce said. "We'll choose the best route based on the situation at the time."

Pointing to the map, Pierce outlined three possible escape routes, all aiming for the eastern border of the Congo. The first went straight east, to the town of Bunia; the second went southeast, past a town called Beni and over the border to Uganda; and the third went south, near

Goma, and then over to Rwanda. Any other routes were out of the question. If they went west, the huge size of the country itself would prevent their escape.

"What do you think?"

"I agree we should go east, but we don't have much time," Yeager replied. "We only have five days' worth of rations left. We could survive by hunting, but that would take up most of the day. We'd never escape."

"That shouldn't be a problem. I'm not saying it's a hundred percent sure thing, but we've arranged supplies and transportation at spots along the way."

"Are you serious?" Garrett said, impressed. "But remember, that's not all we have to worry about. The more time passes, the more countermeasures the Pentagon will come up with. If there's any delay at all it'll just make it harder for us to fight back."

"Then let's take the shortest route. We'll set a course due east. Just before Bunia we have a car waiting, in a town called Komanda. Considering the road, it should take less time than going southeast. We'll be on foot until we reach Komanda."

One hundred kilometers—a three-day march. "Contact Zeta," Yeager said to Garrett. "Tell them Meyers has contracted malaria and that Angel will be postponed."

"Roger that."

They still had five days left on the Operation Guardian schedule. If they could deceive the Pentagon they should be able to escape the Congo before anyone noticed. "I want all of you to turn off your GPS before we leave this camp. Otherwise they'll know our position."

Mick immediately objected. "How are we supposed to navigate? There aren't any landmarks in the jungle. We're supposed to find a spot a hundred kilometers away with just a compass and pacing it out?"

"Esimo will be with us part of the way," Pierce said.

"Esimo?"

As everyone stared down at him, Akili's father smiled modestly.

"That's even worse. The guy doesn't even have a compass."

"Esimo knows the jungle best," Pierce said sternly. "A lot more than you do."

"Don't complain. You'll be able to go home," Meyers scolded Mick.

He turned to Pierce. "You said Japan's our final destination. After we get out of the Congo, how are we supposed to get there?"

"I have a couple of ideas, but at this point it's premature to decide on a route. I want you to do everything you can to get us past the border first. That's the biggest obstacle we face right now."

"Got it."

Yeager glanced at his watch. "We'll leave at oh six hundred. Finish eating by then. And don't forget about the satellite overhead."

Just as they were breaking up they heard an electric buzz. Pierce took a small computer out of a waist pack. This was a different computer from the one he used to communicate with Akili. The black computer was linked to his satellite phone.

As he stared at the display, Pierce's face gradually clouded over.

"E-mail?" Garrett asked. "From who?"

"Don't ask."

"You have somebody abroad helping you out?"

"I can't give you the name, but yes, we have somebody providing information."

"What did he say?"

"The enemy forces are stronger than we expected. And they've already noticed what we're up to." Pierce shut the display. "Operation Nemesis has entered the emergency response phase. We've all been designated terrorists, and there's a ten-million-dollar bounty on our heads. All the insurgent groups in this region will be out to get us now."

But not one of the Operation Guardian soldiers was shaken by the news.

"Can we change our escape route to the south?" Meyers asked.

"Negative," Garrett said, shaking his head. "There are forces that control the south, too. If we head there they'll get us from both sides."

Garrett unfolded the map and studied it. "The eastern border is a good hundred kilometers long. Even with tens of thousands of troops that guard it we should be able to find a way through. We'll stick to the plan and head east."

"Mr. Yoshinobu Suzuki, please come to the seventh-floor counter."

The announcement was repeated so many times it was getting annoying. Kento was standing in a huge bookstore in Shinjuku, one that boasted the largest selection of any bookstore in Tokyo. Tonight, as soon as Jeong-hoon arrived at his place, they would begin development of the drug to treat PAECS, and he was searching for some specialized texts. With the university library off-limits to him, he needed to get the reference materials they would need to develop the drug.

"Mr. Yoshinobu Suzuki..."

The thick scholarly books were all expensive. But money was no object for him now, and he could buy any books he needed, thanks to the ATM card under the name of Yoshinobu Suzuki.

"Would Mr. Yoshinobu Suzuki please come to the seventh-floor counter?"

Startled, Kento looked up.

Yoshinobu Suzuki?

Suzuki was a common enough last name, but it couldn't be a coincidence that the first name was the same. Somebody was paging him.

But *who?*

Was it a police trap? Kento was about to dash away when he realized that a trap made no sense. The police wouldn't know he had an ATM card under that name. If they did they would have frozen the account so he couldn't withdraw cash. And one other thing was odd—being paged here meant that whoever it was knew he was here, in this bookstore. If they were detectives, wouldn't they just arrest him?

Kento tried to calm down. The chain of events that had occurred after the first message from his father had all followed a rigorous logic. If there were a third party who knew the name Yoshinobu Suzuki, then this had to be someone with inside knowledge of what his father had been planning.

Maybe I have an ally, Kento concluded. Maybe it's the same person who warned me to get out of my apartment the morning the detectives stormed in. But there was something else Kento didn't understand about that phone call, besides what was actually said. His phone hadn't indicated UNKNOWN CALLER but OUT OF AREA. Which meant that the call was likely from abroad. That would also explain the caller's unnatural Japanese. Was this person in Japan now, trying to get in touch with him?

Kento returned the book he was looking at to the shelf. Whoever had paged him must be counting on him to decide that it wasn't a detective.

The full bookshelves blocked his view of the store. Kento left the pharmacology section and walked toward the checkout counter, doing his best to act calm and casual. From between the bookshelves he could see only clerks at the counter, no other customers.

One of the uniformed women at the counter glanced at her watch, went over to a microphone, and began speaking into it. "Mr. Yoshinobu Suzuki. Mr. Yoshinobu Suzuki—"

Kento made up his mind and walked over to the counter.

"My name is Suzuki," he said, and the clerk at the microphone turned around.

"Oh, Mr. Suzuki. We found something you lost."

"Lost?"

"Isn't this yours?" she said, holding out a cell phone.

"I'm sorry, but I had to open it to see whose it was," the woman said, indicating the screen. The profile column listed a cell phone number, e-mail address, and the name Yoshinobu Suzuki in Chinese characters. "I haven't looked at anything else, of course."

"Thank you very much," Kento said. He knew he had to react normally to this unexpected event. "Where was it?"

"In front of the organic chemistry shelf."

"Who found it?"

"We did."

"It was on the floor?"

"Yes."

"Thank you. I appreciate it."

Kento reached out to take the phone, but before he could the clerk said, "Just to make sure, do you have any identification to verify your name?"

"My name?" It took everything he had not to show his distress. "My name... Well, all I have on me right now is an ATM card."

"That would be fine."

Kento took the cash card out of his wallet and showed it to her.

"Thank you," the woman said with a smile, and handed him the cell phone.

Kento went to the register next to the counter and paid for his books. As he headed for the elevator he broke out in a cold sweat. He had to get out of this building as soon as he could, go to a coffee shop somewhere, and check out this phone. Why would someone go to all this trouble?

Just then the phone rang shrilly, and he nearly jumped out of his skin.

The name on the incoming call was POPPY—his dog when he was a child. Whoever was calling was telling him he was on his side. Kento hurried over to the entrance to the staircase beside the elevator and took the call.

"Hello?"

"Is this Kento?" an eerie voice asked. The voice was low, the frequency changed by a machine, sounding like it was rumbling up from the bowels of the earth. "I'm going to tell you something very important right now, so listen carefully to every word."

Kento didn't dare ask who it was. The person's Japanese was fluent, so it wasn't a foreigner. Apparently he had two collaborators, one in Japan and one abroad.

"Don't worry about this phone being tapped. Go ahead and use it as you'd like."

This person must have seen him getting the "lost" phone. He was here in this building. Kento leaned out and scanned the bookstore floor but didn't see any customers using cell phones.

"However," the low voice went on, "when you do make a call, choose the person carefully. It's dangerous to call your family and friends. Your call will be traced from their phones."

"Then there isn't much point in having it, is there?"

"No—there is a point. I can contact you anytime."

"You're on my side?"

"That's right." Despite the abnormal, machine-generated voice, Kento could sense an intimacy in its tone.

"What is your name?"

"Poppy," the voice said with a chuckle.

"Can I ask you a question?"

"It depends."

Kento cupped his hand around the phone and spoke in a low voice. "Is section five of the Heisman Report actually happening now?"

"A very good question. You're a quick study. So you've read the report?"

"Yes."

"What I just said was the answer to your question."

Kento took this as an affirmative.

"Leave the phone on at all times so you can receive calls. Even when you're sleeping. Understand?"

"Okay."

"And when you go out from the lab in Machida, never take the train. Starting tomorrow detectives will be watching the turnstiles at the station."

Kento shuddered. They were closing in. But how had they tracked him? It must have been the smart card issued by the railroad company, which he'd used when he rode the trains. He would have to question everything around him now if he wanted to stay safe. "If I can't use the train, then how should I get around?"

"Taxis are safe. You have plenty of money. Stay away from other places as well. Not just Machida station, but keep away from your apartment, the university campus, the university hospital, and your parents' home. The police are staking out those places. There are ten detectives searching for you now. Do you understand?"

"I understand."

"I'll get in touch again. I'll give you instructions soon on how to use the small laptop."

"Small laptop? The black one that won't turn on?"

But the person had already hung up. Kento opened the phone's contacts list. There was only one person listed: Poppy. He hit the dial button, but the person had already turned off his phone. Looking around the bookstore for Poppy wouldn't help, because he didn't know what he looked like. All he could do was wait until Poppy called again about the black laptop.

But why did the person hide his real voice? Was it someone whose voice he'd recognize? Someone he knew?

Kento walked down the stairs and out onto the streets of Shinjuku. Just getting a telecommunications device was all it took to pull him out of his isolation and reconnect him with the world, and he felt a wave of relief.

As he walked down the main street he decided he should phone the people he'd been postponing calling. He took out the memo on which he'd written all the phone numbers. Before he called anyone, though, he mentally checked, as Poppy had told him, whom it would be safe to call. Had the police found out yet about his connection with Sugai, the newspaper reporter? He thought it was probably okay to call him, but as he was passing by a phone booth he decided to play it safe and call him from there.

He inserted the coin and dialed the number, but Sugai didn't answer right away, as he usually did. The phone rang ten times before he heard the familiar voice.

"Hi, this is Kento."

"Ah, Kento."

He could hear, faintly in the background, the sound of a crowd. "Mr. Sugai, where are you now?"

"I've gone out," his father's old friend said. "But it's fine to call me. You wanted to know about that woman researcher, Yuri Sakai?"

"Did you find out anything about her?"

"I'm not sure this is whom you want, but I found only one person who's the right age. In the Tokyo Medical Society list of members there is someone with the same first and last names."

"She's a doctor?" Kento remembered the woman who'd approached him outside the dark campus. A not-very-memorable face, no makeup, a sort of fresh, neat appearance. He could imagine her being a doctor.

"In the phone book there was an ad for a medical facility she was running. Apparently a small clinic she and her father operated."

"What is her area of specialty?"

"OB-GYN."

That was unexpected. If it had been internal medicine or cardiology, then he could see her having something to do with PAECS. "If I go to that medical facility, then, I can meet her?"

"No. Her name was in the Medical Society members' list eight years ago. But not after that. It seems she left the society and shut down the clinic."

"What happened?"

"I have no idea. I'll look into it more. With any luck I'll find out what the connection was between her and your father."

"Sorry for all the trouble," Kento said. He was encouraged by the support Sugai provided. "I really want to thank you so much for all your help."

"Why so formal?" Sugai asked with a laugh, and after they said good-bye, he hung up.

Kento exited the phone booth and walked toward Shinjuku station. Was there some other way of finding out more about Yuri Sakai? He could kick himself for not having memorized the license plate number of her minivan. Just then his cell phone rang.

Kento halted. The screen said OUT OF AREA, and he tensed up. A call from abroad. Perhaps the foreigner who'd warned him about the police, he thought as he slipped into a nearby alley, pushed the accept button, and held the phone to his ear.

"Hello?" a woman's voice said in English, which flustered him. For some reason Kento pictured a beautiful blonde.

"He-hello?" Kento faltered.

The woman rattled on and on, and Kento couldn't catch any of it except for the fact that she was in a panic.

Struggling to communicate in English, he repeated a typical phrase he'd learned. "Could you speak more slowly, please?"

There was a pause, and then the woman spoke. "Who are you?"

"Me? My name is Kento Koga."

"Kento? Where are you now? What I mean is, where am I calling?"

Kento thought he'd misunderstood her. "Just a minute, please. I don't understand what you're saying."

"I don't understand what I'm doing, either," the woman said, sounding like she'd calmed down now. "Kento, listen carefully. I just got a call from somebody I don't know. He told me this number and told me to call. Told me to report on my son's condition. He said if I did, you'd be able to save my son."

"I'd save your son?"

"That's right. Is he wrong?"

Suddenly one of the pieces of the puzzle fell into place in Kento's mind. *An American will show up at some point.*

"May I ask your name?"

"I'm Lydia. Lydia Yeager."

"Lydia Ayga?"

The woman slowly sounded it out for him. "It's *Yea-ger.*"

"Mrs. Yeager," Kento repeated, paying attention to the *r*. "Are you American?"

"Yes, but I'm in Lisbon right now."

Lisbon—that was where the most advanced research on PAECS was taking place. "For your child's treatment?"

"Yes. That's right!" Lydia Yeager said, raising her voice. As if she'd finally gotten her point across. And finally found the way to save her son.

"Do you know a Japanese person named Seiji Koga?" Kento asked.

"No, I don't."

"Where is your husband?"

"Jon? He's abroad for his work, and I can't contact him. I don't know if he knows that Japanese person or not."

"What is your husband's work? Does he study viruses?"

"No," Lydia said, and hesitated. "He's with a private defense contractor."

Kento had her repeat this a few times, but he still couldn't grasp what these terms meant. Something to do with the military, he concluded.

"Do you know about us?" Lydia asked. "About Jon—Jonathan Yeager? Or me? Or our son, Justin?"

Justin Yeager—Kento added the name to his list of those whose lives he could save, right after Maika Kobayashi. "No, I don't know about you. I think one of my father's friends must have brought us together. Who told you to call me?"

"An American, I think. An older man, with an East Coast accent."

Maybe he was the one who'd called Kento to warn him.

"Do you understand the situation now?" Lydia asked.

"Yes," Kento replied.

"How are you going to save my son?"

"I'm going to—develop a new drug," Kento said, and as soon as he did he felt a weight bearing down on his shoulders. If he failed at making this new medicine, the woman on the other end of the line would be beyond hope.

"And that drug will save Justin?" Lydia asked, her tone dismal. "Let me tell you what's going on. The test results are very bad. The doctor says Justin may not survive until next month."

Kento was speechless, as though he'd been punched in the stomach. Justin's condition was the same as Maika's. There was less than a month until the deadline set by his father. If he didn't finish the drug by February 28, two children would die.

"I'm begging you. Save my son."

Lydia didn't sound weak and pitiful. Kento sensed a forceful willpower ready to confront the disease that was ravaging her child. Thoughts of his own mother flashed through his mind. This strength to protect one's child must be a virtue common to all mankind, one that crossed all boundaries of language, religion, and race. Kento knew he had to reward this courageous mother from a far-off country.

"Mrs. Yeager," Kento said, staring up to the sky. He gulped quietly, so she wouldn't notice. The words he spoke next were the biggest gamble of his life. "You have my promise. I will save your son."

4.

RUBENS WAS SEATED on his sofa at home, bathed in the light from a nearby lamp.

It was 2:00 a.m. East Coast time; 8:00 a.m. in the Congo.

He'd gone home to grab a nap, but there were too many problems he had to deal with, and sleep was out of the question. He was itemizing these problems on a legal pad.

Rubens couldn't make up his mind. He wanted to avoid any deaths in the operation he'd designed, but at this point he was unsure about Nous. Should they let him survive? Either way, they couldn't let Operation Nemesis spin out of control. They had to anticipate what their opponent would do and beat him to the punch. If their conjecture were correct, Nous planned to get out of the country, using the mercenaries to protect him. Rubens looked down at the legal pad.

Where will Pierce and the others go to escape the Congo?

This was the pressing question. Africa was huge, and CIA operatives couldn't cover it all. If Pierce and his group got out of Africa they'd be nearly untraceable. The only saving grace for Operation Nemesis was the state of transportation in the Congo. For a country as large as all of Europe, the transportation infrastructure was abysmal. There was but one road running east and west, and if you didn't use that you were left with taking a boat or using a plane. And Pierce's group would know that all the strategic points in the network would be under surveillance. So the only thing they could do was walk to the eastern border. Considering the geography, Stokes, their military adviser, had made the right decision to get the local militias involved. Twenty armed insurgent groups blocked any approach to the eastern part of the Ituri jungle. The only way to prevent Pierce's group from fleeing the country was to rely on these unsavory armed groups and their combat efficiency.

Where will they go to escape the African continent?

Once they were out of the Congo, the chances were low that Pierce and the others would remain in Africa. They were all non–Africans and would stand out too much. But where would they go? Rubens looked down at the third item on his list, hoping it would provide a hint.

What was the selection criteria for the four mercenaries?

Nous had wanted these four soldiers to guard him, going so far as to help kill all the other candidates for Operation Guardian. In the reasons for their selection, Rubens concluded, lay the key to understanding the escape plan. As Nous had thought, Yeager and Garrett had backgrounds that made them willing to betray their employer. But what about the other two? Why choose Kashiwabara and Meyers?

Rubens pulled a report out of his briefcase and reviewed the selection process.

Three other candidates died in Iraq before Mikihiko Kashiwabara's name moved to the top of the list. What distinguished Kashiwabara from them? Their technical skills as mercenaries were all comparable, including their airborne rating and combat experience. The only thing setting them apart was their language skills. Only Kashiwabara was able to use Japanese, his native language. Rubens remembered the academic paper that Seiji Koga had written. Unlike most scholarly papers, it was written in Japanese. In the international scientific world English was the lingua franca, which meant that Dr. Koga was probably not very skilled in English. So possibly Kashiwabara had been selected to serve as a go-between with Koga. If that hypothesis were correct, then because Dr. Koga died, his son, Kento, was now the contact in Japan. The report from the DIA stated that Kento Koga was able to speak English. In other words, the unfortunate death of Dr. Koga meant that there was no longer any need for Kashiwabara.

Rubens pushed these thoughts further. He had no proof, but were Pierce and the others heading to Dr. Koga's homeland, Japan? On his legal pad he wrote *Japan?*

This Japanese soldier, Kashiwabara, had an alarming background. A special notation in the report said that ten years earlier, his father had been beaten to death and his mother severely injured. His mother, though, who would have seen the attacker, refused to testify, and the crime remained unsolved. Kashiwabara joined the Foreign Legion soon after the attack. Disturbing information, though there wasn't enough detail for Rubens to conclude anything definitive. But he decided it wouldn't affect Operation Nemesis and turned to the next report.

Scott Meyers. Four other candidates were killed in Iraq before Meyers, a former air force pararescue jumper, was included in Operation Guardian. What Meyers excelled at, as his background indicated, was medical treatment and combat search-and-rescue techniques. He was probably selected for his skills in crisis management, but his résumé revealed one other thing none of the other Guardian members had: a pilot's license. It was entirely possible that Nous and his group were going to get out of Africa by plane.

An electronic buzzing interrupted his thoughts, and Rubens, groaning, picked up his cell phone. The call was from the DIA agent in the operations center. "Were you asleep?" the man asked.

"No; it's okay. Did you finish your investigation?"

"Yes. As you requested, I looked into all the ships owned by Pierce Shipping. Only two ships will dock in Africa in the next month. The ports are Alexandria, Egypt, and Mombasa, in Kenya."

"What about the Arabian Peninsula?"

"They have multiple tankers that regularly pass through there, but the next ones aren't scheduled for another two months."

"Are either of the ships docking in Egypt or Kenya heading to the Far East?"

"The one stopping in Kenya is scheduled to continue on to India and then return to the United States."

To Japan via India, Rubens thought. If they continued due east after crossing the border out of the Congo, they'd arrive at the Kenyan port. "Have the Agency monitor the two ports. Make Kenya your top priority."

"Understood."

"What about any planes that Pierce Shipping owns?"

"They just have one private jet for use by their executives. There's no indication at present that it's headed to Africa. We'll continue to monitor it."

"This includes any affiliated companies, too, I assume?"

"It does. We've looked into all of them. Including subcontractors."

"One more thing. Check to see if anyone at Pierce Shipping plans to charter or purchase a plane."

Before Rubens had gotten the words out the agent responded. "We're already on it. There's no indication of any movement there."

"I see. Thank you."

So the chances were slim that Pierce and the group would exit Africa by plane. The only other choice was by ship. If they could cut off all sea routes, then they could contain them. Rubens hung up and stared down again at the legal pad.

Counterintelligence.

There was no room for doubt anymore: Nous was hacking top-secret US intelligence. But the need-to-know principle stood in Rubens's way, making it impossible for him to devise any effective counterintelligence measures. He didn't know what sort of system the NSA's Echelon was or anything about its domestic black wiretapping ops, and no information about them was divulged to him. The one thing he did know was that these intelligence agencies ran complex information infrastructures that made centralized communications control out of the question. Unless they did something to stop it, the fact that Operation Nemesis had entered its emergency response phase would surely leak out to Nous.

The only measure he could come up with was a makeshift one. They would incorporate false phone intel in their system to confuse their opponent.

His cell phone rang again. The call was from Eric Burton, FBI liaison. "We have a problem," he said. "Can you come back to the operations center right away?"

Rubens wasn't too keen on going back in. Outside his window it had started snowing. "Where are you?" he asked.

"FBI headquarters," Burton said.

"Can you come to my home?"

"Sorry. We need a secure room."

What could have happened? Rubens wondered. "How about the conference room at the Schneider Institute? It's close by for both of us."

"Sounds good."

Rubens reluctantly got to his feet and grabbed the keys to his Audi.

Twenty minutes later Rubens and Burton were face-to-face in the windowless conference room, the same room where Rubens had first seen Pierce's intercepted e-mail.

"Something bad's come up. I haven't told anybody else yet," Burton began, and took a manila envelope from his attaché case. "It's about the phone call from a telephone booth in New York City. The one warning Kento Koga."

Rubens instinctively leaned forward. "You found out something?"

"The call was made from a phone booth on Broadway, a spot where there's a lot of foot traffic. It was made at four p.m. on Saturday, five a.m. Japan time. At four ten on the same day a security camera in a drugstore two blocks away caught someone walking down the street, someone connected with Operation Nemesis."

Rubens didn't hesitate. "Eldridge?"

Instead of answering, Burton took out several photographs from the envelope and showed them to Rubens. Through a shop window, a camera aimed at the entrance to the store captured an image of a middle-aged man walking down the street.

"The FBI has enhanced the original image, which was kind of grainy."

One glance and Rubens knew who it was. He was surprised, but only for an instant, as if deep down he'd been expecting this.

Burton gazed at him fixedly, awaiting instructions.

"By itself this isn't proof," Rubens said. "He could just have been there by coincidence."

"Then let's get the people at Crypto City onto it," Burton suggested.

The largest intelligence organization in the world, the NSA, is so huge it occupies its own town in a corner of Maryland. This district, not shown on any map, consists of more than fifty large buildings that hold more than sixty thousand employees and other workers. Their goal is to intercept communications from all over the globe, decrypt codes, and collect any information that could possibly benefit the United States. The NSA's other field of expertise is developing technology to counter cyberwarfare.

"If anyone can figure it out, those guys can," Burton added.

After Jeong-hoon called, Kento went outside to wait for him. Jeong-hoon came by motorcycle, and the road that led to the apartment where the lab was located was so dark and narrow that he was surprised to find an apartment building there. The two-story wooden structure didn't have a security light on outside, so it was no wonder he couldn't find it on his own.

He parked his motorcycle at the bottom of the outside stairs, and Kento led him up to apartment 202. When Jeong-hoon saw the lab equipment filling the small room, his eyes went wide. "Wow. Since I met you, it's been one surprise after another."

"You're going to be even more surprised when you hear this," Kento said, and brought him up to speed on what had happened.

Jeong-hoon seemed a little dubious at first, but with drug development software in hand that exceeded anything humans could come up with, he had to take it seriously. He sat there, pondering what he'd just heard. "Human evolution like that—I couldn't say one way or another if it's possible. But as you said, all we can do is use GIFT to try to create a new drug. Otherwise the illness is incurable."

Kento was relieved that Jeong-hoon agreed with him. "Didn't you used to work at an American military base?"

"I did. Dragon Hill it was called."

"What do you think about the wiretapping? Am I just being paranoid?"

"I can't say for sure, but technologically it's possible. America and England created a joint intelligence collection system called Echelon that operates all over the world. In the Far East there's a monitoring antenna at the Misawa base in Japan, and there's a huge electronic wave–interception satellite over Indonesia. Underwater cables are all tapped, too, so there's really no safe form of communication."

Kento was dumbfounded. What had happened to the world he thought he lived in? He'd been so oblivious. Were people just allowed to live within a tiny enclosure that a handful of people who controlled the world had constructed? He had no problem if this made the world safer for everyone, but the people who created the system were far from merciful gods. They were human beings. Rub them the wrong way and they had the potential to brutally crush you. And right now all this was coming down on top of him. He was shocked at how America was taking the lead in trampling on basic human rights. What ever happened to private communications?

"Since Echelon could also be used in industrial espionage, the EU raised this as a problem at their meeting, but they didn't know much about how the system works."

"That really creeps me out," Kento said. The whole idea truly made him uncomfortable. "It's pretty hypocritical for America to talk about democracy."

"I think so, too, but it's not just the Americans. Nothing people do is perfect. All the systems people create—the law, economics—none of them is perfect. It's like buggy software. Once you find the bugs you have to slap a patch on it. If humans really are Homo sapiens—wise men—a hundred years from now the world should be a better place."

"I hope so, but we've got problems facing us right now. Echelon is watching us. I still don't know whether it's right to get you involved."

"I already am." Jeong-hoon smiled his usual gentle smile. "And I want to help those sick children, too."

His positive attitude encouraged Kento.

"Then let's do it," Jeong-hoon said, taking out the laptop with GIFT installed on it from his backpack.

Kento cleared the table so there would be space for the laptop. The laptop was up and running, the screen showing the computer-graphics image of mutant GPR769. The image looked like a living being itself, with the receptors slowly moving along the cell membrane.

"GIFT's basic methodology is no different from existing drug de-velopment software," Jeong-hoon explained, sounding very much the researcher. "As you can see, the receptor's shape is already determined. The next step is to identify the chemicals that will bind perfectly with this pocket."

"And that will be the drug."

"Correct. There are two types of methods we can choose from to decide the chemical structure of the drug. There's de novo—designing the structure from scratch—or there's virtual screening, choosing a highly active structure from existing chemical compounds."

"Which do you think is better?"

"Let's go with de novo. The structure of the compound it comes up with may be really complex, but because that's not my field I'll let you decide."

"Okay."

As they did before, they connected the laptop to the Internet, and Jeong-hoon sat down in front of it. "What's really amazing about this software is that you just indicate what results you want and it does the rest."

"It's totally automatic?"

"Yeah," Jeong-hoon said happily. "Let's set the drug activation strength at one hundred percent."

Jeong-hoon checked that section of the dialogue box and switched from the mouse to the keyboard. As his fingers flew across the keyboard the screen changed at blinding speed to a ribbon model of the receptor, then to an atomic coordinates chart filled with letters and numbers.

"If we indicate the spot where the binding will most easily happen, then GIFT will do the rest of the calculations," Jeong-hoon explained. "Okay: now make us a cure!" he said, and punched ENTER.

REMAINING TIME: 01:41:13 the screen said.

"An hour and forty minutes? This *is* amazing!"

Jeong-hoon was overjoyed. Kento envied him for being so ecstatic. If only I could enjoy research this much, he thought, how different my life would be. Jeong-hoon's beaming face reminded him of his father's mysterious smile when he'd told him that research was the one thing he could never give up. But what had his father found so engrossing? It never seemed to Kento that his life as a researcher was all that fulfilling.

"Are you hungry?" Jeong-hoon asked.

"Yeah, I am. You want to grab a bite?"

They went out to a nearby ramen shop. As they walked down the dark street Kento kept a sharp eye out but didn't see any sign of the police.

They sat down in the restaurant and ordered a meal. The restaurant stayed open late, so after they finished they were able to linger and discuss their next steps. If GIFT were able to successfully design the drug, that would be the first step. Then they'd have to actually synthesize it, do experiments linking it with the receptor, and perform simple pharmacological drug trials using the mice.

"I don't think the reagents we have in the apartment will be enough," Kento said. "We need to figure out how we can get hold of some."

"Won't reagent suppliers sell them to us?"

"They don't take orders from individuals."

"Let me go to the university and see what I can do. I'll contact some friends in other labs and see if they can help."

"Great. But even if we're able to synthesize it successfully, how do we handle the rest of the work? We need to culture cells and test them on mice."

"I don't have any clinical background, either, so we'll just have to study up and do our best. I'll go see Doi and find out from him."

Kento mentally pictured Doi, who'd introduced him to Jeong-hoon. He was a laid-back, casual sort of guy, but very focused when it came to his research. He should be able to help out.

They still had some time before the results were in, and Kento decided to ask a question he'd been pondering for some time. "When I'm with you, Jeong-hoon, I don't feel uncomfortable at all. But don't you find a lot of differences between Koreans and Japanese?"

"Hmm," Jeong-hoon said, his head tilted to one side as he gave it some thought.

"Say whatever you want. I don't mind."

"Well, to give you one example," Jeong-hoon said, turning to Kento. "There's a special emotion that only the Koreans have found a word for. A kind of unusual feeling that Americans, Chinese, and Japanese don't understand. In Korean we call it *jeong*."

"*Jeong?*"

"Right. It's written with the Chinese character and pronounced *jo* in Japanese, which means 'feeling.'"

"Then Japanese have it, too, since we use the same word."

"No; it's very different from what *jo* means in Japanese. It's hard to explain."

Kento was curious. "Could you try?"

"Well, I guess it's like a force that connects one person with another. When we have something to do with a person we're connected through *jeong*, whether or not we like that person."

"Is it like intimacy or benevolence?"

"It's not something as elegant as that. *Jeong* can be annoying sometimes. Because you can be connected by *jeong* with someone no matter how much you dislike him. In other words, we can't completely reject that person. That's what most Korean movies and TV dramas are about—*jeong*."

"Really?" Kento had seen a few Korean films but had never noticed that. It was surprising that people can watch the same movie and see completely different things.

"*Jeong* is also the connection between people and things. . . . Does this help?"

Kento tried to understand *jeong* on an emotional level, but no feelings rose from deep within him. "No. I'm afraid I don't get it."

"See?" Jeong-hoon said with a laugh. "Only someone who understands *jeong* can understand the meaning of the word. If you don't know what a word is pointing to, you can't understand the word."

Just like scientific vocabulary, Kento mused. A person who doesn't understand it never gets it, no matter how much you explain it to him. It lies at the limits of what that person can understand. "It seems like the distance between people in Korea is closer than it is in Japan."

"I guess so."

Was the sort of gentle atmosphere he always felt around Jeong-hoon a result of *jeong?* Kento wondered.

Jeong-hoon glanced at his watch. "GIFT should be finished with its calculations soon."

As Kento got to his feet a thought struck him: someday I want to be a person who understands *jeong*.

They paid their bill, left the restaurant, and—again taking care not to be followed—returned to the haunted house–like apartment building.

On the table in the small room, the screen of the white laptop glowed faintly. Kento switched on the light in the room, and he and Jeong-hoon peered at the screen. What leaped out at them was four letters:

NONE

"None?" Jeong-hoon exclaimed. "What does that mean—none?"

"Don't ask me."

"That's strange. Hold on a second."

Jeong-hoon focused, laserlike, on the laptop. He fiddled with it for a while, and a chemical formula appeared on the screen. It was a simple structure consisting of a core nucleus surrounded by a benzene ring, multiple other rings, and appendant functional groups. GIFT had given a result, but the receptor was only 3 percent activated. This structure wouldn't cure the disease.

"Is it telling us to retool it to optimize it?" Kento asked.

"No. If that were the case, then I don't understand why it would say 'none.' Doing it de novo should produce a little bit better answer than that." Jeong-hoon considered the situation. "Let's forget de novo and do virtual screening."

As before, he inputted instructions into GIFT and hit ENTER. This time it indicated nine hours and twenty minutes until the calculations were complete.

"Normally calculations like this would take months," Jeong-hoon said with a laugh. "In the morning, when the results are in, you'll call me?"

"Will do."

"I'll come back tomorrow night."

Kento glanced at his watch. It was already near 11:00 p.m. Jeong-hoon had his own work to do, and he felt bad for keeping him so late. "Thanks for everything, Jeong-hoon."

"I'm doing it because I enjoy it," the Korean prodigy said, his face lighting up in an affable smile. "See you soon," he said, and left the little lab.

As the roar of Jeong-hoon's motorcycle faded away, the apartment suddenly felt empty and lonely. Kento realized again how fortunate he was to have someone to help him. Not that he could depend solely on Jeong-hoon. He had a lot of work to do, and braced himself for the tasks ahead. He sat at his desk until near dawn, poring over specialized texts, then slid into his sleeping bag for a few short hours of rest.

In the morning, he felt as if he had dreamed, but about what he couldn't recall. He had set the alarm on his watch, and it rang him awake when GIFT's calculations were over.

Eight o'clock.

With the blackout curtains closed, the room was as dark as it had been when he fell asleep. Kento crawled out of his sleeping bag, switched on the light, and went over to the computer. What sort of response would GIFT provide? He said a prayer that it would come up with a structure with a high activation. He turned to the LED display.

Four letters lit up the screen.

NONE

5.

WHEN ESIMO, AKILI, and Nigel Pierce left the hunting camp, the Mbuti seemed devastated, as if it were the end of the world. Young and old, men and women, their faces grief-stricken, broke down in tears as they said good-bye.

At first Yeager looked at them with sympathy, but the clamor went on so long that he grew impatient to set off.

On the first day of their march through the jungle, Pierce explained the circumstances behind the Mbuti reluctance to say good-bye. In order not to be attacked in a Pentagon-led raid, they had decided to disperse to other bands. In other words, Esimo and the others leaving was the signal for them all to scatter. They were also afraid for Akili, going through the jungle at such a tender age. For the Pygmies, a race of hunters, the jungle was filled with danger, and their children were strictly forbidden to go off into it.

The mercenaries assumed a diamond-shaped battle formation, with Akili and Pierce in the middle. In the front were Esimo, their guide, and Mick, on point.

In addition to food and clothes, Pierce had stuffed his backpack full of a couple of laptops, solar electric panels, and a number of satellite phones. Garrett figured these were to make sure they maintained a line of communication outside Africa. Even if Echelon intercepted a call and the phone company cut the line, they could switch to another phone and restore communications. Besides all this heavy equipment, Pierce had a cloth slung diagonally across his shoulder in which he carried Akili, and all this weight tended to make the thin anthropologist lag behind.

Akili showed no sadness at leaving the others and just gazed around at his surroundings as they marched through the jungle. The expression in his eyes was so strange that to Yeager it looked like he was planning some scheme or other.

Yeager was also bothered by the way Esimo acted. He was an excellent guide, confidently striding through the thick jungle, but occasionally he would deliberately fold a leaf in two and place it on the ground so that it formed an arrowlike mark. If an enemy force took after them in this direction the leaves would be perfect signals, showing the way. Also, when they took a break Esimo would lie on the ground near his son and smoke marijuana.

"They have their own way of doing things," Pierce told Yeager. "Leaf markers like that are found all over the jungle. The marijuana they smoke heightens their sense of hearing when they hunt. Unlike us, though, they don't get high."

"There's something else," Yeager said, pointing to the coals that Esimo kept wrapped in a large leaf. When the foliage above them was sparse they risked being spotted by the infrared sensor on the satellite, but Pierce insisted on letting him carry the coals and wouldn't back down. It's a necessity, he explained.

"Couldn't we just give him a lighter?" Yeager said, but Pierce wouldn't listen.

"Don't worry," he said. "We can track the satellite."

Yeager thought his stubborn attitude odd, but he went along. Esimo's timid yet friendly smile kept him from taking a hard line.

The first day they covered thirty kilometers before nightfall. On his two-hour sentry shift Yeager watched Akili as he slept, deeply snuggled up next to his father. When his eyes were closed it lessened some of the strangeness of his appearance.

Still, Yeager found it odd how each person reacted differently to Akili. Akili had developed mysterious intellectual powers but had yet to acquire what you might call a full-fledged personality. Like a human infant, he was a blank slate, not yet good or bad. Did this mean, then, that the totally opposite impressions Meyers and Mick had of him reflected Meyers's and Mick's own mental states? This supposition sprang from Yeager's experiences in the military. When the Special Forces were deployed overseas and came into contact with people who had a different skin color and language, it was the soldiers with an inferiority complex who looked down on the locals the most. A similar psychological process might be at work when it came to their views on Akili.

As he gazed at Akili's defenseless sleeping face, Yeager remembered how he felt when he was first blessed with a precious child. More than anything he wanted him to grow up to be an honest and decent person. Akili might be a different race from humans, but he was born with intelligence and a developing personality, and Yeager hoped he would grow up the same way—with a strong, decent spirit. But if he had the same childish combativeness that lurked inside Yeager himself—after all, lethal weapons were all it took to make him feel almighty—then Mick could be right: Akili could turn out to be very dangerous indeed. Akili was born from a human being, so it was entirely possible he could turn out that way.

Dawn came, and they began the second day of their march. They took a short break every hour, and Yeager used the time to learn a little more about the Pygmies.

"Do Pygmies ever go to war?" he asked.

"No, they don't," Pierce promptly answered. "As far as I know the only thing close to war was the internal strife that took place about fifty years ago. A conflict started within a band, and they ended up splitting into two groups."

"In other words they're natural pacifists?"

"They're much wiser than we are. The Pygmies know that fighting among people will endanger the group. So when there's somebody who doesn't fit into the group, or when, say, there are quarrels between a couple, they move the people involved to another band, and the friction disappears."

"Don't they fight over sources of food?"

"No; it never happens," Pierce said flatly. "Each band has clearly defined territory, and the group shares equally in whatever they kill. This is different from what we would call Communism. It's based on a superior wisdom. First, the hunter who brought down the game has the right of ownership. But he portions out shares to the other hunters with him and those who stayed behind in the camp. This complicated distribution system means that the meat goes equally to all. It satisfies the covetousness of the person who distinguished himself without allowing him to monopolize the wealth."

Pierce clearly admired the Pygmies' way of life. "You seem to really be taken by them," Yeager said.

"I am. By the way, the word *Mbuti*—the name Esimo and the others use for themselves—means 'human being.'" In the gloom of the jungle, as they rested for a few moments, this was the first time the bearded anthropologist had spoken in a friendly tone. "Yeager," he went on, "have you heard of a company called Pierce Shipping?"

"Yes."

"I'm the heir to that firm."

Yeager was taken aback. Pierce—almost malnourished by his primitive lifestyle, dressed in ragged clothes—hardly looked like the scion of a distinguished family. "You must be rich, then."

"I'm lucky enough to have the research funds I need," said Pierce modestly.

"Why didn't you take over the business?"

"When I was young I planned to. Anthropology was just a hobby. But I realized I wasn't cut out to run a huge corporation. That sort of world is just too corrupt." A look of disgust and defeat crossed Pierce's features. "Money attracts the worst sort of people. Bankers and people from investment firms only want to shake hands with somebody who's made a fortune. And lawyers—they're leeches who suck out wealth instead of blood. They all want to rob other people of their riches. I couldn't stand the sight of them anymore, so I went back to the research I love. Research on people who—to me, at least—are the finest people in the world."

Garrett had started listening in on their conversation, and he glanced at his watch. "Sorry to interrupt, but we'd better get going."

Yeager got to his feet. "You should have been born a Pygmy," he said, with a hint of sarcasm. "Instead of the heir to a huge corporation."

Pierce smiled thinly and gave an unexpected response. "No. I don't think so. I'm no silly tree hugger. I use computers, and when I get sick I seek the most advanced treatment. I can't separate myself from almighty science. It's ridiculous to think that primitive society is a utopia forgotten by modern man. I can't live forever in a world where you can die from appendicitis." His eyes shone with a mix of feelings, somewhere between sadness and admiration. "The Pygmies have survived in this harsh environment for tens of thousands of years. They evolved physically and cooperate and share the food they need each day. Pretty amazing, wouldn't you say?"

"It is," Yeager agreed. He prayed that the blood of Akili's peace-loving ancestors still flowed through him.

About ten minutes into their march the trees abruptly ended, and their field of vision opened up. In front of them, below a narrow dirt bank, lay the brownish Ituri River. The river was one hundred meters wide, the water in it high and pulsing downstream. On the opposite bank, too, a wall of trees came down nearly to the river. The Ituri was like a thick blood vessel threading its way through the jungle.

Esimo pointed at something on the shore, timidly calling the mercenaries' attention to it. It was a dugout canoe carved out of a large tree, with a couple of oars, casually lying there on the bank.

Yeager was once again amazed at Esimo's abilities. Without a map or compass he'd led them right to the spot where the canoe was. Yeager, former Special Forces, had no clue how he'd navigated through the jungle, which was bereft of any landmarks.

"Two things to be careful of here," Pierce told the men. "First, the crocodiles in the river. They've eaten several locals here, so watch out. Second, once we're on the other side, we'll come out near farming villages. There may be armed insurgents nearby."

Yeager and the others had been battle-ready ever since they left the Kanga band camp. "Right. Let's cross," Yeager said.

The canoe could only hold four people and their equipment, so it took two trips to get them all across. Once on the other side they walked for about ten kilometers, at which point the vegetation was clearly different from before. They could see cultivated land through the trees and knew they were nearing a farm village near the road.

Yeager called a halt and checked their position on the map. Villages were spread every few kilometers along the unpaved road, and the village before them was Amanbere. Small houses with dirt walls lined both sides of the road. They had sixty kilometers left, as the crow flies, to their goal, the town of Komanda.

"Do you know what the satellite's doing?" Yeager asked.

Pierce pulled a small laptop out of his waist pack and checked. "It'll be over us in forty minutes."

"Let's cross over the road between villages so no one notices us."

"Wouldn't it be safer to wait until night?"

"It's not even noon yet. We can't wait that long."

They quickly worked out a route and, still in diamond-shaped battle formation, started again through the forest.

But just as they were detouring behind Amanbere, Esimo, a startled expression on his face, turned to look back at Pierce. Mick, beside Esimo, looked at him suspiciously, then faced forward again, himself taken aback. Mick signaled a halt and pointed to his ear, signaling that he heard something.

Yeager listened carefully. From where the road stretched off to the north he caught the faint sound of drums.

Pierce focused on the sound for a time. "Damn," he said in a soft voice. "A militia's headed this way."

"How do you know?"

"Those are talking drums of the Bila people. They communicate using drum sounds to stand in for the inflections of speech. They can transmit pretty complex information."

"Does it say how big the militia is?"

"No, it doesn't, but they're a bloodthirsty group. They've massacred other tribes. Normally they'd be operating in the north."

The mercenaries exchanged glances.

"Are they after us?" Mick asked.

"That would be my guess," Garrett said, and nodded.

They heard shrill yells from the Amanbere village. The talking drums' message had been received. From far off they watched as people ran out of their houses, spoke to each other, and ran about in panicked confusion.

Yeager put down his backpack and put his headset on. "Hide Esimo and Akili in the woods," he ordered Pierce. "Have them lie facedown."

Akili clearly understood what was happening. He clung to his father's waist and looked at him with frightened eyes.

"Can't we run away?" Pierce asked.

"We'll check to see when the militia's passed," Yeager said. "This is safer than running around at random," he added, trying to reassure him.

Pierce nodded tensely and escorted the Pygmy father and son behind a large tree. Meyers stayed behind to guard them, while Yeager, Mick, and Garrett flicked the safeties off on their rifles and headed toward the edge of the forest. Beyond where the underbrush thinned out was an expanse of cultivated land, and two hundred meters beyond that was a row of houses. Through his military binoculars Yeager could see people running back toward the village from elsewhere and the terrified looks on their faces.

Run away! Yeager said to himself. If you don't hurry you'll all get killed!

Just then there was a burst of upbeat music totally out of place in the tense scene. Loud music, a mix of African folk music and rock. Yeager followed the music north with his binoculars and saw three pickup trucks, trailing dust and loaded with Africans, barrel into the village. A heavy-caliber machine gun was mounted on the bed of the lead truck. The jostling crowd of militia in the trucks were dressed in mismatched field uniforms they had probably plundered.

"Forty-three men," Garrett reported.

Mick continued. "One heavy-caliber machine gun, three light machine guns, plenty of AKs, some pistols, hatchets, axes, and spears."

The villagers, who were gathered in one spot, screamed and scattered. Several who were too late to escape were sent flying, struck by the armed vehicles.

The villagers began fleeing for their lives toward the forest. A family ran in Yeager's direction—father, mother, and five children. But the field was wide open and provided no cover—the worst possible place to run. Soldiers leaped off the trucks, aimed their guns at the retreating family, and opened up on full automatic. Blood showered up toward the bright sky as the parents and children, one after the other, collapsed. As the bullets struck them their shouts changed to bloodcurdling howls— not the calls of humans who had lost all hope, but the screams of dying animals.

"Meyers!" Yeager said into his wireless microphone. *"Have Pierce and the others cover up their ears."*

"Roger that."

In the middle of the field, beside the family writhing in agony, a boy, uninjured, was sobbing. Eight or nine, about the same age as Justin. The militia aimed a merciless hail of bullets at him, and his head exploded.

"Yeager," Meyers's voice said in his headset. *"Pierce is asking whether we're going to help the villagers."*

"Negative," Yeager said, suppressing the desire to vomit. *"They outnumber us ten to one, so there's no way we can take them on."*

Garrett, next to Yeager, gave a low groan. "What the hell. Look at their pendants."

All the militia had accessories hanging around their necks, strings of human ears and penises. Some of them had attached them to their rifles. Yeager remembered hearing how US soldiers in Vietnam had done the same thing.

Until five minutes ago Amanbere had been a peaceful village, but now it was a war zone. Not a war of ideology or clash of religions, but straightforward, naked war, stripped of all pretense. The militia burst into the houses of people of a different race and began looting their food, fuel, and belongings. The villagers were rounded up in the village square, where the women were raped in front of the rest. The soldiers' lust for anything female was indiscriminate, as infants and old women suffered the same fate.

The violence soon escalated, and the soldiers, their penises still stiff, plunged their bayonets into the vaginas of the women they'd raped, the same method used by Japanese soldiers in Nanjing against the Chinese. When he'd been in the military Yeager had been trained not to lose his composure when he saw scenes like this. Part of his training involved watching snuff films showing Russian soldiers massacring prisoners. But if the slaughter he was witnessing now had been any closer to where he was, he doubted he could maintain his cool. At any rate, he knew that as long as he lived he would never forget this gruesome scene.

The actions of these men, letting their violent nature run wild, were not those of a particular race. Winners in wartime always become fierce and crazed and slaughter those of a different race as a way of making clear which group is inferior. As these militia sliced off the villagers' hands and legs and beheaded them, their actions were one with all the genocides that had ever been carried out in history by various races, peoples, and human beings. Humans are fully capable of creating their own hell on earth. But never heaven.

If a journalist were here, he could report this massacre. The article would plant the seed of a desire for peace in the hearts of those who read it, at the same time arousing their taste for the macabre, for the frightening. They knew that those who were slaughtered were the same living beings as they, yet those who produced and consumed this vulgar entertainment would view themselves alone as privileged and be content with merely mouthing platitudes about peace.

Every adult in Amanbere village was murdered. The children watched their parents being slaughtered and were then herded into one place, where the teenage girls were separated out and loaded onto trucks. To be sex slaves, no doubt. One boy tried to escape, tripped over a severed head, and fell, and a militia soldier attacked him with a hatchet, splitting his skull in two. The other children, nearly insane with fear, watched the brains spill out of their friend's head. They all knew their turn was next. The soldiers, armed with heavy weapons and sharp blades, surrounded them.

Yeager had reached his limit. These barbarians had to be killed. He lifted his rifle and drew a bead on the militia's leader.

"Don't do it, Yeager," Mick whispered. "You'll put us all in danger."

Yeager felt sick to his stomach when he looked at the Japanese man's face. "So the only thing you can shoot are apes?"

"*What?!*"

"Mick's right," Garrett said in a subdued voice. "I want to help those children, too, but there's nothing we can do," he added regretfully.

Needing to dampen the rage that threatened to explode in him, Yeager looked back at the forest, to those he was supposed to protect. Those big eyes were staring back. From below where Meyers stood Akili peered up at him, then turned his enigmatic gaze to the village in the distance. The soldiers had begun slaughtering the children.

Yeager shuddered. They couldn't let Akili see this atrocity. He wasn't just concerned about the child's feelings. It felt as if the tables had turned. Just as they had watched the chimpanzee rip apart one of its young, Akili was observing the slaughter of humans by humans. A foreign intelligence was gazing at the character of this ambiguous creature that, while possessing the concept of morality, easily gave in to its baser, brutal nature.

"Meyers," Yeager hurriedly spoke into his mike. They couldn't have Akili knowing how inferior a creature humans were. *"Akili's watching."*

Meyers turned around, noticed Akili leaning out, and led him back under the tree. It was Pierce's turn to crawl out from behind the tree. He gestured to Yeager and the others to come back. Yeager wondered what was going on, and Pierce, clearly panicked, grabbed away Meyers's headset and spoke into it. *"Get back here! The satellite's picking you up!"*

"What the hell?" Yeager looked at his watch. They still had twenty minutes before the reconnaissance satellite was supposed to be overhead. He made his way back to the forest, careful not to be detected by the militia. Pierce was gazing at his laptop, on which was a satellite image of the village and its surroundings. In one corner of the screen Garrett and Mick were visible, prone, observing the village.

Yeager called them back on the mike and edged closer to Pierce. "I thought we still had time."

"We might have been fooled by misinformation. We have to get out of here before they analyze the image and pinpoint us."

"Which direction should we go?" Garrett said as he ran over. "We need to know what's going on. Can you enlarge the satellite image?"

Pierce scaled down the image so it showed a section ten kilometers square. North and south of Amanbere was a scattering of villages along the road. When he enlarged each area they could make out a line of heavily armed vehicles, an antigovernment force separate from the militia.

"Damn," Yeager said. "More enemies. There're three groups we have to deal with now." He frowned. The path to the east, the direction they should proceed, was blocked by several armed groups.

"Hey," Mick called out. "Check out what they're doing."

The mercenaries trained their binoculars on the village. Several children were still alive, yet the militia had stopped their killing. The one who looked to be their leader leaned inside a truck and was speaking into a wireless microphone. He suddenly spun around and stared hard in the direction where Yeager and the others were.

"This isn't good," Meyers said. "Maybe he got the satellite intel."

The Pentagon had apparently already located them and had, via the arms dealer, informed the militia of their position.

The militia leader signaled his troops. One of the soldiers mounted the truck and opened up with a blast from the heavy-caliber machine gun. The mercenaries ducked for cover behind the trees. The line of fire mowed down the bushes to their left and was getting closer.

Pierce was terrified. "Stay calm," Yeager told him. "And don't move."

The flying bullets sprayed up the fallen leaves around them, but Akili didn't stir and held tight to his father.

As the curtain of bullets passed overhead, Yeager and the others began to withdraw, leading the three people under their protection, one by one, deeper into the jungle. The militia grew more active. They excitedly pointed in their direction and, with all the weapons they could carry, ran off across the field. Apparently they had noticed movement in the underbrush.

"Run!" Yeager commanded, keeping his voice low. "Go back to our original route!"

Guarded by Meyers, Pierce and the two Mbuti began running.

The militia moved across the open field, and Garrett and Mick set their rifles on full auto and hit them with covering fire. Ten or so of them fell dead, halting the enemy's advance.

Yeager drew a bead on the militia leader and squeezed the trigger. The second he fired, the satisfying sensation that he'd made a direct hit ran straight from his right hand to his brain. The bullet took a lower path than he'd hoped for, but his quarry didn't escape. The target's camouflage uniform fluttered, and a red stain spread out from inside. The 7.6mm bullet, flying at supersonic speed, ripped into the man's lower abdomen, shredding his genitals and bladder, and causing instant death. His shouts were strangled as he doubled over and crumpled to the ground.

This was the first time since Yeager had become a soldier that he'd killed someone he could see with his naked eye. He didn't feel guilty but exhilarated. He'd given these cruel animals what they deserved. Kill them! Blow those savages to hell!

One after another Yeager shot down four of the soldiers who had stood there stock-still, then he fell back.

Seven o'clock in the evening.

His cell phone rang, and Kento looked up from the textbook on blood gas analysis he'd been studying. Jeong-hoon should be arriving soon. Thinking he was calling to say he'd be late, Kento picked up the phone, which was plugged into its charger. The LED screen said POPPY.

When he hurriedly said hello, the low, machine-generated voice he'd heard before responded. "Take out the laptop that doesn't turn on, right away."

The black laptop. *Finally*, Kento thought, excited at the prospect of solving this long-standing riddle.

Poppy seemed impatient. Kento pulled the computer over from a corner of the desk, cluttered with lab equipment, and opened the display.

"The apartment you're in in Machida right now has high-speed Internet. You know that?"

The last time Jeong-hoon was over he'd connected to the Internet. "I know."

"After you connect the laptop to the cable, turn on the start button."

He did as he was told and waited, but all he saw was the same blue screen as always. "The machine's frozen."

"No, it's not. It's on normally. There's a button on the screen to input the password."

"I don't see anything like that."

"The background, the entry field, and letters are all the same color. Protective coloration."

So that's why it was all blue! Kento felt a little let down by this simple trick.

"That laptop is already connected to the Internet. I'll tell you the password and you type it in, and make sure you get it right."

The password Poppy told him was *genushitosei*, all in lowercase. A random line of letters, Kento thought—or was there some regularity hidden within it? He couldn't tell.

"Once you've inputted that, hit the enter key."

He did, but the screen remained the same.

"Here's the second password."

Poppy again told him a meaningless line of letters: *uimakaitagotou.*

As soon as he typed this in and hit the enter key, the screen suddenly came alive. The tiny display showed another world. The sounds from the speakers, though, revealed chaos. Rustling sounds, like something rubbing together, and people gasping, struggling to catch their breath.

"What do you see?" the low voice asked.

"A video image. I'm not sure, but it seems like somebody's running through a forest."

"That's a live feed from the war zone."

"War zone?"

"It's what's happening right now in the Congo."

When he heard the name of the country his father had worked in, Kento felt confused. Were all these mysterious things that had happened connected to what was going on in the middle of the African continent?

"Press the control key and the *X* key at the same time to change the image."

Kento did, and the live feed from the war zone switched to a monochrome aerial view. It looked at first like a still photo, but when he looked closer he saw it was a video. A satellite video, like ones he'd seen on the TV news. The audio, though, remained the same, transmitting the sounds of war.

Poppy taught him how to enlarge and reduce the images and left him with this: "If the people on the video ask you questions, answer them. Just face the laptop and talk. This machine uses an unbreakable encryption, so don't worry about it being tapped."

"Wait a second. What is going on here?"

"It's a rescue operation for an evolved human being. And you hold its fate in your hands."

"What the——" he cried out, and the line went dead.

Kento gazed, open-mouthed, at the satellite image. He soon understood what he was viewing—the jungle photographed from above. The dappled pattern he thought was the dark surface of the sea was actually a thick canopy of trees. Below this he caught glimpses of white dots. He enlarged the view and saw, like grains of rice, the white, high-signature silhouettes of people.

These people were probably the ones in the other video, he thought, and switched back to the first screen. The image was still blurry, probably because it was taken by someone who was running as he filmed. For an instant a muscular Caucasian man appeared in the center of the screen. He was carrying a rifle. The man looked at the camera and yelled, in English, "What the hell are you doing?"

Kento was startled, as if the man were yelling at him, and he closely followed the images. "We haven't made a connection yet," another voice replied, and a man's heavily bearded face loomed into view. The man who was running with the camera. The man, wearing a headset, stared closely at the camera, as if he could actually see Kento. "Are you Kento Koga?" he asked.

Unsure what was going on, Kento replied in English. "Yes."

"I can see you from here, too," the man gasped as he continued to run, shifting in and out of view. "This is an Internet videophone."

Kento looked up at the top of the laptop and saw that the internal camera was lit up. The man was seeing him in his Machida apartment in real time. "Who are you?"

"Nigel Pierce. I was a friend of your father."

"My father?" Kento peered at the man on the screen and saw that he was agitated. His eyes were unblinking and terrified.

"Halt!" a voice offscreen shouted, that of the man with the rifle, and the camera stopped moving. "What's the situation?" the deep voice said, irritated.

Pierce turned to Kento and spoke rapidly. "Switch your screen to the satellite view. We don't have time to check it ourselves, so just tell me what you see."

Kento switched over the screen as Poppy had instructed him. Nigel Pierce disappeared, replaced again by the view from the satellite. The audio, though, remained the same.

"We're in the center of your screen. Can you see other white dots?"

"They appear and disappear."

"What is the direction and distance?"

Kento struggled to interpret the scale. "Northeast one kilometer, and southeast nine hundred meters. And a moment ago I saw another dot to the east."

"Three groups?" Pierce was clearly shocked. He asked another question, but his voice shook so badly that Kento couldn't make out the English.

"What did you say?" he asked several times, and another voice came on. Surprisingly, a native speaker of Japanese.

"Where are the ones to the east? What distance?"

The man's tone sounded threatening. Kento was puzzled about who it was, but responded in his native language.

"About two minutes ago, the distance is, uh—about five hundred meters."

"Don't tell me *about*, tell me *exactly*."

Kento was offended. "I can't tell you that."

"You idiot," the unseen Japanese railed. "Can you see the dots now?"

"No. They're hidden under the trees."

"Continue giving us updates," the Japanese man's voice commanded, then faded away. Pierce was back, in English.

"Kento, did you talk with Lydia Yeager?"

Kento found it hard to follow this abrupt change in topic. "I—I did," he finally said.

"Is her son, Justin, still alive?"

"Yes," Kento replied, and sensed another presence in his room. Startled, he looked up and saw Jeong-hoon standing at the front door. He'd told Jeong-hoon to just come in without knocking. Jeong-hoon was smiling, wondering what was going on.

"Would you stay there?" Kento said, motioning to Jeong-hoon to stand back, and Pierce, sounding suspicious, asked, "Is somebody else there with you?"

"No," Kento quickly lied. *Do it alone, without telling anyone.* He couldn't let them know he was betraying his father's final instructions. "It's just me."

"Okay, then. Give me another update. In English."

"All right."

"Are the dots getting closer to the center of the screen?"

Kento turned back to the computer display, but all he could see now was the dark shadow of trees. "I don't know. They're all under the trees now."

A groan filtered out through the speakers, a mix of distress and impatience.

"When the white dots reappear, tell me," Pierce said, and turned to Yeager. "Justin's still alive."

With all the tension he was feeling from the enemy pursuit, Yeager was caught off guard by this news. "Who were you communicating with?"

"An ally in Japan."

Of all people, Yeager thought bitterly. Why does it have to be Japs? If they got to Japan, wouldn't it all be a bunch of bastards like Mick waiting for them? "Did you find out where the enemy is?"

Pierce shook his head, his face pale. "They disappeared under the trees."

"Quiet," Mick said, concerned about what was to the east. "Those militia troops must be on to us. They might catch up with us any minute."

They were now facing three different groups of enemies. Other armed groups approaching from north and south of Amanbere village had entered the jungle to hunt them down.

"Then let's head southwest."

Pierce translated Yeager's command to Esimo, who replied in a low voice. Pierce frowned and quietly told the rest of them what he'd said. "Hold on. Esimo said we should sit tight. He seems to have pinpointed the enemies' positions."

"What'd you say?"

The mercenaries looked down at the little man, no bigger than a child to them. Esimo was like a changed person, down on one knee, unmoving. The usual sad expression on his face had vanished, replaced by a distant, aloof sense, as if the mysterious power of the jungle now resided within him. Eyes narrowed, he slowly moved his head from side to side like an antenna. Yeager realized he was heightening his sense of hearing.

Esimo reached out an arm, pointed in three directions—northeast, east, and southeast—and whispered something to Pierce.

"The enemy to the east is the closest," Pierce said, interpreting. The terrified anthropologist's shoulders were trembling as he slowly lay down on the ground. "They're within the range where the Pygmies use nets, within two hundred meters."

The others all got down low and aimed their rifles at the dense trees. "Yeager."

At Meyers's whisper Yeager turned to the side and found Akili tugging at the sleeve of the medic's combat uniform. "Seems like Akili wants to say something."

Pierce pushed the small laptop in front of Akili. The boy began typing, and Yeager read out the message.

Throw some grenades sixty meters out, east-southeast.

Yeager immediately knew what Akili was thinking. A diversion. Yeager was amazed a tiny child could come up with an idea like this.

"Will it work?"

The three-year-old tactician nodded.

"Are you sure? Won't it just give away our position?" he insisted, but Akili's face remained full of confidence. Yeager was overwhelmed by the glint of brutality in his eyes. Yeager was uneasy, apprehensive that a hatred toward humans was quickly growing in the child's heart.

Akili gave a second command. Throw the grenades fifty meters in front of you. Hurry.

Yeager, rifle in hand, quietly made his way into the jungle. The remaining three mercenaries took up a defensive position. Yeager started to hear the approaching militia. The enemy was less than a hundred meters away.

He removed a grenade from his tactical gear, pulled the pin, and threw it, aiming for the spot Akili had designated. As the grenade described a parabola above them, they all hit the ground. The grenade soundlessly dropped onto the humus-rich soil; there was a second of silence, then the explosion hit. Countless metal fragments ripped through the surrounding trees and immediately, diagonally left and forward of his position, at ten o'clock, there was a roar of automatic fire. The militia, which had come so close to them, were firing in the direction of the grenade explosion. The hail of bullets from the side ripped apart the leaves on the trees, sending them swirling to the ground. More firing came from the front, but this time from the right. Two armed groups approaching from different directions were firing, shooting at each other over the spot where the grenade exploded.

From partial information Akili had correctly predicted the movement of these two groups. Astonished at the child's ability, Yeager made his way back to the others. He didn't need to worry about making any noise now. The group left this spot and headed toward the southwest.

They ran on, so hard they could feel their muscles groan as they plunged through the forest. Pierce, communicating with their Japanese "ally," reported that the third enemy group, to the northeast, was heading their way. But as they forged ahead under the thick foliage, trying to avoid detection by the satellite, they couldn't determine their present location. Without an accurate readout of latitude and longitude, they had no idea how far away or in what direction the enemy was positioned.

Esimo's sense of direction was all they could rely on. The Mbuti, adapted to life in the jungle, was able, to an amazing degree, to retrace the route they had taken in the morning. One by one he gathered up the leaves he'd used as markers at strategic points, and an hour into their flight the jungle finally came to an end and they emerged on the banks of the Ituri River.

If only they could cross the river they could shake off the enemy's pursuit. But as they took a short breather Yeager looked over at the opposite shore, about a hundred meters away, and was shocked to see the dugout canoe over there. Local people had apparently used the boat themselves to cross over and had left it there.

"Where's another boat?" Yeager asked Esimo, through Pierce's translation.

Pierce translated his response into English. "There are boats upstream and downstream, but they're far away. It'll take too long to walk there."

"I've pinpointed our location," Garrett said, pointing to a bend in the river on the map. "We're right here. What's the enemy doing?"

Through his headset Pierce communicated with Japan and then looked at the map. "This is info from three minutes ago. The enemy is here."

He pointed to a spot two kilometers behind their position. It was along the same route they'd taken.

"They're on our trail," Mick said. "We have twenty minutes before they catch up."

Yeager exchanged glances with the others and was conscious of eyes watching him. Two huge eyes silently observing this human being. Yeager began taking off his heavy equipment and laying it on the ground. "I'll go get the boat."

Pierce raised an eyebrow. "You're going to swim? I told you—there are crocodiles."

"Then say a prayer for me."

With just his pistol in his leg holster Yeager stood on the muddy bank. The rough surface of the river rushed downstream. The water was too dirty to see what lay beneath it.

As he stepped into the lukewarm water in his trekking boots Meyers yelled for him to stop. "Insurance," he said. "Fire in the hole!"

Meyers threw a grenade about ten meters offshore. There was a muffled explosion, and, with a flash, the water rose up, a bulge becoming a straight line. A pack of crocodiles, about ten of them. Half of them twisted their huge bodies and slithered up the banks. The mercenaries held up their rifles and formed a protective circle around Pierce and the Mbuti father and son. Yeager was grateful to Meyers for his quick thinking and plunged into the river.

He did the crawl, moving through the muddy water. The current was much stronger than it had looked. If he relaxed for even an instant he'd be dragged far downstream. As he swam with every ounce of strength through the opaque water, something bumped against his stomach. He could feel through his shirt that it was something alive. Probably a fish. Not a crocodile. He focused on his goal, holding the panic in check. He had to reach the far shore and save his companions. He had to show Akili that people like this did exist.

As he passed the middle of the wide river his clothes started getting waterlogged. Strangely, the physical pain made him accept everything else he'd ever suffered in his life. His parents' divorce, signing up for the army, his precious son's battle with an incurable disease—all he had struggled with in life was condensed in the weight and pressure of this muddy water. *Fine.* Yeager spat out the word as he struggled through the water. I *will* cross this river. Not for anyone else, but for Justin.

If only he could show Justin, not Akili, what he was doing. This is what your father is willing to do for you—risk drowning in order to save your life.

He treaded water, greedily gulping down air, and when he wiped the dirty water off his face the shore was surprisingly close. Less than twenty meters. He willed himself the rest of the way, until finally his feet and hands touched the muddy bottom. On all fours, gasping for breath, Yeager pulled himself to his feet. He looked left and right to see where he'd swum to. He'd drifted far downstream, away from the canoe. He needed to hurry across in the boat and get Akili and the others to the other side.

Yeager was running through the muddy shallows when in front of him a huge mouth opened wide. The crocodile's mammoth snout closed and opened like a spring-loaded trap and darted forward to snap at its prey. Yeager, pistol already drawn, pointed it at the croc's head and fired rapidly. The first five shots shredded its nervous system. Its brain function gone, the huge, writhing body sent up a sheet of spray as it leaped into the air. Yeager fired off a coup de grâce of five more shots.

Yeager looked down at motionless monster, its hard skin dripping blood. "That's what you get for messing with me," he muttered.

Kento had been staring at the satellite image so long that he had no idea how the Congo war on the ground was going. The occasional voices came over the speakers, but a low, groaning background noise drowned them out, and he couldn't catch what they were saying.

Twenty minutes had passed since their last communication when he heard men cheering. The situation must have taken a decided turn for the better. Kento switched to the other view, and a bearded man's face loomed up at him. There was a large river behind him.

"You did a good job, Kento," Pierce said from the Congo jungle. "I'm going to cut the connection for a while." He turned to someone off camera. "Cut the connection with Kento."

For the first time Kento realized that a third person was monitoring their communication. Most likely Poppy. The power to the small laptop turned off by itself, and the live feed from the battlefront was gone.

"What *was* that?" Jeong-hoon asked. He'd been standing to the side of the desk so as not to appear on camera.

"I don't really know myself."

"That satellite image was real," Jeong-hoon said. He'd worked at a US military base and knew. "I'm starting to think you're telling the truth."

"You still don't believe me?"

"Well, nothing's for sure until we make that drug."

He was right. Kento shifted in his chair and struggled to refocus on the drug. This Nigel Pierce, who claimed to be a friend of his father; a rescue operation to save an evolved type of human; war in the Congo—the clues he'd been assembling were starting to jell into a vague outline. There were four people involved in the plan. His father and Pierce, the person who warned him by phone from abroad, and this Japanese, who went by the name of Poppy. Somehow Poppy seemed to be running things, but Kento had no clue to his identity.

One other thing was clear now that he understood the function of the small laptop: what Yuri Sakai was after when she showed up that night on the university campus. She wanted to grab it away so she could sever the line of communication between Japan and the Congo.

"So what happened? How'd it turn out?" Urged on by Jeong-hoon, Kento pulled himself together. It was a strange sensation, as if his soul had been called back from Africa to his little apartment in Machida. He opened the white laptop and showed it to Jeong-hoon. "Even with virtual screening, no druglike structure came out."

Jeong-hoon stared at the laptop with GIFT installed, at the word NONE. "That's weird."

Kento knew what Jeong-hoon was thinking. GIFT must have investigated several million known chemical compounds in the search for a substance that would bind with a mutated receptor. If it did, it should have had a hit for at least one druglike structure. "So is this software fake after all?"

"No. For us GIFT is like a self-evident truth. We simply have to believe it. If we doubt it, then we have to give up on making the drug."

Jeong-hoon, glued to the laptop, manipulated it as he'd done before. "This is strange. There are several candidates that have a low activation structure."

"If the agonist has some efficacy, it should at least bind, right?"

"Right. Though they're all under two percent efficacy."

"That's only natural with virtual screening. The assumption is that you replace the functional groups and enhance the efficacy."

"Okay, but then why did GIFT show NONE?" Jeong-hoon called up the image of the receptor on the screen. "This is a docking simulation. One of the candidate compounds is binding."

On the screen was a transparent image of a long, thin mutant GPR769 piercing a cell membrane. Another small compound had entered the translucent pocket. As Jeong-hoon had the low-activation compounds bind one after another, the shape of the receptor changed a little, twisting, getting thinner, the terminal part sticking into the cell membrane, moving slightly.

"Ah!" Jeong-hoon called out, and turned to Kento. "I finally figured it out! It's not just the binding site that changes but the entire conformation."

"What do you mean?"

Jeong-hoon, punctuating his words with gestures, explained. "When a ligand binds, normal receptors shrink inward. This change moves the terminal part of the receptor and activates a different protein. But replacing only one amino acid in this receptor makes not just the binding part but the entire shape get distorted. So no matter what compound binds to it, it doesn't shrivel, as it normally would."

Kento understood what Jeong-hoon was getting at. "So the question is what keeps this receptor from moving?"

Jeong-hoon nodded. "That's the reason why PAECS hasn't been cured. That's one of the secrets of mutant GPR769. And we're the only ones in the whole world who've uncovered it!"

Despite Jeong-hoon's excitement, Kento was worried. He glanced around the shabby little lab his father had left him and felt hopeless. "If that's true, then we'll never be able to make the drug, right?"

Jeong-hoon remained silent for a long while, his eyes unfocused as he meditated.

In Kento's mind he saw the usually flexible receptor turning into a rigid counterfeit. "It's impossible to cure that disease. No matter what drug we synthesize, the receptor itself won't move. So it's impossible to create a drug specifically targeting it."

Jeong-hoon raised his head, and after some seeming hesitation went ahead and spoke. "Kento, can I say one thing?"

"What?"

"The people who created the history of science weren't those who said something was impossible."

These words of reproof from mild-mannered Jeong-hoon managed to make their way past the barriers Kento had erected and strike something deep inside him.

"We're the only ones who can save those sick children," Jeong-hoon said. "Maybe it's impossible, but I can't simply abandon them."

Kento had been on the verge of giving up completely, but when he thought of the names of two of these children, Maika Kobayashi and Justin Yeager, he stopped short. "Okay," he said finally. "Let's do it."

Jeong-hoon smiled.

By chance the two of them happened to incline their heads at the same moment and stare up at the wood grain of the ceiling. They sat there, side by side, as if staring up at the stars, racking their brains. To an outsider these two young men would just seem to be letting their minds wander. But this is precisely what scientists do.

After a half hour Jeong-hoon stood up and began pacing in the narrow space between the lab table and the wall. He muttered technical terms, half in Korean, half in Japanese. Kento was at the lab table, head in hands, facing down, legs fidgeting, getting up at one point to splash some cold water on his face at the sink. How could they get this microscopic receptor—one ten-thousandth of a millimeter in size—to do what they wanted?

"We must be overlooking something," Jeong-hoon said. He was standing at the closet, staring at the cages filled with mice on the upper shelf. "I don't get it. But something is off."

"Off? What, exactly?"

"I don't know. I feel sort of imprisoned. Like I'm inside a wall or something."

He must mean he's hit a mental roadblock, Kento thought.

"Instead of creating a drug, how about gene therapy?"

"I think that's even less possible. And there's no time."

Jeong-hoon let out a pained groan. "Can't we get rid of our preconceptions and think outside the box?"

His words awakened an image in Kento's mind. Of eyes watching them from the outside. The eyes of the person who created GIFT, the one with an intelligence that went beyond anything human. "We have to create the drug. There has to be a way to make an agonist."

"How can you be so sure?" Jeong-hoon asked.

"Everything that's happened since my father died has been perfectly planned. And being given GIFT was part of this, so we should be able to use it to create the drug."

"GIFT?" Jeong-hoon exclaimed, as if finally realizing the existence of this almighty software program. "That's right. The key to solving this has to be GIFT. We just have to do what only GIFT can. What existing software can't. Hold on a second."

Jeong-hoon put a hand to his forehead, frowning, and didn't move. The apartment—in fact, the whole building—was suddenly deathly quiet, as if deserted.

Jeong-hoon's eyes now focused on something far away, his trancelike stare seeing something not of this world. Scientists must all look like this, Kento thought, when they've finally found the answer to a difficult problem.

"An allosteric site," Jeong-hoon exclaimed, gooseflesh rising on his cheeks. "A new method no one else has tried. We can cure the disease that way."

Kento knew the term *allosteric site*. It meant a place on an enzyme, other than the chemically active one, where a drug may bind. Drugs bind with receptors not just in the central depression. Even on the outside of receptors, when molecules with the right chemical and physical properties are exposed, if one synthesizes the appropriate chemical compound one can make it bind to this variant site. As Kento considered this he finally began to understand. "In other words, you bind the compound to the outside of the receptor and change the entire shape?"

Jeong-hoon nodded. "And even then, if the receptor isn't activated, there is a final step. We input the desired result into GIFT, and it will design another agonist to correspond to a second site important to activating the receptor. We designate not just the ligand binding site but also a distinct and separate site, the allosteric site, which controls receptor conformation and plays a role in receptor activation. Thus we have an allosteric site that binds one agonist—an allosteric effector— and partially fixes the distortion in the mutant receptor and another agonist that binds the mutant ligand binding site."

"So we make two kinds of drugs?"

"Exactly. I guess you'd call it an allosteric drug. It's a new approach that no pharmaceuticals company has ever tried. But with GIFT we can do it."

With the limited time they had, though, could they really synthesize two new drugs? Kento was worried, but decided to follow Jeong-hoon's example and swallow back any doubts about doing the impossible. And change his bad habit of giving up before he even did anything.

Jeong-hoon sat down and began working with GIFT. He entered the conditions that would call up the mutant receptor again, pressed ENTER, and the screen said REMAINING TIME: 42:15:34. The answer would come in two days.

"I wasn't sure where to put the allosteric site, so I just indicated a general area. If it doesn't work out then we'll have to do it all over again."

Kento's impatience finally emerged, and he weakly complained. "But if we have to do the calculations over and over we'll run out of time to synthesize it."

"That's the gamble we're taking," Jeong-hoon said, a stern look on his face.

A thought came to Kento. The tightrope that he'd barely been able to cross lay before him once more. Another risk, like all the ones he'd taken ever since he leaped off the balcony of his apartment and barely escaped with his life.

6.

AFTER ELLEN SAW her husband off to work, as always, at the front door, she stood there, feeling a vague apprehension. It was something Mel had said as he left.

"I might have to disappear for a while," her husband of almost forty years had told her. "But don't worry. I'll be back in a few days."

Ellen had frowned, uncomprehending, and he'd kissed her and headed for the garage. Recently Mel had started blurting out jokes, and she wondered if this was another one. During the last six months his working hours had become irregular, and every time she questioned him about this he made her laugh with a line straight out of a spy movie: "It's government work." Of course she knew he was working for the government. His family was proud of the official title he held. But he never explained why he had to be this swamped with work.

What in the world was Mel doing? And where was he doing it?

The Ford sedan slowly pulled into the road as a light snow fell, and Mel gave her a farewell smile and drove off. As she stood at the front door Ellen thought about that strange machine, a small laptop computer that had been delivered to their house at the end of the summer last year. Her husband's sole hobby was playing around with machines, and she figured he must have bought it through the mail. But Mel had stared at the computer as though he had no idea where it had come from. Then he took it to his study.

Mel's personality had changed since then. He'd become less talkative, and though he was often lost in thought, after he acquired that computer he went around with a happy smile, as if all life's worries were a thing of the past. She'd questioned him about the computer, but he'd put her off, saying, "You wouldn't understand even if I explained it to you." Her husband had a brilliant mind, and she was used to this stock explanation. Ellen didn't care so much what was in the computer; rather, she was concerned that there was some secret that lay behind her husband's expression. But his carefree smile made her realize this was a groundless fear. She gave up trying to find out more.

He kept the laptop in a strange place—in a kitchen drawer. Now, anxious about what was going on, Ellen thought about taking out the laptop and switching it on. Unlike her husband, though, Ellen was all thumbs when it came to digital technology. And she knew it would probably be difficult to sneak a look at what was on the computer without leaving a trace behind.

Mel flipped on his turn signal and made a left at the intersection down the road. As Ellen was going back into her warm house she saw a large van start to move. The black vehicle had been parked on their road, and it was moving off, not following her husband's car but heading in her direction. She remembered one other enigmatic thing her husband had said, jokingly, to her.

"If some men come here and try to push their way in," he'd said as he put the laptop back in the kitchen drawer, "cook this computer."

"Cook the computer?" she'd asked.

"Toss it in the microwave and turn it on," Mel had explained.

The black van glided toward her, coming to a halt just past their front yard. Ellen's unease turned to fear. Men she'd never seen before emerged from the van, and she felt weak in the knees. The scene she'd often seen in thriller movies was, she realized, pretty realistic. The four men, striding toward her through the front yard, all had on sunglasses and dark suits.

"Good morning."

The low greeting from the man in the lead wasn't friendly in the least. Ellen stepped back and was able to get back inside the house.

"Do you mind?" The group ignored the frightened Ellen and rushed up to the front door. "You're Mrs. Gardner?"

"Yes," Ellen replied.

"Special Agent Morrell of the FBI," the man said, showing her his ID, and the other three quickly identified themselves. "We're sorry to trouble you, but could you let us inside?"

This was exactly the kind of situation her husband had been talking about. "What is this all about?" she asked, trying to keep her voice from shaking.

"It's about your husband."

"My husband? You do know that he's science adviser to the president of the United States?"

"Yes. We're well aware this is Dr. Melvin Gardner's residence. That's why we're asking."

At this point Ellen was less concerned with checking the purpose of their visit than with following her husband's instructions. Over nearly forty years of marriage her husband had always done whatever she'd wanted. It was time to repay his kindness.

"We have a warrant. I can go over the details once we're inside. May we come in?"

Instead of nodding Ellen slammed the door in their faces. She did it so quickly that she didn't see whether Morrell's expression changed. She hurriedly locked the door and ran back inside the house. There were loud knocks, unexpectedly, from the back door, too. But there was no time to check whether she was hearing things, and she raced to the kitchen. She tugged open the drawer next to the sink and pulled out the small black laptop. Just as her husband had instructed her, she put it inside the microwave and turned on the timer. Lightninglike sparks flew out around the little computer. Afraid it and the entire microwave might explode, Ellen stepped away. But right then a thick arm reached out and switched off the timer.

Startled, Ellen turned around to find eight men filling the kitchen. It was so crowded she felt she might be crushed.

"Don't interfere," Special Agent Morrell said. "You'll put your husband in an even worse position."

One of the men reached inside the microwave and extracted the half-cooked computer.

"What did Mel do?" Ellen asked. "Did he do something to offend the president?"

"He's under suspicion of leaking classified information. We have proof."

"Is he going to be arrested?"

302

Morrell waited one beat, then nodded. "Yes. He's being taken into custody as we speak."

"But even if he disappears for a while, he'll be back in a few days."

"Hmm?" The lawman's interest was aroused. "Why do you say that?"

"He said so before he left the house. 'I'll be back in a few days.' And my husband is always right." Ellen's trust in her husband was unwavering. "He won the National Medal of Science, you know. Don't underestimate him."

He chose the Map Room for their meeting as a final act of consideration for the adviser he'd considered a friend. Unlike the Oval Office and the Cabinet Room, the Map Room was a place where they could talk in a more relaxed atmosphere.

President Burns strode down the first-floor hallway of the White House and opened the door to the room where his science and technology adviser was waiting. Dr. Gardner was seated in one of a pair of Chippendale armchairs before the fireplace. His handcuffs were off. Though he was in the middle of being transported to FBI headquarters, he looked relaxed and unperturbed. In fact there was a dignity about him that fit in well with the rococo interior of the room. Gardner's brilliant career might be crashing down around him, but Burns found it very odd that he could remain so calm.

Burns had his Secret Service detail wait outside, and when he and Gardner were alone he sat down diagonally across from him. Burns crossed his legs, sighed, and slowly began to speak.

"Professor, what is this all about?"

Gardner replied, his tone polite as always. "I have no idea, Mr. President. Good question—what *is* going on?"

"According to reports I received, you're suspected of leaking secrets about Operation Nemesis."

"Am I going to be put on trial?"

"If things continue the way they're going, yes," Burns said, shooting him a concerned look. He wanted Dr. Gardner to know that he was being treated exceptionally kindly considering the circumstances. The president himself was giving him the opportunity to offer an explanation.

"The only thing I can think of is that I was walking down Broadway in New York on Saturday evening. But that doesn't prove anything. In a trial I'd be found innocent."

"The situation is more serious than you imagine." Burns was unsure how much he should explain. Another special access program he'd set in motion allowed the NSA, in collusion with private communications providers, to tap all communications within the United States without a warrant. Gardner's treasonous actions had been caught up in that wiretap network.

"You're telling me you've found proof, using a method I can't conceive of?"

Burns opened his mouth, about to affirm this without revealing the nitty-gritty of their methods, when Gardner repeated, "You insist you have proof?"

Gardner's unusually assertive tone raised doubts in Burns's mind. This wasn't like a criminal suspect suddenly turning aggressive at the last minute. Burns grew cautious. He gazed dubiously at this gentleman with his calm demeanor and went on. "You seem to have serious doubts that we have evidence of your guilt."

A smile rose to Gardner's face. "I know you're very busy, but I wonder if you'd indulge me and hear about a little hobby of mine."

Burns looked at his watch. He needed to get to his next meeting with the State Department rep who'd written their forthcoming white paper on human rights. They had to consider what written criticism the United States should direct at Chinese and North Korean human rights violations. But he couldn't shake the feeling that Gardner was delivering an unspoken threat. "All right," Burns finally said. "I'll give you five minutes."

"Ever since I was a child I've enjoyed fooling around with machines," Gardner began. "Even now what I enjoy most is buying parts and assembling my own computers. Last weekend I went around to some electronics stores and bought a CPU and hard drive. These were all brand-new parts, and I selected them at random."

"At random." Burns repeated the somewhat unsettling choice of words.

"Right. I got home and assembled the computer from these new parts, installed the operating system, and bought the latest security patch, which I downloaded onto an external storage device. I put in other security software as well. I ran a virus scan, but of course found nothing, because the machine is brand new and has never been connected to an outside line." Gardner raised an index finger to get the president's attention. "Here's the important part. I put a short message into that new computer, one that I'd created on another computer. A message in Japanese I made using an off-the-shelf translation program. A crude translation I made as a last resort if we had to urgently get in touch with the Japanese. Later on I found out that that person can speak English, so it was a waste of time."

Burns expected Gardner to confess to his crime at this point, and he silently waited for him to continue.

"As the final step to get the computer ready, I hooked it up to a router. I installed an alert system so I could monitor all communications. Then I connected this brand-new computer to the Internet. I didn't access any site or send or receive any mail; I just left it for a while and then cut the connection. But surprisingly, for some reason it automatically sent the message I'd made in Japanese. I checked the alert system, but there was no evidence of a zero-day attack."

Gardner looked up to see how the president reacted. Burns knew next to nothing about things digital, so he couldn't fully follow Gardner's explanation, yet there was one thing in particular he couldn't fathom: the fact that Gardner hadn't sent or received any e-mail. If that were true, then how did the NSA get hold of proof against him?

"The message in question, then, was saved in a brand-new machine, and though the computer was connected to the Internet no sites were accessed and no communications were carried out. And there was no cyberattack exploiting an unknown vulnerability. In spite of all this, for proof to be found from my computer there can only be, technically speaking, one possible explanation. There has to be a back door built into all the operating systems made in America and used throughout the world—a back door that allows US intelligence agencies to access them."

An instinctive cautiousness made Burns freeze. He maintained a serious expression, not raising a single eyebrow in response, erasing all clues to the inner workings of his mind.

"If I were prosecuted, I think I would repeat the story I just told you in court. While showing a video I made of the entire process."

Burns couldn't judge whether the technical description Gardner had offered was accurate or not. His calm demeanor could be a bluff. Burns weighed the risks. Gardner could be put on trial by a secret military tribunal, but locking him away forever wouldn't be easy. However, if he removed Gardner from Operation Nemesis and from the president's inner circle, that would swiftly remove the threat. Wouldn't that be sufficient?

"There must have been some kind of mistake," Burns said. "I don't think there is sufficient proof to have arrested you."

"Can I believe you?"

"Of course. Let's get the attorney general in here and draw up the papers dismissing the indictment. We will not hold you responsible in this incident. You have my word."

Gardner still looked unconvinced, so Burns stood up, looked out in the hallway, and called over Acres, his chief of staff. Burns ordered him to write a memo dismissing the indictment against Gardner, and Acres, and the FBI agent standing by, both looked confused. Burns shut the door and went back to the fireplace. "This should get you released from custody and back home soon."

"I appreciate it," the National Medal of Science winner replied. "I'm sure my wife must be worried."

"I'll have to relieve you of your duties as adviser, however."

"I understand."

Negotiations concluded, Burns crossed his legs, trying to calm down. The anger he felt at being forced to give in was somewhat lessened by the admiration he felt at how brilliantly he'd been played. "I wonder if you'll indulge me and hear what I have to say now."

Gardner nodded guardedly. "Of course."

"What I'm about to say is entirely hypothetical," Burns emphasized. He had no ulterior motives and simply wanted to satisfy his curiosity. "Suppose there is a scientist. He undergoes a thorough background check and obtains a high-ranking post in the government. He's in his sixties, a warm person with a brilliant record who's respected by everyone around him. He lives a very modest lifestyle for one of his position, is not excessively greedy for fame or money, and cares for his family above all. A model citizen. But for some reason this man betrays his country. He isn't motivated by money or goods, and he isn't black-mailed because of some dark secret he's hiding. So why does he do it? Why would he do something so dangerous?"

"Maybe he gets well compensated for it."

"But according to investigators his estate hasn't increased by a dime. And he hasn't received any other benefits—fine meals, expensive liquor, women, or some privileged position. He sold out his country but got nothing in return."

"Mr. President, you don't seem to understand scientists. We are an especially greedy type of people."

Gardner stared straight at Burns. The president noticed that the look in the scientist's eye had changed.

"Our instinctual desire is a thirst for knowledge. This is as strong as, or maybe stronger than, ordinary people's desire for food or sex. We have an inborn desire to *know*." As he spoke, the scientist's eyes sparkled. Burns was astonished at the savage, hungry look in his eyes. Melvin Gardner had discarded the mask he usually wore, that of a faithful, sincere man, and was now showing his true colors. And Gardner did not possess the type of surface cunning of those greedy men who frantically pursued the money game. Instead he let this unusually powerful desire show, honestly and openly, with no attempt to hide it.

"More than anyone else, we want to understand—the riddles hidden in prime numbers, a theory that describes the entire universe, the secret of the beginning of life. But those aren't what I really wanted to know. I wanted to know about man. Whether the Homo sapiens brain has the intellect to explain the universe or whether it will forever be unable to comprehend it. Whether in this battle of brains, with nature as our opponent, there's any chance that someday we'll prevail."

"And you found the answer?"

"I did. A small computer was sent to me. From where I don't know. I used it to communicate, and someone on the other end gave me those answers. At first I thought it was some kind of joke, but eventually I realized I was dealing with a fearful intelligence, and I came to believe. The 'strong anthropic principle' that some physicists advocate is simple egotism. The one who can correctly grasp the universe is not human. There's someone that comes *after* us."

"Are you telling me the person you communicated with was— Nous?" Burns said, using the code name of the being he had ordered killed.

Gardner didn't answer. "Please Mr. President, let me perform my final task as science adviser. You know, fifty years or so ago President Truman asked Albert Einstein if aliens were to land on earth how we should deal with them. Einstein advised him that we shouldn't attack. You won't defeat intelligent life that surpasses human beings."

Were he and his staff underestimating the biological threat that had suddenly appeared in central Africa? Burns wondered. As he always did when he felt anxious, he sat up straight and looked down at his opponent. "Are you saying, then, that Operation Nemesis was a mistake?"

"I am. Your decision to kill this new intelligence that has appeared on earth was a total mistake. You should halt Operation Nemesis immediately."

Since Burns had taken office, no one had ever spoken to him like this. "So," he said coldly. "That's why you tried to save Nous? Even if it meant betraying your country?"

Gardner shook his head sadly, as if upset by this hopeless display of distrust and intolerance. "I didn't do it for this country alone but for all mankind. If we attack Nous he will use all his power to retaliate in order to save his species. And if that happens, we will be wiped out."

"Exterminated?"

"That depends on how brutal he turns out to be."

To break the oppressive atmosphere Burns tried cracking a joke. "If he's as moral as we are, there's nothing to worry about."

There was a trace of scorn in Gardner's eyes as he looked at his country's leader, but this was quickly replaced by a look of weariness. "At first this is what I thought. If Nous is really an evolved human he wouldn't try to wipe us out right away. He would need to take over the knowledge and technology mankind has accumulated, and he'd need reproductive partners in order to increase his race's numbers—assuming crossbreeding is possible, that is. But Operation Nemesis has put us in a grave position. If intelligent beings discover that there are others in the world trying to kill them, what do you think will happen?"

"I can't imagine."

"It's easy to picture. Think about a human child. The family is a small child's only world. How will that child react if he discovers an enemy in the family who tyrannizes him? If this weak, childlike mind is thrown into a violent environment with no one to protect him, what will happen to him?"

As Gardner said, Burns could easily picture this. He remembered himself as a small child and his father towering over him like a giant. A kind of uncontrollable anger toward Gardner welled up in him just then, from deep in his unconscious. "Are you saying that no decent person can come out of that kind of environment? That seems kind of a prejudiced thing for a scientist to say."

"I'm talking about risk factors. Many people overcome problems in their environment and become solid citizens, it's true. Others sublimate their anger and become successful. But in some cases the anger they direct toward the outside world connects with an innate propensity for violence and they commit vicious crimes. The kind of people who shoot up their workplaces. They want to destroy themselves and the world. Operation Nemesis is doing just that—planting fear and anxiety, and anger, in Nous's heart and trying to demolish his self-respect. Imprinting the idea in his mind that the world hates him. If the operation continues, Nous will wind up with his tremendous intellect intact but with a broken spirit." The scientist fixed his gaze on the president. "What's really terrifying is not intellect, much less military force. The most frightening thing in this world is the personalities of the people who use them."

After a forty-minute drive in his Audi, Rubens arrived at NSA headquarters at Fort Meade, in Maryland. He parked his car in one corner of the huge seventeen-thousand-space parking lot and looked up at the imposing main building, the symbol of Crypto City. It was a pitch-black glass-covered building, the actual shape of which was hidden within. The black glass outer structure and the inner defensive shield weren't just to prevent furtive outside surveillance but were themselves counterespionage equipment used to block electric and audio waves produced within the building.

Rubens went to the visitor screening station, passed through a rigorous identity check, and was given a badge that said PRIORITY VISITOR, for important guests. As if waiting for him to finish, a plump man who'd been standing off to one side walked over. "Mr. Rubens? I'm Logan with the W Group."

An employee of the NSA Operations Directorate. The W Group's full designation was the office of Global Issues and Weapons Systems. Logan wore a blue badge, which signified that he had access to the highest-level secret codes. "This way, please," he said, unlocking a revolving door that led to the interior of the building and motioning Rubens inside. They were heading to Operations Building 1. The walls along the corridor were lined with printed warnings about the need to maintain security.

"Sounds like you've had some serious problems," Logan said as they walked.

The affair with Gardner. The NSA really did know everything. "Did you hear anything about how the dismissal of the indictment came about?"

"That's the part we don't know anything about."

Dr. Gardner must have sensed that the investigation led to him and come up with a way to turn the tables and bring himself back from the brink of disaster. But what exactly he did to achieve this was unclear. Since he was released without being interrogated, the whole affair was shrouded in mystery. Apart from that, the fact that Gardner had revolted against Operation Nemesis came as a mild shock to Rubens. Obviously Gardner had concluded that the operation was a grave mistake.

Logan stopped in the corridor and knocked at a door. Inside was a conference table, where three staff members were already seated. They ranged in age from their twenties to their forties. All had the same blue ID badge, and none of them wore a suit. After some perfunctory greetings they got down to business.

The first to speak was the oldest employee, a man named Jurgens. "This is the laptop computer we confiscated from Melvin Gardner's home. It's a commercial Taiwan product, sold last summer in an electronics store in Tokyo. It's impossible to trace who purchased it, however."

"What about the contents?" Rubens asked.

"The hard drive was severely damaged by electromagnetic waves."

"Will it be difficult to restore? I want to know about any communications log."

"All that data's been destroyed."

Rubens was crestfallen. What Gardner and Nous had discussed would remain a riddle forever.

"There is one thing," Jurgens continued. "The LPS—Laboratory for Physical Sciences—was able to recover about fifteen megabytes of data."

"What's on it?"

"We were able to determine a lot of interesting things." Jurgens let one of his colleagues continue.

Durant, a man in his thirties, took up the story. "Of the fifteen megabytes, three were, we think, part of the operating system code. But this isn't like any existing operating system we've ever seen."

"Meaning?"

"What's installed on that machine is an entirely original operating system. Probably a system created from scratch to prevent anyone from hacking the computer. That's the reason, I think, why the computer used to communicate between the Congo and Japan can't be hacked."

"No vulnerabilities that can be exploited?"

"That's right. It's an extremely secure system. I think that small laptop was made specifically for communications purposes."

Even if communications were intercepted, the encryption was unbreakable, and if someone tried to hack it he'd be rejected. Rubens wanted to find out what the world's largest intelligence organization intended to do. "The only alternative would be to get to the provider and cut the communications, right?"

"That's one way, but if the user's got another provider ready then it's just a vicious circle."

They'd already tried.

"Anything else?"

Jurgens gave a meaningful smile. "There's the twelve megabytes of information that remain. Fisher will fill you in."

Fisher was in his twenties and wore thick glasses. "I copied the twelve megabytes of information we could extract from the computer onto a disk."

Fisher placed a single CD-ROM disk on the table. VRK was printed on the front of the disk, a secret classification.

"The code means 'very restricted knowledge,'" Fisher nervously explained. He seemed like a student, but was apparently a mathematician. "Would you like to see the contents? I don't think you'll understand much of it, though."

"What's recorded in it?"

"A random number sequence."

"What?" Rubens exclaimed.

"Pseudorandom numbers, I would think, and it's not clear what algorithm created it."

This was surprising. Like a child who's received a better Christmas present than he ever imagined, Rubens gazed hard at the CD-ROM. "So this is the key to breaking the code?"

"Yes. They use these random numbers to encrypt and decrypt undeciphered text. I applied this random number sequence to all the communications we've intercepted up till now."

"And? Were you able to decipher anything?"

"Not a thing."

Rubens wasn't disappointed. He could grasp the NSA's intentions. "But if you use this random number sequence you'll be able to decipher any future communications?"

"Correct."

"We ambush them, in other words," Jurgens said. "I advise letting them continue communications between the Congo and Japan. We'll intercept the coms, and at some point we should get some valuable intel. Like the enemy's present position."

Twelve megabytes of information was the equivalent of several dozen printed books. The operation had begun to unravel, but it now looked like they could get a handle on it again. "Okay. Let's go in that direction," Rubens said. "Thank you for all your help."

"You're welcome," Jurgens said, smiling. "There's one more bit of info that should be helpful. Around six a.m. yesterday the amount of communications between the Congo and Japan increased to a level we haven't seen before."

Rubens calculated the time difference. This was the time period when the three armed forces in the eastern Congo would have been pursuing Nous and his group.

"So you think the enemy's control center is in Japan?"

"That's what we've concluded. The control tower, so to speak, is in Japan, and is sending instructions to Nigel Pierce in the Congo."

Was Kento Koga calling the shots on the rescue operation from Japan? The CIA suspected there was one more person of interest in Japan, though they weren't able to confirm it. Rubens recalled the question that had been tugging at him for a long time. "I have one more question for all of you," he said.

"What's that?"

"The situation regarding the development of the supercomputer."

"If you mean Blue Gene, it's completed," the third man, Durant, replied. "We've beaten the Japanese to it."

"Wasn't that machine created to develop things like three-dimensional structures of proteins?"

"That's the level of computing power we were aiming for. If we can understand the correct structure of proteins, we'll be able to control most medical patents. America will dominate the medical field." Durant shrugged his shoulders. "The thing is, the biomechanical structure turned out to be more complex than we thought. Even with the computing power of Blue Gene, we're no match for it."

"So you're not able to accurately determine the shape of receptors, for example?"

"We're not. We just don't have enough computing power. We can only hope for a major breakthrough with algorithms, but right now it's impossible. I suspect we need another twenty or thirty years to get to the point where we can do that."

Since Kento Koga had set out to develop a drug to treat PAECS, there must be a high chance he'd succeed. With Nous's intellect involved this was a certainty. The report the Japanese police had sent confirmed Rubens's suspicions. When it looked like his apartment was going to be searched because his father was involved in some crime,

Kento had asked the detective this: "Was it research data he supposedly stole? Not software?"

Which implied that Seiji Koga had left his son some software. Probably CADD software—a computer-aided drug design program. If this led to the development of a drug to treat a disease that contemporary science couldn't cure, it meant that they had vastly underestimated Nous's intellectual capacity. At a mere three years of age, he'd gone light-years beyond the limits of human intelligence.

But was this really possible? Rubens began to experience an instinctive feeling of dread toward this unknown being. At the same time, though, a different kind of anxiety raised its head. Weren't they overlooking something critical?

"Is everything all right?" Durant asked the silent Rubens. "If you have any other questions we'd be happy to answer them."

"Give me a minute," Rubens said with a smile, trying to pin down the source of his anxiety.

An incurable disease that strikes children. The development of a special drug to treat it. He'd investigated both these points thoroughly. A strategy to get one of the mercenaries, Jonathan Yeager, to betray them. However . . . Rubens let his thoughts go a step further. Curing a disease like that was a high hurdle for Nous to overcome. Why didn't he choose a simpler method? Like using money to win the mercenaries over to his side? There must be another reason why he had to develop this drug to treat the disease. The instant this thought crossed his mind, Rubens felt like his heart stopped.

"You'll excuse me," Rubens said, trying not to let his excitement show as he rose. He asked them where the restroom was, left the conference room, and walked down the deserted hallway.

Rubens entered a cubicle in the restroom and, standing beside the toilet bowl, pondered the moral dilemma he was suddenly faced with.

If they pushed on with the emergency response phase of Operation Nemesis and took Kento Koga into custody, the development of the new drug would grind to a halt. Indirectly, this would lead to the death of children struggling with a terrible disease. Worldwide, there were an estimated one hundred thousand people suffering from PAECS, the same as the number of people killed in the Iraq War, which the Burns administration had started.

So what are you going to do? Rubens heard this unvoiced question. Nous had, without doing any moral damage to them, taken one hundred thousand people hostage. And in doing so was testing his opponents' conscience, asking Rubens's side if they were willing to interfere with the work Kento Koga was doing and turn their backs on the children suffering from the disease.

For the first time in his life Rubens was confronting an intelligence so profound it made him tremble. They might rack their brains to come up with a strategy, but Nous's response was always shrewder, more acute than they could ever have expected. And all the countermeasures he was taking had been neatly mapped out before Operation Nemesis had even been set in motion. The more Rubens felt himself at a disadvantage, the more his impatience led him in a dangerous direction.

Shouldn't we wipe out Nous? It's too dangerous to let him live.

Did Jonathan Yeager understand what was going on? That his animal instinct to protect his child was being manipulated by Nous?

Rubens left the cubicle, washed his face at the sink, and felt refreshed. The counterintelligence measures in Japan targeting Kento Koga were beyond his authority to stop. He could advise Eldridge, the operational supervisor, to put a halt to them, but he didn't think this quintessential bureaucrat would listen to him. Eldridge didn't mind sacrificing the lives of one hundred thousand children as long as he kept on President Burns's good side. It was the same when the cabinet approved the invasion of Iraq. They didn't care how many people died as long as they safeguarded their power and position.

So there was only one way to protect these sick children, Rubens concluded—successfully carrying out the original aims of Operation Nemesis. Destroy Nous, and once this threat to the United States was eliminated, they would most likely back off on the investigation into the Japanese grad student.

When he arrived back in the conference room, Jurgens was holding an STE secure phone, a digital phone that encrypted phone conversations in real time. "You have a call," he said.

"Thanks," Rubens said, and took the phone. The call was from the operations center, from the DIA representative, Avery.

"I can't get in touch with Eldridge and was wondering if he's with you," Avery said.

This was a primitive code they had agreed on ahead of time. If Nous happened to intercept their conversation, he wouldn't be able to pin-point the meaning.

"No," Rubens replied, to which Avery said, casually, "Maybe he went to the movies."

So the emergency response phase of Operation Nemesis had entered stage two. If Eldridge had supposedly "gone to a museum," that meant a problem had arisen. "The movies" signified that all the preparations for the operation were complete.

"We need the supervisor's approval," Avery said, asking Rubens to green-light it.

"If it isn't a pressing matter, then proceed."

"All right," Avery said, and hung up.

This short conversation set in motion a second sweep by the American air force stationed in Kenya. They had made preparations for this without going through the usual communications channels, so chances were slim that Nous had gotten wind of it. This operation would most likely mean that Nous, the anthropologist, and the mercenaries would all be annihilated.

Rubens pictured their dead bodies rotting in the jungle. He tried his best to summon up a sense of shame. He hoped he never got used to a job in which he had to order the deaths of other people. The last thing he wanted was to turn into another Gregory S. Burns. But he knew he was just deceiving himself, and he forced any sense of guilt from his mind. This was the only way to save the lives of one hundred thousand sick children. And among those children was Justin Yeager. Jonathan Yeager was going to die in exchange for his son's life.

7.

"PIERCE, GET UP."

It was 5:00 a.m., and Yeager, on guard duty, shook the anthropologist as he lay curled up on a bed of leaves. Pierce let out a small groan and opened his eyes. The other men and Akili were all asleep.

"What is it?" Pierce asked grumpily.

"I hear drums," Yeager said in a low voice, and Pierce turned to the darkness in the east. A low, percussive sound penetrated the predawn jungle and reached them.

"Can you make it out?"

Pierce listened to the faint sounds, but shook his head. "It's too far away."

The day before they had barely shaken off their armed pursuers, but they'd been pushed back deep into the Ituri jungle. They were more than fifteen kilometers away from the nearest village.

"Are the armed insurgents on the move again?"

Pierce didn't answer, but poured out some water from his canteen into his hand and splashed it on his face, then took his small laptop out of his backpack. As if this were a signal, Akili, lying next to him, sat up. His big eyes shone in the darkness. Before he'd even realized it, Yeager had assumed a defensive posture.

Pierce booted up the computer and received some new information. An e-mail sent by his Japanese "ally."

"Any news?"

"Nothing important. Just an e-mail to Akili."

"To Akili?"

Pierce turned the laptop toward Akili. Akili put on a headset and gazed at the display.

Yeager was getting good at reading the boy's expressions. Right now the odd-looking child's face showed he was happy, as though he were entranced by some children's TV show. His interest aroused, Yeager peered at the screen, where he saw a strange sort of writing, different from an alphabet.

"What is that?"

He meant to ask Akili, but Pierce replied. "He's practicing language."

"What language? Chinese?"

"It's a form of Japanese."

Akili, headset on, nodded from time to time. It seemed he was hearing a spoken lesson as well.

"What does it say?"

"I don't know Japanese. *Arigato* and *sayonara*, maybe?" Pierce stood up and listened again to the talking drums. "But we should be leaving soon. I have a bad feeling about this."

"Agreed."

The two of them split up and went to wake their colleagues. They'd been in the jungle a week now, and the men were all starting to reek.

Yeager brought Mick over to the spot where Akili was intently gazing at the screen and had him take a look. "Is this Japanese?"

Mick followed the writing with his eyes. "I think so," he said.

"What's it about?"

"I don't know."

"You don't know? Can't you read?"

Mick glared at Yeager. "What's written here is all about chemistry or numbers. But the content is too difficult. And some of the sentences are kind of weird."

"You can't translate even one word?"

"It's impossible. It's all technical vocabulary." Mick looked at Akili uneasily. "What's up with this guy's brain?"

"Don't interrupt him when he's studying," Pierce said. They left the three-year-old alone.

They quickly washed up, wolfed down breakfast, then scanned the map to decide on their route. The sound of the drums was coming from the route they had originally planned on taking, so they gave up on going toward Komanda and switched to the southeast, with Beni as their objective. "At the airport near Beni we can arrange for a small airplane with supplies on board," Pierce informed them.

The drumming continued while they buried any traces of their camp and prepared to leave, and Yeager got uneasy. For drums to go on like this for so long, transmitting a message from village to village, something really huge must have happened. But no matter how carefully he listened he couldn't make out the sound of gunfire or bombardment.

They hoisted their backpacks, and Pierce explained the route they planned to take to Esimo. Akili, eyes glued to the computer, suddenly stood up. He motioned Pierce over.

"New data?" Pierce asked. As he stared at the display his expression grew visibly gloomy.

"Did something happen?" Garrett asked.

"The emergency response phase of Operation Nemesis has entered stage two. A large-scale sweep of the area," Pierce said, taking out a map and explaining it to them. "Five armed groups have left the road and advanced into the jungle. Four thousand troops altogether. They're heading west, searching for us."

He pointed to the route the enemy was taking, which cut across north of where they were.

"That's good for us. Then the south is completely clear. We head straight for Beni."

Pierce shook his head decisively. "No. This isn't good at all. This route intersects the Pygmy camp. They plan to smash the Mbuti band."

The mercenaries exchanged looks. They were all remembering the awful story they'd been told in their briefing. About Pygmies being preyed on and cannibalized.

"It'll be genocide," Pierce said miserably. "The Pygmies in this region may be wiped out."

Perhaps sensing something wrong, Esimo started asking a question in a high-pitched voice. Akili stared fixedly at his upset father. As Pierce reluctantly began explaining the situation, Garrett slowly asked, "What do we do?"

"There's nothing we can do," Mick answered at once. "We can't fight four thousand troops."

"So we're just going to stand by and watch all of Esimo and Akili's people be slaughtered?" Meyers asked.

"Don't be stupid," Mick spat out. "Don't you remember what happened yesterday? We stood by and watched the villagers in Amanbere get wiped out." He laughed scornfully. "You're such a hypocrite."

"You bastard!" Meyers started to grab Mick, but a shrill voice brought him up short. Esimo, gesturing with both hands, was complaining about something.

"He wants us to let him go back," Pierce translated. "He wants to go back to his people."

Yeager shook his head. "Out of the question. He'll be killed."

"But can't we do something?" Pierce said, speaking on behalf of Esimo and his pent-up anger. "There's got to be a way to save the Pygmies."

"The only thing we can do is escape," Yeager said. Considering the enemy's strength and position, it was the only choice. "If he wants to save Akili, we have to abandon the other Pygmies."

"Hold on," Garrett said. "Everybody slow down and take a deep breath. There is one way we can save Esimo's tribe."

"How?"

"By turning on our GPS."

The mercenaries silently considered his idea, but Pierce couldn't follow. "If we turn on our GPS," Garrett explained, "Zeta Security will know our position. And that information will go through the Pentagon to the enemy forces north of us. They'll reroute to the south and should miss the area where the Mbuti camp is."

Pierce understood, but he also realized the risks involved. He looked grim. "If that happens, then four thousand enemy troops will be headed straight at us."

"I'm afraid so."

Yeager looked at the map and calculated the distance between them and the enemy. "The closest troops are more than ten kilometers away. We might be able to escape."

"Think we should?" Garrett asked.

"Let's do it," Meyers replied, forestalling Mick's objections. "If you don't want to, then go ahead and escape on your own."

Mick gave a thin, sullen smile, but didn't object.

Garrett laid down his backpack. He kept only the wireless headset and left the other satellite communications equipment they wouldn't need. He took some of Pierce's equipment to lighten the older man's load. Garrett picked up the GPS. "I'll turn it on for just ten seconds," he said. "Then let's get out of here. It'll be a race against the enemy. I'll read out the GPS number, so could somebody write it down?"

Meyers took out a pencil and waterproof memo pad. "Go."

Garrett turned on the device and read out the latitude and longitude on the small display. As Meyers wrote down the figures, Yeager spread out his map and plotted their present position. At that very moment, Zeta Security in South Africa must be hurriedly making contact with the Pentagon.

"Okay, let's get out of here."

Garrett switched off the GPS, and the soldiers formed up in their usual diamond-shaped battle formation and headed southeast. They would try to cover as much distance as possible today. Yeager, covering the right flank, had just done a safety check of the area when there was a sudden, huge explosion. No warning, no whistle of a shell. The shock from behind ran right through him, and the heat and blast waves sent him flying forward.

His head landed in a small stream, and though his face was scraped, he remained conscious. He slapped the side of his head, trying to get his hearing back. He struggled to his feet and saw that the spot where they'd been, fifty meters behind him, had been turned into a ragged crater carved out of the jungle, the mowed-down bushes radiating out from the core of the blast.

He got down in a prone firing position, but he had no idea where the enemy had opened fire from. He looked up, saw the branches of the trees above him snapped away, and shuddered. The enemy was in the air. An unmanned reconnaissance Predator drone, six hundred meters up, had fired a Hellfire missile at them. The pilot was at an air force base in Nevada, remotely piloting the drone on the other side of the world as though he were playing a video game.

The other mercenaries, collapsed on the ground, were moaning and cursing.

"Akili! Akili!"

Esimo, at the head of the formation and the least injured, yelled out his son's name. Akili's small body had been thrown away from Pierce, and he was seated on a layer of fallen leaves, crying his eyes out.

"Take care of Pierce! And watch out for UAVs!" Yeager yelled to the other three. Then he tossed his backpack aside and raced to Akili's side. The tree canopy above the boy was sparse, and there was nothing to block the view from above. If the infrared camera acquired him, another Hellfire missile would zero in on the three-year-old.

Yeager scooped up Akili in his arms, scrambled behind a large tree, and at that very instant the second explosion hit. Traveling at supersonic speed, the missile made no sound at all until it hit, at the exact spot where Akili had been sitting. The large tree covered them, and they were able to withstand the blast wave and flames, though Yeager's insides were shaken by the shock wave.

"Predators only carry two missiles!" Meyers shouted. He was hugging the ground behind another tree. "He won't fire again! But don't let them see you!"

Yeager was trying his best to calm Akili. As he used to do with Justin, he held him in his arms and gently rocked him. He's as warm and soft as my son, he realized. He patted the boy's head, and the thought suddenly struck him: he's exactly like Justin. He would have been born a normal child but for a genetic mutation that made him have to flee for his life. Through no fault of his own, through no desire of his own.

"Akili! Akili!" Esimo shouted as he ran over. Behind him, Pierce and the wounded mercenaries limped their way over.

Yeager handed the still-shaken Akili to his father and turned to Meyers. "You okay?"

Blood was trickling out of Meyers's mouth. "Yeah. Just a small cut."

Both of them still had a ringing in their ears and had to shout. Meyers lowered his medical bag and started checking out the others' injuries. Akili, Esimo, and Mick had no visible wounds. Their eardrums were fine, too. Pierce, who'd lost consciousness for a brief moment, had suffered the same sorts of bruises and lacerations that Yeager had, but he was okay. The most pitiful-looking of the group was Garrett, who'd been in the rear of the formation. The backs of his legs were bloody, ripped apart with shrapnel. Fortunately his backpack had protected the rest of his body.

"No broken bones. And your major blood vessels are fine," Meyers said as he tested Garrett. "When we stop the bleeding you should be okay."

"Do you think you can walk?" Yeager asked, and Garrett nodded.

Pierce, looking stunned, took out the small laptop he used for communication. He pushed the on switch, and when the display came on he breathed a huge sigh of relief. This small machine was, for all of them, a lifeline.

"As soon as Garrett's patched up, we'll get out of here," Yeager said, and Mick cut in.

"What the hell is going on here? I thought we were supposed to know what the Pentagon was up to!"

Pierce came over and shot Mick an annoyed look.

"There's a limit to what information we can gather and process," Pierce said. "The enemy is taking advantage of our blind spot."

"Damn it. From the very beginning you didn't know anything, did you? You trust this guy, and nothing's going to go right."

"Shut up, you son of a bitch!"

At Pierce's angry shout, even Garrett, getting his wounds treated, looked up in surprise.

"We've done the best we can!" Pierce shouted. "An idiot like you doesn't have the right to criticize me!"

"What the hell? Say that again, you shithead!"

Mick's English wasn't always good, but he had a wealth of swear words. The shouting match immediately escalated.

"Enough!" Yeager shouted, pushing his way between them. He pinned Mick's arms back and tried to pull him away. But the fight was quickly over. Pierce, still yelling his threats, suddenly grimaced and broke down in tears. Since the massacre at Amanbere village, he had found his life in danger a number of times, and his nerves couldn't take it anymore. Yeager put his arm around the anthropologist and led him away from the others.

"I'm sorry," Pierce said, muffling his teary voice. "I know something's wrong with me."

"You've never gone through this before. You've got to hang in there. If you fall apart, we're all in big trouble."

Pierce nodded and sighed. "I never knew war could be this terrifying."

Esimo came over, Akili in his arms. He looked up worriedly at Pierce, and they exchanged a few words. Esimo was trying to comfort his friend. And he started addressing Yeager.

Pierce had somehow recovered his composure enough to translate. "He said, 'Thank you for saving my son.'"

Yeager smiled in spite of himself. He felt a little calmer. "You're welcome."

Esimo smiled back and said something to Pierce. He seemed to be imploring him about something. Pierce listened, a perplexed look on his face.

"What is he saying?"

"He wants to take Akili and go back to their band."

That was out of the question. If Akili went back to the area where the camp was, they'd all be killed. He knew they'd already decided what course to take, yet Yeager felt a great deal of sympathy for this tiny father. His fate was to live apart from his son. "Tell him this. If you take your son back to the camp, the Mbuti people will all be in danger."

A wave of desperate sadness swept over Esimo's face as he heard this. He stared down, and after some hesitation, seemed to make up his mind. "If that's the case, then can I go back alone?"

Yeager understood the struggle he was going through. On the one hand Esimo wanted to stay with his son, but on the other he was worried sick about his tribe members, the ones who had committed their lives to each other, who had always stood together.

Yeager was faced with a very practical problem. If they lost their guide, Esimo, what then? He turned to Pierce. "Any new intel?"

Pierce fingered the laptop and gazed at the display. "There's a reconnaissance report from a PKO unit. The insurgents in the north are already headed our way. They've been radioing our GPS coordinates."

Yeager checked his map. Their landmark before they got to the town of Beni in the southeast was the Ibina River in the south, so they should be able to get there without Esimo's help. But with the arrival of the

Predator drones the situation had grown much more strained. They'd be completely exposed when they tried to cross the broad Ibina, targeted by the Hellfire missiles. If the enemy force pushed down from the north, they'd be cut off at the river.

Either way, Esimo's role as guide was over, and he had to get back to his tribe. For his sake and safety it was best to let him go sooner rather than later. "Tell Esimo he can go back to the camp. But unless he circles around to the west the enemy might find him."

Pierce translated this into Kimbuti, and Esimo expressed his thanks. Yeager went back to the others, explained the situation, and gave them a little time to say good-bye.

Garrett and Meyers, and even the sullen Mick, thanked Esimo for all he'd done. The mercenaries would never forget how the tiny Mbuti man had saved them.

One by one Esimo shook their hands. Pierce bent down and gave him a hug. Though from polar opposite worlds, the two men were clearly close friends.

The Mbuti man smiled bashfully the whole time he was saying good-bye, but when he was about to leave and handed Akili over to Pierce, a short, shrill cry broke forth from him, a profound sorrow emanating from the depths of his being.

Akili reached out, as if to keep his father from leaving. In tears, Esimo walked off, but after a few steps he turned to Akili.

Watching this, the mercenaries were startled by a small voice from the grotesque-looking child. Until now the child had never said a word, but now, in Pierce's arms, his mouth was moving, desperately calling out to his father.

"Epa..."

This wasn't some whimsical, meaningless sound an infant made. Awkwardly, Akili sounded out a single word, over and over.

"Epa...Epa..."

Pierce's eyes went wide in surprise, then he shook his head sadly and spoke to the mercenaries.

"In their language *epa* means 'father.' Akili is calling out 'Father, Father.'"

Yeager pictured his son, lying ill in a hospital in Lisbon. As Justin lay there, writhing in pain, desperately gasping for air, he must be calling out for his father, too.

"Tell this to Esimo," Yeager said, fighting to keep his emotions in check. "We'll protect Akili. Someday you will be able to see him again, so take care of yourself until then."

When he heard this, Esimo said "thank you" again and again, gave his child one last hug, and then ran off. Akili was in tears, and the mercenaries took turns soothing him.

Esimo was finally swallowed up by the jungle, and the men felt as if the spirit of the jungle that had been protecting them had vanished. But they had no time to wax sentimental. If they didn't get a move on, the enemy would be upon them in less than an hour. Garrett had been patched up, and Yeager signaled them to move out. "Let's go," he said.

Garrett got to his feet. "He lost something," he said, and picked up a large leaf from the ground. Inside the rolled-up leaf were the coals that Esimo had so treasured.

"That's the fire of life for them," Pierce said. "I've lived with the Pygmies for a long time, and there's one riddle I've never solved. I've never seen them light a fire other than by using coals. That fire may have been burning in this jungle and handed down by them for tens of thousands of years."

Esimo had gone back to his people and their warm fire. Yeager prayed that the Pygmies' fire of life would burn forever.

8.

KENTO STAYED HOLED up in his tiny lab, fighting hunger. On top of the desk, the two laptops his father had left him were up and operating.

The GIFT countdown continued. By tomorrow night he would know the structure of the new drug.

The black laptop was connected again with the Congo. As before, he had a call from Poppy and was instructed to pass along updated intel to Nigel Pierce. But the satellite image only lasted fifteen minutes before it cut out. It then reappeared, only intermittently showing the situation in the Congo. They were apparently employing multiple earth-orbit satellites, switching from one to another. And they were using different types of cameras, too, as a normal video image was replaced by an infrared image, only to switch to a strange monochrome screen.

Every time there was a close-up of the sea of trees, Kento peered intently at the screen, hoping to catch some new information, but the trees blocked his view, and he couldn't see what lay beneath.

"Isn't there a reconnaissance image taken at a lower altitude?" Pierce asked him.

"No, there isn't," Kento replied. Everything he saw was high-altitude imagery.

A long silence followed. Soon after the reconnaissance images faded, Kento's cell phone rang. OUT OF AREA, the display said. The regular call from Lisbon. Once more amazed by the reach of global communications, Kento answered.

"Here are today's readings," Lydia Yeager's melancholy voice said.

The numbers she gave were Justin's blood gas results. Checking the arterial blood indicated how well Justin's lungs were functioning. Kento noted down these three indicators in his notepad.

"How are things at your end?" Lydia asked.

"The drug development is proceeding."

"I hope to hear some good news," Lydia said, and hung up.

Kento compared the arterial oxygen pressure value and the pH she'd given him and, using the dissociation curve published in a specialized text, calculated the degree of arterial oxygen saturation. This was the value that showed the amount of oxygen in the blood. In late-stage PAECS there is hemorrhaging from the lungs, and the oxygen saturation level rapidly decreases, leading to death. The ratio of decrease is set, so if you plot the change in value you are able to calculate very accurately how much time the patient has left. In Justin Yeager's case this meant seventeen days. Unless he took the new drug by March 3, Japan time, he'd be dead.

The deadline that his father had given him, the end of February, had accurately predicted Justin's condition. This, too, had to be the work of a superhuman intelligence.

Kento wanted to know Maika Kobayashi's readings as well, but the university hospital was under surveillance, and he couldn't get in touch with his friend Dr. Yoshihara. All he could do was pray that she would hold out until the drug was ready.

The black laptop, the one used to communicate, gave a short beep. He had mail. A message appeared on the screen, and Kento typed in his reply to Pierce on the other side of the world, telling him he had new information.

Pierce, breathing heavily as he walked through the jungle, said through the voice link, "Could you read it to me?"

The message was in English, and as he read it aloud Kento mentally translated it into Japanese. It seemed to be a record of a radio message, and it said, "We found no bodies in the missile impact zone."

"Okay, got it. Thank you, Kento."

"What is this?"

"It's a transmission from the enemy, intercepted by the PKO," Pierce replied.

Kento was on standby again. He saved the message and then stared at the small laptop. A thought suddenly hit him. If the computer had e-mail function, wouldn't it have a record of past communications?

Why his father had gotten involved in all this was a mystery. And this was a great opportunity to answer that. He began scrolling through the computer, the unfamiliar operating system slowing him down. He cautiously moved the mouse and accessed the data on the hard drive, and a new window opened with a long list of file names, all in English. He had no idea where to begin, so he located the search function, typed in his father's name in Western-style letters, and clicked FULL TEXT SEARCH.

A list of files immediately popped up, all reports on his father's personal history. The letterhead on the reports was the same: Defense Intelligence Agency. Kento wasn't familiar with the name, so he looked it up on his electronic dictionary and learned it was a US government espionage service.

But why would a spy organization's documents be on this laptop? The question threw him momentarily, but then he understood. Poppy must have hacked into the US government's communications network and accessed the DIA's documents. If he could download images from military reconnaissance satellites, this was a piece of cake.

He scanned the documents further and found his father's academic article included, in Japanese. His report on investigations into viral infections among the Mbuti Pygmies. The DIA analyst added this note: At the same time and the same place, Dr. Nigel Pierce was staying there doing anthropology fieldwork. I see, Kento thought. So his father and Pierce met each other in 1996, in Zaire, the former name of the Democratic Republic of the Congo. In the report was an item entitled Other foreigners staying there at the time. Kento skimmed through the list, and when he came across another Japanese name he yelped in surprise.

Dr. Yuri Sakai

So this inconspicuous woman was in eastern Zaire at the same time. Had she and his father met each other there, worlds away from Japan? Kento had a bad feeling about this. The word *affair*, which his mother had let slip, came roaring back into his mind.

Kento called up the search function and typed in this mysterious female doctor's name. One document, complete with a photo, popped up on-screen.

Kento scrutinized the image. The photo was of a woman in her thirties. A photo taken for a passport or some sort of ID. She looked a little younger than he remembered, but the small face, with no makeup, definitely belonged to the woman he talked with on campus.

The report's letterhead said CENTRAL INTELLIGENCE AGENCY. So the CIA had been investigating Yuri Sakai. Kento read through the background investigation report.

Yuri Sakai, doctor of medicine

January 9, 1964: Born in Meguro, Tokyo

1989: Graduated from Joshin University medical department

1991: Employed at the private clinic operated by her father, the Sakai Clinic

All this matched what the newspaper reporter Sugai had found out. The rest of the report, though, contained new information.

1995: Participated in the nonprofit international medical support organization World Medical Rescue Group

1996: As a staff member of this group, was assigned to eastern Zaire; with the start of the civil war there, returned to Japan

1998: After the death of her father, closed the Sakai Clinic and participated in volunteer efforts to help the poor who do not receive adequate medical treatment

Other information:

No Japanese criminal record

No financial difficulties

Tax record follows

Family record is appended

Kento wasn't sure what *family record* referred to, so he scrolled down until he saw a Japanese document. It was a typical *koseki*, or official family record. An English translation was attached, but of course he didn't need that. The first thing he wanted to know was her present address, but it wasn't listed. He searched through the record of her parents' names and home address and came across a startling fact.

On November 4, 1996, according to the record, Yuri Sakai gave birth to a baby. That was not all. The baby was a girl named Ema. The column for the father's name was blank. And there was no record of a marriage. In other words, Yuri Sakai, unmarried, gave birth to her daughter without acknowledging the father. No way! Kento thought. Ema was born in 1996. The same year she and his father, Seiji, had been in Zaire.

Kento groaned. The suspicion that his father had had an affair was confirmed in the worst possible way. He had a half sister. While he was still alive, his father often came home late, telling his wife that he was tutoring a shut-in child, when in reality he was visiting his own daughter. An image that came back to him seemed to support this conjecture. On the night he met Yuri Sakai, he sensed another person inside her parked van. That might have been her child.

Kento scanned the laptop's contents, desperately hoping to find something that would deny this, but that was all he could find.

He stood up and restlessly began pacing the small apartment. Sugai must be continuing his background check on Yuri Sakai. How much did he know? Even if he knew all this, wouldn't he hide it from Kento? For his part, Kento wasn't about to let his mother know.

He scratched his head, polished his dirty glasses, and went back to the computer. This secret past that threatened to shake the Koga family provided the answer to other questions: Why the CIA had investigated Yuri. And why Yuri tried to snatch this laptop away from him. The CIA had something on Yuri, which is why she approached Kento. And even now, somewhere in Tokyo, she was trying to track him down.

Uneasily, Kento called up the search function and typed in a third name.

Kento Koga

He hit the enter key, and a list of documents containing his name flashed on the screen. He called up the first report, from the DIA, and shuddered when he saw it. They were hidden photos taken of him. A close-up taken with a telephoto lens that showed him talking with Marina Kawai on campus.

The background report on him was accurate, down to the smallest detail. Included was a report on his friends and acquaintances provided by the Japanese police. Kento went through the names on the list one by one. Luckily, Sugai and Jeong-hoon Lee's names weren't on it. The United States hadn't caught on that he had some powerful reinforcements, so he could still contact them without putting them at risk.

There was also a report of the messages between the Japanese police and the CIA concerning the door-to-door search of the Machida district. Can't you check all the residences? the CIA asked, to which the Public Security Bureau replied, Considering the population density of Machida, it's impossible to cover with just ten investigators. For the time being, at least, this little lab should be safe.

The final document contained some language he couldn't follow. An order was given to the paramilitary department of the Special Operations Group of the CIA: Kento Koga, already designated a terrorist, will be handed over from the local police and sentenced to special rendition following our extradition treaty. The destination is Syria.

Kento didn't understand the meaning of *rendition*, so he checked his electronic dictionary. The only definition that seemed to apply was "the handing over of an escaped prisoner."

Why Syria? He had no idea, but the awful threat pressing down on him was clear enough. If the police caught him, he wouldn't just be sent to prison. He'd be sent abroad, and he might never see Japan again.

He remembered the words his father had left him with: *I'd like you to do the research alone. Don't tell anybody. But if you find yourself in danger, give it all up right away.*

His hands were shaking. Why was this happening when all he wanted to do was save sick children? But even if he stopped trying to develop the new drug, nothing would change, would it? The US intelligence agencies and the Japanese police would never stop looking for him.

He opened the first document again, the photograph of him and Marina together. Her smiling face seemed to be sending him a message: *Don't give up.* Whatever the future held, he had no other choice.

The cell phone rang, snapping him out of his thoughts. "Don't waste your time looking at superfluous things," the voice on the other end said. The low, machine-generated voice of Poppy.

Kento was shocked. "You're monitoring this computer?"

"I am," Poppy replied, and the screen started changing on its own. One by one the files on the hard drive were erased. The small laptop was apparently connected through the Internet to Poppy's host computer. Just don't erase the photo of Marina, Kento thought. But it, too, vanished.

"I'll send you whatever you need. You just focus on your work."

"Can I ask you something?"

"What?"

Kento did his best to keep his voice from quavering. "If I'm arrested, are they going to kill me?"

"They will. But before they do that, they'll torture you."

Kento pictured his fingernails getting ripped off, and he started to feel queasy.

"Just follow my instructions and there will be nothing to worry about. If you don't want to die, do what I say."

He had to trust Poppy. "All right."

"We have a new satellite image coming in. Get in touch with Pierce." With this command, Poppy hung up.

Kento turned back to his task. The monochrome high-altitude image of the jungle showed a large river stretching from east to west.

Pierce was speaking, and he sounded exhausted. "We've just arrived at the Ibina River. A large town, Beni, is off to our southeast."

The satellite image showed a large gray patch, as if a giant had ripped out a section of the jungle. This must be Beni. Pierce and the others were about thirty kilometers northwest of the town.

"There should be a road that runs north from Beni. Do you see any movement along it?"

Kento enlarged the image. There was a line of cars, and around them a large number of people with rifles. "Looks like an army."

"How many people?"

"There are too many to count."

Pierce was silent for a moment. "We'll check it out on our end. Stand by."

The Ibina River rushed by beyond the stand of trees. In the darkness of the jungle, where the sun didn't reach, Yeager and the others were cornered. There was an escape route south if they could cross the river, but crossing the river meant being exposed to Predator drones.

"The east is completely closed off. There's about a thousand men there," Pierce said, looking up from the laptop computer. "If we head toward Beni we'll run right into them."

Wary of the troops pushing down from the north, Mick said, "Crossing the river's our only hope."

Yeager turned to Pierce. "Any word on the Predators?"

"Our Japanese ally is trying, but nothing yet. The drones are under a different chain of command from Operation Nemesis."

Yeager scanned the map again to confirm the hopeless situation. To the north and east were enemy forces; to the south were Predators waiting to pounce. To the west the meandering Ibina River was a wall blocking their way. Could there be any way out? Yeager wondered, and his eyes met those of Akili, seated on the ground.

"Any good ideas?" he asked, but Akili's expression remained frozen, and he didn't open his mouth. After all the life-threatening experiences the boy had gone through, and after having lost his father, the strange-looking little child appeared to have gone into emotional lockdown.

Pierce was staring at the computer screen. "Japan's sent us a change of tactics," he said. "The route to the airfield in Beni is cut off. There's someone standing by in the south who'll be sent north. We'll head south, and after we meet up we'll go past a town called Rutshuru and get out of the country that way."

Yeager traced the change of plans on the map. The route would take them into Uganda. They'd given up on the first two plans, and their fate now lay in this final option. "But what do we do right now? Cross the river?"

"If we wait here for a while, by tomorrow morning our safety will be assured."

"Safety will be assured? What does that mean?"

"We'll be able to chase away the Predators."

The mercenaries looked doubtful. Meyers spoke for the group. "That's impossible. Unless you've got some surface-to-air missiles stashed away."

"You have to trust our Japanese ally," Pierce said sharply. His expression grew gloomy. "But even if we get across the river safely, if the rebel force in the south starts to advance we'll clash head-on with them. That's our final and most difficult obstacle."

"Is the army in the south the LRA? The Lord's Resistance Army?"

"I'm afraid so."

The LRA was the largest and most feared fighting force in the region, an army that had raped and slaughtered hundreds of thousands of people.

"We're going to die here," Mick said. "In this stinking jungle. What are we going to do about wills?"

No one replied. Things were too desperate to waste their breath.

Pierce called to Yeager. "Come over here," he said. "There's somebody I'd like you to meet."

Meet somebody? In this jungle? What the hell? Yeager thought.

"Check out the computer."

Yeager faced the small display, and Pierce touched a key. The satellite image vanished, replaced by a young Asian man's face.

"Kento," Pierce said into the headset mike. "I'd like to introduce you to someone."

A young man wearing small-framed glasses appeared on the screen. A skinny kid who didn't strike Yeager as someone he could count on.

"Who's this? Our Japanese ally isn't this kid, is it?"

"No. He's a researcher, developing a new drug to treat PAECS."

"Give me a break. This guy's still in high school."

"No. He's twenty-four and in grad school in Tokyo. His name's Kento Koga."

Dubious, Yeager stared at the face of this researcher who was trying to save his son.

Kento felt overwhelmed by the brawny American who appeared on the screen. His face was deeply scarred, the shoulders under his battle fatigues so thick and muscular it looked like he was sheathed in armor. This was the soldier he'd caught glimpses of on the computer when he talked with Pierce. The soldier's sunken eyes glistened as he silently stared at Kento.

"This is Jonathan Yeager," Pierce said off camera. "He's Justin's father."

His father? It's *his* son I'm trying to save? As Kento recovered from his surprise, Pierce put the headset on Yeager's head.

"Kento?" Yeager asked in a low voice, and Kento hurriedly nodded.

"Are you really developing a drug?"

"Y-yes."

Yeager's expression remained stern. Kento realized the man didn't trust him.

"Do you know anything about Justin's condition?"

"Yes, I do. I just talked with your wife on the phone."

"With Lydia? How is Justin? Tell me exactly what she said."

Kento hesitated. "From the test results they say he has seventeen days left."

Yeager glanced down for a brief moment, but when he looked up again his expression was determined, combative even. "Will your drug be ready in time?"

Maybe, Kento was about to say, but then searched for other words. If he gave a vague reply it felt like Yeager would reach right out through the screen and bash him in the face. "Yes. It will be ready in time."

Yeager looked relieved. His face looked more like a father's now. One riddle had been solved.

An American will show up at some point.

"Are you trying to get to Japan?"

"Yeah, that's the plan. But..." Yeager lowered his voice a notch. "We're in a lot of danger here. I don't know if we'll make it to Japan. I might not be able to see my family again. Do you understand what I'm saying?"

Jonathan Yeager was ready to die. "Yes," Kento said.

"If it comes to that, would you tell my wife and son that I did everything I could to save Justin?"

Kento studied the bloodied, muddy face of the soldier. It was obvious that as a father Yeager was fighting with all he had to save his son. This realization surprised Kento, and he asked a simple, naive question. If he were speaking in Japanese the question would have sounded unnatural, but he had no problem asking it in English. "Do you love your son?"

"Of course," Yeager replied, shooting him a dubious look. "Why are you asking that? Your father loves you, doesn't he?"

"I don't know."

"You don't know? What do you mean?"

Kento was stuck for a reply, and Yeager went on. "You don't have a father?"

"He died not long ago," Kento replied, and cursed his fate. His father died, and his situation got desperate, to the point where his life was now in danger.

"I'm sorry to hear that," Yeager said, clearly concerned. "My life got messed up after my parents split up. But somehow I've been able to make it."

I'm not that strong a person, Kento wanted to tell him.

"I doubted my father's love, too," Yeager went on. "But since I had my own child I've understood. A father loves his child and wants to protect him. No matter what." He gave a cynical laugh. "Not as much as a mother, though."

Kento remembered how strong his wife, Lydia, had been, and he understood what a good family Yeager had built.

"Anyway, I want to save my son. Please—hurry and develop that drug. I'm grateful for all you're doing." Yeager handed the headset back to Pierce.

Pierce's bearded face loomed onto the screen. "Can I ask you some questions?" Kento said.

"Sure, for a couple of minutes," Pierce said, and glanced at his watch. "The random number sequence we use to encode video communication is used up pretty fast. So please make it quick."

"It's about my father. Why was he involved?"

"We met here in the Congo nine years ago. That's how I got to be a part of this."

"Was my father trying to save evolved humans, too?"

"It ended up that way, yes. At first it was purely academic interest. But once he knew we needed to develop a new drug, he took that on, well aware of the risks. He really wanted to help sick children."

Kento couldn't believe his father had that kind of zeal. "Really?"

Pierce nodded. "It seems like you didn't know your father very well. Dr. Koga was very concerned because he wasn't able to achieve much in his own field. So he leaped at the chance to develop a new drug. He felt very deeply that a scientist's mission was to serve others."

This was just the flip side of his inferiority complex, Kento thought spitefully.

"Your father realized he was in danger and chose you to carry on the work. He was sure that his son would be able to accomplish it. Your father was very proud that you were studying pharmacology."

Kento still didn't seem convinced, and Pierce continued. "Your father was an honest scientist. The fact that you're doing your best now to create the drug is proof of that. You've inherited his passion."

But there was something that kept Kento from accepting this praise of his father.

"Do you know a Japanese woman named Yuri Sakai?" he asked.

Pierce's expression instantly changed, a sudden look of alarm in his eyes. "Yes—I know her."

"She was in the Congo nine years ago, wasn't she? What kind of relationship did she have with my father?"

"It's best that you don't know anything about Yuri Sakai. Getting close to her is dangerous. Just leave her alone."

"But why? I have a right to know about my father," Kento persisted, but Pierce cut him off.

"We have to end the transmission now. Go back to developing the new drug. If anything happens, I'll get in touch."

The host computer remotely shut down his little laptop, and the room was suddenly silent. Kento felt lonely, like the last person left on earth. But this wasn't a new feeling. He'd been left behind, forlorn and helpless, ever since the moment in the hospital in Mitaka when he said farewell to his father.

His face reflected in the blacked-out monitor reminded him of his father. The story wasn't over just yet. The other computer his father had left him was still pursuing the chemical structure of the new drug.

You're the guardian now, his father was telling him. With science your only weapon, protect the lives of one hundred thousand children.

This might be the final message he'd left his son. But what kind of person was his father, anyway?

9.

ANDY ROCKWELL HAD a secret hobby. It had started in high school, but he had lacked the money needed to invest in it, and once he was in college he was too busy studying, so for years he had to be content with the most basic equipment. Finally, after he was hired by a bank in Sacramento and started getting a regular salary, he could freely use his money to pursue his interest, and he dedicated a corner of his apartment to this hobby.

He purchased three high-speed computers with oversize screens, a joystick and rudder, and a surround-sound system—an investment of ten thousand dollars. Afraid that people would think him weird, he decided not to let his coworkers know about this interest. Whenever he had a free moment, Andy was in the cockpit of a virtual fighter jet buzzing around the world.

In less than a year he'd graduated from World War I biplanes to the latest passenger jets, able to freely manipulate almost any aircraft. His favorite scenario was piloting an F-16 in aerial combat, where he'd shot down countless Russian fighter jets. Simulation technology software improved by the year, and when he watched the scenery on his multiple monitors, he really did feel like he was master of the skies.

Just about the time he'd exhausted all the available software, he received an e-mail ad from a site where he'd purchased a throttle lever.

A revolution in online gaming! A new, ultrarealistic flight simulation!

Intrigued, Andy immediately accessed the site. He was mainly interested in what kind of aircraft they used, but for some reason that fact wasn't revealed. There was a flight manual, however, which discussed the use of a "master arm," so he knew it had to be some sort

340

of fighter aircraft. Probably an air raid mission to wipe out terrorists on the ground, he mused. What was different about this game was that the takeoff time was strictly preset. Eight thousand players had taken the challenge, it said, but not a single one had completed the mission.

I'm the only one who can do it! Andy thought, suddenly filled with the desire to try. He created a log-in password and prepared for the mission, which would take place at a set time the following day.

At 1:00 p.m. the next day, Saturday, Andy was ensconced in the pilot's seat in his apartment. He logged in, and all three of his screens were filled with a runway spreading out before him. The view from the cockpit. But the image disappointed him. Was this what they meant by "ultrarealistic"? The computer graphics were poorly done. And when the takeoff time arrived, the view changed on its own as the aircraft took off on autopilot.

Andy kicked himself for being reeled in by this poor-quality site. He thought about logging off but decided to see what happened. The picture quality might be poor, but the movement of the aircraft as it took off was very realistic. Suddenly the screens on the left and right changed to a different image. There was a command on the left-hand screen: Switch to manual when you reach 10,000 feet. On the right-hand display was an image of the ground, probably taken by a camera fixed to the underbelly of the aircraft. From the unclear monochrome imagery, the aircraft seemed to be flying over a desert or savanna.

The left-hand monitor blinked on another command: After switching to manual, quickly descend and maintain altitude below 500 feet.

Gradually Andy began to have hopes for the game. He realized that this game might be ultrarealistic after all.

The aircraft continued to climb and reached ten thousand feet. Andy switched to manual, following the instructions he'd studied the night before. He rapidly descended, all the while keeping an eye on the altimeter. Visual information and the feel of the joystick matched, and he felt as if he were flying an actual aircraft. It was a prop plane. The body was light, and the ground speed was slow, only ninety knots, or 165 kilometers, per hour.

I've hit the jackpot! Andy thought excitedly. He was piloting an aircraft that had never been used in online games before. This aircraft, flying ultralow to slip past radar, had to be an unmanned Predator drone. The images in front and from below were those of the infrared camera Predators are equipped with.

Andy was totally carried away by the game. Trying to resist the thrill of crashing, he skimmed along just above the surface of the desert. After an hour he was instructed to climb to seven thousand feet. Andy pulled the joystick toward him and brought the nose up. After he leveled out he waggled the plane from side to side, adjusted the throttle, getting a feel for how the plane handled. Two hours later the plane felt like part of him, and he was confident he could handle it in any situation.

The monitor that gave him the flight path instructed him to descend to two thousand feet. He pushed the joystick forward and lowered the nose toward the mass of mountains below. Once he crossed the mountains the scenery abruptly changed, and he saw a modern city ahead. Low-rise dwellings surrounded a central clump of high-rise buildings. Where was this? The Middle East? Africa?

As the plane headed over the city the right-hand monitor showed a line of cars heading down a road. A straight line of sixteen cars proceeding down what looked like a highway.

A short command shot up on the left-hand monitor.

Attack the sixth limousine.

Three long hours into the flight, and he finally had a target. Andy followed the line of cars and went into attack mode. If this were a real Predator it would be the operator's job to fire the missile, not the pilot's. But this was a game, and he'd have to handle both tasks himself.

He took his left hand off the throttle lever and punched in numbers on the keyboard to aim the missile. White crosshairs appeared on the right-hand monitor, centered on the sixth limousine in the line. The long motorcade seemed to suddenly speed up, but the crosshairs remained right on target. Andy drew a square frame around the black body of the limousine. The laser-guided missile was ready to go.

Andy rested his right thumb on the trigger button on the joystick. Push his thumb down a few millimeters, and the Hellfire antitank missile would blow the target to bits.

The mission was just about accomplished. And he was the only one who could carry it out, he proudly told himself. Andy started to press down on the trigger. And right then a doubt struck him. The scene on his screen—wasn't this in the United States?

Vice President Chamberlain had finished a campaign stop in Phoenix, Arizona, and was on his way to Sky Harbor International Airport, riding in the sixth limousine in an escorted motorcade.

His speech on human rights was far from a rousing success, but he had a different aim in visiting this city. The chairman of the energy company Chamberlain used to be CEO of had come to this region. The night before Chamberlain had met him secretly at his hotel and received some excellent news about business conditions.

Since the start of the Iraq War this company's stock had gone way up. After President Burns declared victory, the reconstruction of Iraq had gotten up to speed, and companies that contracted to rebuild the country's infrastructure saw their stock continue to skyrocket to unheard-of levels. With the prospect of massive government-backed investments, and with the Defense Department putting in orders to the tune of seven billion dollars, this company's revenue was set to shoot up 80 percent. This was truly good news for Chamberlain. The company's political contributions were bound to increase.

Still, once he became a central figure in the military-industrial complex he was surprised at the simplistic logic that lay behind the ability to control people. Fear was the key. All policy makers who wanted to profit from war had to do was exaggerate the threat from another country and promote this among the citizenry. As long as they hid the basis for their decisions behind a wall of official secrecy, the mass media would play along and spread the notion of grave peril to the nation. That's all it took to be able to shift a huge amount of tax revenue into the Defense Department and to have the salaries of munitions companies' executives soar. And this fear that had been planted among US citizens also crossed borders, with other countries following America's lead and ramping up their defense budgets. Suspicion bred suspicion, and tensions between countries mounted higher than the reality warranted. In some cases war would even break out, creating a limitless source of funds that would profit a targeted cadre of people. And politicians reaped an added benefit: an external threat increasing their approval ratings.

Eisenhower foresaw this situation, and in his final speech as president he warned the nation of the danger of the military-industrial complex, though the message fell on deaf ears. As long as there are companies in every nation greedy to profit from war, war will never disappear from this world.

Chamberlain, lost in thought, suddenly raised his head. The scenery outside, barely visible through the five-inch-thick protective glass, seemed to be rushing by at a tremendous speed. The armored limousine had suddenly sped up, though the completely soundproof interior remained as quiet as ever. Chamberlain used the microphone to speak to the Secret Service agent beyond the partition. "Why are we going so fast?"

"No need to worry, sir," the voice on the speaker said. "We just should get to the airport as soon as we can."

"Did something happen?"

Just then the secure phone beside the rear seat rang. Chamberlain waved off the agent next to him, and he picked it up himself.

"The Department of Homeland Security just got in touch with us," his secretary back in the White House said. "A Predator drone on a training mission from Creech Air Force Base is missing."

"What are you telling me?"

"Soon after an unmanned aircraft left its base they lost control of it, and it quickly started to descend. They believe it crashed, but a search hasn't located any wreckage."

They should extend the range of their search, Chamberlain thought. "What does that have to do with me?"

"The aircraft is armed. Radar also picked up a small aircraft that crossed over from Nevada into Arizona."

Creech Air Force Base was outside of Las Vegas, only three hundred miles from Phoenix. Chamberlain unconsciously glanced up at the ceiling of the limo.

"But the flight path is the one filed for a Cessna owned by a private corporation, so we think the chances that the aircraft on radar is the Predator are pretty low."

"Did they try radioing the pilot of the Cessna?"

"They did, but he didn't respond to air traffic control."

Chamberlain was starting to get worried. Predators were very small and flew at high altitude, and there was no way to confirm their presence even if they flew right over you.

"You think the Predator was hijacked?" he asked. And right then, without warning, an antitank missile pierced the roof of the limousine. For a split second, the missile was in his lap, but before his brain could react, his whole body was blown to bits by the explosion. Everything went black, and Chamberlain was dead. The missile was well named, for hellfire incinerated everything, instantaneously vaporizing the huge amount of blood that shot up. Right then a second missile hit. Chamberlain's head, already wrenched off his body, was pulverized. Everything from his nose on up became charred bone, and it flew through the air, smashed into the bulletproof glass of the limousine three cars back, then rolled onto the pavement.

The powerful man had lined his pockets with war profits. Now his corpse was mute testimony to the superiority of American weaponry.

Rubens drove his rental car fast, over the speed limit, as he raced down the back roads of southern Indiana. Around him were old electric poles, stands of dead trees, and a few houses dotting the landscape. The upper half of his windshield showed a cloudy sky.

After the news of Vice President Chamberlain's death came in, Washington was in chaos. President Burns took refuge in the White House emergency bunker, the Presidential Emergency Operations Center, while his family was put under protection in a Secret Service facility. All agencies connected to Homeland Security mobilized their staffs, trying to ascertain exactly what had happened, but everyone was clearly in panic mode. Before the facts were known, neocons in the administration demanded that a nuclear strike be carried out on Islamic extremists' sanctuaries.

At first Rubens, too, thought this latest terrorist attack was the work of Islamic fundamentalists. But once he found out that all the unmanned drones deployed around the world were grounded after the attack, he knew who had murdered the vice president. Right this very minute, in central Africa, Nous and his group must have evaded the eyes of any Predator and crossed the Ibina River to safety.

Rubens pulled his car off to the shoulder, looked in the rearview mirror, and waited until the car behind him passed. No one seemed to be tailing him. He pulled out a map and checked the location of the person he was visiting.

After Operation Nemesis commenced, two US citizens were put under tight surveillance. One was the cultural anthropologist that Nigel Pierce had e-mailed with the news that he'd discovered a superhuman. This person, Dennis Schaefer, was an old man under medical care for liver damage. Both the NSA and CIA reported that there was nothing suspicious about this elderly anthropologist.

The person Rubens was going to visit was the other one. He knew there were risks involved in what he was doing, but he had no choice. The situation had gone dangerously downhill, and there wasn't a moment to spare. After Dr. Gardner was forced out as science adviser, there was only one other person he could consult.

He continued down the narrow one-lane road, came to an area with only a sprinkling of houses, and found a small house surrounded by deciduous trees. Rubens parked by the side of the road and headed toward the front door of the white two-story wooden house.

He casually glanced around, but of course he had no idea where the CIA surveillance team might be concealed.

He knocked, and before there was even an answering voice, the door opened. Rubens gazed at the small old man before him. "Are you Dr. Joseph Heisman?"

"I am," the reply came back in a low, husky voice.

This scholar, author of the Heisman Report thirty years before, had left the front lines of research and was now in his midseventies. He had on a woolen robe over an old denim shirt. His short white hair was sparse, and his doubtful look was unexpectedly stern. His eyes kept people at a distance, and Rubens couldn't decide if this was because of his lifelong search to see behind the laws of nature or whether it was a vestige of a struggle against the world.

"It's a great honor to meet you," Rubens said, holding out a copy of Heisman's book *An Outline of the History of Science*. "I've enjoyed your books since I was in college. I heard you lived here and was hoping you could autograph my copy."

Rubens opened the cover. His Defense Department–issued ID card was taped to the title page. Heisman's expression didn't change as he stared at the card.

"I won't keep you long. Do you think we could go inside?"

"Of course. Come in," Heisman said.

Inside was a central staircase, to the right was a dining area and kitchen, and to the left was a tidy living room decorated with photos of his family, including those of his grandchildren. Rubens hadn't seen a car parked outside and figured that Heisman's wife must have gone out shopping.

"So?" Heisman asked before they'd had a chance to settle down.

As he stood in the middle of the room, Rubens checked the windows and the scenery outside. As they spoke, a laser listening device was detecting vibrations in the windowpanes and reproducing those waves. Rubens was concerned about Heisman's safety.

"My name is Arthur Rubens. I work at the Pentagon now, but I'm a senior analyst at the Schneider Institute. In addition to getting your autograph, I have something I'd like to ask your advice about." As he said this, he took out a card tucked inside the pages of the book and showed it to Heisman. **You are under surveillance by the US government. Please answer no to all the questions I'm going to ask you now.**

Rubens waited for him to read it, then continued. "Would you give me more details about what you wrote about in the Heisman Report?"

"No," Heisman replied. "Getting involved with those stupid people in Washington was the biggest mistake of my life. The last thing I want to do is relive those days."

The emotional reaction didn't seem like an act. Rubens hoped these weren't his true feelings.

"I just have a couple of questions I'd like to ask."

"I have nothing to say."

"Just five minutes of your time?"

"No."

"Really? Well, I'm very sorry to have bothered you."

Thus Rubens established that Heisman had not been told anything about the special access program. Rubens went on, expressing an admiration for Heisman that was real, not part of the camouflage. "What I said at the front door a moment ago was true. When I was in college reading your book really enlightened me. Would you mind signing it before I go?"

Rubens held out a second card along with the book.

To avoid audio surveillance, do you have a more secluded room we could go to? Even a bathroom would be fine.

"Of course," Heisman replied. "Since you've come all this way, I'd like to give you one of my other books, too. Let's go into my library."

"Thank you. That's very kind of you."

Rubens followed the old man past the kitchen toward the rear of the house. There was a small room, a sort of addition to the house that stuck out into the backyard. The room was filled with bookcases, not just lining the walls but also filling the middle of the room. Surrounded by thousands of volumes, Rubens felt as if he were getting a glimpse into the great mind of the scholar.

Heisman shut the door behind him and switched on the light. "The windows are all blocked by bookshelves," he said. "There are no chairs or heating. Is this all right?"

"This is perfect," Rubens answered. Under the naked lightbulb, Rubens felt like a teenager meeting a rock star he was crazy about. "I'm sorry I have to do everything in such a roundabout way. It's for your own safety."

"Why should I be under surveillance?" Heisman asked gruffly. "What evidence did the court base their wiretap on?"

"There's no warrant. That's just Gregory Burns's way of doing things."

"Is this the Soviet Union? Or North Korea? What a pathetic, idiotic president." Heisman spat out the words. "Gödel was right."

"Gödel?" Rubens was startled for a moment to hear the genius theoretician's name. He immediately recalled a well-known anecdote from the history of science.

Kurt Gödel, who shocked the mathematical world by proving the incompleteness of natural number theory, left Nazi-controlled Austria and fled to America. In order to obtain US citizenship he had to pass an interview with a judge, so Gödel, ever the serious scholar, thoroughly studied the US Constitution. And he made a startling discovery. Examined logically, the Constitution contains a major contradiction. Behind its advocacy of democracy, it also created a system whereby a dictator can legally be created. And of all things, Gödel chose the moment of his interview with the judge to give a mini lecture about what he'd found. Fortunately, his guarantor and friend, Albert Einstein, had arranged things ahead of time with the judge, so Gödel passed and became a US citizen with no problems.

This was just an amusing anecdote from the history of science, but now, in the twenty-first century, it was no longer funny. A dictator who saw himself above the law had actually materialized. The original role of the attorney general and the president's other legal advisers was to scrutinize the legality of any decisions he made, but these safety precautions no longer functioned. Under the Burns administration, the job of lawyers was to distort legal interpretations so they suited the will of the president. The administration was a complete dictatorship in which the president, commander in chief of all the armed forces, could, in the course of his duties, ignore the law.

We've already lost to the Islamic fundamentalists, Rubens thought. The country that valued freedom above all was no more. Why is it that the more politicians try to protect a democratic system the deeper they fall into totalitarianism? Was freedom within a nation nothing more than an illusion?

"To get back to what I was talking about—" Rubens began, but Heisman cut him off.

"Am I under surveillance because of that report I wrote?"

"That's right."

"Section five has actually come true, hasn't it?"

Rubens tried not to be surprised each time Heisman revealed how sharp his mind was. "Correct."

"Where did it happen? Not in the Amazon, I would think. In Southeast Asia? Or was it in Africa?"

"Why do you exclude the Amazon?"

"Minority groups in the Amazon perform infanticide on any deformed children. If a new human species were born, they'd kill it right away."

Rubens was startled at these words. In the two hundred thousand years of human history, until about a hundred years ago—before modern medicine—an infant in any culture that looked different from others was killed. Infanticide was a type of artificial selection. If any evolved individual had appeared it must have been killed, too. Human beings, always eager to exclude those who are different, might have nipped evolution in the bud.

Then why this time did the Mbuti allow a child whose head was shaped so differently from theirs to live? Had the Mbuti created a culture that accepted deformed children? Rubens had no idea.

"As you have surmised, the site is in Africa, in the Congo. It's a Pygmy child, already three years old. Right now a secret mission is being led by the White House, and they've put you under surveillance because there's been a leak."

Rubens explained the mission and background of Operation Nemesis, trying to be succinct yet hit all the highlights. Heisman stood stock-still under the overhead light, for all the world like a statue of a philosopher. When he heard that the Pygmy child was given the code name Nous, he smiled. "A nice name," he said. "And what do you think is the cause of this evolution?" he asked.

"This is just a guess, but I think it's a mutation in the transcription factor. There's a possibility that there was also a neutral mutation in a different gene. But even if we were to analyze Nous's complete genome, present-day science wouldn't be able to explain the mechanism by which a mutated gene created an evolved brain. This would be even more true if it had an effect on epigenetics."

Heisman nodded. "Continue," he urged. Finally, after he'd heard Rubens tell the story, the testy gleam returned to his eyes. "This is delightful. That a mere three-year-old child can torment a superpower that much."

"The reason I came here today was to see if you could give me any advice."

"I have none to give," Heisman said, spurning him. "My only regret is not being able to see the president crying his eyes out."

"Professor," Rubens said, forcing himself to be calm. "You don't seem to like this administration very much."

"Not just this administration. I hate anyone in power. They're a necessary evil, I suppose, but they've gone too far. I might even go so far as to say I hate human beings."

Deep down, Rubens knew he felt the same way. "Why?"

"Of all living creatures, Homo sapiens is the only species that commits genocide against its own kind. That's the definition of humans. Human nature equals cruelty. The other kinds of humans that used to live on the earth—early man and Neanderthals—were wiped out by modern man."

"So it was not our intelligence that led us to survive but our cruelty?"

"That's the way I see it. The Neanderthals had a larger brain capacity than we do. One thing we can say for sure is that modern man does not want to coexist with other types of humans."

Rubens knew this wasn't some hasty conclusion. It was a fact that many unearthed Neanderthal bones revealed wounds caused by violence, even traces of having been eaten. Forty thousand years ago on the European continent, only two types of animals possessed the intelligence to cook their catch—the Neanderthals and modern man.

"It's a reasonable hypothesis," Heisman went on. "The Europeans who advanced into North and South America killed ninety percent of the native inhabitants through war or epidemic. Most of the tribes were exterminated. And on the African continent, in order to capture ten million slaves, many times that number of people were killed. They were the same species as their captors, but the captors didn't care. Modern man treated other races very badly."

When he remembered the history of the Congo, Rubens felt depressed. Slavery wasn't the only calamity that befell that country. In the Congo—once the private possession of King Leopold II of Belgium—anyone who resisted the government's tyranny was killed by having his hands cut off. Before long the Belgians' racial discrimination ran rampant, and people collected the severed wrists of those they killed. Ten million people, from infants to the elderly, were slaughtered. Up until the twentieth century only the African continent was left behind by development because the slave trade and cruel colonial control had stolen away the most valuable resource of all—its people.

"Humans can't understand that they and other races are the same species. They distinguish themselves by skin color, nationality, religion—even by narrow groupings such as geographical region and family—and see these as their defining features. Individuals from different groups are viewed with hostility, as if they were a different species. This isn't a rational decision but a biological characteristic. The human brain inherently distinguishes different beings and views them as a danger. To me this is proof enough of humans' cruelty."

Rubens could understand Heisman's point. "In other words this behavior is preserved in the species because it aids survival. Conversely, if a person isn't on his guard against another race, then he'll be killed by that other race."

"True. It's the same logic as when a type of animal that isn't afraid of snakes is then bitten by poisonous snakes, and its numbers decrease. The result is that individuals who *are* afraid of snakes will survive in greater numbers, and most of their descendants will have an instinctive fear of snakes."

"But don't we also have a desire for peace?"

"It's much easier to call for world peace than it is to get along with one's neighbor," Heisman replied sarcastically. "Look, war is just another form of cannibalism. Humans use their intelligence to try to hide their instinct for cannibalism. They mix in various kinds of sophistry to justify it—politics, religion, ideology, patriotism—but deep down they have the same desires as animals. People killing other people to defend their territory and chimpanzees going crazy and becoming violent when their domain is invaded—how are these any different?"

"Then how do you account for altruistic acts? Some people do what we'd consider unselfish good deeds." As he said this Rubens pictured a seedy-looking Japanese—Kento Koga, whose photo was attached to the report by the DIA. That young man, unappealing and obviously unattractive to women—why would he continue developing a new drug even though he knew it put him in grave danger?

"I'm not denying that people also have a good side. But good deeds are seen as virtuous precisely because they run counter to human nature. If these were biologically normal acts, we wouldn't praise them. The only way people can show how good their country is is by not killing people from other countries. But human beings today can't even do that."

Rubens knew his debate skills might not be enough to refute Heisman's deep-seated distrust of humans. Heisman might even be hoping that his report would come true, that mankind would be wiped out.

"I'm sorry, but I can't cooperate with the Pentagon's operation. If a new type of human being has appeared, I see it as cause for celebration. Modern men are pitiful beings that have spent most of the last two hundred thousand years killing each other. This situation, in which humans can only coexist by threatening each other with weapons of mass destruction, shows the limits of human morality. It's time we hand over the planet to the next generation of beings."

"But Professor . . ." Without intending to, Rubens sounded like he was pleading. He was driven into a corner, and he knew he had to appeal to Heisman's intellect. "There's another reason besides the one I gave you for my visit today. Can I have a little more of your time?"

"Ask what you want, but my mind is made up."

"There's going to be an official announcement tonight, but Vice President Chamberlain was assassinated earlier today."

Heisman must have been surprised by this news, but his only reaction was a raised eyebrow.

Rubens explained the details about the hijacking of the unmanned drone and how Nous and his companions were held up in the Congo. "What I'm going to tell you now is highly classified, so please keep it secret. The NSA tracked the hacking of the air force computer network and soon identified where the signal came from. The Predator was hijacked by——"

"Islamic fundamentalists?"

"No. It was the Chinese People's Liberation Army. The cyberattack was led by the Fourth Bureau of its General Staff Department."

Heisman's eyes lost focus.

"But only those involved in Operation Nemesis know who was really behind it. Nous. The problem is there's no proof. The American government believes it was cyberterrorism executed by China. If it comes to a military confrontation between the United States and China, all of Asia—the so-called arc of instability—will get involved, along with

Russia, Europe, the Arab countries, and Israel. It could actually lead to another world war."

"But in that case..." Heisman began, and then fell silent, staring at Rubens.

"That's correct. The one who could launch the first nuclear strike is the president of the United States."

Silence descended on the stacks. Rubens cursed the fragility of human peace. Why, he thought, do we have to live in constant fear of humans killing each other? This anxiety has never let up, from the time when human beings first appeared to the present, an unbroken chain of two hundred thousand long years. The sole enemy human beings have is their own species—other humans. "At this rate item three in the Heisman Report might take place. Even if it's limited use of nuclear weapons, once the first one explodes it's just a question of time before mankind's extinct."

Heisman was silent for a while, then looked up. "All right," he said. "I'll answer your questions. Ask anything you want."

Rubens thanked him and plunged ahead. "What chance of success does Operation Nemesis have?"

"Zero. We have no chance of winning against an evolved intelligence."

"If that's true, then what's our best strategy?"

"Find out Nous's intentions."

"His intentions? But is that even possible? According to your report he possesses mental qualities that are incomprehensible to us."

"No; Nous completely grasps our cognitive abilities. And he's giving us a problem we can solve. He's communicating with us."

Looking back on all that had transpired, Rubens saw how true this was. Nous could figure out everything they'd been thinking.

"We have no chance of winning, so we have to understand Nous's intentions and choose the best way of losing. Do that and we should be able to avoid complete ruin. When it comes to deciding how best to lose, we have only two choices."

Rubens put his hands to his forehead, racking his brain. For the first time in his life he was mentally outclassed. "Just a minute. What do you mean?"

"You still don't get it? He didn't kill the vice president out of anger. Through the drone incident he was telling us the strategy he's adopting."

"Nous's strategy?"

"Right. Think of the power relationship between us and Nous. For humans beings, who is it whose wisdom we're no match for?"

Only one answer came to Rubens. "God."

"Correct. The power relationship between humans and superhumans is the same as that between people and God. Because the opponent strikes back with a power that exceeds that of human intellect. Nous chose God's strategy. First he tried to cooperate with humans. If humans reject his overtures, then he retaliates in force. But if they then try to cooperate, he immediately returns to cooperation himself. And he doesn't have a desire for revenge. Doesn't the God of the Bible use the same strategy to win over humans?"

Rubens was astounded. Nous's strategy, which Heisman had seen through, was very similar to that of the prisoner's dilemma and the tit-for-tat strategy discovered in computer simulations. "So God is subtle but not malicious?"

Heisman gave a faint laugh but then frowned. "Because we chose attack as our first move, our opponent opposed us. If we continue to attack, we'll suffer even worse counterattacks. All that awaits us is our annihilation. If we say we want to cooperate, though, we'll be forgiven. The control-and-submission relationship doesn't change at all. We have no chance of winning, and the only thing we can do is prostrate ourselves before him."

"So your conclusion is that we should stop Operation Nemesis right away."

"Exactly. Do that and Nous will immediately halt his counterattacks. Somehow he'll get rid of the threat of nuclear war. He has to protect the environment of the earth, otherwise he won't be able to secure his own habitat."

For the first time Rubens noticed a riddle he had missed as well as its answer. If Nous had the ability to hijack a Predator, then why did he attack the vice president instead of manipulating the ones flying above the Congo?

"At the present stage, if Nous is liquidated then the danger of a nuclear war remains."

"Correct. That was his purpose in killing Chamberlain and making it look like the Chinese did it. In order for us to survive as a species, we've been driven to a point where we have to protect Nous's life."

How many times now, Rubens wondered, have I been shocked by the intelligence of this three-year-old?

"If we push Nous into a corner even more, the situation will get even worse. Next he might assassinate some Chinese leader and make it look like the United States was behind it. But it's a mistake to blame him from an ethical standpoint. Humans, too, would fight back if attacked by chimpanzees. Without any moral qualms. It's the same thing."

An ape shot by a human's hunting rifle, Rubens mused, would probably die without ever understanding what had happened to it.

"So the only thing we can do is protect Nous. That's all I can teach you. Is that enough?"

"Yes. Thank you so much for all your advice," Rubens said, thoroughly chagrined now by the decision he'd made to eliminate Nous. "It's been very helpful."

Heisman held out his hand. "Give me the book. They'll think it suspicious if I don't sign it."

Thankful for his consideration, Rubens held out a copy of *An Outline of the History of Science,* along with a pen. As Heisman reached out to take them his left sleeve moved up on his arm, and Rubens almost cried out at what he saw. Heisman had a faded tattoo on the inside of his left arm. A single letter followed by four numbers: A1712. An inmate identification number given to those who had been in Auschwitz.

Six million people had been murdered by the Nazis just because they were Jewish. Rubens calculated backwards and figured that Heisman must have been a teenager at the time of the Holocaust. He wondered what had happened to his family and recalled that there was not a single old photo in the row of photos in the living room.

At the time of the Cold War Heisman had joined an American government advisory body, but he had been a rebellious scientist, arguing against the use of war. He was the greatest intellect of his generation, someone who had taught Rubens the true fascination and appeal of science. Rubens stole a furtive glance at Heisman's hand as he signed the book, imagining that hand back then, smaller, doing forced labor from morning until night as his friends and family were, one after another, murdered. Did this hand remember the last time he touched his mother?

A sudden surge of gratitude welled up in Rubens's heart—gratitude toward this old man who had fought against a cruel fate and had survived, and gratitude toward the life he had protected to the end. Rubens wanted to tell this curt, misanthropic Jewish scientist how much he respected him and how much affection he had for him.

"Here you are."

Heisman handed back the book and looked up at Rubens with a wondering look on his face. Rubens was blinking back tears. Heisman glanced at his left arm and seemed to guess what Rubens was feeling. He flipped the underlined, well-worn pages of the book. "You really seemed to have liked my book," he said. "Thank you for that."

"No—thank *you*. Your work will continue to influence later generations."

Heisman nodded, the stern look now gone, and he spoke calmly, as if speaking to a friend. "The six and a half billion people on the earth right now will, in about a hundred years, all be dead. So why do they have to keep killing each other?"

"Maybe because there are so many people who don't hide their true character."

Heisman smiled. "Don't just study history. All it does is glorify massacres done by stupid people obsessed with power, transforming them into heroic tales."

"True."

"There's one more thing I'd like to add about your operation."

"Please."

"You're overlooking one very critical problem."

Rubens frowned at the unexpected comment. Were there still other problems?

"But you can just let this point be. It's not going to have that much of an effect on anything. Consider this a kind of quiz. Try to find the answer while you're working."

Rubens racked his brain, going back over the details of the operation, but nothing came to mind. "Can you give me a hint?"

"Why is Nous trying to find a cure for an intractable disease?"

Rubens had referred to this when he was explaining the situation to Heisman. In his view Nous had two objectives: to get Yeager, whose son suffered from the disease, on his side, and to use the children with the disease as hostages to ensure Kento Koga's safety. "Is there a hidden aim other than what I discussed?"

"There is. From Nous's perspective, developing this special drug was the most rational solution of all."

"Solution? Are you saying that he's given us other puzzles that need to be solved?"

Heisman nodded and smiled significantly. "As you've monitored the operation, haven't you thought something was not right? Hasn't there been some small question that's tugged at you, unconsciously?"

Now that he mentioned it, Rubens was sure there had been. But like a dream from a few days before, this question lay below the conscious level and wouldn't come into focus.

Heisman gazed at Rubens, his look a mix of innocence and spitefulness. The face of a professor who's just assigned his student a knotty problem to solve. "Let this be your homework. Here's one more hint: you're underestimating your enemy's intellect. Be very, *very* cautious."

10.

GIFT'S COUNTDOWN WAS down to seconds now.

"Fifty-nine seconds," Jeong-hoon announced. They would soon know the structure of the drug.

As he stared at the laptop screen, Kento felt secretly frightened. If GIFT displayed NONE, then he wouldn't be able to save those sick children. But if it did show an answer, the task of developing the new drug would switch from Jeong-hoon, who'd taken the lead up until now, to him. And Kento had no confidence at all that he'd be able to pull it off.

Thirty seconds to go. Kento intentionally started taking shallow breaths. Taking in only half the amount of oxygen as he normally did, he soon found himself nearly suffocating. This was the pain of alveolar hypoventilation. The children with PAECS were forced by this suffering into a hopeless battle, for years. Kento pictured Maika Kobayashi and tried to summon back his sense of mission as a pharmacologist. He had to control this deadly disease and save her.

"Ten seconds."

Jeong-hoon's voice pulled him back to GIFT.

"Five seconds, four, three, two, one," they counted down together, and when it reached zero they were glued to the display.

A new window filled the screen. "There it is!" Jeong-hoon yelled.

The display showed a list of compounds. The answer GIFT had come up with far exceeded their expectations. There were twenty candidates that should be 100 percent active. The list included each drug's pharmacokinetics, and when they clicked on this there were detailed predicted values on absorption, discharge, and toxicity, as well as a list of existing drugs whose simultaneous use was contraindicated.

"I feel like I'm dreaming," Jeong-hoon said. He clung to the computer screen, excitedly poring over the possible candidates. Once he'd gone through them, he said, "I think any of them would pass as a drug, but there's one thing I'm concerned about. This, for instance."

Jeong-hoon called up one of the candidates and pointed at a heading that said METABOLISM. "This medicine acts differently depending on the person. It looks like the effectiveness of the drug depends on differences in the genes that produce metabolic enzymes. For certain people this drug is completely metabolized in the liver, and not enough of it reaches the lungs."

"In other words, it can only be used for people with a set base sequence."

"Right. And there are all sorts of other issues, like certain drugs that produce renal toxicity in some patients."

Since they didn't know the base sequence of either Justin Yeager or Maika Kobayashi, these drugs were dangerous. "Isn't there a drug that will work for everyone?"

"There are eight types in the list that I think should be safe. If you click here the structures will appear, so could you run through them and check whether they can be synthesized?"

"On it."

It was Kento's turn finally. He drew a deep breath, took Jeong-hoon's place in the chair, and faced the software that surpassed human intelligence. When he clicked the consecutive numbers on the list, two structural formulas appeared: one was for an allosteric effector that could change the shape of the receptor, and the other was for an agonist that would bind the mutant ligand binding site. Elements such as carbon, hydrogen, oxygen, and nitrogen were bonded to each other in a hexagonal cyclic structure with a sort of zigzag of pendent functional groups. These were the structures of each drug.

Kento stared at the structures and mentally tried to perform a retrosynthetic analysis. To synthesize the drug that GIFT had shown them, he would have to use reagents to transform existing compounds in a step-by-step fashion into the final product, the target drug. Retrosynthesis involved devising a synthetic pathway from the starting material to the final drug, but in reverse. By doing this he could estimate which reagents and conditions were necessary and in what order.

Kento began by eliminating the candidate materials that had asymmetry. He did this because these might produce, in addition to the structure he was aiming at, mirror-image isomers. In the process of synthesizing, avoiding "Looking-glass milk" was very time-consuming. Next he looked for parts where simple reactions such as amidation, oxidation, and reduction might easily take place. He examined each reaction's yield, looking to see if, for example, there was reduction of ketone or whether there were hydrocarbons with halogen or heteroatoms attached. He consulted the reference books he'd bought, but there were still too many things that were unclear.

"I don't have enough information," Kento said. "If I could use the university computers I could access their databases."

"Do you mean this?" Jeong-hoon promptly asked, and called up the database function from GIFT's menu. The screen changed, and the exact chemical information site Kento was hoping for appeared.

"What do we do about an ID and password?"

"You can log in as is. GIFT is apparently illegally accessing the site."

Kento was beyond worrying about minor details. Using this site he could get data on one hundred million compounds and could search for more than twenty million known organic chemical reactions.

He quickly went to the editing software that allowed him to write chemical structure formulas and entered the reactions that he envisioned. But all of them were off, and he didn't arrive at a synthetic pathway that he could feel confident about. As this struggle continued, anxiety built up. Maybe this really was beyond someone like him, a second-year MA student. But he only had sixteen days left to create two types of drugs. Delay was unacceptable.

He decided to leave the candidates that didn't look promising for later and go through the remaining materials in order. But one by one, he gave up hope. Tormented by a feeling of impotence, he arrived at the final candidate. Lamenting his lack of knowledge, Kento opened up the eighth structure formula.

The agonist that appeared on the screen was a long, thin structure with two benzene rings and one heterocyclic compound, plus sulfur, nitrogen, and amino groups bonded to it. The three cyclic structures would probably form a functional group that would bind specifically to mutant GPR769. Although the allosteric drug used together with it was of a different composition and structure, it was also made up of three cyclic compounds.

As soon as Kento saw the combination of these two, his eyes were riveted to the screen. He had little to base it on, but his gut told him he would be able to synthesize this. Formulas sprang up one after another in his mind, and he wrote each down in his notebook and checked its reactions one by one.

An hour later he looked up. "I think it will work," he said. Though some vague areas still remained in the synthetic pathway, both types of drugs could be created from the starting material in about seven reactions. The remaining issue would be the amount of time it would take to synthesize them. But Kento was hopeful they could make it in time.

"So it's the eighth one?" Jeong-hoon said cheerfully. "That's the best one, too, in terms of predicted pharmacokinetic values. Its bioavailability is ninety-eight percent."

Jeong-hoon looked like a real researcher now as he began a brisk and detailed explanation. As Kento listened to information about the blood concentration half-life, among other things, he pictured the finished drug. They wouldn't administer it intravenously but orally. Ten milligrams once per day; five milligrams for infants. And the medicine would take effect within thirty minutes of being ingested.

"What about toxicity?"

"Extremely low. It's not carcinogenic or teratogenic, either, and long-term toxicity is safer than that of aspirin. However, besides mutant GPR769, this drug will also bind with twelve other receptors that are similar in shape."

The drug's side effects, then, would be that it would act on other proteins besides the target.

"But there will be a very low percentage of activation. GIFT has concluded that the drug is safe."

"So there are hardly any side effects?"

"That's what it looks like."

It all seemed so ideal. But could he really trust this? Kento felt apprehensive.

"What should we do?" Jeong-hoon asked. "You want to go with the eighth candidate?"

In his hesitation Kento recalled the words of Professor Sonoda. The professor had developed numerous new drugs and had often commented to his students between classes that "With a drug where all goes well in development, it's as though the god of medicine had preordained that everything will work out."

Kento decided to follow his professor's rule of thumb and believe in divine intervention. This god was ordering them as pharmacologists to save all the people in the world suffering from the disease.

"Let's go with it."

"Great," Jeong-hoon said, nodding vigorously. "I was just thinking: Shouldn't we pick a name for the drug?"

"You're right." Kento looked at the structural formula and inclined his head. If they followed the usual naming protocols the name of the compound would be ridiculously long. "How about calling the agonist GIFT 1 and the allosteric GIFT 2?"

"I like it," Jeong-hoon said, and smiled. "It'll be a gift to children."

Because they were concurrently synthesizing two kinds of drugs they needed not only more reagents but also more lab equipment. They would wait until morning, and then he and Jeong-hoon would split up to procure what they needed.

Jeong-hoon had done his part wonderfully, and he looked exhausted. "Do you mind if I get some sleep?" he asked.

Kento glanced at his watch and saw it was 3:00 a.m. already. "Sure."

Jeong-hoon lay down under their table-cum-lab-bench, using his backpack as a pillow and his leather jacket as a blanket.

Kento took off his glasses and rubbed his oily face with his sleeve. Suddenly he looked at the small black laptop. Since yesterday there had been no messages from the Congo.

How was Jonathan Yeager? he wondered.

The small black laptop had become Kento's portal to an unreal world. These past few days he'd been buying the newspaper, checking the international section, but there were no reports on a war in the Congo. If there really was mass fighting there, why was the Japanese media ignoring it? As long as the press didn't report on events on the other side of the world, it was as if nothing at all was happening. He felt like he no longer understood what was happening in the world he lived in.

Kento prayed that Jonathan Yeager had survived. It would be too tragic if Justin Yeager conquered his disease only to find his father dead.

Yeager opened his eyes in the darkness. Someone was whispering his name. He sat up on the tarp and had trouble remembering whom that voice belonged to. The accumulated exhaustion had not just dulled his body but his mind as well.

"Wake up."

Awake now, Yeager remembered the events of the last twenty-four hours. It had been a whole day and night since the threat of the Predators had vanished. They'd crossed the Ibina River, and Yeager and the others had headed south through the jungle. Pierce had given no explanation for why the armed unmanned surveillance aircraft had left the skies over the Congo, and the mercenaries hadn't pushed him to explain. Their concern was a more imminent threat. The Lord's Resistance Army, the LRA, which occupied the wildlife preserve to the south, had started advancing north, as if to cut off their route.

It was 2:30 a.m. Yeager confirmed with Meyers, on sentry duty, that everything was okay, then asked Pierce what he had found out.

"Take a look at this."

On the ground in this dark primeval forest, the small laptop emitted a faint glow. Next to it, Akili was curled up, fast asleep. As Meyers had said, Akili looked like a kitten when he was asleep. Careful not to wake him, Yeager moved around so he could view the display.

"We've finally acquired images from the surveillance satellite. This image is from fifteen minutes ago."

Yeager stared at the screen and was jolted wide awake. The satellite imagery had captured numerous heat sources, which indicated people. And the numbers looked to be in the tens of thousands.

"These aren't all the enemy. The ones spread out to the northeast are local villagers. With armed forces pressing down on them from the north and south, they've become refugees."

"So they're trying to escape into the jungle?"

"Looks like it," Pierce said, and pointed at the screen. "The enemy that was chasing us is more than thirty kilometers away to the north. We've basically shaken them off. The south is the problem. The LRA wants to wipe us out, and they're coming up right next to us."

Pierce's finger traced the north-south main road, and then a branch road heading to the south. "They're spread out more than ten kilometers."

Yeager clicked his tongue in frustration. The enemy was a bigger force than he'd imagined. And the site where they'd camped was inside the enemy formation. They were cut off on two sides, the east and the south. Once morning came the enemy troops would be back in the jungle in force.

"Why are they so intent on killing us?"

"They'll get a huge amount of money. Plus they'll get on America's good side."

"This sucks."

"Not really. This is a chance for us." Pierce's tone was forceful. "The LRA is the final barrier. If we can break through them, there'll be no other armed groups to deal with. We'll be able to get out of the country."

"But that won't be easy."

"No, but we'll manage," Pierce said. His finger moved on the satellite image, jumping over the LRA forces that filled the road and pointing to the south. "There's a town called Butembo, forty kilometers south. I have a vehicle filled with supplies waiting there. After we call the driver he should be up around here in less than thirty minutes. If we can take the SUV, Uganda's very close. We could get out of the Congo sometime this morning."

"Who's driving the SUV?"

"A young man we've employed temporarily. A Ugandan tourist guide."

"Sounds promising," Yeager said, but to him Pierce's plan seemed like an empty dream. "The problem is the LRA's formation. There must be more than a division deployed—fifteen to twenty thousand troops. How are we supposed to break out of here?"

"That's why we'll force our way through the enemy's center." Pierce swiftly called up a different document on the screen. "Take a look at this. Our ally in Japan hacked into this and came up with a PKO unit's battle plan."

"PKO?" This was unexpected. Yeager read through the UN peace-keeping force's secret document, which outlined a surprise attack against the main force of the LRA at 6:00 a.m. today. "You've got to be kidding. Would UN forces do something like that?"

"Anything goes in the Congo. Ten days ago the LRA ambushed them, and the PKO forces lost nine men. This is payback."

"Most of the PKO is made up of Pakistani soldiers, correct?"

"That's right."

This was an infamous PKO force that had sexually abused local women refugees. They were definitely a group that could undertake a retaliatory attack. Yeager, careful to not let the light filter out, shone his flashlight on his map. The attack was to take place on the center of the L-shaped formation, the junction of the main road and the branch road. If the Pakistani forces severed the formation at this point, a route to the south would open up. They might have a chance after all.

Yeager studied the battle plan. The Pakistanis weren't planning a frontal showdown but a hit-and-run attack. A warning to the LRA not to fool with them. The entire attack was planned to take only fifteen minutes.

"This is our only chance." Yeager had to agree. "Speed is the key here. We need to get close right now."

Meyers, who'd overheard them, went to wake up Garrett and Mick.

As Yeager briefed them, they raised a number of objections to this high-risk plan. But the more they examined it, the more they understood that this was their only chance. Trying to do an end run around the enemy's formation would take time, and they ran the risk that the force from the north would catch up with them. And they only had two meals' worth of rations left. They didn't have even a day to spare before they would need to reach their supplies.

Finally they all agreed that their only choice was to break through the enemy's dragnet. They put on their night vision equipment, taking care not to drain the batteries, and hurriedly prepared to depart. They'd used up a lot of rations, so their equipment had lightened to twenty kilograms.

Yeager looked at the sleeping Akili. "Shouldn't we let him eat something?"

"Better to let him sleep," Pierce said. He picked up Akili and placed him in the sling he'd fashioned in front of him.

"Once the fighting starts," Yeager said, "I want you to cover his eyes and ears."

They were eight kilometers from their objective. In the darkness of the predawn jungle they used their flashlights for a while, setting the output level at dim, then switched to night vision equipment for the last half of the journey.

By 0500 a faint light had crept over the jungle. They halted, and Garrett and Mick went off to reconnoiter. In less than a half hour they were back to report.

"The main road is swarming with LRA troops."

"Can we get past them?" Pierce asked.

"No way. There're sentries everywhere."

Garrett pointed to the map. "This is our precise location. If we want to cross at the junction, we'd better go a little more to the southeast."

"How close should we get?" Meyers asked.

Yeager considered all the risks. "Let's halt at four hundred meters away."

"Right at the edge."

"We'll be in rifle range. Watch out for stray bullets."

The four soldiers lined up in single-file battle formation, with Pierce and Akili bringing up the rear, and headed toward their staging area. The scenery around them remained the same, and they couldn't see more than twenty meters ahead.

"Wait here," Yeager said. "Mick and I will go ahead. We'll check out the situation, and we'll radio you about the timing."

"But our radios only have a range of two hundred meters," Garrett reminded him. "We have to get closer."

Reluctantly they moved closer to the enemy line. They designated a spot with a stand of large trees as their staging area, and the others stayed there while Yeager and Mick moved closer to the enemy line.

The main road was off to their left, parallel to the direction they were moving in. The branch road cut across it straight ahead. Both roads were carved out of the jungle and had a wall of trees soaring on either side. Their field of vision in the jungle was close to zero, so Yeager and Mick had to walk to a spot some twenty meters from the branch road. They figured they were a hundred meters from the junction of the two roads.

Yeager hid behind a huge tree and gingerly leaned out to check out what lay ahead. A line of LRA vehicles was halted on the muddy one-lane road. There were troop transport trucks, and the troops had gotten out of them and were standing around smoking and preparing meals. Unlike the militia they'd encountered up until now, these troops were dressed in matching uniforms and even wore berets.

Mick lowered his backpack and took out his claymore antipersonnel mines, some C-4 explosive, and a detonator. He pointed to the four corners around them, indicating that he'd set up booby traps.

Yeager nodded and climbed up the tree to view the scene from a better vantage point. He clambered five meters up, above the bush layer, and clearly saw the junction of the main and branch roads. He scanned with his binoculars and saw Russian-made tanks, armored personnel carriers, and countless weapons in the hands of the soldiers— mortars, rocket-propelled grenades, heavy machine guns, and AK-47 assault rifles—"poor man's weapons" that had made their way into the country for various purposes from China, the former Communist countries, and from the West. In this part of the country these killing tools outnumbered people's other possessions.

Ten minutes until the PKO's zero hour. Yeager switched from a rifle to his silencer-equipped pistol and shifted to a position where he could cover Mick. No way I'm going to die here, he thought.

Yeager was sure of one thing. Everything in his life up until now was for one single purpose.

To help him survive this.

It was 10:30 p.m. when Rubens got the emergency summons from the White House. "Be prepared to brief the president directly on Operation Nemesis," Eldridge instructed him, and Rubens hurriedly left the command post.

After his meeting with Heisman, Rubens had tried hard through many channels to make a direct appeal to the president. And now it seemed they'd finally listened to his request. But it was premature to celebrate. In the Congo the strongest, and worst, armed force had successfully encircled Nous. The successful conclusion of Operation Nemesis was imminent and the elimination of the superhuman a certainty.

Though it was late at night, the Defense Department was crowded. On the first floor Rubens passed Defense Secretary Lattimer, surrounded by his entourage, hurrying to the Pentagon's operations center, the National Military Command Center. This was the unit that would be the first to receive a nuclear strike order from the president.

Since Vice President Chamberlain's assassination, the US military's alert status had been raised to DEFCON 3. All military communications were encrypted with a secret call sign to defend against interception by an enemy country. If the unit tasked with cyberwarfare were put on the same alert status, then DEFCON 1, which meant full-scale war, would most likely be implemented.

Rubens got in his Audi and headed for the center of the city. As he drove he speculated on why he'd been summoned this late at night. The National Security Council had been convened at the White House for several days in a row, and the members were considering all the possible diplomatic and military options against China. The fact that he'd been summoned in between these meetings must mean that the White House was starting to have at least some concern for Operation Nemesis. There must be someone else in the administration who had the idea that Rubens had—namely, that the assassination of the vice president was not the work of the Chinese but of this new intelligence born in the Congo. If that were true, then Rubens had gained an ally. But who could it be? A powerful figure who could persuade the president to put a halt to Operation Nemesis? Rubens could only hope.

Rubens arrived at the White House and underwent a thorough ID check and body scan before he was given permission to enter the West Wing. He was led to a small lobby beyond a door guarded by two marines. This was a room that could hold about ten people, and the interior furnishings made it look less like a public space than an elegant private room, a cramped little parlor off in the corner of some wealthy person's mansion.

A receptionist sat behind a desk at the entrance. When Rubens said his name, the sole occupant of the room rose from the sofa next to the wall.

"You must be Rubens."

The man wore a suit and had silver hair and a mustache, and when Rubens saw him he was taken by surprise. It was the director of the CIA, Robert Holland.

"It's an honor to meet you, sir," Rubens said, and shook the intelligence agency chief's hand. Holland motioned him to a red leather chair.

"We don't have much time, so let's get right to it," Holland said, shooting a glance at the receptionist. He spoke so quietly Rubens had to lean forward to hear him. "How is the operation coming?"

"We've entered the final stage of the emergency response phase," Rubens replied, and glanced at the wall clock. It was 11:00 p.m.—5:00 a.m. in the Congo. This briefing with the president would be his last chance. "The largest military force in the region has completely encircled Nous. They'll begin wiping them out in two hours."

"Do you think our target will survive?"

"No."

Holland nodded and shot him a reproachful glance. "I hear that you went to see Dr. Heisman."

"Yes," Rubens freely admitted. He knew full well the CIA's network had him under surveillance.

"What did he say?"

"Nothing, really."

"Fine."

Holland's swift reply told him that the director was not an enemy.

"If you insist that Dr. Heisman remain silent, that's fine with me," Holland said. "I need your opinion. You think that the tragedy involving Chamberlain was not the work of the Chinese but originated in the Congo?"

"I do."

"Then is there still room to change Operation Nemesis?"

"There is. We have to protect Nous right away. And not kill him."

Holland looked like he'd anticipated this response. "But we don't know their exact location, do we?"

"If we send our assets stationed in Djibouti to the Congo, rescue could be possible. Nigel Pierce is using a satellite phone, so if the army's Intelligence Support Activity can acquire the signal they can pinpoint the location. And we can have two Delta Force platoons rescue them."

"But that's different from sending in unmanned aerial vehicles. It will take a few days just to coordinate permission to travel through their airspace. And we can't have a US military presence right in the middle of the Great War in Africa."

"Then we should immediately lift the terrorist designation from the operatives and let the military forces there know this: That killing them won't earn them one cent. That much we should be able to do immediately."

But Holland only scowled.

Rubens lowered his voice even more. "Director, isn't there something about this mission you've kept from me, even though I'm the one who planned it? Why were we told to eliminate Warren Garrett?"

"Because he's a traitor," the CIA director said bitterly. "He was collecting proof of special renditions and was filing a case with the International Criminal Court against the president."

Rubens was shocked. Shocked at the other objective hidden in Operation Nemesis. And at Warren Garrett's reckless plans—and his courage.

Holland was about to continue when the inner door opened. Acres, the president's chief of staff, appeared. "The president will see you now. Please step into the Oval Office."

As he and Holland stood up, Rubens whispered to Holland, "If we don't hurry, we'll be forced into a situation we can't handle."

"I understand," Holland said quickly. "We've underestimated the threat from the Congo. But it's very difficult to change the plans."

Rubens felt depressed. Was it really necessary to continue Operation Nemesis to the point where Warren Garrett was killed? While they were taking care of that, the world would be forced into an even more dangerous position.

They followed Acres down a narrow corridor, at the end of which was a chair. A sturdy-looking man was seated in it with a handcuff around his left wrist. This handcuff was connected to another on a briefcase at the man's feet. This briefcase was the nuclear football. Officers from the three major armed services were always on standby near the president so he could order a nuclear strike at any time.

Acres knocked on the door, and as Rubens waited next to him he thought of the long path that brought him here. He'd first taken an interest in the psychopathology of those in power while working in the Santa Fe research lab, and now, after many twists and turns, he was finally about to meet the greatest research subject of all. The kind of king of destruction found throughout history, the mad king who, in the present case, held a missile launch button in one hand while shooting depleted uranium bullets with the other.

Acres opened the door, and before them lay the Oval Office. President Burns looked over at them from behind his desk. He had on a dark blue suit and a tie of a similar color. Daily workouts had given him a firm body. Contrary to what you'd expect from such a supremely powerful figure, though, his eyes flitted around in a hesitant, timid way.

"This is Arthur Rubens, the person in charge of strategy for Operation Nemesis."

As Holland introduced him, Burns walked to the center of the room. For no clear reason, fear welled up in Rubens, and he struggled to suppress it. He had to contain the human reaction of blind obedience to authority, or else he'd never be able to uncover the other person's true colors.

The president shot Rubens a sullen glance. "So?" he said to the CIA director. "I'd be happy if you tell me the operation is completed. What's the situation now?"

"The operation is just about finished."

"And you'll get rid of the threat in the Congo?"

"Yes."

"Well, that's good news."

Burns motioned them to sit, and sat down on the sofa. He was clearly tired. "Why, when I'm so busy, do I have to hear about this low-priority plan? Are there some other issues?"

"The reason I asked you to meet with us tonight, Mr. President, is to let you know of the possibility of a connection between the hijacking of the drone and Operation Nemesis."

Burns's eyes tensed. Rubens was confused by this sudden change in expression. His eyes were exactly those of a child afraid of being scolded by his father. Was the president afraid of something?

"What do you mean? You're not saying that child—Nous—did it, are you?"

"I'm saying it's a possibility."

"Do you have any hard proof?"

"It was just a little too slick the way China surfaced so quickly as the source. In the past when the US Central Command's network was hacked, we never found out where the attack came from. If China's cyberwarfare unit did this, then they have the technology to conceal it."

"That's ridiculous. Saying that a three-year-old—a Pygmy child, no less—did this is much more unbelievable, wouldn't you say?" Burns went on. "When I say 'a Pygmy child,' understand, I just mean they're not civilized. That's all."

"But if he reached the level of abilities mentioned in the Heisman Report—"

"I can't believe that's possible."

Rubens couldn't overlook how worked up Burns was. The skin around his eyes flushed. The fear that had assaulted Burns before had now turned to open hostility.

Holland calmly began to try to persuade the president of the need to modify Operation Nemesis. Rubens, seated beside him, focused on analyzing the fluctuation in Burns's emotional state. To successfully persuade him he would need to pinpoint what he was afraid of and what was the object of his anger. Was he racist? Neo-Nazis and white supremacists had similar mind-sets, in that their violent impulses were transformed into a political ideology that became the pretext for phony right-wing groups. It was all a manifestation of twisted pride, of people whose pasts kept them from affirming their individual identities. Instead they sought refuge in the group, identifying with the organization. They saw the group as superior and their affiliation with it as proving their own superiority. It was clear that their interests were directed entirely inward, since their most vicious attacks were aimed at comrades who raised objections to their principles and positions, at members who should have completely affirmed the organization. For Burns, too, who was devoted to neoconservatism, it was undeniable that he uncritically affirmed the group to which he belonged. But what was hard to figure out about him was the kind of barely controlled anger he had displayed earlier. In America it would be a fatal mistake for any politician to openly display racism. If Burns possessed a strong racial prejudice that made him lose self-control, it would have been impossible for him to have hidden this in his political activities up until now. Most likely he was not a racist. Even if he did have a slight sense of discrimination, he was smart enough to keep it in check.

The CIA director's briefing continued until Burns frowned and cut him off. "I simply can't believe that one child could throw the United States into crisis. Aren't we humans the highest intelligence on earth?"

"But if we accept that, then the whole premise of the mission falls apart. Operation Nemesis's mission was supposed to be to remove the threat to mankind posed by this new intelligence."

"My approval of the mission was based solely on my desire to get rid of the threat that our codes would be broken. Nothing more, nothing less. It just happens that this child has an extraordinary mathematical ability, right?"

"If that's true then we still have the option to use that ability to help our country. We protect Nous and use his ability to decrypt codes. Also . . ." Holland hesitated. "Nous is the only one we save. There's no need to rescue the four mercenaries and the anthropologist."

This was a huge concession on Holland's part, but Burns brushed it aside. "No. There's no need to change the operation."

Political decisions might appear to be done rationally, but in reality the decision maker's personality plays a huge role. And in the president's decisive attitude, Rubens detected a bias in his character. Some personal belief must be motivating his insistence on wiping out Nous. But what was it? Rubens knew the only possible answer and was beginning to think it was impossible to change Operation Nemesis. Before Burns became a politician he'd been an alcoholic, had prayed to God to help him, and he'd recovered.

"Your name's Arthur?" Burns turned to glare at Rubens.

"Yes, sir."

"Arthur, I'm disappointed in you. Why is it taking this long to deal with one child? Are you that incompetent?"

"Compared to Nous, all of mankind is incompetent."

As he spoke these challenging words Rubens sensed Holland tense up. Perhaps taken by surprise, the president stared hard at the young analyst.

"Please let me tell you about the type of enemy we are confronting." Rubens changed his tone and explained the analysis found in the Heisman Report, without mentioning Heisman by name. He realized there was a hidden land mine in what he said, and, as he expected, Burns stepped right on it. When he heard that Nous was using what Heisman had called God's strategy, the president reacted immediately.

"I don't want to hear that kind of idiocy!"

Burns was obviously upset and was about to say more when Holland hurriedly reprimanded Rubens. "That is an inappropriate example. Stick to a political analysis."

"I apologize," Rubens said. "I agree it was inappropriate. However—"

Holland calmly took over. *Don't say another word* was his unspoken message. "What Rubens is trying to say is that if we stop our attack, there's a possibility that the threat will vanish."

The president turned a jaundiced eye on Holland, looking like he wished he'd disappear. Rubens stared at this man, known as a devout Christian, who prayed every time he plotted the Iraq War. At his feet, lit by a light from above, lay a dark shadow known as intolerance. But this didn't make Burns so unusual. Imagining an omniscient, omnipotent being and regarding people of other religions as enemies is a common Homo sapiens trait. People decide whether others are friends or enemies not just based on skin color or language but also on what god they worship. And God is a convenient being who can even wipe away the crime of mass murder, as long as one repents.

Rubens was gradually understanding the workings of the president's mind. For Burns, an evolved human being would be his newest enemy, a substitute for those of another faith.

"That's enough," the president said, standing up in the middle of

Holland's remarks. He'd lost patience. "Your assessment of this threat is considerably exaggerated. Just like the situation with Iraq. Where were the WMDs? Stop deceiving me with a threat that doesn't exist."

Rubens could sense both a guilty conscience and a desire to shift responsibility. The president's confident demeanor when he spoke publicly about the Iraq invasion was a complete act.

"I'm not saying the use of force against Iraq was a mistake," Burns said as he headed back to his desk. His haughty attitude whenever he insisted on justifying his decision only revealed how deep-seated his guilty conscience really was. "We liberated the Iraqi people from a tyrannical government and gave them their freedom."

America has gotten too damn big, Rubens mused. It is too much responsibility for one person to be in charge of this enormous country. Given more power than he deserved, Burns had been driven to use it any way he wanted, and this had turned to violence. He panicked at the disaster his decision had brought about, was tortured by a sense of guilt, and sought salvation. However...

If humanity evolves, then human beings will no longer be made in God's image. And if they lose God's favor and love, then their sins will no longer be forgiven. Burns's soul would forever bear the sin of killing one hundred thousand Iraqi citizens. And that was not all. Burns projected his own image onto that of this unknown new intelligence. When a person has a commanding type of power—be it great authority or intelligence—he can lose control and use his power for violence. Burns knew this well, and firsthand. That's why he feared his opponent and wanted to take the first move by attacking it—before this being who was not God brought down his own judgment. Before what killed Vice President Chamberlain came down from the skies and struck *him* down.

Rubens looked squarely at the supreme authority standing before him.

Throughout his life Burns could never escape his troubled relationship with his father. After failing in business he became an alcoholic, then sought salvation from God and turned his life around. He was a Christian who could never love his enemy.

This middle-aged man, Gregory S. Burns, was actually quite ordinary.

"I'd like to change the topic," Burns said as he straightened various documents piled on his desk. "Can Arthur leave the room, so we can speak alone? It's about Mason."

"Ah, I see," Holland replied. Thomas Mason, the House majority leader, had apparently been selected to be the new vice president.

"Could you wait outside?" Holland said, and Rubens obediently turned to leave.

"Mr. President, I apologize for what I said," Rubens said. "I'm only concerned about doing what's best in the present crisis, and I'm afraid I said something I shouldn't have. I hope you'll excuse me."

"Just take care of the threat from the Congo," is all Burns said, and waved him away.

Rubens left the Oval Office. Outside, the Yankee White officer with the nuclear football at his feet was seated there as before. Rubens walked down the narrow hallway, back to the lobby.

He sat down on the sofa, let out a big sigh, and buried his head in his hands. Up until now he'd felt that deterring war involved dealing with the madness of political leaders. Because no matter how many nuclear missiles a country might possess, in order for them to be a threat you need a person who could push the switch. But the commander in chief he'd just met was an ordinary person. A typical example of the human species. In other words, given enough power, anyone might pick up the nuclear launch switch. A person without imagination could, as long as it happened indirectly and far away, easily start a war and kill untold masses of people.

Rubens looked back again on his journey, which had started at the Santa Fe research lab. Dr. Heisman's insight remained foremost in his mind.

Human beings, who have constantly killed each other over the past two hundred thousand years, are always afraid of invasion by other groups. Constantly jumping at shadows kept them in a nearly paranoid state, leading them to create nations as a defense system. Mankind universally possesses this psychological state, so it's regarded as normal. It's simply the "human condition." And the reason we cannot achieve complete peace is because inside each one of us lies proof positive that the Other is dangerous. All humans are willing to hurt others in order to snatch away food, resources, and land. We project our true colors onto our enemies, fear them, and attack them. And in using violence against others, the nation and religion are the support systems that pardon our actions. Our vicious deeds are defensible because people outside that framework are aliens. The enemy.

Humans are able to shut their eyes to this immorality because there is no other intelligence that criticizes slaughter within the same species. Even God encourages the killing of heathens.

But now things were different. A different kind of intelligence, one that denounces internecine struggle, had appeared on the African continent. And in order for people to show any sort of dignity toward this being, who was closer to God than men were, they had to turn their backs on their own animal nature and maintain peace.

But wasn't that impossible?

"Rubens."

He looked up and saw Holland standing above him. The CIA director had a sour look. "What were you thinking? You've ruined everything."

"I'm very sorry."

"We were just talking about what to do with you."

"Am I fired?" Rubens was ready to accept the worst.

"No. You'll stay in your present job."

Rubens thought this was odd, but then he realized that safety measures were still in place. If the mission failed, he could be the sacrificial victim who would take responsibility.

"However, all command authority will rest with Eldridge. You'll just sit in the command center."

"I see."

Holland brusquely headed toward the exit of the West Wing.

When Rubens came out onto the entranceway, a piercingly cold wind struck his cheeks. The CIA limousine was already waiting, but Holland didn't get in the car. Instead he motioned Rubens aside, away from the Secret Service agents.

"Listen, Arthur," the director said in a low voice. "What I'm about to say is not an order. I don't have the right to interfere in an operation spearheaded by the Defense Department."

"All right."

Holland looked around him, and when he was satisfied it was safe, he spoke. "Save Nous."

Rubens stared at the top intelligence official.

"This operation is too much for Eldridge. He'll eventually have to rely on you. When that happens, do what you can."

"Yes, sir," Rubens replied, straightening himself as he spoke.

Holland turned and walked back to the limousine.

Rubens looked at his watch. It was 6:00 a.m. in the Congo. On the other side of the world Nous was facing a terrible crisis, and there was nothing Rubens could do about it. All he could do was hope that Jonathan Yeager and his party could rout the largest armed group in the Congo.

The battle about to begin, Rubens thought, though small in scale, might well decide the fate of the world.

And Nous would be witness to the worst side of these animals called humans.

His digital watch showed 6:00 a.m., the PKO unit's zero hour.

From his perch in the tree Yeager checked the situation, but there was no sign of an attack. On the ground, Mick remained motionless as he observed the battle line of the Lord's Resistance Army.

"Nothing yet?" Garrett's voice asked over the radio.

Yeager pushed the send button twice, the signal to wait. Just then there was an explosion in the direction of the main road. Yeager trained his binoculars there and saw black smoke pluming up from a wrecked tank. LRA soldiers nearby were shouting and pointing to the south. Hostilities had finally started. Yeager looked back at the side road twenty meters ahead. The unit blocking the road ran back to the personnel carrier and grabbed their weapons.

There was sporadic gunfire, punctuated by a series of explosions on the main road. Missiles from far away were destroying one armored vehicle after another on the main road. Blood sprayed up, and body parts—arms, legs, torsos—flew into the air. With a piercing shriek countless mortar shells rained down on the soldiers.

Mick looked up at Yeager above him, waiting for the signal to proceed. The unit in front of him was still maintaining battle formation, and he shook his head. The enemy was surprisingly disciplined. If Yeager and his team weren't careful, they'd have the tables turned on them.

About three minutes after the attack began, the force on the main road started to scatter. Above them a black Cobra AH-1 attack helicopter rushed by like the wind, spraying the ground with its Gatling gun. Tracer bullets precisely followed the enemy ranks, ripping apart the bodies of the soldiers and sending them flying. The attack by the Pakistanis totally deviated from the rules of engagement for PKOs. Yeager spotted another Cobra. As the AH-1 hovered, it aimed for the branch road intersecting the main road.

In a low but piercing voice Yeager spoke into the mike. *"Go!"*

"Roger that," Garrett's voice said from two hundred meters back.

A barrage of TOW antitank missiles blasted out from under the wings of the attack helicopter and devastated the line of troops. One missile landed nearby, and Yeager was almost thrown out of the tree. On the road in front of him the LRA troops were firing back, but their rifles were no match for the weapons of the PKO. The attack helicopter rained machine-gun bullets as it drew closer, and the enemy unit in front scattered wildly into the jungle, seeking to escape.

Yeager signaled Mick. At the same moment, the four booby traps they'd set exploded, and the enemy that had been pressing down on them was driven back. Yeager and Mick used their silenced pistols to, one by one, shoot the soldiers who remained alive, wiping out the enemy twenty meters to the left and right. An escape route had finally opened.

Yeager clambered down from the tree just as Garrett and the others caught up with them. Pierce was carrying Akili in his arms, his mouth wide open, panting for breath. Akili appeared to be awake, but his kittenlike eyes were shut tight.

The attack helicopter swept low over the side road, accompanied by explosions, reddish earth swirling into the air as it roared away. They couldn't see well for all the dust, but Yeager recognized the opportunity. "Let's go!" he yelled.

Assault rifles in hand, the mercenaries leaped out onto the side road. They broke into two groups, covering both sides. Pierce, carrying Akili, raced across the road in the gap between them. In the space of five seconds Garrett and Meyers shot down four enemy soldiers who spotted them, and Mick jumped up on a personnel carrier, grabbed an RPG, a sniper rifle, and other weapons, and stuffed them in his backpack. The four mercenaries crossed the road and ran into the jungle after Pierce.

Routed enemy soldiers appeared between the trees, and each time the mercenaries exchanged fire with them, killing them with rifles and grenade launchers. As they exchanged fire a bullet from behind them sliced off a piece of Yeager's shoulder, but for a battlefield wound it wasn't serious. Yeager shot back, not even feeling the pain, gunning down the soldier who shot him with three bullets.

The mercenaries formed a tight protective circle around Pierce and Akili, so they were unharmed. They all ran like mad toward the south, and the gunfire faded into the distance. It appeared that the threat from the LRA was now behind them. As he ran for all he was worth, Pierce gasped, "We had a satellite image from ten minutes ago. It showed a separate group of about two hundred straight ahead."

"LRA?" Yeager yelled back.

"Yes."

The Pakistani army had overlooked this force at the front lines. "How far?"

"Five hundred meters."

As if to back up Pierce's words, they heard Kalashnikovs firing ahead of them. Yeager grimaced. At this rate they would run right into them. "Where's the supply vehicle?"

"It's heading down the main road toward us, but with the PKO troops there it can only get about two kilometers from here."

Should they forge ahead or detour around? Either way a force larger than a company was waiting for them. If two hundred enemy troops were deployed into the jungle it was inevitable they'd get caught in their net. Maybe the best plan was to gather in one place and try to fight it out.

As Yeager pondered this, they came out onto a village carved out of the jungle. There was a circular common area and a row of simple mud-wall dwellings. And standing out among them was a large redbrick building.

"What's that?"

"A Catholic mission church."

The church looked like it could be a bulwark against the enemy. Yeager swept the village with his eyes. Maybe all the villagers had become refugees, since the place was deserted.

"Okay. We'll wait for the enemy inside that church."

"What?" Garrett shot back. "If they find us, we'll have no place to run."

"No—we won't hide. We'll attack them and lure them out of the jungle. When the Pakistanis see them, they'll take care of them for us."

Garrett, convinced, glanced at his watch. "The PKO attack will be over in seven minutes. We have to hurry."

Yeager and Mick went first and raced to the church. The church was a large, blocklike building, and though flat, its roof was high, so overall it was as tall as a two-story building. Yeager plastered himself against the wall and tried peering into the church through the window, but the glass was sooty and he couldn't see a thing. He and Mick edged along the wall to the wooden front door. A hubcap was hanging from the door, perhaps a charm of some kind.

The two men exchanged glances and together kicked down the door and rushed into the church. They swung their rifles in all directions in case enemy troops were inside, and as they did Yeager involuntarily backed away. There were a huge number of people inside, but all of them were dead and decomposing. Bodies of all ages—from babies to the elderly—littered the floor, and a black cloud of flies hung over the chapel. The stink of death pressed back terribly on Yeager and Mick, driving them out of the church.

"Man, that's sick," Mick said, grimacing.

Yeager caught his breath and then flew into a rage. "The Pakistani army is too soft on them. Those LRA assholes should be slaughtered. Every single one of them."

"With that smell we can't go inside," Mick said. Like a skin diver, he took a huge gulp of air, went back inside the church, grabbed a ladder that was leaning against a wall, and quickly dragged it outside. "Let's climb up to the roof," he said.

Yeager nodded and motioned Garrett and the others to join them. Intermittent gunfire sounded from the jungle where the enemy was hidden. When they reached the roof they had a 360-degree panorama. The jungle spread out as far as they could see, covering the earth like the surface of the ocean. Off to the east rose the glacier-capped peaks of the Rwenzori Mountains. To the north the Pakistani army's helicopters continued their attack, mopping up before returning to base.

Yeager saw the rest of them up to the roof, pulled up the ladder so the enemy couldn't follow, and assigned them positions. He had Pierce watch the north, while he and the others took up a position so they could concentrate their fire on the enemy to the south. Garrett and Meyers, deployed to the left and right of the roof, were also to keep an eye out on the east and west. Assuming they might not be able to hear orders when the firing started, they put on their wireless headsets.

From the jungle across the hundred-meter square they saw numerous muzzle flashes and heard many women screaming. This separate LRA company wasn't fighting the Pakistani ground forces but were apparently continuing to massacre villagers they'd taken captive, eliminating any witnesses to their massacres before the Pakistanis found them.

Yeager's hatred for the enemy was growing by the minute. He swore he'd make them pay for their atrocities. The four mercenaries rested their rifles on the edge of the roof and began firing simultaneously at the jungle, where the enemy was hidden. They aimed at the edge of the jungle, since some of the villagers might still be alive. After they'd emptied their thirty-round clips, they saw figures among the dark trees. The enemy had taken notice.

"Save your ammo," Yeager shouted into his headset, his final order before the battle. *"Let's hold out until the PKO gets here."*

They reloaded and again took aim. In the dark jungle a group of enemy soldiers dimly appeared, looking like stalks of wheat waving in the wind, and suddenly spilled out.

Yeager drew a bead on the foremost group and was about to squeeze the trigger when all hell erupted. The group charging toward them, wildly firing their AK-47 assault rifles, were children. Little boys, around ten years old, shrilly yelling, plowed forward to kill him.

Half a year ago, on a sunny day, Oneka's life changed forever.

Until then he was a normal child. Born and raised in a small village along the road, he had a lazy father, a hardworking mother, and an older brother and younger sister near his own age. In the morning the children would go to draw water, then skip off to elementary school, help their mother in the fields, and play with friends from the village. Their only real pleasures were going to market once every two weeks and occasionally having chicken for dinner. When a feast like this was laid before them on the dirt floor of their one-room dwelling, his brother, Obuya, and sister, Atieno, smiled from ear to ear, and the three of them would happily share their food with each other.

On the day when the devil came to their village, Oneka was playing outside the house. He and Obuya were kicking a ball back and forth. Atieno was sitting in front of the house, singing a song and watching her brothers, when her tiny voice was drowned out by screaming. At the edge of the village a woman was shrieking. This wasn't the kind of shouting heard when couples were fighting but a fearful scream that froze anyone who heard it.

Oneka and his brother went out to the road to see what was happening. A speeding truck roared by, quickly stopping as it let out three soldiers in front of each house. It was advancing toward them.

"Dad! Mom!" Obuya yelled for his parents.

His mother, working in the fields behind the house, and his father, taking a nap, ran up to them, their faces strained. At that very moment the vehicle stopped in front of Oneka, and three men with guns leaped out from the bed of the truck.

"Run!" his father yelled as he grabbed up Atieno, who was right next to him. One of the soldiers charged at him and stuck the bayonet clear through Atieno in her father's arms.

Oneka felt he was in a nightmare. Atieno was just singing. She wasn't doing anything wrong. So why would they...

His little sister collapsed. His father had no time to mourn his daughter's death. The knife that had pierced Atieno had stabbed through his chest, too. His father moaned in pain, clutched at his wound, and fell writhing to the ground.

The tallest soldier walked over to Oneka's mother, crouched on the ground in shock, and said, "I'm taking your sons." His mother didn't respond. She was shaking, and she couldn't speak. Another soldier came up to his older brother and held out a knife. "Rape your mother and then slash her throat," he commanded. Obuya, his eyes wide, shook his head. As if waiting for this, the three soldiers fell on him with hatchets.

Oneka shut his eyes, but even with his face down, he could hear his brother's screams and the sound of his still-living body being cut apart.

Oneka was sobbing when he felt a heavy knife in his hand. That devil's voice again spoke. "Rape your mother and slash her throat. Otherwise we'll kill you like we did your brother."

Through eyes clouded by tears he saw his brother's mutilated torso. Oneka didn't want to die. He turned to his mother and saw she'd turned pale.

"Do it," the devil said, yanking down Oneka's pants and rubbing his little penis.

His mother kept on sobbing until her son had finished the brutal acts he'd needed to do to save his life.

When it was all done, Oneka had become a different person. It felt like he was watching this world from another. They loaded him onto the truck, and as it sped down the dusty road he saw his father writhing on the ground, crying his heart out. I'll never come back here again, Oneka thought.

Along with ten other children from the village, Oneka was taken to a training camp. And he was made into a soldier and dragged into a war. Several hundred children were gathered in rows of simple tents in a corner of a grassy plain. Since they were not allowed to bathe, an awful stink hung over the area.

When training started, children who made even the smallest mistake were killed on the spot. Children who tripped and fell were beaten to death, and some children had kerosene poured over them and were set on fire, screaming like animals as they died. Oneka didn't want to be killed, so he silently set about every task he was given, from cleaning dismantled rifles to practicing charging the enemy. Three months later he was sent out to participate in actual fighting, in which he attacked a village just like his own and helped steal food, fuel, and women. The devil who kidnapped him, their leader, who had the jungle name Bloody General, tied the captured villagers to trees and then, saying he wanted to train the children to be brave, had them run these people through with bayonets. Oneka killed several of them.

"Now we just need to be patient." A boy named Rokani in his group kept saying this in the evening after they had killed people. "The American army will come soon and rescue us."

"The American army?"

"Yeah. American soldiers will punish bad people. Also, do you know the words 'The pen is mightier than the sword'?"

Oneka shook his head.

"Newspaper reporters are stronger than any army. The power of the pen will surely save us."

But the American army did not come, and the pen was unequal to the sword. Unable to wait any longer, one night Rokani tried to escape from the camp, was caught, and the leader called Oneka over and ordered him to beat this escaped soldier to death with a club. Oneka smashed his friend's head in and killed him. Oneka no longer trusted anyone, no longer had any feelings. He didn't care anymore. This was Oneka's war.

In the attack two days ago he didn't hesitate to kill the villagers who had gathered at the church. The child soldiers were ordered to cut open the people they'd killed and eat their hearts and livers. The young women were taken away to the jungle as playthings of the leaders. But this morning something totally unexpected happened. Shells started to fall from far away, and battle helicopters had attacked them. Oneka and the others were ordered to take down the tents they'd set up in the village square and escape into the jungle. Once they withdrew, the killing of the village women began. The five leaders seemed panicked. Oneka had a sudden thought. Maybe this was the American army attacking. If it were, wouldn't they kill an evil person like himself? Because they were even shooting at the women who were crying and begging for mercy.

"Battle formation!" the Bloody General suddenly shouted.

Oneka realized for the first time that they were directly under attack. His comrades nearest the square were being shot down. Oneka turned to the direction of the attack. A handful of people on the roof of the church were shooting at them.

"Attack the church! Kill every one of them!"

The children loaded their assault rifles and lined up in battle formation facing the church.

The Bloody General lowered his raised arm. "All troops—*charge!*"

The two hundred yelled as one and began racing toward the church across the square. Oneka was in the lead group. As always, he felt no fear. All he had to do was kill. As he ran, spraying the roof with his AK-47, the sweet odor of gunpowder faded and the scent of soil came to him. It made him think of his hometown. Memories of his family that he'd tried to recall but couldn't up until now opened the lock on his heart and rushed back to him.

The aroma of soil changed into the aroma of his sweet, gentle mother. Oneka felt as though his mother were holding him. Enveloped by her softness and warmth, he found it strange that she wasn't angry. *I raped her and killed her, but does she still love me?*

Oneka started to cry. The tears flew away as he ran.

If only I hadn't been born a human being.

I wish I'd been a bird or an animal so Dad and Mom and my brother and sister and I could snuggle up and live happily together.

The enemy was shooting back. A man on the roof was shooting at them, full auto. To his left Oneka heard a bullet, at tremendous speed, shatter a skull. Out of the corner of his eye he saw children around him being cut down, and he thought: *I am going to die, too.*

The muzzle flash from a gun aimed at him. After that he saw nothing, felt nothing, as his head flew off and he died.

Mick aimed his rifle at the mass of children and began neutralization fire. The front row of children was mowed down, blood spraying in the air. The group behind them tripped over the bodies of their comrades and toppled over.

"Cease fire!" Yeager yelled into his headset.

But Mick ignored the order. *"Come on, you motherfuckers!"* he shouted angrily, and continued to gun them down. When he was out of ammo he yelled *"Reloading!"* and rammed in another clip. As he was doing this, the children who had stumbled over the dead bodies managed to scramble over them and began charging again. Garrett and

Meyers were compelled to keep on firing, though both of them fired warning shots. The bullets landing at their feet formed a line the children couldn't cross, and their advance finally ground to a halt.

"Hold your fire!" Yeager ordered, and he pulled the pin on a grenade. Checking the kill zone, he tossed it ahead of the children. The child soldiers hit the ground at the explosion, but he figured it was far enough away to prevent their getting hurt even if some of them remained standing.

The younger children's crying and screaming reverberated throughout the square. Yeager hoped the terrifying experience would make them quickly withdraw. For Yeager's plan had already backfired. The Pakistani army had intentionally overlooked this company of child soldiers. They couldn't count on the PKO's help. If the battle went on much longer it would turn into mass extermination.

As if responding to his thoughts, several of the children got up, turned around, and were heading back to the jungle. Yeager had the faint hope that the whole force of soldiers would withdraw, but this hope was soon crushed. Tracers flew out of the jungle, downing the retreating children. Yeager could barely keep from vomiting at the awful scene.

Realizing that even if they retreated they would be killed, the child soldiers roused themselves to another desperate, disorderly, banzai-like charge. As they rushed toward the church they became a moving target in the square, where there was no cover. Though the soldiers were children, the weapons they carried were real, and the random fire from their AK-47s became overwhelming as it rained down on Yeager and the others. Hundreds of rounds slammed into the edge of the roof where they were crouched, steadily ripping it away. And then the last row of soldiers came to a halt; several of them shouldered antitank rockets.

"RPG!" Meyers yelled as he scrambled to the back of the roof. Rockets sped straight for them, landing on the left side of the roof. The ground shook as shards of brick exploded into the air, and right at Meyers's feet a section of the roof collapsed. Meyers nearly fell to his death, but he managed to cling to the remaining section of flooring with his upper body. An awful stink of dead bodies rose up from the chapel be-

low. Meyers somehow hung on, and he clambered up and crawled over to Yeager's side.

"*If we don't do something we're gonna die!*" Meyers yelled.

Across from Yeager, Mick was shooting his captured RPG back at the children. It exploded in the midst of them, sending severed heads and organs flying in all directions.

"*Cease fire! Cease fire!*" Yeager yelled, but Mick ignored his order, relentlessly blasting the enemy with his AK-47.

"*Come on, you bastards! I'm going to blast every one of you to pieces!*"

Mick's voice sounded choked up with joy. His brain was secreting stress-relieving neurochemicals, producing a combat high. He screamed obscenities at the African children as he sprayed them with bullets.

A burning liquid rose up from Yeager's stomach. The child soldiers had advanced to the middle of the square, but nearly half of them had been gunned down by Mick.

A second RPG exploded on the left side of the church, convulsing the floor of the roof. One more hit and the whole building would collapse.

Mick exchanged his AK-47 for a grenade launcher.

"*Damn it, Mick, don't shoot!*"

"*Shut the hell up! This is war!*" Mick yelled back, and fired the grenade launcher. The grenade exploded at the feet of the front line of troops, killing or wounding seven children.

I have to shoot, Yeager decided. I have no choice. Even if it means eternal punishment, I have to pull the trigger.

"*This is war, all right,*" Yeager yelled. Then he pulled out his pistol and shot Mick right through the temple.

The 9mm bullet didn't go all the way through. It ricocheted around his cranium, completely destroying his brain. Mick, half seated, was instantly killed, and he fell down, face-first. Darkish blood flowed from his head and nostrils, even after he was dead.

Meyers and Garrett stared, dumbfounded, at the body of their comrade. Yeager's right hand, which had pulled the trigger, felt as if it were splattered with Mick's brains.

"*Garrett, fire warning shots to get them to stop. You can use grenades, too, if you want.*" Yeager shouted out one order after another. "*Meyers, fire the grenade launcher.*"

The grenade launcher was passed to Meyers, and he frowned and stared at Yeager.

"Fire at the back of the jungle. Flush out the commanders who are hiding there!"

"Roger that!"

Meyers checked the angle and shot off a 40mm grenade. Yeager picked up the Dragunov sniper rifle they'd captured, squinted through the optical sight, aimed at a large tree on the edge of the jungle, and fired. He lowered the rifle, checked where his bullet had struck, and adjusted the sight.

The surviving children were inching toward the church, their eyes glistening malevolently. These were the eyes of children who had witnessed unimaginable violence and loss, and Yeager saw in them broken spirits, utterly unrecoverable.

Several of the child soldiers starting throwing grenades. They didn't reach the roof, though the explosions right below them further weakened the walls of the church, already on the brink of collapse.

As they desperately continued to return fire, Garrett yelled, *"We can't stop them! Do it now!"*

Meyers changed the point of impact of the grenade he launched from deep in the forest to just in front of it, but the hidden officers still hadn't shown themselves.

Perhaps sensing that their enemy wasn't planning to kill them, the children steadily ran faster. Thirty more meters before they reached the church. One child shoved his way through the mound of dead bodies and came up with an RPG launcher. One blast from that and the mercenaries would be destroyed. Yeager reluctantly hoisted the sniper rifle, ready to shoot the boy's leg at any moment.

Yeager sensed someone beside him. He looked up, startled, thinking that Mick, who should be dead, might have started moving again. A grotesque-looking child was standing there. Akili had come over to his side without his realizing it and was staring at the ground below. His face was just like that of the child soldiers, twisted in hatred.

Yeager, in prone shooting position, yelled, "Get down!"

Akili didn't obey, but knelt down beside Mick's corpse and took something out of his backpack. The roll of ten thousand dollars that was his spending money. Akili broke the band with his tiny hands and scattered the two hundred fifty-dollar bills off the roof.

The shower of bills floated on the wind and fluttered down from the church to the square. The children cowered when they first saw something falling down on them, but when they understood it was money they began scrambling to collect it. With a faint smile Akili watched as they threw aside their weapons and fought each other for the cash. He looked as if he had seen through human greed and was mocking it.

"Yeager!"

At Meyers's shout Yeager quickly aimed his rifle again. The officers, who were letting the child soldiers kill each other, had finally emerged at the edge of the jungle, driven out by the continual explosions. Five men, all wearing berets. One of them was covered in blood, no doubt wounded by the grenades.

Yeager didn't hesitate. He pulled the trigger, and one of the men's heads slammed backward. Before his listless body hit the ground Yeager squeezed off a second shot on another man. It was too bad he had to administer a fatal blow with a single shot. He wished there were a crueler way of making these devils suffer.

The remaining three men, realizing there was a sniper, began to hustle back to the jungle. Yeager was able to bring down two of them, but he ran out of ammo. As the final blood-covered officer was racing into a grove of trees, a grenade Meyers had launched landed right at his feet. The grenade exploded, sending hundreds of pieces of shrapnel into him, and he collapsed like a limp rag.

Yeager leaned over the edge of the roof and yelled down. "Your leaders are dead! Run away!"

The little soldiers all stopped and looked up at the voice.

Garrett yelled down Yeager's message, translating it into Swahili.

The children came to their senses, picked up their rifles, and restarted their attack, but Yeager and Garrett, lying low, continued to yell. "Your leaders are gone! You won't be killed! Run away right now!"

The firing tapered off and soon stopped completely. Yeager held up a signal mirror that he pulled out of his pocket and checked out the square. The children looked back at the jungle, saw the dead bodies of their leaders, exchanged looks and a few words, then scattered in all directions.

It didn't take long for the battlefield to be deserted. The children had abandoned their weapons and run away.

Yeager checked again. "They've withdrawn!" he reported, and sat up. He felt woozy.

Akili, staring hard at Mick's corpse, looked up at Yeager and smiled eerily. Yeager felt he couldn't take any more, and didn't make the effort to try to delve into what Akili was thinking. He silently lifted up the tiny body and handed him over to Pierce, who had raced over from the north side.

The mercenaries pulled anything that could identify Mick from his backpack and divided his food and ammunition.

"Don't worry about it. This is war," Garrett said, staring down at Mick's body, trying to console Yeager. "A total clusterfuck."

Meyers nodded in agreement.

Yeager didn't say anything, but he was grateful to them. He thought for a moment about the Japanese man he'd killed. About this person named Mikihiko Kashiwabara, who had come to the battlefield without a single photo of family or friends. A man who lived a life filled with hatred, loved by no one.

"Let's head out," Meyers said, and ran across the roof. They lowered the ladder to the ground and descended the north side of the church.

"I just had a message from the vehicle that's waiting for us," Pierce said. "The PKO is heading back to base. They'll pass us coming this way. They should be here soon."

"What kind of vehicle is it?" Yeager asked.

"A Land Cruiser. Let's wait a hundred meters from here, at the main road."

With Yeager and Garrett taking point, Meyers bringing up the rear, and Pierce and Akili in the middle, they headed east. About a hundred dead bodies of the children lay in the square in front of the church. Yeager couldn't hold it in any longer and vomited.

Garrett looked back. "Let's hurry," he urged them, and started to speed up. Right then he halted, as if he'd run right into a huge, heavy object, and gingerly held his right side. He fell to his knees and collapsed forward.

Yeager lay facedown on the liquid he'd just vomited. *"Sniper at three o'clock,"* he yelled at Meyers through his headset.

It was in the direction of the body-littered square. Yeager aimed his assault rifle and saw a boy, more dead than alive, stand up. He looked like he was drowning in a sea of dead bodies. Garrett was facedown, groaning in pain.

"Hold on, Garrett. Meyers will be here soon," Yeager said, trying to encourage him, then turned back to the square.

The boy had probably been hit by an RPG, for his left arm was torn off and one eye was crushed. He managed to hold up his AK-47 with the remaining arm, but his vacant expression showed that he was steadily losing consciousness. He desperately continued to fire, randomly spraying bullets.

Why? Yeager asked himself. Why do that child and I have to kill each other?

Despite the sporadic fire, Yeager ran over to Garrett and pulled him behind the wall of a nearby house.

"Shit! It hurts!" Garrett gasped.

Yeager pulled off Garrett's equipment, opened his battle fatigues, and checked the wound. Blood was gushing out from his right ribs. The bullet was lodged near his liver. The kinetic energy of the bullet had ripped apart all his organs.

Garrett's face was deathly pale, his breathing shallow. Yeager placed his backpack under Garrett's legs to raise them, treating him for shock.

"Damn." Garrett's voice was husky. "I got shot by a kid."

"It's okay. It's not a bad wound. Hang in there."

When Yeager put pressure on the wound to try to stop the bleeding Garrett twisted away in agony. Yeager pulled out a morphine needle from the medical kit and glanced over at their medic. Meyers was stuck behind the church, shielding Pierce and Akili, but finally started running toward Yeager.

"Am I going to die here?" Garrett asked faintly. "God, I wish I had done something good with my life."

"You say that because you *are* a good person."

"No...I transported lots of people to other countries to be tortured....Syria and Uzbekistan—"

Yeager cut him off. "Not because you wanted to. You could have escaped by yourself from this jungle. But you stayed with us because of my son, right?"

No response.

Garrett closed his eyes, stopped breathing, and lay there, a calm look on his face.

Yeager touched his carotid artery to check that his heart had stopped and tried CPR, though he knew it was a lost cause. It was all Yeager could do to keep from asking aloud if Garrett's soul had heard his last words.

Meyers arrived, checked Garrett's pulse and breathing, examined his pupils, and stopped Yeager from massaging his heart. The young medic looked stricken. He helplessly shook his head and announced the death of his comrade.

"Jesus," Pierce muttered bitterly.

"What happened to the kid?" Yeager asked.

"He collapsed and hasn't moved," Meyers said. "I think he's dead."

The two of them stood there for a while, mouths closed in silent prayer, then Yeager searched through Garrett's backpack and extracted a photograph of a woman about Garrett's age and an envelope, probably a will. It said TO JUDY, and there was an address in northern Virginia. Yeager carefully placed it in his pants pocket.

"Aren't you going to bury him?" Pierce asked. "He helped save the Mbuti."

There wasn't a minute to lose, but Yeager couldn't stand the thought of leaving Garrett's body exposed like that. He looked around, but the enemy had completely vanished.

"Let's bury him," Meyers said. "It shouldn't take long if the three of us do it."

Yeager nodded, and he and Meyers dragged the body off to the jungle. They dug a hole with their folding entrenching tools, laid Garrett's body inside, and noted the spot on a map.

As they were about to shovel dirt over the body, Meyers and Pierce bowed, and each said a short prayer. Yeager was watching the one person who didn't seem sad. In Pierce's arms, Akili looked happy, as if he were fascinated by his first glimpse of a religious ceremony.

Was that all the child was feeling? Yeager wondered. Was the dead body just an object to him? He grabbed Akili's chin. It felt just like a human child's. Akili looked up at him fearfully. Yeager turned the three-year-old's head toward Garrett's corpse. "Listen carefully, Akili. I have no idea what you're thinking or feeling. Maybe you think we humans are a stupid race. But never forget this one person. He died trying to save you. He sacrificed his most precious gift for you."

Tears welled up in Akili's eyes. Yeager remembered his own son's face when he scolded him. This was necessary discipline, he felt. "From now on you will carry Warren Garrett's life with you. Which means you have to live a good life like his. You understand what I'm saying?"

Akili gave a tiny nod—as though if he didn't, the mistreatment would continue.

"All right, then," Yeager said, and let go. Akili still seemed frightened, so he patted the boy's huge head. Yeager turned to the other two. "Let's blow this country."

After they finished burying Garrett, the now-four-person group mustered what was left of their energy and stamina and marched off into the jungle. The PKO force was already back at its base in the south, and the remaining LRA soldiers and villagers had scattered to the winds. As they moved steadily through the hushed jungle, next to a stream they saw a mass of butterflies take flight in the sunlight filtering through the trees. As if countless flowers were wildly dancing.

The world is this beautiful, Yeager thought. Though on the same planet there's this vermin called man.

Before they left the jungle Pierce took out his laptop and made sure the reconnaissance satellite wasn't observing them. "All clear," he announced.

When they emerged onto the muddy main road a Land Cruiser parked to the south started its engine and drove toward them. Admonishing himself not to let his guard down, Yeager nevertheless couldn't help but breathe a huge sigh of relief.

The large SUV came to a halt in front of them, and a young black man called out to them from the driver's side. "Are you Roger? British?"

"That's right," Pierce replied. "You're Sanyu?"

"Yes."

"I'm really happy to meet you, Sanyu."

"Me, too," Sanyu said cheerfully, but when he looked at the two men in battle fatigues his face stiffened. And when he saw Akili in Pierce's arms, his eyes grew wide.

"This child is ill," Pierce explained. "I'll tell you all the rest in time. More important, do you have all the supplies on board?"

"Ah, yes," the young man, lively again, said as he jumped out of the driver's seat and opened the door. The luggage compartment was piled high with boxes of food and clothes.

The men took out a box of mineral water, went into the jungle, and washed their whole bodies. They quickly shaved and changed clothes and now looked much more presentable. They put an infant's cap down low on Akili so it covered his odd-shaped head and eyes.

Pierce distributed counterfeit journalist credentials and fake passports to the men, and they were ready to leave the country. "We'll cross over into Uganda via Rutshuru," he explained.

"What about after that?" Meyers asked. "How do we get out of Africa?"

"I had several plans, but right now we're back to square one. We don't have as much fighting power as we used to. But don't worry— our ally in Japan will come up with a plan." By "fighting power," he meant that two operatives had died.

Just to be sure, when they crossed over the Congo border the four of them would leave Sanyu in the car and proceed on foot, detouring around the checkpoint. Until then, Meyers drove, with Yeager beside him and the other three in the backseat. They set off in the Land Cruiser.

As he watched the Ituri Forest pass by Yeager unconsciously wiped his right hand on his pants. He still felt the sensation he'd had when he shot Mick, as if he'd been splattered by his brains.

Since I came into this country have I done anything right? Yeager wondered. Have I sunk to the level of the enemy we fought and killed one of my own out of egotism? If Mick hadn't attacked the child soldiers from the roof, we might have all been wiped out. Mick had decided this was a battle for sheer survival, and wasn't he the one who made the right choice? Shouldn't I apologize to Mick, who'd saved us from danger? For forcing him to play the villain?

Bitter regret for his hatred of Mick was swelling up inside him. Regret for killing Mick and abandoning his body. He felt an indelible sense of guilt he'd never get rid of, and tears welled up in his eyes. The fragility of life, the nauseating nature of man, the powerlessness of good saddened and disgusted him—as did he himself and his own inability to judge right from wrong. Silently, he began to weep.

"Yeager," Meyers said from the driver's seat. The young medic's voice was shaking. "Suck it up. I'm holding it back myself."

Yeager wiped away the tears and looked ahead again with watchful eyes, but now he heard sobbing coming from the backseat. It was Pierce, as a wave of relief washed over his frayed nerves. Akili began crying, too, his guardian's tears inducing his own. The large tears rolling out of his catlike eyes were proof that his feelings were the same as those of humans. The fear of this complete Other that had haunted Yeager abated a little.

Sanyu, the only one clueless about what was going on, looked puzzled. "Are all of you all right?"

Realizing how silly they must look, the two mercenaries in the front seat were finally able to laugh.

PART 3

OUT OF AFRICA

1.

KENTO STAYED LOCKED away in the blacked-out room, barely eating or sleeping, continuing to work on the drugs. He had no idea if it was day or night.

A week had passed since he'd begun the synthesis process. There had been no calls from Poppy and thus no communication with the Congo, which let Kento focus solely on his experiments. Once, as he crawled into his sleeping bag on the floor for a short nap, an ominous thought crossed his mind. Maybe Jonathan Yeager and Nigel Pierce had already died in Africa. Or did not hearing from them mean that they were all right?

The synthesis of the new drug had gone smoothly until yesterday. The starting materials needed to make the two drugs—GIFT 1 and GIFT 2—had, through three separate reactions, transformed themselves into intermediate products with completely different chemical structures. When each reaction finished, Kento separated and refined the resulting chemical compound and sent the materials over to Jeong-hoon at the university. In the basement of the pharmacology building were nuclear magnetic resonance and X-ray structural analysis equipment, and using these would tell them whether the product was what they were after. Jeong-hoon messengered them by motorcycle a number of times between Machida and the university in Kinshi-cho.

Between last night and today the synthesis process reached a critical juncture. In the synthesis route for GIFT 1 there was a reaction Kento couldn't find in a search of academic articles, so he had to come up with the reagent and reaction conditions on his own. Justin Yeager had less than ten days to live, and he knew he couldn't make a mistake. Before this, Kento had spent several days studying texts on reaction mechanisms, racking his brain to come up with a promising experimental plan and put it into practice. As he put the reagent and catalyst in the beaker his hands trembled slightly. The reaction had taken twelve hours, so he separated the product in the late afternoon and had Jeong-hoon messenger the reagent by motorcycle. Now he was waiting for the results of the analysis.

As he prepared for the next reaction he felt a strange sense of elation. Trying reactions that no one had ever done before, he was finally part of the world of organic synthesis. The drug development he was involved in was more than enough to win several Nobel Prizes, but he also felt the weight of those who had preceded him—as if he were building on and being supported by the accumulated reactions performed by nameless earlier scientists. Not only was he now able to join these predecessors but maybe someday someone else would also use his reactions to create another new drug. For Kento this was an exciting prospect.

A motorcycle pulled up outside, and he raised his head. Jeong-hoon had arrived. He heard him bound up the outside staircase, and Kento went to the front door to greet his friend.

"I got the results," Jeong-hoon said as soon as he opened the door. Too impatient to remove his shoes and come inside, Jeong-hoon stood there, lowered his backpack, and yanked out a stack of printouts. They couldn't use faxes, so all documents had to be hand-delivered.

Kento went back into the room and eagerly read through the three types of results—analyses of mass spectrometry, infrared spectrometry, and nuclear magnetic resonance.

The first sample seemed to be the compound they were looking for. Everything was consistent—not just the molecular weight, mass, and atomic composition but also the functional group shown by infrared spectrometry as well.

Keeping his impatience in check, he scanned the NMR chart. A straight line along the horizontal axis intermittently peaked in several spots. This indicated there were no impurities. It was clear there was a benzene ring present; the arrangement of protons was also clear, and he could mentally picture the chemical structural formula that would fit the analysis results. There was no discrepancy. No matter who interpreted the results, only one structural formula could be derived from these readings. He checked it many times to make sure there was no mistake. Kento raised a fist. "We did it!"

"Fantastic!" Jeong-hoon, who had come into the room in the meantime, happily clapped his hands.

"Three more reaction steps, and GIFT will be complete!"

Jeong-hoon was beaming from ear to ear. "My little present," he said, holding out a bag full of hamburgers and energy drinks.

Kento gratefully accepted the food. All he'd had these days was sweet rolls and ramen, and he was tired of them. But there was something left to do before he unwrapped his hamburger. Just to be absolutely sure, he checked the analysis results of the by-products. And when he did, he found something surprising. A very different compound had been synthesized, not what he'd anticipated. An unexpected reaction must have taken place in the beaker.

Kento finally understood what Professor Sonoda, his adviser, had always told him: check the side reactions. If you only are concerned about the main reaction, you might overlook an unexpected discovery lurking in the background. In the university lab it often happened that a grad student would go to report on his work, and only Professor Sonoda would be excited while the grad student would stand there blankly. When Professor Sonoda came across these unexpected phenomena he detected the presence of an unknown reaction, which aroused his curiosity. Now Kento was feeling the same excitement as his mentor, and he felt he'd taken a major step forward into the world of organic synthesis.

"You look happy," Jeong-hoon said, smiling. "Why don't we eat?"

"You go ahead." Kento walked back to the lab bench. "I need to get the next reaction ready to go."

"Can I help with anything?"

"Could you measure the mice's oxygen saturation?"

"I'm on it."

Jeong-hoon looked into the closet, pulse oximeter in hand. "Kento," he called out.

Kento turned around. Jeong-hoon was pointing to a lifeless mouse in the cage. "One of them's dead."

It was a transgenic mouse, one that had artificially been given

PAECS. The tag on the mouse's ear read 4-05. Kento looked through his lab notes at the graph showing arterial blood oxygen saturation, which he recorded every six hours. Number 4-05 was the mouse whose symptoms were the worst.

He had deliberately not given the lab animals names so he didn't become attached to them, but still Kento felt a heaviness inside. Silently apologizing to the little creature, he noted DEAD at the end of the graph.

"I'll take this to the university," Jeong-hoon said, reluctantly pulling the dead body out. Jeong-hoon, in a more theoretical field, wasn't used to handling lab animals. "If we extract the genes and insert CHO cells," he said, referring to cells from a Chinese hamster ovary, "we can make cells that can be used in the binding assay." They would put mutant GPR769 on the cell membrane so that the genes that caused the illness manifested in those cells.

"You know how to do that?"

"No, but I'll ask Doi. I'll be careful when I ask, and I won't use your name."

"Treat him to a meal at the school cafeteria. That's all it'll take," Kento said with a laugh.

"There's one more thing I'm concerned about, Kento."

"What?"

"The two children we're trying to help. Maika Kobayashi is in the university hospital, and Justin Yeager's in a hospital in Lisbon, right?"

"That's right." Kento had constantly been worried about Maika's condition. He wasn't able to get the results of her tests, so he wasn't sure if she was still alive, let alone how long she had to live. Even if he had Jeong-hoon try to visit her, she was in the ICU, and only close relatives were allowed in.

"The problem is Justin," Jeong-hoon went on. "I looked into it, and mailing the drug to Portugal would take, at the fastest, two days."

"Two days?"

Kento realized he'd overlooked something critical. He'd always thought that the American who would visit him would be Jonathan Yeager, and he'd just hand over the drug to him. Even if they completed the drug before the deadline, the time it took to get it to Justin would make it too late. Now that all communications with the Congo had ceased, he was starting to doubt that Yeager would even show up. A terrible scenario crossed his mind again—that Yeager had been killed in battle.

"If we mail it we'll have to move the deadline up two days."

Jeong-hoon nodded. "That means we only have seven days left."

Kento thought about the remaining reaction, and the binding assay and pharmacological tests on the mice, and felt the blood draining out of his head.

"We have to speed things up."

"The fast chromatography machine I ordered will be here tomorrow," Kento said, trying to be hopeful. He'd paid 1.5 million yen for the used machine. "That should reduce the time by quite a lot."

"By how much?"

"Eighteen hours."

"That still leaves us thirty hours short."

They looked at each other, silently trying to come up with a plan.

"Worst case," Kento said, "after the drug's synthesized we'll have to send it off without any verification process."

"Without even a minimal check? Then we can't verify if GIFT's projection is correct."

"But if we don't make it in time..." Kento swallowed back the rest of the sentence.

The dead mouse lay on the edge of the lab table. If the new drug didn't arrive in time in Lisbon, Justin Yeager would suffer the same fate as this tiny animal.

After the fighting in the eastern Congo, twenty kilometers north of Butembo, Nous and the others vanished from Operation Nemesis's surveillance network.

What had happened to them in the battle ten days earlier?

Rubens sat down at his seat in the operations center and studied the last report from MONUC, the United Nations Organization Mission in the Democratic Republic of the Congo.

Among the hundred and forty-nine bodies discovered at the site of the massacre in Manjoa village, forty-eight were local villagers, ninety-five

were child soldiers kidnapped in northern Uganda, five bodies were LRA troops, and the last body was that of what appears to be an Asian male. This Asian had no passport or other ID, and we were unable to identify him. This person was the only one who had fallen on the church roof, and inspection of the body revealed the cause of death as a shot fired into the head from extremely close range. Twelve wounded child soldiers testified that they had exchanged fire with a small group on the roof of the church. It is unclear why the Asian man's group was staying in this region…

The report had a photo attached, and when he looked at it Rubens knew right away who it was: Mikihiko Kashiwabara.

The operation he'd formulated finally had its first casualty.

Rubens looked up from the document and gazed vacantly around the operations center, trying to control the confused feelings swirling around inside him.

Why did the Japanese mercenary die? If the autopsy was correct, there was a high possibility he wasn't killed by the enemy but by his own men. And not friendly fire, but an execution. Maybe Mikihiko Kashiwabara had screwed up and put his people in danger.

Whatever the truth, the fact remained that Rubens had now joined the ranks of those who killed. And if Yeager and the others killed the young soldiers to protect themselves, then Rubens might be responsible for those deaths as well. But maybe he shouldn't think that way. Wasn't he merely a cog in the machine that was Operation Nemesis? Maybe the real murderer was the one who called the shots, President Burns.

Rubens brushed that speculation aside. Nous had escaped from a desperate situation. Right after the battle at Manjoa village, their reconnaissance satellite had detected an SUV racing away from the scene. The vehicle was last seen entering Butembo, a town of some two hundred thousand people, and then it disappeared. And over the last ten days they'd had no clues as to Nous's whereabouts.

If only this situation could continue. Rubens could only hope. If it did, Operation Nemesis would die out spontaneously.

"Arthur." Eldridge was standing in front of his desk. Above the loosened tie his face was weary. On the verge of success, they'd let Nous escape, and Eldridge, on whom all the authority for the operation had devolved, was now constantly seeking Rubens's advice. Exactly as Holland, the CIA director, had predicted.

"Where are they headed? Any idea? Even a guess."

"At this stage I really couldn't say." He wanted nothing more than to confuse Eldridge and let Nous escape to someplace safe, but he had no information to base any decision on. "There's no trace of the vehicle containing Yeager and the others crossing stations in either Uganda or Rwanda."

"But it makes sense, right, to assume they left the Congo?" Eldridge said. "If they did, they could only be heading north or east."

"Why do you say that?"

Eldridge pointed to a screen on which there was a map of Africa. "Ships from Pierce Shipping are heading to Egypt and Kenya. That's their only means of transport. If they head elsewhere it'll be much harder for them to escape from Africa."

"The CIA has Alexandria and Mombasa under surveillance. And Nous must know that. I don't think he's going to head into a danger zone."

"But then there's no other place they can go. They've been designated terrorists. They can't pass through international airports or port facilities in Africa."

Eldridge was right. And Yeager's group had one more obstacle. Even if they had made phony passports and disguised themselves, they still wouldn't be able to hide Nous. If they chartered a private plane, there would be a baggage inspection when they boarded. They couldn't try to sneak the three-year-old in their carry-on luggage.

"I wonder if they have some sort of safe house in Africa they could hide out in for a long time." As Eldridge said this the outside line rang. Rubens took the call, which turned out to be from Logan, the NSA employee.

"I can't say this with one hundred percent certainty," Logan began, "but it looks like the broken-off communications between the Congo and Japan have resumed."

"Really?"

"Yes. We intercepted a message on a satellite phone that we can't decode. From the position of the satellite that intercepted the signal, the monitored targets have left the Congo and are already near Zimbabwe."

"Zimbabwe?" Rubens turned to the map of the African continent. Zimbabwe was far to the south, bordering the Republic of South Africa. "So they're in the southern part of Africa?"

"We're certain of it."

Rubens had his doubts. Wherever Nous was heading, it certainly wasn't south. The southern part of Africa, where the continent tapered off to a point, offered no escape route.

"We'll try reading the communication using the random number sequence. I'll call you as soon as we know anything."

"Thanks," Rubens said, but inside he was uneasy. If they did manage to decrypt the message, they'd be able to pinpoint Nous's location.

After he hung up and reported this to Eldridge, the director perked up. "They're underestimating what the NSA is capable of. They're like trapped rats now. Concentrate all CIA assets in the south."

With this, Operation Nemesis, on the verge of spontaneously fading away, took on new life. The operation to assassinate Nous would continue until he was eliminated.

After making it out of the Congo, Yeager, Meyers, and Sanyu took turns driving the Land Cruiser in three shifts—eight hours driving, eight hours on watch, and eight hours resting.

The route Pierce indicated went south. For Yeager it was an unexpected choice, because he'd been thinking they would exit the continent via the Indian Ocean. But Pierce, when asked, refused to reveal any details. He seemed leery of having an outsider, Sanyu, hear their plans. For his part, Sanyu was an outstanding companion on this long journey, his easygoing replies brightening up the often gloomy atmosphere in the car.

As they forged on south, the sun, which should have been straight overhead, steadily crept closer to the northern horizon. As they raced down the unchanging savanna, they felt the Ituri jungle, that place of such suffering, vanishing behind them, and for some reason this made Yeager feel vaguely sad. Africa was said to cast a spell over visitors, a power that kept them in thrall and wouldn't let them go. And Yeager might be the latest victim of this so-called African poison.

The Land Cruiser sometimes passed small villages, where they saw locals, and at night they ran through pitch-black mountain roads. They drove from Tanzania to Zambia and through Zimbabwe, heading always for the southern tip of Africa. Twice while driving at night they were attacked by armed robbers, but a few bursts from their AK-47s were enough to drive them away. Several of these poor men, unfortunate in their choice of whom to rob, must have been wounded by the full-auto blasts at their feet.

But what depressed them was not these incidents or the long, exhausting drive but rather Akili's crying at night. The odd-looking child seemed to have lost the ability to sleep soundly. Soon after he fell asleep he would feverishly cry out and start sweating, and they knew that he was having nightmares of being abandoned. This would happen every few hours, and finally, crying mightily, he would snap wide awake. When Pierce was awake he would hold him and comfort him, and when he was asleep Sanyu would take over. Meyers suspected malaria and checked him, but physically Akili was fine. The problem was purely emotional.

Yeager had the same fears as he did when his child began his long battle with disease. How would this affect the boy in the future? Even if they succeeded in escaping to Japan and could keep Akili safe, there was no family there to welcome him. Would he continue to develop his extraordinary intellectual powers, but with a broken spirit?

Near the border of Zimbabwe and the Republic of South Africa, the Land Cruiser came to a halt. Sanyu would drive it across the border while Yeager and the others walked across. Smuggling people across the border into South Africa was much easier than ever before. The electric fence that ran along the boundary was not turned on, and there were scattered holes one could climb through. In order to secure labor for its booming economy, South Africa accepted unlimited numbers of immigrants from Zimbabwe. Yeager decided to cross at night, and in their night vision goggles they saw the flashlights of Zimbabweans stealthily crossing the border for work.

Yeager and the others walked through the sparse bushes until they met up again with Sanyu and the Land Cruiser. They boarded and drove straight through to Johannesburg, five hundred kilometers away. They arrived in the suburbs and saw, in the clear morning air, the sky-line of the huge city, with its millions of people. They got out of the SUV and gazed intently at the mass of buildings covering this broad plain. They were struck with a momentary illusion that they'd slipped through time, suddenly catapulting from a primeval world to a civilized society.

"This is where we say good-bye, Sanyu," Pierce said, handing the young Ugandan a roll of South African rands for his return trip. "There's a bus stop nearby. Go to the airport and fly back to your coun-try."

"I understand," Sanyu said, his face a mix of reluctance and relief that this great adventure was over.

For Yeager and Meyers, the young black man was an angel who had rescued them from the pit of hell.

"The rest of the money should be in your account by the time you get home."

Sanyu's face lit up at Pierce's words. "Thank you very much. Now I can quit being a carpenter and study computers."

"Carpenter? Aren't you a tour guide?"

"Actually," Sanyu said hurriedly, "carpentry is my main job."

"It doesn't matter. You did a great job," Pierce said with a smile. "Make sure you keep all this a secret. Best not to let anyone know you've become wealthy."

"I understand."

Yeager and Meyers each shook Sanyu's hand.

"Thank you for everything, Sanyu."

"Stay well, now."

"Thank you. I wish the same for all of you."

Sanyu stepped out of the SUV with his bag of clothes, and the last thing he did was pat Akili on the head. "You be a good boy."

Akili started to fuss. Yeager took this as a good sign, that Akili could feel so friendly toward Sanyu.

The Ugandan carpenter fairly skipped as he walked off toward the bus stop. He turned around many times, flashing them a broad smile.

410

It had been so long since Yeager had seen someone happy, and after he boarded the SUV he continued to gaze at Sanyu's retreating figure in the rearview mirror.

Pierce spoke up in the lonely car. "Since we were held up in the Congo we're way behind schedule. We should have arrived in Japan by now."

Meyers, in the passenger seat, spoke up. "So: how are we going to get to Japan?"

"First let's get this car going," Pierce, in the backseat, said. "We'll go through Johannesburg, get on National Route twelve, and continue southwest."

Yeager started the engine and began driving. "Is there a safe airport or harbor?"

"No. All the places from which we could leave Africa are under surveillance."

"Then what do you propose? Are we going to stay put?"

"Meyers, you have a pilot's license, don't you?"

"I do." The young Meyers used to be in the air force. "Before I went into pararescue I flew transports."

"I'm going to have you fly a commercial jet."

Meyers, about to take a drink of water from a plastic bottle, choked. "A commercial jet? But I only have experience with prop planes!"

"I have a manual. The plane you'll fly is a special prototype Boeing 737 with long-range fuel capacity. About the same size as a transport plane."

"What kind of plane is that?" Yeager asked.

"It only holds about a hundred passengers. A small jet. It has extra fuel tanks, though, so it has a considerable range."

As Pierce explained this, Meyers considered the possibility of piloting it. "I guess if I really push myself, I might be able to do it," he said. "I mean, it won't be the friendly skies or anything, but..." He turned to face Pierce. "Where's the plane? Is it a charter?"

"No. We're going to hijack it," the anthropologist announced, and continued before the mercenaries could object. "Listen, I know you'll think the plan I'm going to tell you is crazy, but our ally in Japan came up with it. This is our best option. Our only option. With the fighting power we have now, we don't have any other choice."

"But what airport are we going to snatch the plane at? They'll stop us at the boarding gate as soon as we try to hijack a plane."

"We got it covered. There's one airfield that's not under CIA surveillance."

"Where?"

"Where you trained for Operation Guardian. At Zeta Security."

The unexpected reply had Yeager searching his memory. He recalled the runway, beyond the armory, where transport planes took off and landed. "We're going back to Cape Town?"

"Correct. A CIA-owned plane lands there to secretly bring in ammunition. That's the one we'll hijack."

"Hold on," Meyers said. "Suppose it works out and we hijack it. What then? Where are we going to land? There's no place to run. If the Special Forces storm in, it's all over."

"It'll all be done in secret. We'll tie up the crew outside before we take off and hijack an empty plane. Nobody will send out a signal that the plane's been taken."

"But if we deviate from the flight plan, they'll know right away. Even if we take off with just the four of us aboard, we'll have to keep to the CIA-designated flight path."

"We'll follow that route for a while. The flight plan they submitted takes them to Brazil, but over the Atlantic we'll be changing our route to Miami."

"Miami?" Yeager couldn't help but laugh. "Japan's in the opposite direction. Why go to America? Any plane that deviates from its flight plan and invades US airspace is going to be shot down."

"And that kind of aircraft isn't going to make it all the way to Miami, is it?" Meyers asked.

"We have enough range. The published specs from the manufacturer have twenty percent extra built in. This special prototype can make it the twelve thousand kilometers to Miami."

"Did our so-called Japanese ally calculate this?" Yeager asked sarcastically.

"That's right."

"You sure he's all there? I mean, we might have enough fuel, but there's no way we can repel fighters."

Pierce stood his ground. "This is the best possible plan, believe me. The one with the least unknowns. But timing is critical. I'll tell you all the details, so just listen to me for a minute, okay?"

"Okay. The floor's yours."

Pierce leaned forward from the backseat and outlined the details of the strategy, starting with how they would infiltrate Zeta Security.

2.

IN TWO DAYS Justin Yeager would be dead.

Kento had been working without sleep on the synthesis process, all the while receiving phone calls from Lydia Yeager. But the test numbers didn't look good. The most advanced stopgap measures had little effect on the terminal symptoms, and as predicted Justin's symptoms were only getting worse. If they could lengthen his life by just one day they would have time to send the drug to Portugal, but this wasn't going to happen.

It was 1:00 a.m. on March 1. Kento felt hopeless as he let Jeong-hoon in.

"Here's the NMR, and these are the MASS and IR." As Jeong-hoon passed Kento the sheaf of printouts, he noticed how depressed he was. "What happened?"

Kento checked the analysis results, saw that the synthesis was going well, and was about to perform the final reaction. "The experiment's on track. Just as we planned. But we weren't able to make up the thirty hours."

Jeong-hoon's expression turned gloomy. "We won't make it in time?"

Kento shook his head.

"Both GIFT 1 and GIFT 2?"

"GIFT 2 is okay. GIFT 1's the problem. This last reaction takes twenty-four hours. We have to send it to Portugal by this evening, but the reaction won't be finished until the middle of the night. Then we have to do refining and structure determination, and with all that, there's no way we'll make it in time. I just don't see how we can save Justin."

Jeong-hoon let out a pained groan, and after that silence reigned in the little room crammed with lab equipment.

As he went about the final reaction, Kento felt a deep regret. If he had only started the experiments as soon as he received his father's e-mail, he could have made it in time. Maybe Justin Yeager wouldn't have survived, he thought weakly, but at least he could have saved Maika Kobayashi. He looked at his friend. Behind his glasses, a researcher's special gleam came to Jeong-hoon's eyes.

"What's the exact time the drug will be ready?" he asked.

"Including the structure determination, twelve noon on March second."

"Then we can make it."

"How?"

"Do you have a passport?"

"No, I don't."

Jeong-hoon made up his mind. "Then I'll go."

"What are you talking about?" Kento had no idea.

"I'll fly to Lisbon with the drug."

Kento stared, dumbfounded, at his partner.

Jeong-hoon pulled out his laptop, got online, and accessed an airline's website. "See? Don't give up just yet. If I take the ten p.m. flight on March second I'll get there in time. It flies from Narita airport to Paris, then on to Lisbon. It'll only take eighteen hours."

Kento did a quick mental calculation. "Then the drug will arrive in Lisbon at four p.m., March third, Japan time?"

"That's right."

There would be a seven-hour gap between the time the drug was completed and the time Jeong-hoon needed to head to the airport.

"We can run a verification using cells and the mice."

"Exactly. We'll have enough time to save Justin."

"*Yes!*" Kento shouted, and he and Jeong-hoon leaped around the room. Jeong-hoon had saved him once again.

"Will you let Justin's mother know when I'm arriving?"

"Of course. I'll give you the money for the plane, so go first class. You'll get through customs faster that way."

"VIP treatment." Jeong-hoon smiled.

Kento felt a new lease on life, and he turned to begin the final reaction. A small piece of equipment called a magnetic stirrer began stirring the liquid in the flask. Inside, countless microscopic compounds were reacting with each other, changing composition, creating a cure for PAECS.

Kento stared into swirling liquid, and a thought struck him.

By tomorrow night it will all be over.

The goal now in sight, the long, desperate high-wire act was drawing to a close.

Kento worked the entire night, finally finishing the synthesis of GIFT 2, and sent over a sample to the university first thing in the morning.

After a short nap he had good news from Jeong-hoon. Spectral analysis showed GIFT 2 was complete. The allosteric drug was ready. The reaction was still continuing for GIFT 1, the critical agonist. Now it was a waiting game. He had nothing special to do until late at night.

Kento lay his weary body down on the tatami mat and stared up at the ceiling. The experiment his father had left him would be finished tomorrow. He had no idea what would happen to him when it was all over. Would he have to be a criminal on the run forever? Calls from Poppy had stopped some time ago, so he had no idea what the situation was.

Kento was unsure what to do. Besides the experiment, there was one other thing he'd left undone. This might be the last chance he had to unravel the mysteries surrounding his father.

He checked the address on the Internet, the only clue he had to Yuri Sakai's whereabouts. The place was in Sendagaya, in Shibuya, a one-hour trip from here.

He pulled on his coat and staggered outside. He hadn't been out in a few days, and the bright sunshine left him dizzy. He went down the outside staircase and walked along the wintry street. Were detectives still watching the turnstiles at Machida station? No one seemed to be following him.

He headed in the opposite direction from the station. As he waited on the sidewalk along the highway for a taxi to pass by, he took out his cell phone and called Sugai, the reporter. It wasn't yet noon, and he was afraid Sugai might not be in the office, but he answered right away.

"Hello?"

"Hello, this is Kento Koga."

His father's old friend seemed surprised. "Kento? I hadn't heard from you in so long, I was wondering what was going on."

"I'm sorry I haven't called. Did you find out anything about Yuri Sakai?"

"No, nothing, I'm afraid."

"I see." Kento wasn't discouraged. He knew he'd have to track her down himself.

"Where are you now?"

"Right now? Well—"

As he wondered if he should tell him he was in Machida, Sugai interrupted. "It's okay, no need to answer. I'd like to see you soon. What's your schedule like?"

Kento wasn't sure how to answer this, either. "I can't make any plans right now. I should know my schedule in a couple of days."

"All right." Sugai lowered his voice. "Kento, you need to get away from where you are. Immediately."

Kento shuddered. "Excuse me?"

"You can't stay where you are. You've got to get out of there."

"What are you talking about?" Just then a taxi approached.

"I'll tell you more when I see you. Try to get in touch with me soon."

Kento was left puzzled, but said, "Okay," and flagged down the cab.

"Talk to you later," Sugai replied, and hung up quickly, as if he were being urged to do so.

Still wondering what Sugai's real intentions were, Kento got into the taxi. "Sendagaya, in Shibuya," he told the driver.

"What part of Sendagaya?" the driver asked.

"The building that houses the World Medical Rescue Group." He recited the address he had on the memo.

"That's near the National Noh Theatre. Is it okay if we take the highway?"

"Sure."

The driver pulled away from the curb.

Kento leaned back in the seat, and as he passively watched the scenery flash by outside he reviewed his conversation with Sugai. He glanced uneasily through the rear window, but he didn't see anyone following him.

Why had Sugai said that? As a reporter, had he heard from someone that Kento was a criminal and was on the run from the police? Even if he had, Kento couldn't understand why he'd tell him "get away from where you are." He started to worry that the call had been traced, and to be on the safe side he powered off his cell phone.

The heater in the taxi was putting him to sleep. Kento gave up thinking and was about to nod off when his eyes snapped wide open.

Wait a second. Could Sugai be *Poppy?*

Poppy used software to disguise his voice, which must mean that Kento would recognize the voice otherwise. And he could think of no one other than Sugai who could have known about his late father's plans.

But something about this hypothesis didn't sit well. The phone call indicated that Sugai knew about the police's movements and was warning him. But then why didn't he call him first using Poppy's voice?

In the end Kento didn't nap at all, and the taxi entered the heart of the city, wending its way down the narrow streets of Sendagaya. The building he was looking for was on the corner of a row of low-rise office buildings.

Kento got out of the taxi and went into the lobby of the six-story building. World Medical Rescue Group, Room 501 was on the list of tenants, and Kento walked over to the elevator bank. The interior of the building was practical and no-nonsense, and other than the carpeting it was no different from the pharmacology building at the university.

Kento got off at the fifth floor, walked down the hallway with its fluorescent lighting, and came to room 501. Beyond the frosted-glass door he could see people moving about inside. There was no intercom, so he knocked twice and opened the door.

"Yes?" a woman at the reception desk said before he could get a word out. She was standing, holding a stack of files.

"Excuse me, my name is Kento Koga... There's something I need to ask you."

The expression of the woman, in her early thirties, didn't change. "And this would be concerning...?" she asked.

"There was a doctor, a Yuri Sakai, who used to be with your organization."

"Yuri Sakai?" The woman inclined her head. "When was she with us?"

"Nine years ago. She was sent to Zaire—the Democratic Republic of the Congo."

"I see," the woman replied, sounding as if she were reviewing the distant past. "Could you wait here a minute?" she said, and, files in hand, went to the rear of the office.

The World Medical Rescue Group office consisted of ten desks, a partitioned-off area for receiving guests, and a small room behind a door that appeared to be a conference room. The receptionist went to the farthest desk and was talking with a man in his fifties. As they spoke they shot glances back at Kento. I just hope they don't get suspicious, he thought.

The man stood up from his desk and walked toward him. He wore a neatly tailored suit, and his slightly heavy build and thinning hair gave him a dignified presence.

"Mr.—Koga, is it?"

"Yes, Kento Koga."

"Kento Koga," the man repeated. "My name's Ando. I'm the office manager here." He proffered a business card.

Kento wasn't sure of the proper etiquette for exchanging cards, but he went ahead and received it in both hands. In addition to giving his title—office manager—his card indicated that Ando was an MD.

"I understand you were asking about Dr. Yuri Sakai?"

"Yes. My father went to Zaire nine years ago. I heard that at the time Dr. Sakai helped him a lot."

A smile spread over Ando's face. "You aren't Seiji Koga's son by any chance, are you?"

Kento was surprised. "I am. Did you know my father?"

"I did. I was in Zaire myself back then. We had a tough time of it, with the civil war going on."

I really lucked out, Kento thought. Far from being on his guard, Ando was welcoming.

"You know, you look exactly like your father," Ando added, a mild expression in his eyes.

"Really?" Kento reluctantly said.

"We can be more comfortable over here." Ando led him to the guest area. He poured hot coffee for them from a nearby pot. "What did you want to see Dr. Sakai about?"

"I was hoping to find out how to get in touch with her."

"Well, actually," Ando said, turning serious, "a few years after we returned from Africa I lost touch with her. She quit the medical association, and I don't know her address or phone number."

"I see," Kento said, wondering how he should proceed. Ando must have witnessed everything that took place nine years before in Zaire.

"But why are you trying to contact Dr. Sakai? Is your father looking for her?"

"No—it's not that. Actually, my father died last month."

"What?" Ando looked shocked and was at a loss for words. "But he was so young. . . . How did he die?"

"He had an aortic aneurysm."

Ando nodded several times as he exhaled. "I am very sorry to hear that," he said in a pained voice.

"I thought I should let Dr. Sakai know. His experience in Zaire seemed to have left a lasting impression on him, and I thought I could hear from her about those days."

"We had a very hard time back then, that's for sure," Ando said, and smiled faintly, no doubt trying to lighten the mood. "It's right in the middle of the continent. We were based in a town called Beni, in the eastern part of Zaire, and from there we traveled to a lot of other places. Villages along the roads, hamlets deep in the jungle. We went all over helping people who didn't have access to adequate medical treatment. But just as we were about to build several small clinics the civil war broke out."

"I heard that my father went to study HIV infections among the Pygmies. Did he work together with you and Dr. Sakai?"

"No. We met up with Dr. Koga only in the final week we were there."

The final week? That was surprising. "Until then you didn't know him?"

"That's right. There's a Pygmy tribe called the Mbuti. Dr. Koga went to take blood samples from them, and there was a sick person among them. He contacted us about it."

Ando's testimony ran counter to the scenario Kento had imagined. That couldn't have been the first time his father and Yuri Sakai had met. "Then you came back to Japan right afterward?"

Ando nodded. "As I recall it was—that's right, it was Culture Day in Japan. The November third holiday. We barely escaped with our lives from Zaire when war broke out, and I remember thinking what a peaceful country Japan was."

November 3, 1996? Kento was even more confused. According to Yuri Sakai's official family record, her daughter, Ema, was born on November 4 of the same year. She gave birth to a daughter the day after arriving back from Zaire? A child whose father wasn't recorded? Kento went ahead and asked a leading question. "Did Dr. Sakai give birth right after returning to Japan?"

"Give birth?" Ando was nonplussed.

"Yes. My father said that she had a daughter."

"No, that's not possible," Ando said with a laugh. "If Dr. Sakai had been pregnant we would have known. We were all doctors and nurses, after all."

"But I definitely heard that." He wasn't about to back down. He was determined to find out if Yuri Sakai had had an affair with his father and had given birth to his half sister.

Kento was about to continue when Ando raised a hand. "I think you're mistaken. You must be confusing her with another pregnant woman."

"Another pregnant woman?"

For the first time Ando looked dubious. "I'm sorry, it's just that I find it odd. I just talked about this with a newspaper reporter who came to see me the other day."

Kento frowned. "What newspaper was he with?"

"The *Toa* newspaper."

"He wasn't named Sugai by any chance, was he?"

"Yes, that's the name. He said he was with their science bureau. Do you know him?"

"He was a friend of my father." A strange chill ran through him. Why did Sugai tell him he didn't have any new information? Had he found some dark secret of his father's he didn't want his son to know?

But Ando didn't sense Kento's doubts and went on. "That makes perfect sense. Sugai must have heard about Dr. Sakai from your father."

Sugai hadn't heard of Yuri Sakai until Kento told him about her. "What was he trying to find out?"

"He said he wanted to write a human interest story."

"About Yuri Sakai?"

"That's right. After she left the medical association she apparently moved to the city's skid row and was treating day laborers. He said he wanted to write an article about this female doctor who had a tremendous volunteer spirit. Going back to her time in Zaire."

Sugai must have made up some phony story about an article he was writing to extract more information about Yuri Sakai. "Mr. Sugai didn't know Dr. Sakai's address?"

"No. He was having trouble because he couldn't interview her directly."

"What did you talk about?"

"About the other pregnant woman. The one I mentioned. I was intentionally vague about it, though. I'll tell you the real story, but you have to promise to keep it secret. It's a very painful incident for us."

"Of course," Kento said, and leaned forward.

"When Dr. Koga visited us in Zaire, he was with an American academic. An anthropologist studying the Pygmies."

Kento realized whom he was talking about. "Are you talking about Nigel Pierce?"

"Yes. A very kind person, with a stubbly beard. They came to tell us about a sick person in the Mbuti camp they wanted us to examine. We went there and found a pregnant woman in pain in a crude hut. Her name was Anjana, and like the rest of the Pygmies she was about the size of a child. Dr. Sakai examined her, since she's an OB-GYN." Ando paused to take a sip of coffee. "Anjana had a severe case of preeclampsia, but there was no hospital nearby equipped to handle her case. We were about to transport her to a large hospital in a town called Nyankunde when the civil war broke out. We had to withdraw from the area, but we didn't know what to do with Anjana. If we left her, she and her baby would both die, but the main road was cut off, and it didn't look like we could make it to the hospital in Nyankunde."

"So what happened?"

Ando lowered his voice. "What I'm going to tell you now is secret. You understand?"

"Yes."

"In Zaire the Pygmies are viewed as less than human and aren't given citizenship. We discussed it and bribed an official to make a passport for Anjana. So we could take her to Japan to get treatment."

Kento was surprised to hear that his father was part of this bold adventure. He'd never mentioned it after he came back to Japan, because he'd helped smuggle a person out of a country.

"But getting all the paperwork done wasted time, and that proved a fatal delay," Ando said regretfully. "We got to Japan one day later than we planned, and though Anjana was treated at Dr. Sakai's clinic, we were too late. The treatment was pointless, and mother and child both died."

Kento felt sorry, too, for the sad ending, but a riddle soon reared its head. The pregnant Pygmy woman they brought to Japan died, along with the fetus. And Yuri Sakai was not pregnant. Then who was this Ema in Yuri's family record?

"I think Anjana would have been happier dying among her family in the jungle. But at the time we just couldn't abandon her," Ando said wistfully. "Even now I don't know if we did the right thing. At any rate, that was the Zaire mission's final, unfortunate incident. Your father probably didn't tell you the details because it was something he always regretted."

He talked with Ando for nearly an hour after that but got no more helpful clues.

Kento left the office and walked in the direction of Sendagaya station. He'd finally gotten some hard evidence, yet he had no idea how to interpret it. He stopped by a diner near the station and had, for the first time in a long while, a decent hot meal. Then he hailed a cab.

At least he could reject the scenario of having a half sister by a different mother. What Ando told him made it unlikely that his father had had an affair.

Lost in thought, Kento passed where he wanted to get off. He'd told the driver to drop him off next to the highway, where he'd earlier gotten a taxi, but then he remembered Sugai's warning and hurriedly changed destinations. "Just go a bit farther," he told the driver, "and you'll see a narrow alley. Turn in there."

With the new drug nearly complete he needed to be especially cautious. After he got out of the taxi he stood there for a time, checking to see if any other cars stopped nearby. Sure he wasn't being followed, he walked down the narrow road to his apartment building. No one seemed to be following him or lying in wait.

Relieved, Kento was about to climb the outside stairs when a man silently slipped around from the back of the building. Kento felt his heart nearly stop, and he froze.

"Excuse me," the man said. He had a coat on over ordinary clothes. "Are you visiting this building?"

"Uh, yeah," Kento said, hoping to get by with a vague reply.

"Are you a friend of Mr. Yamaguchi on the second floor?"

So the lab was rented in the name of Yamaguchi. "Well, sort of..."

"I'm the landlord."

"Landlord?" Kento gave the man a once-over. He noticed for the first time how old he was, way past the retirement age for a policeman—so he couldn't be a cop.

"Neighbors have been complaining about a bad smell, and I thought it might be coming from Mr. Yamaguchi's place."

Must be the smell of the chemical reagents, Kento realized. They didn't have a fume hood, so he'd attached a thick bellows around the ventilating fan in place of a ventilation system. "I don't think it's coming from there," he said. "What sort of smell is it?"

"A bad smell is all I heard. They say it's different depending on the day."

"I don't think it's from Mr. Yamaguchi's. I've been there many times and never smelled anything." As he said this, Kento tensed up. What would he do if the man asked to see the place?

"Is that right? Okay, then." The landlord didn't press the point. "Maybe it's Shimada on the first floor, then."

Kento started to walk away, greatly relieved, but came to a sudden halt. He turned around. "There's someone else in the building besides apartment two-oh-two?"

"Yes—in the last apartment on the first floor. The place is going to be bulldozed soon, so the rent's cheap."

So there was another unseen resident of the building where his father had his hidden lab. Kento had the weird sensation that someone had been spying on him all along. Was this Shimada person involved in all this, or was he...?

"What sort of person is Shimada?"

"Well, sort of hard to say—"

"A newspaper reporter type, in his fifties?"

"A reporter?" the man said incredulously, and stared at Kento. "No. And it is a woman, not a man. About forty, I'd say."

"A woman," Kento muttered, and, unable to believe it could be true, described her. "Slim, hair down to her shoulders, no makeup?"

"That's the one," the landlord said, giving a big nod. "Why are you asking?"

"It's—it's nothing." Kento faltered, trying not to let the shock show. "I saw someone I'd never seen before and thought she was suspicious."

"She's not suspicious. Not to worry—she lives here," the landlord said with a smile. "I guess I'll come back later," he added as he headed down the narrow private road that led to the main street.

Kento stood there until the old man disappeared from sight, trying to calm down. He turned back to the apartment building but didn't take the staircase. Instead he quietly walked down the first-floor hallway. An outside wall was nearby, so even during the day the hallway was dim.

Kento stood in front of the last apartment, 103, readied himself, and knocked.

No answer. And no sign of anyone behind the flimsy front door.

Kento glanced in both directions to make sure no one was there and twisted the doorknob. It was unlocked, and he pulled it open toward him.

"Hello? Anybody home?" he called out, but no one replied. He hesitated for a moment, then slipped off his shoes and went inside. His were the only shoes at the entrance. The occupant of the apartment seemed to be out.

The layout was the same as 202, his lab. A kitchen, a bathroom, and, farther on, a small room. There was a frying pan on top of the stove, evidence that someone actually lived here.

Kento gingerly walked farther into the apartment and slid open the sliding door to the small room. There was a minimal amount of furniture. A low table and TV; hangers, but no clothes on them. In the closet were two sets of futons, which surprised him. So were two people living here? But the room was as bland and graceless as a cheap hotel. It was less a place where someone lived full-time than a temporary residence.

Why did it seem so bleak and unoccupied? As he tried to figure this out, he noticed there weren't any clothes. No dresser. No luggage, either, which might mean that whoever lived here was on a trip. And then he remembered the unlocked front door. It seemed less likely that the person had gone on a trip than that she had hurriedly run away.

He walked around the room some more, and then he noticed the phone and came to an abrupt halt. The receiver had been altered; there was a device of some kind covering the mouthpiece.

Kento removed the device, studied it, found the tiny switch, and turned it on. He paused, then said "Hello" into it. The voice that came through the speaker in back of the receiver was a low bass, sounding as if it were coming up from the abyss.

Poppy's voice.

He stood stock-still, device in hand, as he pondered this unexpected discovery. Someone whose voice he'd recognize, who knew everything about what his father had been up to—

Yuri Sakai was Poppy.

But would that one piece solve the whole puzzle? Would it explain all that had been happening?

Immediately he thought of the dossier on Yuri Sakai in the small laptop. Maybe the CIA was investigating her not as a possible collaborator but as a suspect. So why had they doubted her to begin with? Nine years ago in Zaire there were many other Japanese doctors besides Yuri. There was only one reason why she would have been singled out. Without Kento realizing it, she'd been feeding him information. And Sugai, the reporter, was the only one he'd told her name to.

The thought upset him, as if he'd been given a hard whack in the head. It wasn't Yuri who was working with the CIA, it was Sugai, the science reporter. Sugai was the one investigating Kento's movements.

If they catch me they'll kill me.

He tried to calm his fears as he reviewed his conversations with Sugai. What had he told him? At least he hadn't revealed the existence of this lab. Sugai didn't know about Jeong-hoon, either. Kento remembered one more important thing. The phone call, Sugai telling him "You've got to get out of there." What was behind those words?

Maybe, Kento conjectured, Sugai just supplied information about him to the CIA, but when he understood the CIA's intentions and knew Kento was in real danger—and realized the phone was tapped— he tried to help him. This thought comforted him a little, but the fact remained that he was in danger.

Had he done anything else that would put him at risk? As Kento tried desperately to recall, he arrived at a possibility.

A tutor to a child who refused to leave the house.

A child who never went outside.

No way, Kento thought, and froze.

Rubens had spent another long day in the command center, and just before midnight two updates came to his attention, one after the other.

The first report was from the CIA, which had news about Kento Koga's whereabouts. They'd intercepted a cell phone signal at the north side of Machida station, the district they believed he was hiding in, and narrowed down the spot to a three-hundred-meter radius. When Rubens learned that the Public Security Bureau of the Tokyo police was focusing their search in this area, he grew impatient. How far had Kento gotten in developing the new drug? That seedy-looking young Japanese researcher was the only chance to save the lives of all those children.

One sentence in the CIA report gave him hope: Our local operative, Scientist, has learned of our intention to locate Kento Koga and is becoming increasingly uncontrollable. We feel there is a distinct possibility that Scientist will actually help the suspect escape, and we are exploring possible measures to deal with this.

Rubens could only pray this Scientist would betray his handlers and take Kento's side.

The second update was from Logan of the NSA, and the contents startled him. The encrypted transmissions from Japan to Africa had finally been decoded.

The moment he received this intel, Rubens raced out of the command center and sped in his Audi to Fort Meade. The time had come to see exactly what information Nous had been transmitting by satellite. If this pinpointed Nous's present position, then Rubens would have to find a way to suppress it.

It was late at night when he arrived at NSA headquarters, but Logan was there to greet him. He passed through the same security checks as before and headed to the conference room. There were three NSA employees in the room, one of whom was the mathematician, Fisher, he'd met before. The other two were new to him.

Logan first introduced him to an elderly man in black-framed glasses. "This is Dr. Kenneth Danford, an expert in linguistics."

Rubens and Danford shook hands. The linguistics scholar's grip was surprisingly strong. He was next introduced to a middle-aged Asian man. "This is Tak Ishida. He specializes in Japanese and Japan-related issues."

Ishida responded in a perfect East Coast accent. Rubens figured he must be a Japanese American. From the way he spoke, Rubens also judged him to be quite well educated. Rubens was impressed by how many different types of people worked for this, the world's largest intelligence organization.

Rubens got right to the point. "So what did you find out?"

Fisher spoke in his usual agitated way. "The random number sequence we got from Melvin Gardner's computer finally proved helpful. But because the random number sequence was broken into three fragments, the message we decrypted was also divided into three types of data. First there was this."

Fisher held out a sheaf of printouts. Rubens took it and glanced through it. It was a Mercator map of the earth, including Africa and North and South America. Beside this were dense rows of numerical values.

"This is a map of the undersea topography and ocean currents in the North Atlantic, including data on water temperatures and tidal currents."

Rubens scanned the printouts. The North Equatorial Current, which flowed west from the west coast of Africa, turned into the Gulf Stream near the North American continent then changed direction and flowed northeast. A great current of seawater that circulated in the North Atlantic. Differences in water temperature were indicated by a gradation from green to red.

"The water temperature this year seems unusually high," Fisher said.

"Isn't this public information from the Internet?"

"It is. Put together from observational data from a number of countries. We've already confirmed the existence of a corresponding website."

"This information was sent from Japan to Africa?" Why would Nous want data on the North Equatorial Current? Was the movement to the southern part of Africa just a diversion? Were they really planning to escape by ship near the equator? If that were true, then they wouldn't be heading to Japan but to North America.

"We have no idea why this information was sent. One of the other two messages we decrypted was audio data, the other text data. Take a listen."

Fisher inserted a CD-ROM into his laptop.

Before the sound started Logan added an explanation. "What you'll hear is a child's voice, we believe. Our analysis indicates it is a girl around five years old."

Rubens was perplexed. "A child's voice? Not a middle-aged woman's?"

"Correct."

Fisher tapped his keyboard, and they could hear a girl speaking. Rubens listened intently and was even more confused. "What language is that?"

"Something close to Japanese," Ishida replied.

"What do you mean 'close'?"

"The accent is standard Japanese, but the message is unintelligible to Japanese."

"How so?"

"The grammar is odd, and she's using lots of vocabulary that doesn't appear in any dictionary. But there was one clue we did get." Ishida passed Rubens the final file. "This is the text data we decrypted at the same time."

Rubens looked over the pages, but they were covered with unfamiliar writing, and he couldn't decipher it. "Is this Japanese, too?"

"Yes. It seems the child's voice is reading this writing. As if she's teaching someone to read. Before I say anything about this cryptic message, may I explain a little bit about Japanese?"

"Go ahead."

"I'll try to keep it short," Ishida said. "Because the Japanese had no writing system until around the third century CE, that period is considered prehistoric. Starting in the fifth century they imported Chinese characters and began using them. At that point the Japanese had not developed the ability for abstract thought, so they also introduced many abstract concepts as words from China. Which explains why nearly half the vocabulary used by present-day Japanese are foreign words from China. Take this, for example." Ishida pulled over his legal pad and wrote down two characters. "Each Chinese character has its own special meaning. Put several together and they form a word and create a new concept. The first part of this word means things like 'not protruding,' 'still' or 'quiet,' or 'nothing happened.' The second part means things like 'adding two things,' 'two things reconciled,' 'a calm and settled situation.' Put these two together and you get the word 平和, which means 'peace.'"

Thought patterns of Westerners and Asians are completely different, Rubens realized. Not that one was superior to the other—just different. "About how many Chinese characters are there?"

"More than one hundred thousand," Ishida readily replied. "But Japanese today use only about two or three thousand."

"And they remember all of them?"

"They do," Ishida said, and smiled. "It might seem irrational, but Chinese characters actually have their advantages. They enter the brain as visual information, so when compared to phonograms there are fewer steps necessary to connect them with semantic meaning. In other words, Chinese characters introduce a lot of interesting possibilities. You can read books and film subtitles faster. You're rewarded for the difficulty of learning them. But I've gotten off topic."

Ishida returned to the decrypted text data and pointed out a few words. The Chinese characters—先論系, 後論系, 暫決解—were for Rubens, of course, just odd-looking figures.

"These ambiguous words seem to be entirely new concepts made by combining Chinese characters. The ones the girl's voice pronounces—such as *senronkei, koronkei, zanketsukai,* and so forth—are new concepts."

"Can't they be translated into English?"

"As I explained, each character has meaning, and based on that I could hazard a guess." Ishida handed over a sheet written in English. "But now an even bigger riddle presents itself."

Rubens tried to carefully read through the English translation, but couldn't follow.

O, O, senronkei [the previous logic or the system that was created by the claim?] *1x1y* sunani koronkei [the latter logic or the system that was created by the claim?] *2x1y along with the time function 3x1y* sunani *1x2y truth-value transforms randomly 2x5y corresponds to emergence* zunani *truth-value and validity transition both linearly and nonlinearly. In order for a solution to the* zanketsukai [a temporary solution?] *that manifests in chaos and the "window" of* chaos it is necessary for there to be a decision based on *choyuchi* [which can be written out in three Chinese characters but is impossible to translate] . . .

"What in the world?" Rubens asked, his eyes glued to the page. What was written there was indeed unclear, but it wasn't pure nonsense, either. "Truth-value transforms randomly?"

"I've never heard of a system of logic like that," Fisher, the mathematician, commented.

"This word *choyuchi*: its meaning is unknown?"

"If you synthesize the meaning of the characters, it means something like 'a subject that makes a decision that transcends nonfixed wisdom and knowledge,' though this is just a tentative translation. Anybody who could comprehend the meaning would have to be someone who already understands *choyuchi*-type things."

Rubens tried connecting some of the fragments to come up with a meaningful thought. "Doesn't this suggest what you might call a kind of complex logic? Something that would correspond to a complex system—like quantum logic, made to parallel quantum theory?"

"But we don't know what kind of axiomatic system the complex logic is based on in this case," Fisher replied.

"I'd like to give an opinion, if I may." Danford, the linguist, had been quiet throughout, but now spoke up. "I was asked to analyze this writing, and at first I thought it was just nonsense. But if you don't get hung up on the semantic content and focus solely on the grammar, you arrive at an odd supposition—namely, that on the grammatical level this might be an entirely original artificial language."

"So it does follow certain rules?"

"It does. The grammar is fundamentally different from the natural language that our brains produce. As I investigated this writing it hit home how one-dimensional our own language is. Whether writing or speech, it proceeds along a one-directional axis of time. But this writing doesn't. It moves back and forth among concepts and propositions that are on a plane and completes the message that way. The x and y coordinates indicate the position on that plane, though it's unclear what the disposition indicates regarding meaning or rules. And if you read to the end you'll notice a z coordinate, which means that the language itself has strata. If we employed this kind of grammar, many paradoxes that puzzle us might disappear."

This very odd conclusion bothered Rubens. "But this message was read by a little girl, wasn't it?"

"Correct."

"Then this isn't just something you read but a language you can speak as well. Such a complex grammar wouldn't be practical."

"You're right. For our brains it would be impossible to speak this language."

"Impossible for our brains?" Rubens felt a sudden shock at Danford's casual turn of phrase. He remembered Heisman's low voice.

You're overlooking one very critical problem.

"If you tried speaking this language you'd soon lose the thread of what you were saying. Because if you don't memorize the position of the concepts and propositions scattered in three dimensions you won't be able to communicate. There's one more thing besides the grammar that I should add," Danford said, oblivious to Rubens's speechless state. He pointed with a pen to two words in the translated text. "In the original text the words *sunani* and *zunani* appear frequently, but these aren't Japanese, I take it."

Ishida shook his head. "Those words don't exist in Japanese. And these aren't written in Chinese characters but in special Japanese phonograms, so it's impossible to reason by analogy what the meaning could be."

"If we focus on the words' function, we see they're used as conjunctions. But, as Mr. Ishida points out, because the meaning is unknown we can only understand them syntactically."

Fisher, seated next to Danford, smiled as if this were all quite interesting. "That makes sense. The more conjunctions the more logical constants, right? The language is different, therefore so is the logic. The person who uses this language has different patterns of thinking from ordinary people."

Danford's conclusion was more practical than that of the young mathematician. "Or else it's an elaborate hoax."

Rubens tried to keep his voice from trembling. "I'll double-check, but the transmission was sent from Japan to Africa, correct? Not the other way around?"

"That's right."

The shock Rubens had felt at first was becoming an overwhelming sense of intellectual excitement. The answer to the puzzle Dr. Heisman had given him was unimaginable.

There was one more evolved human.

Rubens recalled the report by the operative code-named Scientist, which had come in via the CIA. The information they'd gotten at the Tokyo office of the World Medical Rescue Group was the key. "Mr. Ishida?"

"Yes?" The Japanese American turned to him.

"Are you familiar with Japanese law and domestic affairs?"

"A little," Ishida modestly replied.

"In Japan they have an official family register called *koseki*, I believe."

"That's right."

"I heard that people illegally buy and sell *koseki*."

"It happens. Organized crime's involved, because if you obtain another person's *koseki* you can hide your identity."

"How do they go about buying them?"

"They go to places where the homeless and day laborers congregate and find someone willing to sell theirs. People desperate for money will sell their *koseki*."

"If you use the *koseki* you bought, then you can become a different person, right? You can make a contract with an Internet provider, open a bank account, lease a place through a real estate agent?"

"Yes, all those."

"How do they create an individual *koseki*?"

"When a child is born you report it to the city office."

"What documents do you need?"

"You need two documents. A certificate issued by the doctor and a birth certificate."

"Can a relative of the woman who gives birth issue the doctor's certificate? For example, say the woman's father is an OB-GYN. Could he write the certificate?"

"Legally it shouldn't be a problem."

"On a totally different topic, what's the system in Japan for accepting refugees?"

Ishida looked off into space. "Because one conservative party has held power in Japan for the last fifty years, they've not been very keen on accepting foreigners. They accept less than one percent of the refugees the United States does, a level that's essentially inhumane."

"So it's hard to obtain refugee status in Japan?"

"Very. Japan's been harshly criticized for being closed off to refugees."

Rubens spoke more slowly now as he posed a more concrete scenario. "Based on what you've said, let's say a civil war breaks out on another continent and a pregnant woman escapes to Japan. But that woman dies soon after giving birth, leaving behind her daughter. If the guardian, a Japanese woman, wants to care for the child, what can she do?"

Ishida sat in thought for a moment at what was clearly a difficult question. "First she would try to get her refugee status, but there's a high risk of being deported. If the father was still back in her native land, the chances of being deported would increase even more. I can imagine trying to adopt the girl, but then they would have to reveal who the real mother was, and that brings things right back to the question of refugee status." Ishida seemed to be recalling their previous discussion, and a smile came to his face. "This Japanese woman who is the guardian wouldn't happen to have a father who's an OB-GYN, would she?"

"She does."

"In order to protect the child would they be willing to break the law?"

"Of course."

"Then it's simple. Have it look like the pregnant woman died before she gave birth. Then you create a death certificate. That way you can erase the existence of the child who was to become a refugee. Then have the Japanese woman's father write a false birth certificate and register the baby with the town office as her own daughter."

"Is that possible if the fake mother isn't married and the father isn't known?"

"Entirely possible. The column in the *koseki* for the father is just left blank. And the real mother isn't named, either, so no one knows that the report is fake."

Rubens nodded slowly, satisfied.

Language becomes a tool of communication when there are multiple subjects who understand it and can have a meaningful exchange. If a language cryptic to humans is sent and received, that means there must be at least two people who use that language.

Nigel Pierce probably knew in advance that a superhuman might be born among the Kanga band. Because nine years ago the first such individual was born in Japan.

In the midst of civil war in Zaire, a pregnant Pygmy woman was transported to Japan. She died soon after giving birth. Her attending physician, Yuri Sakai, was bent on saving the child and must have submitted the false report that the baby was her daughter. The fact that the child had a congenital abnormality of the head must have aroused her sympathy all the more. But as it grew up this child she thought was deformed displayed an astounding intelligence, and Yuri contacted the anthropologist, Pierce. They investigated the intelligence of this child, named Ema, and found that a different species of human had come into being. Anticipating the birth of a second such child, the two of them began to formulate a plan to rescue that child from the Congo, where the civil war was still raging. Actually by this point the one in charge of the plan might have been none other than Ema Sakai, the sole individual of a new race. For Ema it was imperative to get this second child to Japan. Without another individual to mate with, the line would die out.

From Nous's perspective, developing this special drug was the most rational solution of all.

From just a few clues Dr. Heisman had seen through it all. Ema and Nous probably had the same father but a different mother. It was very possible that their future consanguineous mating might lead to the same tragedy that had befallen Yeager and his wife. Any child born of such a union would run a high risk of inheriting the same etiology gene from both parents. The development of the drug that Seiji Koga had entrusted to his son, Kento, was no doubt the first experiment to deal with a genetic disease brought on by consanguineous marriage.

Rubens mentally calculated how old Ema Sakai would be now. Eight years and four months. Operation Nemesis was not pitted against a three-year-old from some remote, uncivilized place but against an eight-year-old superhuman in an advanced country with access to all kinds of information.

You're underestimating your enemy's intellect.

If a mere three-year-old of an advanced race was able to attain the intellectual powers of human beings, Ema Sakai's mental abilities must far and away exceed ours.

The operation will fail. Rubens was certain of it now. From the encoded message they'd decrypted, it was obvious that Ema's mental powers far surpassed that of Homo sapiens. This eight-year-old perceived a world we could never comprehend.

Over on the African continent, Nous was being protected by an intelligence unknowable to humans, and Rubens felt sure he would make it to Japan. As long as the people supporting him didn't screw up.

Rubens began to worry about Kento Koga. He must be in contact with Yuri Sakai. If he were arrested by the Japanese police, then the investigation would eventually lead the authorities straight to her.

Kento had locked his apartment, yet when he got back there was a brand-new cell phone on the floor just inside the front door. A memo was with it. GET RID OF THE PHONE YOU'VE BEEN USING.

He picked up the phone and checked the display. There had been several incoming calls but no voice messages.

He took off his shoes and was heading into the lab, where GIFT 1 was going through its final reaction, when the new cell phone began ringing. When he answered he heard that low voice again, sounding as if it were coming up from the bowels of the earth.

"Leave your apartment, right away."

"Why?" Kento asked.

"You made a mistake. They traced your phone call to the newspaper reporter and know your location. Five detectives are searching your neighborhood as we speak. It's only a matter of time before they find you."

Cold air brushed his back. If detectives heard about the problem with the bad smell the landlord had mentioned, they'd race right over.

"But..." Kento's voice trembled. "The drug isn't complete yet."

"This is for your own protection."

"You're telling me to give up?"

"I am."

"But there has to be a way. If we take the lab equipment somewhere else..." he began, but realized it was impossible. There were just too many things he'd need to take. If he got hold of a car he'd still have to go in and out of the apartment to carry equipment, and he couldn't help but stand out.

"There's no time. You only have one chance to escape. If you're outside too long there's a high risk they'll find you. Leave the apartment, then walk as fast as you can to the east. Grab a taxi and head to the center of Tokyo. After that I'll tell you where you'll be living."

Kento looked at his watch. There were ten more hours before GIFT 1 was fully synthesized. It would take an additional eight hours after that to separate the final product material and determine the chemical structure. "But I just need one more day to complete the drug!"

"Time's up. Get out of there."

Kento had a sudden mental picture: of Maika Kobayashi, lips bloody, struggling for every breath. He could save her. He knew it. "No. I'm not running away. There's a child I have to save."

"But you're in real danger."

"But you used to save children's lives, too, didn't you? Yuri Sakai."

He couldn't see her face, but he could sense how much his words jolted her. Kento went on. "You came to get the laptop to keep me from getting involved.... You wanted to keep me away from danger, didn't you?"

No reply.

"But I *am* involved. I took my father's laptop, and here I am now. I can't go back. I'm going to finish the drug. And nobody's going to stop me." Kento abruptly hung up.

He waited awhile, but there was no call back. Kento went into the lab and gazed at the flask above the magnetic stirrer.

The detectives must have started their search from the spot next to the highway where he phoned Sugai. There were several housing complexes between there and this apartment. For five people to stop by each one would take at least a day.

Looking up to the heavens, Kento murmured a message to his father.

Dad, I promise I'll fulfill your last wish. So please protect your son.

Let me save those children's lives.

Kento smiled faintly and ended his prayer with these words:

I'm sorry I ever doubted you.

3.

BEFORE THEY ENTERED Cape Town, Yeager and Meyers purchased all
the equipment they would need—batteries, various tools, and black
sweaters and cargo pants, which would be their uniform. Pierce needed
a printer, so he stopped by an Internet café, printed the necessary documents, and handed them over to the two soldiers.

They arrived in their Land Cruiser at a spot overlooking Zeta Security just as the sun was setting. The company's site, a broad open space
in otherwise hilly surroundings, was lit up clearly in the dying rays of
the sun. The main building, resembling a resort hotel, was beyond a
chain-link fence and steel netting. The runway lay behind it.

They stayed inside the car for one final briefing. The data sent from
their Japanese ally covered all the necessary information: a schematic of
the compound, security camera blind spots, the disposition of security
personnel and their numbers, and a list of codes for the electronic key-
pads so they could get into each room. There was also a flight manual
for the Boeing 737, which Meyers had wanted. But the manual, which
Pierce had printed in the Internet café, was so thick that Meyers just
ripped out the pages he needed and worked on memorizing the loca-
tions of cockpit gauges and instruments.

After they'd run through their plans, Yeager looked in the backseat
and saw Akili intently studying a sheaf of papers.

"What are you reading?" Yeager asked, but Akili didn't respond. Akili
didn't seem to be intentionally ignoring him; rather, he was caught up
in reading the material. His upward-turned catlike eyes were reading
through the pages at blinding speed.

"He's looking at a chart of ocean currents in the North Atlantic."

"We're going to be flying, so why worry about currents?"

"It's his trump card," Pierce said. He looked perplexed and less confident himself. "There are aspects of this escape plan I can't understand. We just have to trust our friend in Japan." The anthropologist pulled out the laptop Akili used to communicate. "I installed some voice software. When Akili types in anything now it'll be converted to a voice."

"Sounds like we can have a nice talk," Yeager said.

They opened cans of food, had their final meal in Africa, and drove their car behind Zeta Security, out of sight behind a stand of trees.

The security patrol came by at 21:40, right on schedule, and as soon as it passed by Yeager started up the Land Cruiser. Headlights off, they crossed the road and pulled up alongside the fence. A board bearing the image of a skull against a yellow background hung from the four-meter-high fence, which had ten thousand volts running through it.

Yeager got out, tugged on a pair of rubber gloves, and sat down at the base of the fence. Using a plastic jack, he gingerly lifted the bottom of the fence. For a former Special Forces member, it was an elementary infiltration technique. Once there was enough space between the ground and the fence, Meyers inserted a large plastic board to hold open the gap Yeager had made.

Faceup, Yeager slid between the board and the ground, careful not to touch the electrified fence, and slipped into the Zeta Security compound. As soon as he was in he got to his feet and ran over to the electric power unit, a waist-high metal box locked with a small padlock. Yeager broke the lock, opened the door, found the alarm switch, and turned it off. He next cut the communications cable to the security office and then shut off the power.

Meyers threw a knife at the chain-link fence to make sure the power was off, and then all three of them passed through the opening.

Phase two of their plan went quickly. The four of them moved toward the rear of the main building, zigzagging to stay in the surveillance camera dead zones. Back in Zeta Security after a long while, Yeager felt less tense than nostalgic.

They arrived at the rear of the building at 22:05, five minutes ahead of schedule. In front of them was the concrete armory, and beyond that, bathed in orange light, was the runway.

They held their breath, impatiently waiting for their chance. Red beacon lights shone far off in the sky as the roar of a jet, owned by a dummy corporation, drew near. The plane banked steeply as it glided downward.

When the noise was sufficiently loud, they made their move. They ran to the armory, punched in the code, and the heavy door swung open. Inside, Yeager and Meyers exchanged their AK-47s for silenced M4 carbines. They handed Pierce a loaded pistol, and all of them put on bulletproof vests. None of the vests fit a three-year-old, so Pierce carried Akili on his back. The anthropologist's body would shield the boy.

Once they were outfitted, they brought out a handcart and loaded it up with other items they would need—helmets, goggles, small oxygen tanks, and square parachutes—all equipment they would need for high-altitude high-opening jumps. The two mercenaries were airborne-qualified, so they would hold Pierce and Akili and do a tandem jump. For this they needed to check their harnesses and couplings carefully.

The jet engine roar from the runway reached a crescendo and then quickly subsided. The Boeing jet had landed safely.

Moving to phase three, Yeager leaned out the door of the armory to check out the situation. Just then something happened they hadn't planned for. The rear door of the main building opened, and a tall man emerged. Yeager recognized him right away—Singleton, the director of operations. Yeager had a quick insight: this could save them some trouble. He signaled to Meyers the presence of an enemy, motioned him to follow, and silently slipped out the door.

Singleton seemed headed toward the runway to greet the CIA operatives. Yeager came up behind him, aimed his pistol at the back of his head, and cocked the trigger.

"Hold it right there."

Singleton shuddered and raised his hands. "Who are you?"

"An old friend."

"I can't tell from the voice. Do you mind if I turn around?"

"All right."

The director of operations of the private defense contractor slowly turned. His eyes widened in surprise when he saw Yeager and Meyers pointing their pistols at him. "What happened to Operation Guardian?"

"Two of our guys died."

"*What?!*" A pained expression, slight but still detectable, ran across his features. "Were they infected by the virus?"

This reaction erased any doubts Yeager had. Singleton had heard nothing about the operation's real goals. Yeager no longer felt hostile toward him, though he wasn't feeling much goodwill, either. "The operation's still ongoing. I want you to do exactly what I say."

"What are you talking about? Is this what the Pentagon wants?"

"Interpret it any way you like. Just do what I tell you."

At this point Singleton finally understood this was no joke. "And if I don't?"

"Don't try to resist. You know what kind of men we are."

The unarmed former soldier looked at each of them in turn, frowned, and nodded. "What do I have to do to get out of this alive?"

"Get inside the armory," Yeager commanded.

Ten minutes later, Singleton emerged from the armory and walked alone toward the airfield. Inside the hangar a small passenger jet, thirty meters long, was parked on its spot, wings spread wide as if to display the elegant curves of its fuselage. Nine workers were busy unloading cargo and refueling the aircraft.

Singleton went over to the five men at the base of the gangway. "Welcome to Zeta Security. I'm Mike Singleton, director of operations."

The CIA agents unloading arms and ammunition each introduced themselves, and shook Singleton's hand.

"We've prepared a light meal for you in the mess hall, but could you wait here for a couple minutes?"

"Sure, no problem," the copilot said with a friendly smile.

After he saw that all the containers had been unloaded, Singleton directed the agents. "Gather around over here, if you would."

The men, dressed in overalls, assembled, and Singleton pointed to two of them. "There's a handcart over in the armory with some cargo on it, so could you bring it over here?"

"Okay," the men said, and headed for the armory.

The Boeing pilot looked dubious. "What are you loading onto my plane?"

"We received an order a little while ago to load some extra cargo."

"The order came from Langley?"

"Correct."

One of the agents took a cell phone from his jacket pocket. He's calling the United States to confirm, Singleton realized, and he felt cold sweat drip down his back. "I'm sorry, but please don't use the phone."

"Why not?" the agent asked suspiciously.

"The reason is . . . this," Singleton said, and unbuttoned the front of his shirt. Taped to his chest was a microphone and C-4 explosive with a remote-control detonator attached.

"Everyone here, myself included, has been taken hostage. An armed group is a little ways off, with sniper rifles aimed at us."

The CIA agents stared off toward the runway, but the hangar was too bright, and they couldn't see into the darkness beyond.

"They're monitoring our conversation. Please, everybody, do exactly what I say. Let's start by taking out all your weapons and phones and laying them on the ground."

Suddenly one of the agents made a break for it. But the instant he turned to run, a sharp crack split the air, and a bullet hit his right shoulder. He gave a brief shout, grabbed the wound, and squatted on the floor.

"They're well trained," Singleton said, stating the obvious. "If you don't resist, no one will be killed. I'm telling you, do what I say."

The men reluctantly followed his instructions. They knelt down, underwent a body check, were blindfolded and gagged, then shackled with plastic handcuffs, hands behind their backs. Only the man refueling the plane was left untied, and he was ordered to continue working.

Just then the two men who'd been ordered to the armory appeared, pushing the handcart. Seeing that something was amiss, they came to an abrupt halt. But when they saw the bomb wrapped around Singleton, they realized what was happening. "Hurry up," he ordered them, and they mutely followed instructions. When they finished loading the plane, Singleton ordered them to keep the plane's door open but to roll away the stairway. As soon as they were done they joined the line of hostages.

During the hour it took to refuel, everyone was kept as they were.

★   ★   ★

Once the refueling was over the man refueling the plane moved away from the fuel cap under the wing, and Singleton tied him up. Yeager checked this through his gun sight, stood up from his prone sniper position, exchanged the sniper rifle for the M4 carbine, and cut across the runway.

As he approached the hangar he saw Singleton, the only one standing. "Is this okay?" Singleton asked.

His stilted voice revealed how exhausted and helpless he felt and carried with it, too, a touch of hostility. Though not enough to rouse the anger of his captors.

"You did a good job," Yeager replied, and tied up Singleton's hands with plastic handcuffs.

Meyers, Pierce, and Akili materialized from different directions. Seeing that the hostages wouldn't be able to resist, Meyers lowered his medical bag and began emergency treatment for the man with the shoulder wound. "Don't worry," he told the man. "You'll make it."

Behind the gag the man groaned. He said something, muffled and unclear, though clearly not words of thanks.

Meyers got in a pickup truck in the hangar and started the engine. They loaded the hostages in the back and drove them to the practice area behind the main building. They bound their legs, then Yeager had them locked up inside the shoot house they'd used during their training.

"When is the next practice session?" Yeager asked Singleton.

"The day after tomorrow."

In a couple of days the next group of mercenaries in training would be startled to discover live hostages. Yeager put a blindfold and gag on Singleton. "Just be patient till then," he said, and left the room.

Out in the hallway Pierce looked at his watch. "Good job," he said. "Now let's get out of this country. Out of Africa."

They boarded the pickup truck and drove back to the hangar.

It was now late at night. As they arrived Yeager took another look at the plane. There was no logo of any kind on the white fuselage, just a registration number, N313P.

Meyers took away the chocks and came over. "Help me out," he said.

The two of them went into the hangar, pulled out an expandable ladder, and leaned it up against the entrance to the plane. It was about ten meters high. Meyers went first, clambering up the ladder, then Pierce, carrying Akili on his back, and finally Yeager.

The plane was pitch black inside. Meyers shone his flashlight around the cabin. The cabin had been reconfigured for business purposes, with meeting spaces forward and aft and seats set up in the center around a table rather than along the windows.

They pushed the ladder to the ground and tried closing the door. They didn't know how to shut it, and it took an unexpectedly long time. They were discussing how it was supposed to work when a mechanical voice rang out in the darkness.

Place the door parallel to the fuselage, then push outward.

Akili was using the computer to instruct them. When they moved the thick door as he said, it went smoothly, and they were able to close it.

"You're amazing," Meyers said, patting Akili's head as he moved toward the control cabin.

Faint light filtered in from outside, revealing the gauges surrounding the cockpit.

"This is the first time I've sat in the captain's seat," Meyers said as he lowered himself into the left-hand seat and slid it forward. "Yeager, could you sit next to me?"

"You're sure I can help?"

"Yeah. Shine your light on the gauges."

Meyers unfolded his checklist. "Fuel valves. Auxiliary power switch," he muttered to himself, switching each on, one by one. The lights came on in the cockpit, and the LED displays and gauges were illuminated in a variety of colors.

Meyers went through the same operation twice and got both engines up and running. The cockpit was filled with the roar of the fired-up jet engines.

"That's more like it!" Meyers said happily.

But Yeager was still on edge. "I won't be happy till we take off."

Pierce watched these proceedings and, with Akili in his arms, sat down at the rear of the cockpit. "We're a little ahead of our flight plan, but let's take off."

"Fasten your seat belts," Meyers intoned, sounding very much the captain. He turned forward again. "Here we go."

Meyers pushed the thrust lever forward slightly, and the engines roared to life as the plane slowly began taxiing.

Yeager was startled to see Meyers's hands leave the control stick. He was apparently using a different lever to the left of his seat for taxiing. Wandering to the left and right, the Boeing aircraft made its way unsteadily down the taxiway. The curve just before the runway was a real challenge for the impromptu captain. He moved the plane in fits and starts and was finally able to manage the curve.

The final change of direction accomplished, the Boeing came to a stop. Outside the window their escape route lay straight ahead, illuminated by runway lights.

"Radio frequency, check; flaps set; transponder on . . ." Meyers ran through his final check. "When we're in the air," he said to Yeager, "pull up this lever. That will store the landing gear."

"Anything else?" Yeager asked, searching his minimal knowledge of planes. "Want me to read out the airspeed just before we take off?"

"That's important, but I don't know the exact numbers."

"What?"

Meyers laughed, but his expression was tense. "It's okay. Let's do this. When the airspeed indicator hits one hundred and ninety knots, call out 'VR.'"

"You sure we're okay?"

"Trust me."

Meyers rested his left hand on the control stick and with his right hand moved the thrust lever to ninety degrees. The engines revved up, and the low growl turned to an earsplitting roar.

"All set?" Meyers raised his voice.

"Yep."

"Auto throttle, brakes off."

Meyers pushed the thrust lever to full power, and the Boeing lurched forward at full speed. Yeager was pushed back in his seat. The plane leaned to the left, and fear rose up in his throat. Before he could take a breath, the plane was barreling down the runway, reaching the point where it seemed impossible to stop.

Meyers stared at the line down the middle of the runway and used the rudder pedal at his feet to straighten the plane out. At full thrust, the plane leaned left and right as it charged down the runway. Yeager kept his eyes on the airspeed indicator. They hadn't reached 190 knots yet. He glanced up and saw the end of the runway fast approaching. At this rate they'd plow right into the trees just beyond the runway.

"Meyers!" Yeager yelled, and just then Meyers pulled the control stick. The nose began to rise, but the angle was too shallow. The runway vanished beneath them as the fence surrounding the airfield drew near.

Yeager, sure they were going to die, felt a cold, hollow feeling in the pit of his stomach. A floating feeling. The plane had risen up. The Boeing aircraft cleared the fence by inches, grazed the trees, and soared into the night sky.

The two men in the pilots' seats were silent for a moment. Yeager finally managed to unwind his tense body and push the lever to raise the landing gear. The forward wheels and main landing gear groaned as they folded into the undercarriage. The red light on the instrument panel went out.

His expression frozen, Meyers continued to pull back on the control stick. Finally he came to himself and kept repeating "Hello?" He was apparently communicating with the radar operator at air traffic control. Their whole flight over the Atlantic would be monitored by radar.

After a few words with the controller, Meyers said, "Looks like everything's okay. They don't know we hijacked the plane. In a little while I'll switch over to autopilot."

"You did great, Meyers," Yeager said, praising him. Only a C minus by his book, but at least they'd taken off in one piece. "How long before we get to our destination?"

"It'll take about fourteen hours. Half a day from now our mission will be over."

Yeager nodded and relaxed back into the seat. Out the window, beyond the lights of Cape Town, lay the expanse of ocean. The huge continent he thought they'd never escape was vanishing behind them.

They were finally leaving Africa. The instant he thought this, Yeager felt an invisible power pulling him back. It felt as if the continent, the birthplace of new human beings for millions of years, was reaching out with a massive hand to keep him from escaping. I have to get away, Yeager thought. Have to shake free from this ominous power. This evil fate reaching out to stop me.

He glanced at his watch and saw that the deadline for his son's life had not yet arrived. Justin was still alive. This father-and-son struggle was still ongoing.

Yeager went over their plans again to make sure they hadn't overlooked anything, determined to survive until the final stage, fourteen hours from now.

4.

KENTO HAD COMPLETELY lost any sense of time. He glanced at his watch and saw it was 1:00 a.m. At this time of night the detectives would have to have put their investigation on hold. For the time being this apartment was safe.

A little past the estimated time, he used thin-layer chromatography to check that the reaction was over. The synthesis process to create GIFT 1 was finished.

Kento lifted the flask from the magnetic stirrer and stared at the clear liquid inside. If the experiment were successful, it contained the agonist that would activate mutant GPR769.

Kento used all the knowledge and technical skill he'd learned to close in on a new miracle drug no one else had discovered. To extract the desired material from the reaction solution, he began with great care to do a liquid–liquid extraction. The extraction procedure isolated the nonpolar organic materials of the reaction mixture into a nonpolar organic solvent, leaving behind the unwanted polar constituents in a polar water phase. He then evaporated off the organic solvent, thus concentrating the organic materials, which could then be purified by column chromatography. Through column chromatography, the organic target product could be separated from side products and other unwanted organic materials by eluting off the materials with an appropriate solvent or solvent mixtures.

While running the column, Kento could see with his naked eye three bands of material separating into three distinct layers. Each layer was collected as separate portions into separate flasks.

Soon after dawn the column chromatography was complete. He transferred each fraction into an eggplant flask and evaporated off the solvent with a rotary evaporator, leaving behind a solid with traces of solvent. Kento then used a vacuum desiccator to remove the last traces of solvent.

The solids remaining in each flask had not crystallized but were frothy and amorphous. He finally had the end product. One of these flasks contained GIFT 1.

Before he could get too emotional, Kento picked up his cell phone. It was not yet 9:00 a.m., but Jeong-hoon answered right away.

"Hello?"

"Were you asleep?"

"No. I got up early and have been waiting," Jeong-hoon replied. "How'd it go?"

"It's finished."

"Okay. Now we just have to do structure determination."

"There are three materials, and none of them has crystallized. So we can check them all with NMR. Can I send them to you right now at the university?"

"Sure, go ahead. I've reserved the joint equipment room."

"Along with the samples, I'll include a memo with GIFT 1's structure written down. Can you have the old lady in the joint equipment room check the results?"

By "the old lady in the joint equipment room" he meant a spectrum analysis expert who supervised and maintained the equipment. Her powers of observation were astounding, and no matter how difficult the analysis results, one look at the chart was all she needed to know the chemical structure of the sample. If they asked her to help, she'd be able to discern in an instant which sample was GIFT 1. "If we do that we can save time on sending the results back."

"Exactly. And I've already bought the plane tickets."

Jeong-hoon was set to take off for Lisbon that night.

"We're almost there," Kento said.

"We just have to make sure not to let our guard down."

Kento nodded and told Jeong-hoon the number of his new cell phone. "Use this number from now on."

"Did something happen?" Jeong-hoon asked. "Is everything okay?"

"I think so," was all he could say. "This evening we can talk about the transfer of the drug."

"Got it."

As soon as he hung up Kento got the samples ready to be transported by motorcycle, double-checking he'd labeled them correctly.

They should be able now to save Justin Yeager. The problem was the other person on their list. Was Maika Kobayashi still in the hospital? Or had she already lost her fight with death?

Kento remembered Jeong-hoon's words and roused himself. It was too soon to give up.

It was 11:00 p.m. on the East Coast. Rubens was leaving the Defense Department and had just reached the parking lot when he was called back.

"We need you back," Avery, one of his subordinates in the command center, told him over his cell phone. "We've traced Nous's movements. Looks like they're leaving Africa."

"By ship?"

"No. By plane. A plane owned by Aviation Specialties was hijacked."

Aviation Specialties was a CIA dummy corporation. Rubens, puzzled, hurried back to the basement of the Pentagon.

As soon as he cleared the biometrics scan and was back in the command center, Avery quickly brought him up to date. "A CIA plane smuggling arms and ammunition was taken over by Jonathan Yeager and his group."

"At which airport?"

"The airfield inside Zeta Security."

Rubens was impressed. Private defense contractors' airfields had been an option they'd overlooked.

"Four hours ago a security officer noticed the runway lights were still on, checked the grounds, and found the crew tied up. The hijacked plane is being tracked by radar as we speak."

"What route are they taking? Are they headed to Asia?"

"No. They're heading northwest across the Atlantic."

Rubens was taken aback. So were they heading to North America?

"This route follows exactly the flight plan submitted by Aviation Specialties. If they continue as they are they'll arrive at the airport in Recife."

"Recife?"

"On the eastern edge of Brazil. The point that juts out into the Atlantic. They must be trying to illegally enter the country disguised as CIA operatives."

Their plan can't be that simple, can it? Rubens thought. But if we come up with a response based on this assumption, then we might be able to let Nous get away. As if perfectly timed, a phone call came in from Eldridge. The director of Operation Nemesis couldn't hide his frustration at this unexpected development. He must be worried about his own position, Rubens thought, smiling to himself.

"I'm up to speed," Eldridge said. "I want you to get all our CIA assets in Brazil to the Guararapes airport."

"Should we alert the Brazilian government?"

"No need to. Don't let anybody from the State Department get involved. That would be a huge mistake. Have the intelligence community alone handle it."

"Understood."

"I'm heading over to the command center," Eldridge said. "God, what a disaster!" he added, spitting out the words before he abruptly hung up.

The command center surged to life. Stokes, their military adviser, was already at his post, but before Rubens could say hello another call came in, this time from Holland. Getting a call directly from the director of the CIA gave Rubens a faint sense of hope.

"Rubens, just speak casually. No 'sir' or anything," Holland said straightaway. "Otherwise they'll know who you're talking to."

"Um, sure," Rubens said, trying to keep it casual.

"Did you hear details about what happened at Zeta?"

"No."

"I just spoke with a man named Singleton there. According to him, Warren Garrett is dead."

"He is?"

"That's right. Yeager told him that."

Rubens had one more thing to feel guilty about. This courageous man, who was going to expose the crimes committed by the president of the United States, had fallen victim to Operation Nemesis without achieving his goal. What had incited Garrett to act had to be the same pangs of conscience Rubens was feeling right now. Anger at being duped by those in power and allowing others to die.

"There's a possibility now that the operation will be halted." The CIA director was clearly pleased by the death of this traitor. He was no doubt also happy that Nous had escaped and that the special renditions he'd had a hand in could be buried back in the shadows.

Rubens was angry at Holland for not admitting his guilty conscience, but at this point in time it was wise to have him on his side. Even though the hidden agenda behind Operation Nemesis had reached its objective, he still couldn't be optimistic. A man far more shameless and arrogant than Holland—the most powerful man in the world, an immoral mass murderer—was still hoping to get rid of Nous.

"What do you think?" Holland said. "Will Nous be okay even if agents converge on Guararapes airport? Will he be able to escape?"

"We'll have the minimal number of agents go there." It was best to let the CIA director believe that Yeager and his group were going to smuggle themselves into Brazil. "If he can find an opening, I think he should be all right."

"You're probably right. Okay, then."

"Is this the only step we're taking at present?" Rubens asked.

"Yes. The hijacked plane is over the middle of the Atlantic, so it's out of range of our fighter jets. This Boeing was used in monitoring drug smuggling, so it's equipped with military radar. If we send out AWACS surveillance aircraft the plane will detect it right away. Best to leave them alone till they get to Recife."

"One more thing, just for reference. What's the cruising range of the hijacked plane?"

"A little over eleven thousand kilometers. A rough estimate would take it almost to Miami."

The mention of an American city had Rubens uneasy. "What kind of defensive measures does this plane have?"

"None. Other than the radar it's the same as a business jet. If fighters scramble it'd be helpless. Best not to let the Brazilian government know anything."

Where could Nous be heading? Rubens again found it all puzzling. If they deviated from their flight plan as they neared Recife, the Brazilian air force would scramble jets to intercept them. It would be the same no matter where they tried to escape. The air forces of nearby countries would all mobilize, and if they attempted to escape over the open ocean they'd run out of fuel. The one thing Rubens knew for sure was that they weren't heading toward the US mainland. If they breached US airspace they'd be shot down in a heartbeat.

"How's the radar looking?" Meyers asked from the pilot's seat.

"It's clear." Yeager, in the rear of the cockpit, where he was monitoring the radar, looked up from the screen. "No sign of anything."

Six hours had passed since they took off from Cape Town. It was still dark out, and from their altitude of eleven thousand meters the countless stars sparkling in the night sky looked close enough to touch. Pierce was in the copilot's seat, Akili on his lap, and the boy was tracing each star with his finger, as if making astronomical observations.

"We'll get real busy soon," Pierce said, glancing at his watch. "How's our fuel?"

"It's almost weird how little we've used," Meyers said.

"It's because we're using the westerly currents. We're in the fastest part of the jet stream."

The Boeing didn't deviate enough from its flight plan to arouse suspicion. The figures entered in the autopilot were updated when necessary by their Japanese ally. They'd started to call this unknown Japanese person by the code name Ema. Pierce had come up with the name, which in Kimbuti means "mother."

"Is Ema a meteorologist?"

"She knows everything," Pierce said with a laugh, and turned to Yeager. "How's it going? Everything set?"

"Yep. Could you all come over here?"

They all stood up. The plane, on autopilot, continued on course.

They went into the passenger cabin and began inspecting their parachute gear. The three adults strapped on insulated jackets to protect them from the cold, and Yeager and Meyers helped each other as they put on their parachute containers. They put on their oxygen supply systems and tried out the improvised tandem jump harnesses. Meyers used the V ring and carabiners mounted on the front to link himself to the harness Pierce wore. Now their two bodies were tightly connected.

Akili's head was big enough to fit snugly into an adult-size helmet. The goggles and oxygen mask fit neatly over his face. But because his body was so small they didn't use harnesses for him but instead put him in a backpack, which would hang between Yeager's legs.

"Looks good," Pierce said, satisfied. "In a little while we're going to deviate from our set flight path. If we get any closer to Brazil they'll scramble fighters to intercept us."

They took off their gear and headed back to the flight deck.

Meyers, in the captain's seat, rested his hand on the control stick. "A question."

"What is it?"

"After we veer from the flight plan, are you seriously planning to head north? If we enter the US Air Defense Identification Zone, they'll send interceptor fighters to come after us."

"This is the only flight route that will satisfy all the conditions."

"But if we get shot down, it's all over."

"Ema assures me we'll be okay."

"But just because we're in international waters doesn't mean we can relax. The intercept options for the United States include shooting planes down over the high seas."

"I thought it was strange, too," Pierce agreed. "But Ema's message was clear: there's no worry about your being shot down. Just focus on flying. What we need to concentrate on is arriving at the precise point at the exact time. If we take care of our end, things will work out okay."

Meyers turned to look at Yeager.

"We've come this far, so we don't have any other choice," Yeager said. "We have to trust Ema."

"I don't see how we can drive away attack jets," Meyers said, hand grasping the control stick. "But okay, here we go."

Pierce took Akili and sat down in the rear seat. "All set!" he said.

Meyers pushed the control stick forward. The nose of the Boeing jet, flying at eleven thousand meters, tilted downward toward the ocean, and the plane began a rapid descent.

★　　★　　★

When the hijacked plane disappeared from control radar at 1:00 a.m., traffic on the Washington, DC, secret communications network immediately shot up.

And less than an hour later, all the cabinet members who dealt with national security had assembled in the Situation Room in the basement of the White House.

5.

AS HE WAITED anxiously for Jeong-hoon to contact him, Kento felt more dead than alive. Had they successfully synthesized GIFT 1? Had the final verification with mouse cells gone well? And what about the police looking for him?

If he went outside he ran the risk of the detectives discovering him, so he couldn't lay in a stock of food. For a whole day he hadn't eaten a thing and had managed to tide himself over by licking some sugar. At this late stage in the game he had to stay sharp.

As he struggled with anxiety and an empty stomach, about to give in to sleep, the call he'd been waiting for came in, just before noon.

"It was a success!" Jeong-hoon yelled out over the phone. "GIFT 1 was among the samples!"

Kento snapped wide awake. "What was the label number?"

"GI seven B."

Three flasks were lined up on the table, labeled 7A to 7C. Kento picked up the middle one and gazed at it, deeply moved.

"You did it, Kento!" Jeong-hoon gave him all the credit, despite the crucial role he'd played in developing the new drug.

"No way. I couldn't have done it without you," Kento said, and laughed. "Oh—what about the cells you asked Doi to take care of?"

"That'll take a little longer. They should get to your place around four."

"Okay." Kento reviewed the final schedule. Jeong-hoon would fly to Lisbon this evening. "When are you leaving the university?"

"If I leave at seven, I can be at Narita airport by eight. The flight leaves at ten."

"Then we'll meet in front of the university hospital at seven. I'll bring GIFT with me."

"Sounds good."

As soon as he hung up, Kento got busy. He changed GIFT 1 and GIFT 2 into hydrochlorates, made them water-soluble, adjusted the concentration, and began orally administering this to the mice.

Of the mice in the four cages, twenty-four were normal, while the remaining nineteen had been given PAECS. Kento gave ten from each group the new drug, administering the dosage the GIFT software indicated. One by one he placed the mice in his palm and, using a syringe with a long tube attached, injected the drug directly into the mice's stomachs. He'd practiced this many times, and the process went quickly.

Next he measured arterial oxygen saturation. A simple clip attached to the mice's ears was all it took to get a readout on the amount of oxygen in their bloodstreams. If the mice with disease onset showed an increase in this value, then he'd know the drug was working.

But was this kind of perfunctory pharmacological test enough? Even at this late date Kento had his doubts. Still, with their backs to the wall there was no time to check metabolism and toxicity. All he could do was trust GIFT's calculations.

Thirty minutes after administering the drug, results were already starting to appear. Just as GIFT had predicted. The values for the mice not given the drug continued to decline, and the decline halted for the ones given the drug. But any conclusion at this point was premature. Telling himself to keep calm, Kento went about ordering his experimental notes and transferring the medicine to go to Lisbon into a different container, all the while checking the measurements every half hour.

After an hour, then two, the readings on the charts for the two groups began to clearly diverge. After three hours Kento held the hope that the values for the group treated with the drug would start to rise. And four hours later he was sure of it. The mice were recovering lung function. The pulmonary alveoli had regained ventilatory capacity and were starting to send oxygen throughout the body.

Kento watched in astonishment as mice that had been on the verge of death began moving, albeit unsteadily, and drinking water from the water-supply devices. He couldn't believe his eyes. The new drug's effects were so dramatic it was hard to believe. The concomitant allosteric drug's powers were so tremendous he thought for a moment that maybe it was all a sleep-deprivation-induced hallucination.

Just as he was studying the graphs in his lab notes again to make sure there were no errors, someone started banging loudly on the front door.

Kento was so startled he nearly screamed.

The police.

The detectives had finally zeroed in on his apartment.

But a voice soon shouted out "Messenger service," and all the tension drained from him. The cells that Doi had genetically modified had finally arrived.

When he opened the door the man standing there was clearly a messenger-service employee, not some detective pretending to be one. Kento took the package, locked the door, and returned to the lab.

The package was a small cardboard box, inside of which were four plastic flasks and a few sterilized instruments, plus a memo with notes on the experimental procedures. In what he took to be Doi's handwriting was a detailed explanation of how he did the binding assay.

The flasks contained CHO cells introduced into the genes of the disease-onset mice. The receptor, mutant GPR769, which caused PAECS, had been forcibly expressed on the cell membrane. Moreover, this receptor was fluorescently labeled by a special reagent, so when it was activated it would give off a bluish light. In other words, if GIFT 1 and GIFT 2 made the receptors glow, then the new drug development was a success.

As Kento reviewed the experimental procedure, he was startled for a second because he didn't have the device called a plate reader, but when he saw the words If you simply want to confirm that there is a glow, it can be detected by the naked eye he breathed a sigh of relief.

Now it was just a race against time to get everything ready. This part of the process was outside his area of expertise, so the unfamiliar operations took time. He had difficulty just transferring the cells to a petri dish. He did everything carefully to avoid any mistakes, and in nearly an hour all preparations were complete.

The genetically modified cells were spread around the round, flat glass plate. Using a pipette, Kento drew out some of the GIFT 1 solution and slowly sprinkled some on top of the cells.

Nothing happened right away. If the data from the mice were correct, the G-protein-coupled receptors would activate within thirty minutes, so GIFT should start binding before that.

But thirty minutes later there was still no bluish light. Kento was panicking. Had he made some error? Or had GIFT 1 not bound with the receptors?

He left his desk, went over to the closet, and once more measured the mice. The arterial oxygen saturation levels for the group given the drug had risen even further. So why was there no change in the cells?

Kento looked back at the petri dish, and it suddenly hit him. The room was too bright for the naked eye to detect the faint light given off by the cells. He switched off the overhead fluorescent light, felt his way in the dark, and trained his eyes on the lab bench. And there, in the little glass dish, were countless gleaming blue lights. The realization pierced through him, and all the hairs on his body stood on end.

It was activated.

As he stared wordlessly, the binding of GIFT and the receptors occurred one after another, with new bluish glows lighting up the petri dish.

He'd successfully created a drug no one else had made in human history. Only one person in the world—he, Kento—had, at this instant, confirmed that mutant GPR769 was activating. Nature was showing its hidden, true face to him alone.

A chill ran through Kento, as did a strange sense of euphoria. The human brain must contain a reward system for intellectual discovery, he thought. As he basked in the quiet joy, a smile rose to his face, motivated neither by happiness nor enjoyment. A kind of smile he had never experienced in his life. And a realization hit him: this was the same smile his father had when he'd told him, "Research is the one thing I can never quit doing."

This is what science is all about, Kento realized. His father didn't have any great achievements to his name, but still in the midst of his daily research he'd made many small discoveries that only he was aware of. And this excitement was what kept him going. Unraveling the mysteries of nature had given him—and now his son—a dizzying sense of joy.

As Kento sat there, steeped in bliss, he thought of the other side of science and technology—the terrifying side. The scientists who developed the atomic bomb must have been in thrall to the same sense of joy. It wasn't a desire to kill masses of people that drove them to devote themselves to developing the atomic bomb. Weren't they instead excited by the prospect of making Einstein's prophecy a reality? By bringing a massive new energy source to mankind? The sense of euphoria brought on by challenging the future was, for human society, always a double-edged sword.

Kento stood up. He turned on the light, put on his coat, and got ready to go out. He divided the precious GIFT, portions for Justin Yeager and Maika Kobayashi, into two small containers. A half year's dose for each.

Just then, somebody knocked at the door.

Kento stood still and listened.

A moment later there was another knock on the thin front door. He tried to pretend he wasn't at home, but whoever it was didn't go away. The visitor continued to knock persistently. Perhaps the revolving dial on the electric meter outside told him someone was in the apartment.

But Kento was no longer afraid. The earlier determination to develop the drug, no matter what happened, had now turned to anger. He stuffed the drug, his lab notes, cell phone, and laptop into his backpack and faced the door.

"Who is it?" he called out.

"The police," a man's voice replied. "I have some questions I need to ask you."

"Just a second."

Kento stepped into his shoes, unlocked the door, turned the knob, and opened it.

A thin man was standing there, and when he saw Kento's face his eyes instantly changed. "Are you Kento Koga?"

Kento quickly turned away, held his breath, and threw the test tube he had in his hand at the detective.

The detective let out a painful groan, doubled up, and started vomiting. The test tube Kento had prepared for self-defense contained a compound that, while not very toxic, emitted a horrible smell, so awful that with one drop on your clothes you couldn't ride the subway. And a shower wouldn't simply wash it away. Most likely this detective would be taking tomorrow off from work.

Kento slipped past the detective, still on all fours and throwing up, and ran as fast as he could down the outside staircase. The sun had already set. He glanced at his watch and saw it was 6:00 p.m.

I'm okay, Kento told himself as he searched for a taxi. Jeong-hoon had given himself two hours from the time he arrived at the airport until his flight took off. If he raced to the hospital he'd be in time. Hungry, exhausted, legs wobbly, Kento summoned up his final ounce of strength and ran down the road.

No matter what, you have to deliver the medicine.

And save the lives of Justin and Maika.

The Boeing 737 continued at an extremely low altitude, so low it was on the verge of crashing.

The altimeter showed 330 feet, but to Yeager, now seated in the copilot's seat, it looked like they were sliding down the surface of the ocean. The ocean, solid black until now, was catching the morning rays of the sun, the occasional whitecap showing that dawn had arrived.

Meyers, looking determined, clutched the control stick, undaunted by the alarm telling them they were getting too close to the ground. "Where are we?" he yelled.

"About four hundred and fifty kilometers southeast of Miami," Pierce answered. He peered at the laptop and conveyed instructions from Japan. "Ascend in one minute and twenty-five seconds. Heading east-northeast. We'll get the precise route after we've ascended."

"We're going to ascend here?"

Ascending would mean they would be picked up on radar again.

"Why don't we veer fifty kilometers to the east? It's insane to intentionally ascend into the Air Defense Identification Zone. F-22s will be on us in no time."

"Ema's got everything under control. Just ascend. Yeager, do you remember how to operate the autopilot?"

"Got it."

The autopilot control, on the upper part of the instrument panel, was a simple device controlled by a small lever and switch.

"Everything's down to the second from here on out. As long as we don't make a mistake, we won't be shot down." Pierce glanced down at the laptop on his knee and went on. "We'll start climbing in twenty seconds. Increase speed to four hundred and thirty knots, and ascend fifteen degrees. Then maintain an altitude of thirty-three thousand feet."

"Roger that," Meyers said.

Pierce began the countdown, and at zero Meyers pulled the control stick. The nose left the sea right below them, and they began to climb into the dim sky.

Shouts rang out in the Operation Nemesis command center when the Boeing reappeared on radar. From the amount of fuel the hijacked plane had on board, they had concluded it must have crashed.

Rubens, in the command center, focused on the screen before him. The screen showed a display sent from NORAD and the White House, which were linked by a videoconferencing system. The display showed the Florida peninsula with the position and direction of the Boeing plane flying over the Atlantic indicated by a triangular marker.

Was the plane that suddenly appeared in their airspace really the hijacked CIA aircraft? In the Situation Room of the White House the chairman of the Joint Chiefs of Staff sought confirmation from an air force general.

"It can't be anything else," the general immediately answered. "We'll have interceptors scrambled in less than a minute."

"You're sure the communications network isn't compromised?" The chairman pressed home the point. The air force, after all, had had one of their unmanned Predator drones hijacked.

"We're fine. These are Raptors we're scrambling, not remote-controlled aircraft."

As he watched the shifting situation, Rubens began to feel apprehensive. And when he received confirmation that a squadron of four F-22s had taken off from Eglin Air Force base, his anxiety only increased. The Boeing business jet had no defenses against air-to-air missiles. It was going to be shot down for sure now.

Still—Rubens frowned. Something had gotten stuck in his mind, and he couldn't shake it.

Airspace 450 kilometers, southeast of Miami.

The spot where the Boeing had reappeared must have some signifi-cance. Rubens combed his memory and finally remembered. There had been an incident involving a midlevel executive of a drug cartel. This man had been heading to the United States on his own jet when the pilot lost consciousness and the plane nearly crashed. The drug cartel executive managed to keep the plane level and get it to rise again, but before he did the plane was painted by US air defense radar. And this unidentified small aircraft reemerged onto radar exactly 450 kilometers southeast of Miami.

Gradually Rubens understood Nous's intentions. Because of the drug cartel incident, NORAD was forced to reevaluate the air defense sys-tem. A new action plan, including the stationing of F-22s, must have been transmitted through the military communications network to all related agencies. And Nous—or, rather, Ema in Japan—had hacked into this secret information. And knew what actions the air force would take in response to an unidentified aircraft invading its airspace. The F-22s that had just scrambled had been lured out by Ema.

"The hijacked plane has changed direction," a voice said, and Rubens looked up.

The triangle on the CG display, which had been heading north, was now heading east-northeast. Once again Rubens was left wondering what Nous was up to. The Boeing plane left the Florida peninsula and was returning to the open seas. It was headed toward the Sargasso Sea— dangerous waters, where numerous sailing ships in the age of explora-tion had shipwrecked. If it continued on its present course, the only place it could land would be Bermuda, but if it landed there, they'd have no place to run to on the little island. Nous and his group would suffer one of three fates: they would be shot down by interceptor jets, cornered, or run out of fuel and crash into the ocean.

"The threat is receding," said the chairman of the Joint Chiefs, seek-ing direction from the commander in chief. "How should we proceed if the aircraft leaves the Air Defense Identification Zone?"

"Keep after it," President Burns answered from the videoconference screen. "Understood?"

"Yes, Mr. President," the director of Operation Nemesis replied in a shrill voice. For Eldridge the present situation was nothing less than a nightmare. The operation had gotten completely out of control, and he was no doubt afraid his career prospects were in a death spiral as well.

Rubens stared at the conferencing screen, hoping to see how Holland was reacting. He spotted him among the seated figures. He couldn't make out Holland's expression, but he did see a man hurry over to him and pass him a small note. Holland put on reading glasses and stared at the memo. For an instant the CIA director seemed to freeze. Holland shook his head feebly and spoke to President Burns. "This just came in. America is under attack."

Burns grimaced. *"What?!"*

"Electric power stations in Alaska, Wisconsin, Michigan, and Maine have come under cyberattack and are no longer generating electricity. There have also been irregularities in the control systems at thirty-five nuclear power plants, and they've halted operations."

In both the Situation Room and the Operation Nemesis command center, silence reigned as everyone tried to absorb the shock.

"If they're not restored quickly, tens of thousands of people will freeze to death. And by the way..." Holland hesitated. "The cyberattack began at the exact same time the fighters were scrambled."

So this was their final trump card, Rubens realized. These superhumans had counterattacked mercilessly in order to preserve their race. Ema would do whatever it took to prevent the interceptors from firing their missiles.

The taxi got off the highway at the Kinshi-cho off-ramp. The university hospital was close by. Kento was fifteen minutes behind schedule, but he prayed he'd be in time if he got the drug to Jeong-hoon right away. Jeong-hoon planned to ride his motorcycle to Narita airport so he wouldn't get caught in any traffic jams.

As he was telling the driver the way to the hospital, his cell phone rang. Kento looked at the display and saw it was from Jeong-hoon. He put the phone to his ear, starting to feel anxious that something had happened. "Hello?"

"Kento? Where are you now?"

"Very close. I'll be there in three minutes."

"Hold on," Jeong-hoon said, lowering his voice, as if worried about being overheard. "Maybe you shouldn't come."

"Why not?"

"I'm at the entrance to the hospital, and there's a car that's been parked outside here for a long time. The driver's been watching the entrance."

The chances were good that the police had staked out the hospital. They had kept his parents' house and his lab under surveillance, and now they were watching the university hospital. Kento hurriedly put his hand over the phone. "I'm sorry," he said to the driver, "but would you just pull over someplace?"

"Okay," the driver replied. He changed lanes and pulled over to the side of the road.

Kento turned back to the phone. "The car doesn't look like it's leaving anytime soon?"

"No," Jeong-hoon said. "What should we do? Maybe we should meet somewhere else."

"No. Hold on a second."

If he couldn't slip by the detectives and get into the hospital, he wouldn't be able to deliver the medicine to Maika Kobayashi. Jeong-hoon could take his place, but sending a Korean exchange student nobody knew would be pointless. He'd never get to the ICU, let alone to Maika. Kento was suddenly struck by doubt: Was Maika even still alive? If she had already died, then he'd be putting himself in danger for nothing.

No, Kento decided. I've come this far for her and can't give up hope. "We're going to take another route," he said to the driver. "Please go to the back entrance of the hospital. Turn right after the next street."

"At the second light?" the driver said. He switched on his turn signal and pulled out into traffic.

"Jeong-hoon," Kento said into the phone. "I'm going in through the back entrance. Can you make sure the car at the front stays put?"

"Got it."

"Don't hang up."

Kento pulled earphones out of his backpack and plugged them into the phone jack. He'd be able to talk and keep his hands free.

The taxi turned onto a back street. The taxi's headlights revealed the concrete wall surrounding the university hospital.

Kento leaned forward, checking to see that there were no suspicious cars parked along the road. It looked okay. No detectives seemed to be staking out the place.

The taxi pulled up to the back entrance, and Kento quickly paid the driver and got out. "No movement there?" he asked.

"Everything's fine," he heard Jeong-hoon say.

Kento whispered a short prayer for Maika Kobayashi, then went in the back entrance and spoke to the security guard stationed at the reception desk. "I have a delivery for Dr. Yoshihara in pediatrics."

"And you are . . . ?" the guard asked.

"Doi, from the pharmacology college at Tokyo University of Science and Humanities." Kento's heart skipped a beat. A person was reflected in the glass window of the reception cubicle. The detective, Kadota, who had barged into Kento's apartment with a search warrant. He was getting out of a black car parked in a corner of the parking lot inside the wall and hurrying in Kento's direction.

"All right. Please go ahead," the guard said.

Kento went into the main hospital building and rushed over to the elevators, but then thought better of it. Kadota would be able to see the display above the elevator and know which floor he got off at.

Jeong-hoon's voice came through on the earphones. "Kento? Are you there? The man in the car got out and is running toward the hospital."

"There's a detective right behind me," Kento said as he raced to the door to the stairs. "They know I'm here."

"What should we do?"

"Stay put. After I get the medicine to the ICU on the sixth floor, I'll find a way to get outside."

"Okay."

"I'm going to turn off the phone."

Kento powered off the cell phone and started running up the stairs. He reached the sixth floor, pushed open the metal door, and came out on a long corridor stretching out in the ICU. How much time would he have before the detectives got here? At the other end of the hall was a swinging door, and through the window in the door he could see the bank of elevators. No one was there. He was still okay.

Kento went over to the ICU and peered through the glass wall. He prayed that Maika was still alive as he searched the unit for her and saw a group of people gathered on the left. A doctor and nurses in white and a couple who must be the girl's parents surrounded a bed.

The woman who must be her mother was wiping away tears, while the others stood there, silent, heads down. *No way!* Kento thought, and moved to one side to get a view of the bed through the crowd of people. He could see the girl, hooked up to an IV and an oxygen mask. When he saw her small chest move up and down, Kento wanted to leap for joy. Maika Kobayashi was still alive.

He looked to both sides to make sure he was safe. The detectives hadn't reached this floor yet. He spotted Yoshihara next to the bed and raised his hand to get his attention.

Yoshihara, speaking to a more senior doctor, noticed him. He shot him a bewildered look and started in his direction.

Yoshihara came through the automatic door and out into the hallway and yanked his mask off. He looked annoyed. "Why are you here this late?"

"How is she?"

Yoshihara shook his head listlessly. "I'm afraid it's hopeless. I told her parents she won't make it through the night."

But these discouraging words only encouraged Kento. He'd made it in time. All they needed was thirty minutes for GIFT to show what it was capable of.

"So why are you here? You wanted to visit her?"

"No. I've brought a medicine to treat pulmonary sclerosis."

Yoshihara frowned. "Did I hear you right?"

Kento rummaged through his backpack and pulled out a plastic bag. Inside were numerous plastic containers. "There's a half-year supply here if you give one dose per day, orally. You have to give her this right away."

But Yoshihara only looked more incredulous. "Who made this drug?"

Kento came up with a quick lie. "It's Chinese herbal medicine. It's been tested, and it's safe."

"Give me a break. I've done my homework on this disease. There's no such thing as a Chinese herbal medicine that helps with pulmonary sclerosis."

"I tried it on mice." Kento barely kept himself from yelling. "It takes effect immediately. Give it to her now, and her lungs will revive. Check the pulse oximeter and you'll get the results right away."

"But you haven't done clinical trials yet, have you? If I give her the medicine the hospital ethics committee will be all over me."

"Damn it, who cares about ethics?!" Kento shot back.

Yoshihara looked indignant. "Are you crazy? You really think I can give a patient a medicine I know nothing about?"

"But if you don't do anything she's going to die!"

From down the hallway the elevator chimed. Startled, Kento stared. Past the swinging doors, two nurses exited the elevator. He turned back to Yoshihara. "Look, I tested transgenic mice and their ventilatory capacity. In just thirty minutes their arterial oxygen saturation had started to recover. I'm begging you, give her the medicine!"

"But if they find something odd in the autopsy—"

"There won't *be* an autopsy. She won't be a dead body! Don't you get it? This drug will save her!"

The elevator chimed another arrival. A middle-aged man in a suit emerged. Detective Kadota from the Metropolitan Police Department. He craned his head from side to side, trying to spot his target.

"Damn," Kento muttered. He was out of time. If they grabbed him now he wouldn't be able to get the medicine to Jeong-hoon for Justin Yeager. Kento turned his back on the elevator hall. "Are you going to let her die? Or take a chance on this drug? It's up to you now. But please, I'm begging you—save Maika."

Kento thrust the bag with GIFT toward Yoshihara and headed back to his only escape route, the stairs.

"Wait!" Yoshihara yelled, but Kento, afraid, kept on going. Any hesitation and Kadota would grab him. Anxiety seized him, as if the devil were hot in pursuit. It was already hard to get away from there without being noticed. Kento made a beeline for the stairs and pushed open the door. Now he only had to get down to the first floor, but as he headed down he heard footsteps coming up from below. Hard leather shoes, and he knew it was the other detective who had been staking out the entrance.

At this rate he'd be caught in the middle. He had to head upstairs. But if they came at him from both the stairs and elevators he'd be totally cut off. And then how would he get outside the hospital?

Feeling hopeless and desperate, Kento was racing up the stairs, taking two at a time, when he heard another sound—the roar of a motorcycle engine—from outside the building. At the seventh floor, he flung open the window and looked below. In the security lights, Jeong-hoon was astride his motorcycle, staring up.

When he spotted him, Jeong-hoon took his right hand off the handlebar and made a call-me motion. Kento hurriedly switched on his cell phone. He got a signal and heard Jeong-hoon through his earphones. "You okay?"

"I'm fine," Kento lied. Jeong-hoon was not about to abandon his friend. If he knew the predicament Kento was in, he would rush inside to help. "I'm going to throw you GIFT," Kento said. "Then take off for Narita!"

"Okay!"

Kento leaned out, holding the bag with GIFT inside. He aimed and tossed it down. The white bag flew through the air, and Jeong-hoon, left arm stretched up, neatly snagged it.

"Jeong-hoon, go!"

"Don't worry, I'll save Justin!" he yelled out. Then he flipped his visor closed and roared off into the night.

Kento watched out the window until the motorcycle raced out the back gate. This might be the last time he ever saw his friend.

As the roar of the motorcycle faded, the sound of footsteps coming up the stairs got closer. Kento opened the door and slipped into the seventh-floor corridor, looking for a place to hide. Next to the lavatory was a small equipment locker for mops and other cleaning tools. It was cramped and didn't look like anyone could hide in it, but someone as small as Kento just might be able to squeeze inside.

He clambered into the locker, which was full of buckets, rags, and brooms and smelled like disinfectant. He sat there, rolled up in a ball, clutching his knees. All he could do was pray he got lucky.

★ ★ ★

After Kento had raced away, Yoshihara was about to toss the medicine into the trash. But something his friend had said made him stop.

If you don't do anything she's going to die!

Human pulmonary alveolar epithelial cell sclerosis. A fatal disease that not even cutting-edge medical science could cure. Could drinking this colorless liquid really be all it took to cure it?

In his mind Yoshihara saw Kento, a shadow of his former self, and knew this was no joke. When they'd had drinking parties back in college Kento had always sat in the corner, unable to join in, a nothing guy who blended into the wallpaper. Yet here he was, almost crying, pleading with him to give this medicine to his patient. He'd been pale and ghastly-looking, desperate that Yoshihara listen to him.

If he didn't do anything, Maika Kobayashi was going to die. If she were still alive twenty-four hours from now, it'd be a miracle. Would giving her that liquid make the miracle come true?

Maybe I should try it, Yoshihara began to think. Though this would break every rule in the book.

The automatic door slid open, and the attending physician, nurse, and Maika's father emerged from the ICU. The father, in his midthirties, turned a haggard face to the attending physician and was thanking him for doing all he could for his precious daughter.

The mother had stayed behind in the ICU at the bedside of her daughter, whose face was purplish. Yoshihara looked at the mother and found it incredible how so many tears could come from one person's eyes. The mother might well be whispering her final good-bye to her beloved daughter.

Yoshihara waited until the attending physician had returned to the doctors' office and approached the father. "Mr. Kobayashi, a word?"

"Sure," Maika's father replied weakly, and came over to where there was a bench.

Yoshihara spoke in a low voice so no one else could hear. "What I'm going to tell you now you have to keep secret."

Kobayashi frowned. "What are you talking about?"

"Please. You have to promise me you won't tell anybody."

471

Kobayashi seemed dubious, but said, "All right."

Yoshihara showed him the bag in his hand. "Inside this bag is a Chinese herbal medicine that might be effective against pulmonary sclerosis."

"Huh?" The man had had his hopes crushed so many times, but still a slender thread of anticipation showed on his face. "There really is a drug like that?"

"It hasn't been proved safe, which is why the hospital can't give it to Maika. I can't hand it over to you."

"Then what am I supposed to do?" Kobayashi shot back. His tone made it clear he couldn't stand one more ordeal. "The medicine exists, but we can't use it?"

"No. There *is* a way. I'd like you to sign Maika out of the hospital right away. Then she won't be a patient here. And we won't have to be bound by the hospital's ethics regulations. The minute she's discharged, then we can give her the medicine. Even while she's still in the ICU."

The father was too taken aback to respond, so Yoshihara continued. "You have to get going. It takes thirty minutes for the medicine to work. You've got to do it while she's still alive!"

6.

THE PREDAWN SKY at eleven thousand meters above the Florida peninsula was dyed a mysterious color. The heavens revealed a clear gradation from deep navy blue to orange, while below the ocean was still in darkness.

But for Yeager, in the copilot's seat, this wasn't a time to enjoy the scenery. The low-fuel indicator light had been on for some time now. More than 90 percent of their fuel was gone.

An artificial voice spoke up from the computer behind the pilot's seat. *Change heading to zero-nine-three. Altitude fifteen hundred feet.*

With his unsteady little fingers Akili had typed in their instructions.

"Another steep dive?" Meyers asked.

"Do it," Pierce replied. "Timing is key here."

Meyers inputted the numbers into the autopilot. The control stick moved on its own, banking the Boeing plane to the right as it began its descent. As the nose faced directly east they spotted a slice of the sun peeping up above the horizon.

Yeager gazed at the point of red light and was struck by a thought. A defense strategy to deal with the fighters. Was Ema, their Japanese "control tower," planning to use the sunlight to confuse the infrared guided missiles that would be targeting their engines?

"We're not at our destination yet?" Meyers asked.

"Not yet," Pierce replied.

"Fuel's down below three thousand pounds. We have less than twenty minutes before we crash."

"Don't worry. Everything's going according to plan."

"How about the radar? Are fighters after us?"

"No sign of them scrambling."

"I can't believe it," Meyers said as he left the pilot's seat, trying his best to keep his balance in the descending plane. "No way is the air force going to overlook an unidentified aircraft entering the air defense zone." He hunched over the radar.

"Anything?" Yeager asked.

"No. Nothing."

Yeager felt relieved, but Meyers's face visibly stiffened.

"Problem?"

"This isn't good news. In fact the opposite. They didn't scramble F-15s. These are Raptors we're talking about."

Yeager had heard the nickname. "F-22s?"

"'Fraid so."

Raptors were the latest stealth fighters, invisible to radar. The most powerful fighter jets in history, with an astonishing 144:0 kill ratio in mock battles. And now they had slipped in, unseen, behind the Boeing. Ready to shoot it down.

"They only show up on the radar when they fire a missile," Meyers said. "When you know where they are, it's already too late. Their air-to-air missiles travel at Mach four."

The four-fighter squadron scrambled out of Eglin Air Force Base in Florida continued to fly toward the Sargasso Sea. Cruising speed was Mach 1.8. The weather over the North Atlantic was perfect, not a cloud in the sky, and as the sun rose above the horizon an infinite blue stretched out ahead.

Captain Grimes, the flight leader, felt honored to be part of the mission. As the War on Terror had intensified—after the incident in which the Colombian had violated US airspace, and with the raising of the defense alert to DEFCON 3 following the assassination of the vice president—these latest stealth fighters, still in the testing phase, had been secretly assigned to the Thirty-Third Tactical Fighter Wing. And the scramble this time was the first real action the F-22s had seen.

Grimes was told the target was a hijacked Boeing prototype 737-700ER. The radar image sent by data link clearly showed the plane. It was flying at high altitude, making the occasional minor course correction, 120 kilometers ahead.

Grimes was surprised that the target was sending out such a strong radar signal and knew it must be the kind of military radar a civilian aircraft did not carry. This must have been why the stealth Raptors were given the attack order. But though the target had search capabilities, it was essentially a defenseless business jet. He wondered why they had to take such precautions.

The Boeing, with its odd flight path, suddenly began to descend. With Grimes in the lead, the horizontal formation of Raptors began to descend. The F-22s had already deviated from normal scramble flights and had left the Air Defense Identification Zone behind a while ago.

Grimes was worried about fuel. How far should they follow the plane over the open sea? At this rate they'd have to return to base before they caught up with the target. And he finally understood what orders they would be receiving.

In three minutes the target would be close enough for medium-range air-to-air missiles.

With no radio warning or warning shots, they would be shooting down this target BVR—beyond visual range.

"Four more states have been hit—Nevada, California, Colorado, and New York," Holland intoned, reading from a memo over the videoconference system. "There are also problems with the control system at the Hoover Dam. The oil pipeline in Texas has shut down, and the online systems for all major financial institutions aren't operating."

The cyberattack against the United States was ramping up. Thirty states were now without electricity, and the northern half of the country had been forced back to the frontier era.

If this goes on until morning, Rubens thought, doing some quick mental calculations, all economic activity will be disrupted, not just industrial production and the financial system. Losses to the United States will be in the hundreds of billions. And people freezing to death won't be the only human victims. With the traffic system snarled and violence spreading, countless people will die.

This battle with a superhuman being was becoming a game of chicken. If you wanted to win you had to plow straight ahead, willing to die. But if your opponent adopted the same strategy you'd both crash into each other.

Ema wasn't about to steer away, Rubens believed. To save her species she would barrel straight ahead and step on the gas, for she had to win.

"It's the Chinese! The Chinese are behind this!" Secretary of Defense Lattimer barked. "We have to retaliate!"

"The NSA is investigating the cause, but until they determine which country is behind this let's not jump to any hasty—" As Watkins, director of national intelligence, was saying this, the image on the screen wavered, and the electricity in the command center began to fade. The light soon came back on, but the cabinet members in the White House and everyone in the Operation Nemesis command center were speechless. Electric power had been cut off to the capital, Washington DC.

Auxiliary power switched on in the Situation Room, and President Burns spoke up. "I'd like to hear what the director of the CIA thinks. Are you still harping on that preposterous idea?"

Holland didn't flinch at this attack. "Which idea?"

"That this is also the work of that child."

"There's only one way to find out," Holland said. "We immediately halt Operation Nemesis. For real. I'm asking you to halt all operations and transmit that order to all concerned. If our opponent is really Nous, then he'll hack these transmissions and stop the cyberattack right away."

Burns was silent, and Holland continued. "There's no downside to doing that."

"What do you want us to do?" the air force general broke in. "The F-22s will reach their maximum range soon. If we're going to attack, we have to do it now. We can shoot them down the moment they come in range."

"The enemy's heading due east, right into the sun," Lattimer said. "What kind of missiles are they carrying?"

"AIM-120s. Radar-guided missiles, so the sunlight won't interfere. They *will* be shot down."

"But shooting a plane down over international waters..." Holland said, raising his doubts.

"There are no civilian aircraft nearby," Lattimer cut in. "And who's going to complain if we down a CIA plane?"

But Holland wasn't about to back down. "Look. There's no need to fire any missiles. The hijacked plane is nearly out of fuel. They're heading to Bermuda, but they won't make it. They'll crash into the Sargasso Sea."

"Your orders, Mr. President?" the chairman of the Joint Chiefs of Staff asked, waiting for a decision from his commander in chief. "Do we shoot the plane down, sir?"

As he watched this back-and-forth, Rubens was counting on Burns to act rationally. In a game of chicken, the most logical answer was for one side to keep on coming and the other side to avoid the collision. The one who lost wasn't chicken. The loser was the most rational one. The present situation presented Gregory S. Burns with the greatest decision he'd ever have to make. This creature beyond human intellect was urging the most powerful man in human society to make the right call.

"Let me get this straight." Burns broke the silence, facing Holland. "You're saying this cyberattack is the work of that Pygmy child."

"I am," Holland said.

"Well, he's going to regret he ever attacked the United States," Burns said, and turned to the air force general. "Permission to shoot down. Down the hijacked plane now."

"Yes, Mr. President," the air force general replied.

Rubens knew he was standing at the crossroads of history. All that was dangerous about human society was condensed in this moment. An instant of madness residing in a political leader would put the lives of hundreds of millions of people at risk. A future nuclear war, too, might start the very same way, through a decision by a single mad politician.

Nous must be at the end of his tether. Along with a sense of anxiety, Rubens felt boiling up in him a brutal impulse.

Kill, Rubens said silently to this superhuman intelligence.

Kill, Ema.

Become the goddess Nemesis, who brings divine punishment, and give these arrogant lower creatures exactly what they deserve.

An order appeared on a multifunction display in the glass cockpit: ENGAGE TARGET. Captain Grimes broke radio silence for a moment to relay the command to the other planes in his formation.

The image on the data link showed the enemy plane, flying low, turning north and ascending. A business jet like that could try as much as it wanted to evade them, but there was no way it could avoid an air-to-air missile.

Grimes switched on the master arm. The underbelly hatch opened, and the AIM-120 slipped down from the weapons compartment. This cutting-edge missile was the latest fruit of mankind's intelligence and murderous intentions. The missile flew at Mach 4 and had internal radar, so it would certainly hit its flying target, forty kilometers ahead. In less than one minute the Boeing would be blasted from the sky. Over the past two hundred thousand years humans had continued to evolve more precise and more lethal antipersonnel weapons. Starting with stones and cudgels, they'd now reached weapons of this magnitude.

Grimes switched on radar and locked on to the target. The radar waves let the enemy know for the first time of the Raptor's presence, but it was already too late. There was no way the Boeing could escape.

The head-up display showed SHOOT. Grimes put his thumb on the control stick trigger, called out "Fox three," the medium-range missile's call sign, and pushed down hard on the trigger.

With a roar the air-to-air missile left the mother ship. Flames leaped out as it hurtled across the ocean. Right when it was clear the Raptor was going to feed on its prey, Grimes saw a strange sight. The missile, two kilometers away, was enveloped in a reddish light that had suddenly appeared, and it vanished.

What the hell? Sure enough, the missile had vanished from radar. Was there a glitch in the guidance system? He was about to order the other planes to shoot a second missile, but instead he grunted in surprise. His plane rapidly lost altitude and was suddenly spinning out of control. He made an instant decision and pulled the escape handle between his legs. But his seat didn't eject. An explosion at the rear of the Raptor sent Grimes and the plane spiraling out of the sky.

When he saw the planes suddenly appear on radar where nothing had been before, Yeager felt the hairs stand up on the back of his neck. The enemy was closer than he ever imagined. Within range for air-to-air missiles. The Boeing was making a rapid descent, but wasn't maneuverable enough to shake off a fighter jet. "Enemy planes forty kilometers behind us!" he yelled out.

Meyers, at the controls, turned. "Radar picked them up?"

"Yeah."

"They've locked on to us!" Meyers yelled, and looked helplessly around him. "Missiles are away!"

"Don't panic!" Pierce told the two of them, but his voice, too, was shrill and fearful. "Do not change course! Stick to the plan!"

"Is it just one plane?" Meyers asked Yeager.

Yeager stared at the radar and saw two points of light now, one moving more quickly than the scrambled jets toward them. "There's a second plane now. It's moving at an unbelievable speed!"

"That's a missile! How can we evade it?"

"If it's an infrared guided missile maybe the sun will—"

"No!" Meyers cut in. "At this range it's radar-guided. No mistake: we're going to get hit!"

"Hold on!" Yeager cried out. All indicators on the radar screen had suddenly vanished. "The enemy's disappeared."

"Disappeared? That's impossible. The missile should still be on the screen!"

"Forget about the Raptor!" Pierce yelled. "What's our altitude?"

Meyers checked the instrument panel. "Seventeen thousand feet."

"Good. We'll let the autopilot handle it from now on. We're into the final stage."

"This is it?"

"Right!"

Even if the air-to-air missile were to continue its pursuit, they had no defense. They let the autopilot take over and hustled back to the passenger cabin, fearful they would be shot down at any moment. They hurriedly put on their parachutes. A couple of minutes passed, but the passenger jet was still flying. Yeager was amazed they had not yet been shot down.

Once they had all their equipment on, Pierce glanced at his watch. "We're twenty seconds late. We can't make any mistakes. Everything from now on has to be perfect."

The two mercenaries, parachute containers on their backs, went back to the cockpit. Meyers looked at the altimeter and checked with Pierce. "Decompression will start at thirty-four thousand feet, right?"

The reply came from the laptop Akili was holding. *Change to thirty-three thousand feet. Set heading at oh-one-nine.*

Yeager entered the figures into the autopilot. "Akili, did you drive away the missile?"

The strange-looking boy didn't answer and instead flashed him an unearthly, gremlinlike smile.

When First Lieutenant Murdoch, pilot of the second plane in the formation, saw the squad leader's plane explode, he quickly took evasive maneuvers. He climbed and turned hard left, finally leveling out. The remaining two planes dove to the left and right and again took up formation.

Had Captain Grimes bailed out? Murdoch scanned the ocean, and when he did, he saw an unbelievable sight. The ocean below, for as far as the eye could see, had turned white.

Instinctively sensing danger, Murdoch broke radio silence and told the others to change course. But the third and fourth planes both exploded, one after the other. They suddenly fell from the sky, too quickly for the pilots to eject.

Murdoch again climbed steeply, barely avoiding jagged pieces of the other jets scattering in all directions. The high g-forces thrust him back against his seat, and he nearly blacked out. And something was damaged in his plane. He was losing control of the Raptor.

Wreckage from the other planes was being swallowed up by the white sea. *Why?* The question ran with a shudder through Murdoch as he flew above the ocean, the sole survivor of his squadron. What made the Raptors crash like that, one after another? Faulty maintenance? Or were they attacked?

"This is Alpha One. Eagle Two, do you copy?"

Murdoch replied to the call from headquarters. "Eagle Two, copy."

"Report."

"The other three have crashed. I don't know what's going on."

"Repeat."

"Eagle One, Three, and Four have crashed!" Fear that he would be the next ran up Murdoch's spine.

"Were they shot down?"

"Unclear. Red flames came out of their tailpipes, and they exploded right after. It appears all the pilots are dead."

"And the target?"

"Negative. We did not down it."

"You're ordered to engage."

Murdoch shuddered. To lock on his missile he'd have to point his nose at the discolored sea. He shoved the stick to the left and banked. He'd fly along the edge of the whitish sea. "Roger that."

He switched on his radar, and the image of the Boeing plane emerged. Murdoch locked on to the target, wanting nothing more than to escape this dangerous part of the ocean as soon as he could.

"Fox three," he said, and pushed the trigger. Just then the supposedly smooth sea below him began to turn a cloudy white. His eyes opened in astonishment. The surface of the sea was covered in bubbles. It was foaming up, as if it were boiling. It was an imposing, weird sight, as if a submarine as big as a town were rising to the surface. The missile, a mere one kilometer ahead, turned upward, then down, falling into the seething foam. The sea around where it fell blazed up.

Murdoch tried desperately to avoid the flaming sea, but his controls weren't responding. The uncontrollable Raptor began a rapid descent. Murdoch felt an unseen force taking hold of his plane, yanking it down toward the sea. "The sea is burning! I'm ejecting!"

This was the final communication from the squad.

The Boeing, tilted at an angle, gradually righted itself and leveled out at thirty-three thousand feet.

Standing behind the pilot's seat, Meyers pulled the thrust lever back and lowered the landing gear, causing the plane's airspeed to decrease. The stall warning light came on, making the control stick vibrate.

Yeager checked his helmet strap and lowered his goggles over his eyes. "Put on your oxygen mask and check the flow!"

Akili was inside the backpack, hanging from Yeager's chest. Meyers tugged the mask over Akili's face, turned the control valve, and checked the flow. The oxygen supply system, a lifeline in a high-altitude high-opening jump, was working fine.

Once everyone had nodded, indicating that the system worked, Meyers leaned forward and flipped off the pressurization switch. Oxygen masks dropped from the ceiling, and a new warning light lit up on the instrument panel. But the red light went unnoticed, as the panel was already ablaze with warning lights.

With the pressurized air cut off, the pressure inside the plane plummeted. Without the oxygen masks they would have blacked out in a couple of minutes. As they waited for the pressure inside to equal the pressure outside, Meyers pointed at the fuel gauge. They were nearly out of fuel. Behind his mask Pierce called out in a muffled voice. "T minus thirty seconds!"

They hurried out of the cockpit to the passenger cabin and assembled before the center exit door. The door was right over the wing. Meyers and Pierce connected their harnesses and got in tandem-jump position. Yeager flung open the door, and a violent wind swept the cabin, flinging the hanging oxygen masks around. They'd successfully depressurized the plane, so the four of them weren't sucked outside.

Pierce held his hands out and spread his fingers apart. "Ten seconds!"

For a brief instant the men exchanged looks. Their long battle was drawing to an end. Their eyes reflected gratitude at having survived this far.

"Five seconds!"

Yeager grabbed hold of both sides of the door. In front of him Akili peeked out like a baby kangaroo in its pouch.

"Four! Three! Two!"

At "Zero," Yeager leaped out the door. He'd planned to first land on the wing directly below, but a blast of wind pushed him sideways, rolling him off the wing and tossing him into the sky ten thousand meters above the earth. A shadow flashed above, the horizontal stabilizer, as the plane flew by. A floating sensation raced through his stomach, as if his organs were being sucked upward. Tossed about by air and gravity, his body began to spin violently, but he was finally able to level out and gain control, arms and legs extended as he faced straight down.

He glanced over his shoulder and saw Meyers and Pierce directly above. Behind them, the Boeing was still flying, but its nose suddenly dipped, it lowered one wing, and lost lift. This graceful aircraft, which had seen them safely out of Africa, had finally run out of fuel. The roar of its jet engines died, and it fluttered toward the Sargasso Sea like some gigantic leaf.

Yeager turned back. Far below him lay a blue planet filled with an outrageous amount of water. As he looked at this beautiful globe, a thought came to him.

I'm coming back to earth.

Mother Earth, which nurtures all life.

Back to that gray world where people love each other and hate each other. A world caught between good and evil.

The moment contact with Lieutenant Murdoch was lost, the air force general himself called in the order to deploy pararescue. What had happened to the Raptor squadron? The whole incident was so inexplicable that the National Security Council members around the table were mute.

Soon afterward the Boeing plane disappeared from radar over the ocean, two hundred kilometers from Bermuda.

"What's going on?" Burns said, breaking the silence. "Why did it vanish from radar?"

"The target has probably crashed," the air force general replied.

"You mean it was shot down?"

"No. There's no radar indication of a launched missile. We believe the hijacked plane ran out of fuel and crashed."

"Could they have done an emergency landing in the ocean?"

"No. That didn't happen. It stopped at a certain point and lost altitude, so it had to have crashed."

The president looked at his CIA director. "So Operation Nemesis was a success?"

"Yes," Holland replied, looking half stunned. "The target, Nous, has been eliminated."

As he watched this exchange on the videoconferencing system, Rubens knew one thing for sure. Nous was still alive. One of the qualifications for people to join Operation Guardian was an airborne rating. And besides, there was Nigel Pierce's background to consider.

Just then a report came in that ten southern states had lost electricity. Holland read the memo aloud, then turned to the president. "In order to focus on the present threat, can we close down all activities related to Nemesis?"

Burns stared at the screen in front of him. The radar image showed nothing. "So ordered."

"Not just activities under our direct jurisdiction, but can we have the entire intelligence community back away from what they're doing?"

Burns nodded. "That operation does not exist anymore."

"Did you hear that, Eldridge?" Holland asked from the TV screen. "There were some casualties, but Operation Nemesis was a success. Have all assets stop operations, and lift the terrorist designation for all those involved. Also, halt plans you made in Japan. And halt any steps that were being taken for special rendition."

"Yes, sir," Eldridge replied, and he ordered his subordinates in the command center to contact all relevant agencies. Now the CIA, NSA, DIA, and the FBI would be moving to end operations, and the order came down to assets in the field, in Japan and Africa, to stand down.

The end of Operation Nemesis was like the death of some enormous monster. And, as if waiting for the monster to breathe its last, power stations throughout the United States began to come back online. Even as word came in that, one by one, power was restored in Alaska, Michigan, Maine, and Wisconsin, the Situation Room was not filled with joy. Rather, an atmosphere of unease once more hung over the room.

"Who's starting to turn the power stations back on?" Secretary of Defense Lattimer asked.

No one replied.

"Is it Nous?" Burns asked.

After a pause, Holland voiced a third question. "You want to take him on again?"

The president thought for a moment, then shook his head. "No."

Still in free fall at eight thousand meters, Yeager yanked the rip cord and opened his chute. The square sail opened above him, quickly slowing his rate of descent. Now he could use the toggles on both sides to steer them to their rendezvous point. In HAHO jumps the parachute is opened at high altitude, and then the jumper glides down, so it is possible to cover up to thirty kilometers in horizontal distance. The square parachute was too small to be picked up by radar.

After they had glided through the sky for an hour, their rendezvous point finally loomed into view in the middle of the ocean—a huge cargo ship owned by Pierce Shipping, floating in the ocean like a solitary island.

Our adventure's drawing to an end, Yeager told himself as he aimed for the tops of the containers that filled the deck. It's amazing I ever survived. He was astounded by how well their whole escape from Cape Town had been planned. This person Ema must be pretty damn smart.

An image appeared to him, of a man who was like the spirit of the jungle. Esimo. When he'd told them about his pregnant wife leaving him forever, he'd used the word *mzungu*, pointing at Mick. After his pregnant wife had been taken away by *mzungu*—white—doctors, she never returned to the Ituri jungle.

If the name—Ema—is any indication, she must be a woman. So Akili has an older sister.

The container was rushing up at them. Yeager waited for the right moment, then yanked the toggles down to below his waist to break their descent. His legs hit the top of the container, and the impact jolted through his whole body.

Akili was fine. Meyers and Pierce landed a few seconds later on another container on the deck. Their parachutes, reluctant to part with the wind, billowed out behind them. Yeager and Meyers gave each other a thumbs-up.

The two mercenaries, along with this new species of human, had finally made it out of Africa.

7.

THE AIR FRANCE flight arrived at the Lisbon Portela Airport right on schedule.

Jeong-hoon, in the third row from the front, was the first passenger to deplane. He knew someone was waiting anxiously for his arrival, and he didn't want to waste a minute. He had gone through immigration control already in Paris, so he headed straight for baggage claim.

His bag took a long time to come. Bringing the liquid drug into the cabin wasn't allowed, so he had to check it at the last minute.

Finally his backpack emerged on the conveyor belt, and Jeong-hoon quickly checked inside. None of the capsules inside the plastic case had broken, and none of the liquid had spilled.

Now came customs, the final hurdle. He'd left Japan in such a hurry all he had was the one bag, and he was afraid that would look suspicious, but those in the duty-free line passed through without being checked.

Jeong-hoon hurried out to the arrivals lobby. The smells of a different country enveloped him. Portela airport was small for an international airport, but the glass walls and cathedral ceilings kept it from feeling cramped.

He looked around and spotted her. A blond woman holding a large sign with JUSTIN YEAGER written on it. Jeong-hoon went over to her.

"Are you Mr. Lee?" Lydia Yeager asked him.

She was only in her thirties, but she looked hurt and desperate. She must have been battling death for years with her son, Jeong-hoon imagined. "Yes. Are you Mrs. Yeager?"

"I'm very happy to meet you," Lydia said with a forced smile that was painful to see. At this very moment her son was on the verge of death.

With not a moment to lose, Jeong-hoon pulled out the plastic case. "There's a new kind of drug inside," he explained quickly. "Give Justin one dose per day. That's all you need to do. Refrigerate the rest. There's a half year's supply here, and we'll send more as soon as we can."

"Thank you." Lydia's voice trembled. "But I should pay your airfare. Or give you something for what you've done."

"No. I'm fine. This is—a *gift*. For your son."

Lydia wiped away the tears about to flow down her cheeks.

"You'd better go give the medicine to Justin."

Lydia nodded and ran out to the taxi stand. But she stopped and turned around, allowing herself a precious moment. "You've saved my family."

Jeong-hoon felt as if his life was, for the very first time, headed in the right direction. Studying pharmacology had finally paid off, rewarding him for all the time and effort he'd devoted to this field. A warmth welled up inside him, and he smiled.

"My friend and I made it. My good friend, Kento Koga."

When Kento woke from a long sleep, his body still smelled like disinfectant. The clock showed six, but he had no idea if it was morning or night. Still wrapped in his sleeping bag, he checked the date and realized he had slept for sixteen hours straight.

Not long after he hid in the janitor's closet at the university hospital, a call came in on his cell phone. The screen said Poppy, but he was surprised to hear a normal woman's voice, not the usual low, artificial tone.

"Kento?" It had to be Yuri Sakai. He knew it right away. But with a detective prowling around nearby he couldn't reply. Yuri told him that everything was finished and he didn't need to hide anymore.

Kento was half doubtful, but being curled up in the constricted space was making his muscles scream in pain. He knew he couldn't stay like this any longer, and he tumbled out of the locker.

The hospital hallway was deserted. No doctors or nurses, and no detective, either. Kento hurried down the stairs, but at the sixth floor he stopped, opened the door a crack, and peered in. Yoshihara and Maika Kobayashi's attending physician were rushing toward the ICU. Her parents back in the hallway were staring fixedly at what was going on. A momentary smile flashed across her father's face and Kento knew what had happened. Yoshihara had given her the drug. He'd administered GIFT to this patient on the verge of death.

Kento beamed.

Maika was saved.

He quietly shut the door, walked down to the first floor, and left the hospital through the service entrance. Starving, he bought two box lunches at a nearby convenience store and wolfed them down next to the road. Now where to? His apartment near the university or the lab in Machida?

For some reason he was drawn back to the lab his father had left him, as if this was where he belonged. Kento flagged down a taxi and headed to the opposite end of Tokyo, back to that old, run-down building.

At the front door the detective's vomit and the overpowering stink of the chemical reagent remained. He held his breath, slipped inside, and found everything unchanged. There was no sign that the police had searched his room, and nothing was missing. He finally felt like the danger had passed.

He gazed at the mice who had recovered and felt a wave of joy. He gave the drug to the remaining nine mice, then curled up in his sleeping bag and, overwhelmed by exhaustion, had barely closed his eyes before he was fast asleep.

When he finally woke up he felt like a new person. He crawled out of his sleeping bag, washed his face at the kitchen sink, and was thinking about going to a sauna to take a bath when he looked at his cell phone screen. There were two voice messages. The first was from Jeong-hoon, in his usual cheerful voice.

"Kento? This is Jeong-hoon. I'm in Lisbon. Mission accomplished. I just gave GIFT to Lydia."

Kento smiled broadly as he listened to the rest of the message from his friend.

"I'm taking off for Japan now. I'll call you when I get back."

Jeong-hoon had played such a critical role in the success of their mission, and now he was going to circle the globe in forty hours. Kento was again amazed by his friend's vitality.

The second message was from Yuri Sakai. I'm going to send you an important message, she said, so boot up the black laptop. The password isn't the difficult ones I gave you before, but just the number 1, typed in twice.

Praying it wouldn't be bad news, Kento powered up the machine. He typed in 1 twice on the blue screen, and the mail program came up automatically.

He moved the cursor, clicked open the in box, and cried out. The message was from Seiji Koga, Tama Polytechnic University. The subject heading was To Kento from Dad.

As he did with the message that had set everything in motion, his father had prepared this one for Kento while he was still alive. Kento was about to read it but stopped. These would be the last words his father would ever have for him. He should take his time.

Kento took his hand off the mouse, took a deep breath, then clicked the screen. As before, a message appeared in a small font.

Dear Kento,

If you're reading this it means something unforeseen has happened. I had planned to be back with you and your mother shortly, but apparently this didn't work out. I don't want to even consider this, but I probably won't be able to see you again.

And that's exactly what happened, Kento thought. I'll never see my father again. Never see his tired-looking face or listen to his litany of complaints. Never talk with him or share that knowing smile that only another researcher could understand.

I'm really sorry it came to this. Please take good care of your mother. I have so many more things I'd like to say, too many to write down here. I'm not going to lie to you and tell you I was an ideal father or that I have no regrets in life. Quite the opposite. At the very least I wanted to give you advice so you don't make the same mistakes I did. But now I won't be able to. If I can say one thing, it's that no one can live without making mistakes, and it's up to each person whether he learns from them or not. We grow stronger through the mistakes we've made. Just remember that.

But I need more, Kento thought. If I could just have ten minutes with him again. What would he tell me? What life lessons would he pass on?

Finally, there are some things I'd like to ask you.

Were you able to carry out the research I asked you to do?

Did you save children's lives?

Did you help mankind?

Did you enjoy this step into the unknown?

Did nature reveal a side of herself you never imagined you'd see?

And did it move you more than any work of art?

Your dad's confident you were able to accomplish it.

I'm very proud of you. I hope that in the future you'll continue to grow in your field.

Good-bye, Kento.

Become a great scientist someday, okay?

Love,

Dad

His father's farewell note ended here.
Kento felt the tears streaming down his cheeks and realized how long

he'd been holding back this sadness. He and Jeong-hoon were, with a single drop of medicine, going to save lives, lives that otherwise were hopeless.

I did it, Dad, he said to his father's spirit. I was blessed with a wonderful partner, and somehow we managed to finish. Continue to watch over me. We're going to find a legitimate research-and-development channel and save the lives of one hundred thousand children.

Kento's adventure had only just begun.

EPILOGUE

EARLY SPRING SUNLIGHT filtered into the Rose Garden. President Burns stood at the window of the Oval Office and thought back to the beginning of Operation Nemesis. It had been a different season but the same kind of morning. He'd been standing right here, waiting for the members of his daily briefing team to assemble.

"Mr. President," Chief of Staff Acres said. "Shall we begin?"

Burns turned and saw a familiar lineup, along with one new face. Everything is just as it was on that day, he concluded. Melvin Gardner's successor as presidential science adviser was seated on the sofa, looking distinctly uncomfortable. What was his name again? Lamont?

Burns took his seat, and, as always, Watkins, director of national intelligence, passed him a leather binder. "Today's PDB, sir."

The first critical item dealt with the assassination of the vice president.

An analyst from the NSA who had accompanied Watkins was in charge of briefing the president. "Regarding Vice President Chamberlain's tragic death," he intoned, "we have to admit we were mistaken. We had suspected the Chinese cyberattack unit of having a hand in it, but we found there was more to it than that."

Burns, not exactly a digital expert, cut him off. "Make this as simple as you can."

"Certainly, sir. We concluded that someone hacked into the Chinese People's Liberation Army mainframe and used that as a springboard for the attack on us."

"Then who actually carried it out?"

"Unfortunately, it's been difficult to determine. We can say, though, that it was not the work of the Chinese."

"Are you telling me that whoever assassinated the vice president of the United States didn't leave a single clue behind?"

"I'm afraid so," the analyst admitted with a pained look.

But Burns wasn't angry. He was scared. This unknown person, whoever he was, could come after him next.

Watkins added, "We were overestimating the threat from China. In the National Security Council meeting today I think we'd best discuss a review of our policy toward the Chinese."

CIA director Holland, seated next to him, nodded. "We all agree, I believe, that we should freeze the military options we'd been considering against China."

Burns didn't respond but turned the page in his briefing book and asked about the second item. "We also don't know who's behind the cyberattack on the entire United States?"

The analyst had to confirm this. "I'm sorry to say so, but that's also true. We found out later, too, that another strange thing happened. The attack made a complete shambles of data from all the financial institutions in the country, but now the data's back to normal. If it hadn't been restored, our economy might have collapsed."

"Why would the enemy do that?"

"I'm just speculating, but I think it was a demonstration of power."

Perhaps worried that the analyst had been a bit too frank, Watkins hurriedly cut in. "Right now maintaining order is the most urgent task at hand. We need to make it mandatory for any entity connected with public infrastructure, as well as all financial institutions, of course, to come up with countermeasures against cyberattacks."

"And that will sufficiently protect us?"

No one could answer the president's question.

Burns cleared his throat sullenly and went on to the third item in the report. "Now about this crash of the F-22s. What happened?"

"This gets kind of technical, so I asked Dr. Lamont to join us," Watkins said, and urged the newly appointed presidential science adviser to speak.

Lamont, seated at the end, removed his reading glasses and turned to the president. "The four fighter jets crashed at almost the same time, but this was not the result of an attack. It was the result of a natural disaster."

Burns frowned. "Natural disaster?"

"Correct. The deep seafloor off the Florida peninsula contains large amounts of a substance called methane hydrate. Under extremely cold conditions and high pressure, methane gas that normally would have turned into natural gas gets trapped in water molecules. On the day we scrambled our fighter jets these crystals started to break down, and a huge amount of gas was released into the atmosphere all at once. Unfortunately the F-22s were flying at low altitude through that gas at just the wrong time."

The president looked unconvinced, and Lamont continued. "What happened was the fighter jets and the missiles they fired all had jet engines burning as they passed through the middle of this combustible gas. Either their engines experienced incomplete combustion or they exploded. The pilot's final transmission, 'The sea is burning,' probably indicated that pieces of burning wreckage had ignited the gas gushing out on the surface of the sea."

The officials seated in the Oval Office weren't sure whether to accept the scientist's explanation.

"Is this substance, methane hydrate, found only off Florida?" Holland asked.

"No. It's found in both North and South America and the oceans in the Far East."

"Then shouldn't there be similar accidents all over?"

Lamont shook his head. "Only the sea off Florida meets the right conditions. This has to do with the Gulf Stream. A warm current from the African continent moves west into the Gulf of Mexico, changes direction, and then flows into this area of the ocean. This is the only part of the ocean where methane hydrate is exposed to such high temperatures. This high water temperature itself triggers the release of the gas."

"So," Burns said, "you're telling me that the Raptors' destruction was the result of an unfortunate coincidence?"

"I'm afraid so. Their pass through that area was just bad timing."

"Could this accident have been planned?"

"No; that's impossible," Lamont declared. "No one can predict when large amounts of methane gas will be released. And no human would be able to time it precisely enough to lead supersonic jets to pass through that area right when it happened."

"No human," Burns repeated in a small voice. "Did that young man prepare this report?" he asked Holland.

"Do you mean Arthur Rubens?"

"Yes."

"No, sir. He resigned. Another analyst wrote the report."

Burns nodded and was silent. He felt as though he were being watched.

Eyes that shouldn't be trained on the commander in chief were watching him. Eyes that could see through everything.

Burns thought of Arthur Rubens's gaze during the night briefing in this very room. The young man had gazed at him with the same look.

No; those weren't human eyes.

What made him most afraid was the gaze looking down on him from above. An omniscient, omnipresent gaze that always knew where he was and what he was doing. Vice President Chamberlain hadn't escaped this gaze. Someone had watched him, held him in thrall, and then brought down judgment.

"May we move on to the next item?" Acres asked. "The situation in Iraq?"

This gaze would be with him until the day he died, Burns concluded somberly.

Rubens was seated in the simple yet tasteful living room. The sunshine outside the window showed that even in Indiana spring had arrived. A single thread of steam rose from the teacups that had just been placed on the table.

He was enjoying a peaceful moment with the great scholar. Now there was no need to be concerned that others were listening in.

"So it's safe?" Heisman asked as he lifted the teacup, which his wife had brought in, to his lips.

"Yes. The operation's over. They're calling it a success, though Nous is secretly heading toward Japan as we speak."

Rubens related the details of what happened after the vice president's assassination. When he was done, Heisman gave a satisfied smile. The face of a sensible citizen shouting for joy that a despot had been defeated.

"I also finally figured out the answer to the question you asked me last time," Rubens said. "The answer is that there is a second Nous. Am I right?"

"Correct. From the beginning there was no chance of winning. Tell me, do you know the other's age and whereabouts?"

"All I know is she's in Japan. And that she's eight years old and named Ema Sakai." Rubens explained how the pregnant Pygmy woman came to be in Japan. "My understanding is that Yuri Sakai, who raised Ema, is a very responsible, loving person."

"I'm glad to hear that," Heisman said, nodding. "A mother's love is the foundation of all peace."

"What will they do now?"

Heisman took on a thoughtful, scholarly expression again. "They'll keep out of sight until their race is established. In the meantime they'll study the habits of these lower primates called Homo sapiens and begin exercising their power. But in a hidden way."

"Specifically, what do you imagine them doing?"

"I can't say. I'm one of those lower primates myself, after all," Heisman said with a laugh. "But if I put myself in their place, I think eliminating nuclear weapons would be their first priority. Throughout the world they were born in, they see apes fighting for territory with their fingers on the launch buttons for nuclear missiles. Or else they might target political leaders who seek war and kill them all."

So the meek shall indeed inherit the earth, Rubens mused. "What about in the long term? As you wrote in your report thirty years ago, will we be exterminated?"

"It depends on how brutal they are. And how fast they propagate. Until they reach the numbers needed to sustain their race, they might keep us alive to ensure there's a sufficient workforce."

Rubens recalled an interesting historical example of sexual selection. There are males on the Eurasian continent who have a special Y chromosome, and, using a biological marker called a molecular chronometer, scientists were able to determine the time period and area where this chromosome first appeared. It turned out this matched the route